IT's FOR YOUR OWN GOOD

CONTENT NOTE
It's For Your Own Good is a work of fiction
but it deals with many real issues, including
grief, depression, death and murder.

To the original legends…Mum and Dad.

First published in the UK in 2026 by Usborne Publishing Limited, Usborne House, 83-85 Saffron Hill, London EC1N 8RT, England, usborne.com.

Usborne Verlag, Usborne Publishing Limited, Prüfeninger Str. 20, 93049 Regensburg, Deutschland, VK Nr. 17560

A CIP catalogue record for this book is available from the British Library.

ISBN 9781836048404   10542/1   JFMAM JASOND/26

Printed and bound using 100% renewable electricity at CPI Group (UK) Ltd CR0 4YY.

IT'S FOR YOUR OWN GOOD

KATE FRANCIS

CHAPTER 1

Something stirred the night air in Liv Walker's bedroom.

A warning instinct pulled her out of deep sleep, forcing her thoughts to struggle to the surface. She blinked her eyes open, momentarily confused by the shadows on the ceiling – branches of darkness swaying silently in an unseen breeze.

There was an unfamiliar chill in the room. Had she left the window open?

Reluctantly, she pushed herself onto her side and looked around. It wasn't the window.

There was a faint yellow rectangle of light; the door was wide open. Liv groaned. Why was her door open? She always kept it closed, no exceptions. It was the only way to get some much-needed privacy, and besides, she couldn't sleep with it open like that. It felt too exposed somehow.

A flash of irritation hit her. Damn Mattie. Her bratty little stepsister must have toddled over in the night – probably to steal some make-up or something. She was always coming in and out like she owned the place. Four years old and she already ruled the whole house.

Maybe tomorrow night she would balance a cup of water on the jamb – a small surprise for the little diva. Her stepmom, Carianne, would not be happy. Oh no – she wouldn't like that at all. Her precious princess doused in the middle of the night by her evil stepsister. All hell would break loose. Liv smiled at the thought.

Rubbing her eyes, she shook off the last clinging edges of sleepiness and pushed herself up to sitting. The bed was so cosy, but there was no way she could go back to sleep until she got up and shut the door. Except, of course, once she got up, she'd never get back to sleep.

A shot of familiar midnight angst hit her. She needed sleep. *She needed it.* How was she going to cope in the morning if she hadn't slept? All the things waiting for her the next day started listing themselves in her head, one after another in a fizz of panic. She had to wash her hair, all her clothes were in dirty piles spread across her floor, there was a test she hadn't studied for, another lunchtime detention. Fuck. She couldn't face any of it. She just couldn't – not if she was tired. Not if she hadn't slept.

She reached over to the bedside table for her phone. But it wasn't there. It was probably buried somewhere in the bed sheets; she must have fallen asleep while she was doomscrolling and forgotten to plug it in. Reaching around, she poked the comforter, trying to feel for it.

Something creaked.

It was faint, almost inaudible – but enough. Liv froze, every part of her instantly on alert. The shadows around the doorway deepened as she stared into them, searching. It had to be the house groaning, settling after a long day of summer heat – right? Or maybe Mattie was still here, the little monster, lurking in the corner.

"Mattie, is that you? I'm going to kill you…" she whispered.

Another creak, louder. Too loud.

That was when she saw it. The yellow rectangle of light morphed as a dark shadow pushed into one side of the doorframe. Her mind pushed back, struggling to make sense of what she was seeing. Was she imagining it? Angles? An elbow? A shoulder…?

Fuck. Someone was there. Someone big.

"Who is it?" Liv's voice sounded unnaturally high; her heart was beating too hard. She sat up, rigid, instinctively pulling the sheets around her. "Dad, is that you?"

There was a silence…too long. Not Dad. *Who was it? Who?*

The shadow stretched, extending itself slowly across the floor and onto the bed as a dark figure moved fully into the doorway. The weak light illuminated its large silhouette.

A man.

Fuck.

A stranger.

Fuck.

Something was covering his face. A ski mask.

Fuck no.

Liv kicked out wildly, instinct taking over. She pushed off the bed, stumbling as she tried to find her feet. No plan, no idea what to do. Pure adrenaline driving her – fight or flight.

Two steps. She took two steps away from the bed before she landed smack into something soft and big. Something solid.

Someone else was there. Standing by her bed. There were two of them!

Rough hands grabbed her, catching her easily, pulling her in.

Everything exploded in Liv's head. She thrashed hard, kicking out desperately, but she couldn't break free. She tried to scream but it was too hard to breathe. Fear took over as she felt her wrists gripped tightly. The man from the door was behind her now, pushing up hard against her back, an arm locked around her shoulders. She was trapped between the two of them, she could feel the weight of their bodies, the fabric of their shirts, she could smell them – smell their sweat.

"*Help!*" she managed to get out, her voice cut off as a meaty hand clamped itself over her face.

They were talking. Words she could barely understand.

"Have you got her?"

"Get her."

"I'm trying!"

Liv thrashed out wildly with her free feet, kicking viciously.

"Fuck…she's kicking me."

Without thinking, Liv sank her teeth hard into the vice-like fingers gripping her face.

"Ow!" The person recoiled. "Jesus. She bit me!" It was a woman's voice.

"Calm down already," the man behind Liv growled at her. He twisted her around and in a second, she was on the bed, face down. The man's heavy weight landed hard on top of her, pinning her down, her face pushed into her sheets. Pinpoint flashes of light were breaking behind her eyes. Sheer panic hit her. Was this it? Was this how she was going to die? Sixteen years old and murdered in her own bed.

The man grabbed her hair, pulling her head back. He pushed his face close. She could smell spearmint gum through his knitted ski mask.

"Olivia Walker, settle down. We're not here to harm you." The man's voice was calm. Too calm for *this*. "Now, I'm going to count to three, then you're going to get up and we're going to walk downstairs. Do you understand? You won't get hurt unless you do something stupid. Got it?"

Liv didn't dare move or speak.

Still holding her hair, the man forced her head up and down in a crude nodding motion.

Tears pulled at her eyes. Nothing was making sense.

She felt something cold grip her wrists, a metallic snap. *Handcuffs?*

"Good girl. All right then. Are we ready? On the count…one, two, three." The man slowly peeled his weight off her. She sucked in air, gasping, instantly struggling to push herself away from him. The man laughed. "Feisty. You're gonna have your hands full with this one." He nodded at the woman, who was standing to one side, nursing her hand.

"Just what I need," the woman muttered. "Another dang troublemaker. Come on, Walker. You're mine now, kiddo."

She grabbed an elbow, pulling Liv up. Liv wobbled, her feet unsteady. What the fuck was happening here?

They half-walked, half-dragged her through the yellow doorway. All the house lights were on. She looked around wildly for signs of anyone, trails of blood or weapons – anything to make sense of this. Oh God, what had they done to the others; to Dad, to Carianne and Mattie? Mattie's door was open. She was just a kid, a baby. They wouldn't hurt her, would they? She must be so scared.

They clumsily stumbled down the stairs. The front door was also open. Why were the lights on? If they were kidnapping her, they'd want it dark.

A fuzz of confused thoughts raced through her mind. They knew her name. They said they weren't going to hurt her. Who were they? Kidnappers? Had they targeted her family because they were rich? That would explain why they knew her name. Well, they'd fucked up – her stepmom would rather pay them to keep her than pay a ransom to get her back.

As they stepped through the open doorway, Liv felt a shock of cold night air. A white passenger van was parked in the driveway, lights on, doors open.

She was roughly pushed towards the van. Somebody had to see something; someone had to notice a kidnapping, right in the middle of their fancy cul-de-sac. The nosy neighbours would call the police; they'd write down the licence plate. The police were probably already on the way. Someone would stop this. Someone would help. She looked around wildly, opening her mouth to scream – but stopped cold.

They weren't alone. Standing on their immaculate McMansion lawn, were three people – her dad, Carianne and little Mattie, her chubby arms wrapped tightly around her mother's leg.

Her so-called family.

Watching.

"Dad!" Liv gasped. "Help me!"

James Walker's arms were tightly folded, his chin stuck forward; there was an uncharacteristically hard look on his usually amiable face.

"Dad, help…" Something was wrong. Her father didn't move or speak. He just stood there – impassive. "*Dad!*" They were almost at the van.

That was when she saw it. His green eyes flicked up and for a brief, painful second met hers – cold and locked-in. Defensive. She felt like she had been punched hard in the gut. *Her dad.* Why? Why was he doing this?

"Dad…" Her voice wavered. "Dad, please don't…please…" She was begging; she didn't care. He had to stop it. "Look, I know I fucked up, but please just give me a chance to explain. Don't send me away. Please… *Dad…?*" The words choked in her throat and died. Her father didn't move; he didn't look at her again. Nothing. He just stood there, with Carianne rigidly by his side, one manicured hand resting possessively on his shoulder, the other hand waving at Liv.

She was smiling. *Smiling.*

That was it. Everything left Liv. She sank against the gripping hands. The two masked figures lifted her through the side door of the passenger van, dropping her onto the floor between two rows of seats and smoothly removing her handcuffs. They pulled the van door shut behind her.

There were voices outside, but she couldn't focus. Her mind had shut down. A humming noise was building in her ears. She lay still, her face pushed into the cold metal of the van floor. More doors slammed. An engine kicked in.

She didn't move. She couldn't move. She wouldn't move. The passenger van pulled forward; an indicator ticked. Streetlights flashed over her.

But she lay there, focusing on the only thing that was cutting through the buzzing, ugly mess in her head. The one thing that she could see clearly – her dad turning away from her, letting them do this, letting them drag her away. The hard look in his eyes, that one last defiant glance.

He had done this to her. He had chosen this for her.

Her own father.

Her own fucking father.

CHAPTER 2

Rain streaked across the van's window; occasional streetlights flashed past. Liv's face was pushed against the cold glass, her breath steaming up the surface.

Somehow, she'd managed to scrape herself off the floor and crawl into the row of seats at the back of the van. She had no idea how long they had been driving but it must have been hours. The two dark figures in the front had played through old country songs, alternating with vaguely familiar nineties hip-hop, squabbling each time one track ended over who got to pick next.

The kidnappers were both thickset with low, gravelly voices. They were still wearing their identical ski masks pushed up on their heads like beanies, and seemed inappropriately relaxed, guffawing and joking around like old friends.

Clearly, they had done this before – at least twice.

Because Liv wasn't the only one in the van.

The two other kids were slumped deeply in their seats. Liv had the clearest view of one of them, a tall girl with curly red hair, sitting two rows in front of her. The girl had been sobbing quietly to herself ever since Liv had been unceremoniously dumped on the van's floor. On the rare occasion that she looked up, Liv would sneak a brief glimpse of her profile – high, soft cheekbones, pale white skin and wide-set, tear-soaked eyes.

The boy was harder to make out. He was at the front, in the row behind the driver's seat with his back to them, a grey hoodie pulled low over his head. His face was turned to the window – all Liv could see were a few curls of sun-bleached blond hair escaping from under his hood. Everything about him said to fuck off and leave him alone.

Liv shivered. She was freezing. For the hundredth time she cussed herself for her choice of pyjamas – shorts and a cami-top dotted with tiny blue flowers. It was no better than underwear and she felt horribly, mortifyingly exposed. Being dragged around half-dressed like this tapped into all her worst insecurities. She hated the way she looked on a good day – and this was definitely not a good day.

Wrapping her arms tightly around herself, she contemplated asking Bert and Ernie up front if they could put the heat on. But the memory of them grabbing her and forcing her into the van was still too raw. She'd rather freeze to death than ask them for anything.

Gritting her teeth, she turned back to the window, looking for any landmarks or signs that might give away where they were going, and – more importantly – how to get back home.

Home.

Well, that was a joke.

The oversized McMansion in Flagstaff had never been her home. Not really. Her home – her *true* home – was back in Seattle, with her mom, with her memories, with her best friend, Min.

Fuck.

Liv rested her forehead on the cold window, letting it tap against the glass as the van bumped along the road. It hurt a little. But she didn't mind. It was a distraction from her spiralling thoughts.

It was pointless to think like this. That home – that life – didn't exist any more. It had ended two years ago, on the day her mom died. The day her father left the hospital, unlocked the front door and walked straight into his office, closing the door behind him, leaving Liv alone on the other side. Countless times over the next several weeks, Liv had sat by his office door, listening for him, needing to know she wasn't alone in the empty house, needing someone who would never come. At least, until the day the door opened wide, three months after her mom died. He stepped out, a manic grin on his gaunt, unshaven face, and announced he was getting remarried and that they were moving to Flagstaff, Arizona. A "colleague" had swept in online and given him the attention he'd needed while mourning the death of his wife. Carianne.

Her father's face flashed into her mind. His expression as she was dragged from the house. It didn't bother her that Carianne was clearly delighted that she'd finally got rid of her problematic stepdaughter. But *her dad*, his face resolutely turned away from her, the set of his jaw…

Fuck. That hurt. How could he do that? *How?*

If her mom was still alive, he would never, *ever* have done this. If her mom was alive…

Stop. Liv pulled herself up in her seat, wiping at her eyes. *If* this. *If* that. Fuck *if*. Her mom was gone, and would never know how bad things had become between Liv and her dad. No, her mom had died leaving a perfect little family of love – a perfect little daughter. At least she had taken that with her. None of this could touch her now or hurt her. Wherever she was, she was safe.

Instinctively, Liv rubbed her thumb against a silver ring on her right hand, gently pushing against it and turning it around and around.

Another unreadable road sign flashed past, caught in the headlights. She wasn't sure, but from the scarcity of towns or stops along the empty road, Liv thought they might be heading north, through the desert, towards Utah.

Liv tried to think through what was happening. A while ago, she had gone down a rabbit hole watching content about kids incarcerated at some school for "troubled teens". Is that where she was going? A school? Rehab? *Prison?* No, it couldn't be prison, right? Her lawyer said the charges against her had been dropped. She'd been released with an official warning. It couldn't be that. So, what was it?

Her stomach did a small flip as her head went darker. Her dad and Carianne wouldn't have decided to get rid of her…permanently? She looked at the two goons up front. They weren't *professionals*, were they? No, that was stupid. They wouldn't have professionals drive up to their house in front of all the neighbours. She was being irrational – right?

Oh God. What was happening here?

Where were they taking her?

Pushing her face harder against the window, Liv watched the raindrops dripping like pathetic tears down the glass. She traced one with her finger. The drops were running straight down now, pooling at the bottom of the window.

At long last, the van was slowing down.

"Restroom break," barked the woman. The van pulled off the road into the dimly lit forecourt of a gas station. Pure darkness surrounded them. There was nothing nearby. Just the gas station and the road disappearing out of the halo of light, shrouded under shards of pouring rain.

The middle of nowhere.

The van parked next to a gas pump, and the woman walked to the side door, opening it wide. Cold, wet air sucked into the van.

"Out." The woman stood back, her muscular arms crossed tightly over her broad chest.

This was the first time Liv had managed to get a good look at her. Her face was unnervingly ordinary, like someone you'd be standing in line behind at Costco. She had nondescript features and wispy dyed-black hair, and was wearing a faded yellow T-shirt with a crudely drawn smiley face nestled under an inverted V-shaped hat. Only one thing stood out: she had tattoos running the length of her right arm. It was a mess of dark-arts images – skulls and wolves and a snake wrapping around her arm several times, its head rearing onto the back of her hand.

"Five minutes. Restrooms are inside."

Trying not to look too relieved, Liv slouched out of the van, shivering as the rain pelted her. She kept her eyes down and was careful to steer well clear of snake woman. She needn't have bothered. The woman was busy on her phone and blanked her; probably queueing up another round of achingly loud hip-hop to torture them with.

The tall girl shuffled out next, her crying on a momentary hiatus. Blinking in the rain, she pulled her pink fleece pyjamas around her as she sniffed her way to the gas station store.

A bell dinged as the door swung open.

There was a boy working behind the counter; he could hardly be much older than her, Liv thought. He looked up, an expression of mild curiosity on his face, clearly not used to customers at this hour. He nodded at Liv.

A short, sharp thrill raced up her spine. The woman was still outside on her phone. There was time. She could tell the boy she was being kidnapped and get him to call the police. She just had to make it look casual in case the woman was watching.

Without a phone or money and basically in underwear, Liv didn't bother pretending she was about to buy something. She just walked up to the kid, arms wrapped protectively around herself, still soaked through and shivering with cold.

"I need help," she whispered, keeping her head down, trying to act cool. She had to manage his reaction too. If he panicked when she told him what was going on, the snake woman might suspect something.

The boy looked at her. He had a shock of dark hair that covered the top half of his face. How could he even see like that?

"'Kay." He grinned.

"Please, you have to listen. Don't react when I say this – they're probably watching. But I'm being kidnapped by that man and woman." Liv looked pointedly in the direction of the van. "You need to call the police."

The hair nodded.

"'Kay – gotcha," the boy said, still smiling. It wasn't the right reaction. He seemed unfazed.

"No…seriously. Those two people outside have kidnapped three of us. Please, you have to get help. My name's…" Liv paused here. If she said her real name, where would she end up? Right back home where all of this had started, waiting for the next van to pull up in the middle of the night. "My name's Min Wei. I'm from Seattle."

It was all she could come up with in the moment. She hadn't made any close friends in Flagstaff – not the kind she could call for help in the middle of the night. But her best friend from Seattle wouldn't mind Liv using her name. If she gave the police Min's number, when they called, Liv could explain everything. Min would help. They'd been best friends since the first day of kindergarten and they still talked almost every day. Min's parents were lawyers and had been her mom's best friends for as long as Liv could remember. They were the closest thing Liv had to family – a real family. They would help her out. Of course they would. They'd be so shocked at what her dad had done. Maybe she would be able to go and live with them? At least for a while, until she figured things out.

"Min Wei?" The boy crumpled up his face in confusion. With her mother's bushy middling-brown hair and her Canadian father's pale green eyes and freckles, Liv knew she did not look like her name was Min Wei. Damn it.

"Look, it doesn't matter, all right. The thing is, I've been *kidnapped*."

"'Kay." He nodded again. A hand reached out and pushed the overly long bangs back. For the first time, Liv saw his face clearly. Not as young as she'd thought. Maybe mid-twenties? Definitely unimpressed.

This wasn't going the way she'd hoped. She looked around nervously. The red-haired girl had disappeared in the direction of the restroom. Outside, snake woman wasn't standing by the van any more. *Where was she?*

"Listen," Liv said urgently, resisting the impulse to grab the cashier by his ridiculous floppy hair and shake him into action. She had the horrible feeling that this might be her last chance to escape – especially if they were headed to some school or rehab facility. She had to make him understand that she was serious. "*Please*, just call the police, already. I'm being kidnapped! What part of this are you not getting?"

The doorbell pinged behind her. Liv's heart leaped; a cold chill crept down her back. She didn't need to turn round. She just knew – snake woman was here.

"Yo, Chipmunk," the boy called out to her. "Got yourself another runner here…"

Fuck. He knew her. They must come here all the time with their latest van-load of victims.

"Yeah, thanks, Shane. I figured, the way she hot tailed it outta the van." Chipmunk walked over to the counter and stood next to Liv. "Planning an escape, were ya?"

Liv shook her head, sullenly.

"Good. Cos you can't do a runner from here." Chipmunk grinned conspiratorially at Shane. "Not unless you wanna hike across seventy miles of flatland in a hundred-degree heat, all on your little lonesome. Though I suppose you could follow the road and get yourself flattened by an eighteen-wheeler. No skin off my nose neither way. You run – you're not my liability no more. Dead or alive." Chipmunk turned to look around the small store. The girl from the van had emerged from the restroom and was standing forlornly in the snack aisle. "Now y'all need to finish up and get your butts back on the van, A-SAP. That means you too, Miss Shasta Lee." Chipmunk nodded pointedly at the girl.

The girl squeaked and dropped a bag of Doritos.

Damn it. Liv sighed in her head – not out loud. She wouldn't give Chipmunk the satisfaction. Serving Shane her finest stink eye, she turned and walked to the restroom, slamming and locking the door behind her.

CHAPTER 3

Fuck, fuck, fuck. What was she going to do now? Liv didn't know where they were taking her, but her survival instincts were fired up.

It must be early Friday morning by now. Any way she looked at it, it was unlikely anyone would realize she was missing until after the weekend. She'd skipped enough days of school that no one would think twice if she didn't show up. If she was brutally honest, she couldn't think of anyone in Flagstaff who would notice or care if she disappeared for months, if not for ever. The only person who might actually miss her was Min; but even if Min was worried, it could still take her days to decide what to do.

No, Liv had to be realistic. She was on her own, and she'd watched enough true crime to know her best odds for escape were now, before she got to wherever they were taking her. She couldn't let her imagination go beyond that thought. It was too terrifying. She had to keep in the moment. Out here, in the real world, she still had a fighting chance.

Liv's reflection in the dirty restroom mirror made her jump. Her face was pale with dark circles around her eyes, and her long hair was matted and wild, like a stray dog on an Instagram reel.

She looked like she felt – as though she'd been chewed up and spat out by an angry universe.

Gritting her teeth, she looked around. There wasn't much to see, apart from a narrow window over the washbasin. It was small, but she could potentially fit through it. Chipmunk had shot down the options for escaping but hadn't factored in one thing. Shane-the-hairy-cashier had got himself to work somehow, and he would have to leave at the end of his shift. Whether he had a car, scooter or Uber set-up, Liv was going to hitch a ride out of here and make her way to Seattle – to Min. All she had to do was get through this stupid little window and hide somewhere close by until her ride arrived. Easy. She had a plan.

She clambered onto the washbasin rim. It creaked loudly under her weight. The window was cracked and easy to open. Without thinking, she dove headfirst into the opening, balancing painfully on her stomach. The next part was awkward. She was hanging upside down, legs still inside, cold rain pelting hard on her head and shoulders, dangling over a metre above the ground.

Wriggling around, she tried to get a knee up to the frame, but it didn't fit. The window wasn't wide enough to bend her legs through. She was stuck, half-in, half-out. There was nothing for it – she was going to have to drop headfirst, with nothing to break her fall.

Roll, she told herself. *Drop and roll, you'll be fine.* One hand clung to the frame as she shifted her weight forward. Her other hand came up over her head, ready. There was no scenario in which this wouldn't hurt. It was a really bad idea. But she was committed. She was not going to be locked away by her treacherous father and evil stepmother. They didn't get to win.

Tipping forward, she dangled precariously for a moment before gravity took hold, whipping her through the window, her legs scraping hard on the sill, her knees catching excruciatingly as she fell. Her arm barely broke her fall and she tumbled headlong onto the ground, crashing to a stop against a nearby dumpster.

Ow. She didn't dare move. There was damage, for sure. She just didn't know how bad it was. Slowly she scanned her body, wriggling various bits as she checked them out; knees burning, scratched up but functional. Her forearms had some cuts and bruises, but nothing broken. The rest seemed all right. She grinned. *She'd done it.* She'd escaped! She just needed to find Shane's ride and…

"If I could get me a dollar for every kid who tried that…" The voice crushed Liv's momentary euphoria. Two worn hiking boots moved in front of her face. Chipmunk. "Are we going to need handcuffs again, young missy?"

Slowly, reluctantly, Liv looked up. Chipmunk was looming over her, rain dripping off her nose onto Liv's face. The man was close behind her.

Despair cut through Liv. She'd fucked up. Again. How could this be happening? She just wished she could be home in bed – for this all to be some messed-up nightmare.

Chipmunk squatted down next to her and leaned in.

"Look, missy. I get it. This isn't how either of us wanted to be spending our night. But no one's going to hurt you. You're safe in our hands. I know you don't see it yet, but all this is for your own good."

"Where…where are you taking me?" The adrenaline was wearing off and Liv's voice was shaky; she could hear how pathetic she sounded.

"To a place where you can get the help you need. I'll explain everything when we get there. But for now, you just need to know that this is in your best interest. Trust in the process, and this'll go a heck of a lot easier on all of us."

Liv didn't respond. What was there to say? She'd lost this round. Her father and Carianne had won – for now.

Chipmunk gave a short nod, and before Liv could process what was happening, she was roughly lifted from behind by the man and hustled into the van. The door slammed shut on her for the second time that miserable night. The two goons clambered back into the front seats, their playlist started up loudly, and they were off.

Liv lay curled up on the floor of the van for a long time – tears of frustration mixed with the rain on her face. She was shaking now, though not from cold. Anger and fear mixed together. She was in trouble, big trouble, and she knew it.

Her cami-top and shorts were soaked through from the rain. Folding her arms self-consciously, she dragged herself onto her scraped-up knees, then over to her seat, trying to hold it together. She could hear the other girl, Shasta, back in her seat, sobbing again – great gulping sobs.

There was something on Liv's seat. A folded grey rectangle. Confused, it took a moment to understand what she was looking at. Then it finally registered.

Carefully, she picked up the soft, grey hoodie and slipped it over her head. She pulled her knees up underneath and curled into the cosy fleece, burying her face into the folds. She could smell the faint, reassuring scent of clean laundry and something else – someone else. A warm, earthy scent. Nothing had felt so good in this whole shitty night. Nothing.

Grateful, she looked across at the boy, sitting silently, position unchanged. Without his hoodie on, she could see the back of his neck, the way his floppy, blond hair curled just above the line of his faded black T-shirt, just over his shoulders.

Silently, she thanked him.

There was at least one good thing here. Just the one.

Whatever came next, she wasn't alone.

CHAPTER 4

"Off!"

Liv jumped. She must have dozed off at some point on the long drive. The side door to the van was open. Chipmunk was standing by it, glaring at her.

Rubbing her eyes, Liv stood up, wobbling a little. They'd been driving so long it felt odd to be stationary. The van was empty; the others had left while Liv was still sleeping. She must have been really out of it not to notice.

As she stepped out of the van, she breathed in the air; it was different from before – dusty and dry. It could make your eyes water and your throat itch at the same time.

Yup, it definitely tasted like Utah.

A soft dawn light clipped the tops of a small cluster of bland box-buildings and asphalt parking lots littered along a solitary road that wound tightly into the foothills of a low, scrubby mountain range. They weren't in the desolate emptiness of the previous night's drive, but it could hardly be called civilization, more of a pit stop on the road to nowhere.

Chipmunk led the way into one of the nondescript buildings

under a sign that ominously read: *INTAKE*, with a small logo below it made from the intertwined letters WTC. The building seemed to be empty, lights auto-flickering on as they walked down a long corridor and into a darkened room lined with rows of beige, plastic folding chairs. The two others from the van were already waiting, sitting awkwardly in front of a large screen.

Liv slipped into a seat near the back, grateful for the darkness. Pulling her knees up, she took the opportunity to look around, trying to find clues to her new location. So, was this it? The final destination? It didn't look like a boarding school or rehab, or even a prison. At least not like any she'd seen online.

Shasta was sitting in the front row, slumped low in her seat with her curly red hair falling over her face and her long legs folded awkwardly under her. Her posture hung with dejection and utter misery. She was clearly just as shocked as Liv to find herself sitting in some random office building in the middle of God-knows-where in her pyjamas.

As for the boy, Liv's eyes drifted over to him and lingered. He was at the end of a row, facing forward, one arm draped loosely over the seat back, fingers tapping lightly on it. From where she was sitting, Liv could only see the side of his face: sun-bleached, surfer-dude hair and a tanned jawline with standard-issue freckles. His manner was laid-back and relaxed; his easiness projected an entitled confidence she hadn't felt once in her whole life. Just that small, limited view was enough to tell he was the kind of boy she avoided – they didn't like girls like her, and she didn't like them back. The way of the world, or at least high school.

Liv sighed and looked away.

To be fair, he had given her his hoodie. Fingering the grey sleeve, she breathed in the faint scent that lingered on it. What was it? Something salty and fresh, like a dip in the sea on a sunny day – like summer.

Okay, so the hoodie was nice. Not that it meant she owed him anything. It was his choice to leave it on the seat for her. She'd give it back as soon as she got the chance. So, no big deal.

Without warning, the lights went out and the big screen lit up.

The logo with the letters WTC appeared at the top of the screen, followed by a series of stock images of smiling parents with fake teens, fake hugging and fake hiking in random picturesque scenery.

An unnervingly calm voice-over kicked in:

Welcome. Today is a new dawn in your journey. Under the guidance of our compassionate and trained staff, you will discover the power of Mother Nature, our ultimate healer. With our help, you will uncover your authentic selves and learn to live, thrive and survive. At our Wilderness Therapy Camp…

Oh no – no way. No, no, no…*Wilderness Therapy Camp?* How could this get any worse? *How?*

Liv felt ill. Her twisted stepmother must have laughed herself sick when she signed the papers. Liv didn't have an outdoorsy bone in her body; she loathed hiking and camping with a passion – and Carianne knew it. So, this was her parting gift to her unwanted stepdaughter, a little kicker of added misery. She could have chosen a residential programme or a school at least. But no. *Camping.*

Fuck.

Liv would have preferred prison.

Academic, supportive, immersive…

The promo video was prattling on and on, throwing out endless big words strung together earnestly over the images of grinning models. Liv blanked it out. She needed to think.

Okay, so wilderness therapy…what did she know? Most of the troubled-teen industry stuff she'd seen was about scary residential programmes with cavity searches, solitary confinement and horrific punishments. She didn't know too much about wilderness therapy camps – just that some boy at school had been sent to one for smoking weed. He came back six months later and developed a full-blown fentanyl addiction. She vaguely remembered him telling stories about not showering for months and pooping in holes in the ground. That was all she knew.

It was enough.

Clearly, she wasn't the only one freaking out. Shasta stood up abruptly, turned and walked towards the door. But she was pre-empted. The man from the van stepped out of the shadows, blocking the doorway with his immense bulk.

He didn't need to speak. He just needed to smile – a cold, tight smile that reeked of confident domination. The message was clear: *I own you. You're not leaving.*

The girl dropped into the nearest chair with a small whimper, folding in on herself. She looked as broken as Liv was feeling. This was bad, really bad. But what could they do?

Liv's mind was racing. Was any of this legal? She wished she had her phone. She'd ask ChatGPT, "is it legal for your parents to pay to have you forcibly kidnapped from your bed in the middle of the night and dragged to fucking Utah?" But she already knew the answer. Wouldn't the camps have been shut down by now if it wasn't legal? So, it must be legal – even if not technically moral. But that didn't help her case.

Maybe she could ask for a phone call and beg her dad to reconsider.

But she knew she would have to grovel for forgiveness and there were no guarantees he'd give it – not after what she'd done. Especially considering the fact that (despite what she said) she didn't regret her actions one bit. She would do it again in a heartbeat.

No. She remembered her father's face as she was being dragged to the van – the locked-in, hard look in his eyes. He was fully committed to this. He must have been spoon-fed promos like the one on the screen in front of her. He must have liked what he saw. He must have…right? To send her here?

Liv wrapped her arms around herself tightly.

Fuck it. She'd go to hell before she'd beg for her dad's help. That option was off the table.

So, what else? What could she do?

And with the help of nature's loving hand…blah blah blah…find their path back to a healthy, normal childhood.

Cue drippy music. The letters WTC morphed into the words *Where They Care* as the promo wrapped up with an uplifting finale. After a brief pause, a basic list appeared on the screen. This looked businesslike, and a lot more sinister – no touchy-feels here. Liv had the impression that this was the first thing they were seeing that wasn't aimed at their parents.

The list was titled simply: *The Programme.*

Chipmunk moved up next to the screen, a completely unnecessary microphone now clipped to the neck of her yellow T-shirt. She spread her hands wide and paused, looking at her three new victims.

"All right, campers. It's time to get real." Her low voice caught in the mic and resonated around the empty room. Liv winced. "I haven't been officially introduced. My camp-name is Chipmunk.

I've worked for the WTC for seven years now, in five different camp locations, and I will be your head counsellor for the duration of your stay with us. It's my pleasure to welcome y'all to Camp Smiling Skies!" She threw out a little bark of a "*whoop*" before turning back to the screen and pointing to the list. "Now this is *The Programme*. It's going to be your handbook at camp. You're gonna want to study this list and memorize every word. This is your healing path now. Only when you have completed all four levels of *The Programme*, will you be ready to return to full and meaningful lives at home with your loving families."

Liv shifted uncomfortably in her seat, reluctantly side-eyeing the screen.

THE PROGRAMME

Beginner Level 1: Rock Squirrels
Unlearning bad habits. Re-training the mind.
Silent contemplation.

Intermediate Level 2: Bighorns
Acquiring new skills. Morality re-education.
Service to others.

Intermediate Level 3: Ringtails
Teamwork development. Processing regret.
Atonement.

Advanced Level 4: Condors
Leadership. Promotion of camp values.
Commitment to the new you.

Morality re-education? Atonement? What was this place? A cult? Get your parents to donate the lease to their house or you'll be stuck here for ever. Who would be stupid enough to buy into this shit?

Well – there was Chipmunk. She was reading out the list, word for word, without needing to look at the screen. Clearly, she'd drunk the WTC Kool-Aid.

Liv tried and failed to focus on the words, but a heightened feeling was bubbling inside her head, a pressure in her ears, as she processed the subtext – complete *The Programme* or you won't go home.

Play or stay.

Chipmunk had taken to marching up and down now, thumbs tucked into the belt loops of her trousers. A happy drill sergeant in front of their newest recruits. She pointed at the screen as she passed it.

"Now, you're probably thinking – where am I on this list?" She walked up to the screen and pointed at the wall above it. "You are up here. You aren't even in *The Programme* until you have proven that you are ready to start doing the hard work to fix yourselves. Only when you have shown a willingness to improve will you be eligible to start your journey through recovery." She lowered her finger to point at Beginner Level 1. "You have to earn the right to call yourself a *Rock Squirrel.*"

Liv snorted, loudly.

Everyone turned to look at her.

"Olivia Walker?" Chipmunk said sharply, glaring at her. "Do we have a problem here?" She narrowed her eyes.

"No," Liv muttered sullenly. "Allergies," she added, dropping a theatrical sniff onto the end of her sentence and glaring back. "Chipmunk" didn't suit her. She should have called herself

Rattlesnake or Scorpion. Something mean. Liv liked chipmunks.

There was a long awkward moment as Chipmunk stared at Liv, a familiar look of distaste on her square face. Liv recognized that look. She was being put into a box labelled *troublemaker*. After just a few more encounters, the box's lid would be nailed shut and that's who she would become, once again. Liv Walker – the troublemaker.

Whatever.

Chipmunk pointedly turned to address the others.

"Now, I know y'all are feeling pretty confused right now." She moved in front of the screen, the blue light illuminating the back of her head, creating an ethereal halo around her ski-mask hat. "I know you're scared. I get it. Let me share something with y'all. When I was your age, I had struggles too." The halo slipped to the side as she turned and started pacing up and down. "Oh yes, you may not think it, seeing me now. But I was lost…messed up in my own head, taking drugs and partying like there were no consequences to my actions. Outta control. *Delinquent* – just like y'all." She nodded earnestly, looking around at them in the darkness, clearly trying to make that one hit home.

Liv rolled her eyes and shuffled in her chair, tuning out the words. She didn't need to take this on board. Not from some low-life goon who worked in the troubled teen industry – not exactly a life goal.

Chipmunk continued, "The difference between you and me? I had a reason to be like that. I didn't have a family. I spent my childhood moving from foster home to foster home, and I can tell you, my life was hard. So dang hard. Not like y'all with your big homes and rich-ass families. I know your type. Spoiled, entitled brats. Y'all got everything: good food, a roof over your heads, a family. Goddam it – *a family*. A family that loves you so dang much, they paid more than I earn in a year to send you here – to me. To heal you. Because they care."

Liv glared at her. They clearly had a very different definition of care. Getting your kid forcibly kidnapped in the middle of the night and paying a huge amount of money to get them out of your lives for as long as possible didn't seem *caring* to Liv. Caring was holding them on a bad day and loving them, despite themselves. Caring was her mom. Not this.

Chipmunk was still talking. "…and that's why I'm here – a re-educator for the WTC. Committed to fixing you. Each and every one of you. That is my promise. By the time you have completed *The Programme*, I promise you will be fixed."

Fixed? Like a broken toy?

Liv bit her lip. A cold, empty feeling was settling inside her. How many times had she felt it this past year? Sitting in the principal's office, at the dining room table, at the police station. Her father and Carianne talking about her in front of her, like she wasn't there. A problem child…unacceptable behaviour…consequences… Now here she was in *Utah*, trapped, and it was just more of the same. She'd heard it all before. Too many times.

She was bad – broken.

She needed "fixing".

She got it.

Shifting in her seat, Liv pointedly faced the wall. Tears were prickling behind her eyes, but she wouldn't give in to them. She wouldn't cry. She heard Chipmunk's words droning on, but didn't let them in. Something blocked them, pushed them out of her head before they could take hold and cause more damage. She dug her fingernails into the palms of her hands, focusing on the sharp pain.

"…and with that, do we have any questions?" At long last, Chipmunk was wrapping up her self-indulgent waffle.

Shasta's hand went up, tentatively. It was shaking slightly. Chipmunk nodded in her direction.

"Um…so, when can we go home?" The girl's voice quavered.

"Well, that all depends on you, Miss Shasta. On top of completing your camp activities, you'll have weekly sessions with a psychologist, who will evaluate your mental state. She'll provide an assessment for my approval, before you can graduate. But if you want a rough estimate of how long this takes, some of our best campers have completed *The Programme* in as little as three months."

"*Three months?*" Shasta gave a short whimper of despair and shook her head.

Three months. Liv swallowed down a rising wave of nausea. As little as three months? Oh Jesus. She would miss the rest of junior year. She would miss *too much*. Her grades were bad enough already. There would be no catching up from this. She'd have to retake the whole year…or flunk out of high school. This couldn't be happening.

"No!" Liv heard her own voice, surprising herself. She was standing now. Something inside warned her to just sit down and shut up, but she couldn't. She waved her hand towards the others. "We have rights."

Did they, though? She had no idea. But it was wrong – she knew that much. So wrong. If this were a prison, at least she'd have had a chance to defend herself in court. A chance to tell her side of the story. This just wasn't fair.

"Olivia Walker." With scary, speedy efficiency, Chipmunk covered the space between them.

Liv bundled her hands into fists and tucked them under her arms but didn't sit down. She jutted out her chin defensively. *Bring it.*

"Oh, I know all about you, Miss Olivia Walker. I know everything. I've spoken with your family. I've seen your arrest record. I know what you did…" Chipmunk shook her head disdainfully, leaving it hanging.

Liv looked down. She knew what she'd done too. And she knew she didn't look good on paper. Not good at all.

Chipmunk was smiling, too hard. She leaned in and dropped her voice to a gravelly whisper. "I've seen all sorts come through *The Programme*. Really rough, nasty pieces of work. But believe me, if I'd been your folks, I would have pressed charges, and you wouldn't be in a cushy 'therapy programme'. You'd be in juvenile detention, where you belong…with all the other thieves and criminals."

"*I'm not a thief!*" Liv's cheeks flushed.

There was a familiar tightness in her chest. She couldn't bring herself to look around, to see if the other two were watching this play out – to see what they thought of her.

"Really? Forgive me if I find it hard to believe a known liar." Chipmunk was smiling, clearly aware of the power her words had. "I have a file full of evidence that says you are trouble, Liv Walker. Bad news. But your antisocial behaviour stops here, young lady. Starting today."

Liv's hands were shaking now. With difficulty, she bit her tongue. She couldn't win this. It wouldn't help to deny it. No one ever believed her anyway. It would just look pathetic and the one thing she had learned was to not show weakness. She wouldn't give them the satisfaction.

"I have a question." The voice was close behind Liv.

The boy.

While she had been focused on Chipmunk, he must have moved up behind them.

Chipmunk looked equally surprised to see him standing there.

"Yes, Lucas?" She reluctantly shifted her gaze from Liv and turned to him.

"When do we eat?" Lucas smiled a wide, easy smile. He was tall – much taller than Liv had thought. The surfer-dude impression was accurate – athletic, broad shouldered, tanned. He moved closer until he was standing next to Liv. "It's just I'm hungry as all hell, and I bet you've got some good food lined up for us."

"Of course!" Chipmunk's full attention was on him now. She smiled back, a girlish smile. "Yes, of course. I know y'all are hungry. I've got everything ready. Right after we get you in your uniforms."

"I knew you'd have us covered." Lucas moved forward again, stepping between Chipmunk and Liv. "So, what are we talking here? Bacon and eggs? Pancakes? Please don't say it's avocado toast. I might cry."

Chipmunk actually laughed. "Oh, Lucas Cole. Don't bring a slimy avocado near me! Heck no. I've got some real food for y'all, just as soon as the uniforms are sorted."

"I bet you do. Let's do this!" Somehow Lucas had shifted the direction of the conversation, inching them both towards the door, away from Liv.

Chipmunk propped the door open. The stony-faced man from the van held out a small pile of white envelopes. She took them and nodded.

"Thank you, Lomax. All right, let's move it! Lucas, you go with Lomax. Girls with me."

Lucas went first, walking through the open doorway. For the first time, Liv noticed he had a pronounced limp and bore his weight heavily on his left leg.

As he passed her, Chipmunk counted out three of the envelopes and handed them to him. He stuffed them into his back pocket, then, pausing for just a moment, he looked back across the room, at Liv. She felt the look go right through her. His eyes were unnerving – ice blue and bright – as he coolly took her in for just a second too long. He smiled a sweet dimpled smile before turning to follow Lomax down the hallway.

That look. He knew how to use it. Clearly her first impressions of him had been right. Lucas Cole was a player.

He already had Chipmunk eating out of his hand. And after his little intervention just now, Liv was starting to feel things she didn't want to feel. He was good. Very good.

Liv made a mental note – she was going to have to keep her guard up around Lucas Cole. The boy was dangerous.

CHAPTER 5

"Jewellery," Chipmunk said flatly, holding a drawstring bag in front of Liv.

They were standing in a restroom where a pile of clothes had been set out on the counter. Shasta had been escorted to a separate room, leaving Liv and Chipmunk alone.

"Jewellery? Seriously?" Liv glared at the bag.

"Oh yes. Camp rules. No jewellery allowed." Chipmunk nodded at the bag.

This was so stupid. Why couldn't she wear jewellery for camping? Liv pulled out her earrings angrily and dropped them in the bag. This was so messed up.

"Ahem." Chipmunk cleared her throat pointedly and nodded at Liv's hand. Instantly Liv closed her fist protectively.

"No. Not my ring."

"*All* jewellery. When you complete *The Programme*, it will be returned to you."

"Come on. It's not expensive or anything. I don't mind if it gets damaged." The prickling feeling was back behind her eyes, but she angrily pushed it away. No crying. "Please. The ring was my mom's…" Her words trailed off. She already knew it was pointless.

Chipmunk had a fixed smile on her face. There was nothing there. No emotion. No compassion.

Liv gently touched the small silver ring. A tiny bird was carved into the band – a swallow. Her mom loved swallows, the way they soared joyfully, high above the world, defying gravity and mocking the rules of nature. Every one of her mom's paintings had a tiny swallow hidden in it somewhere, her secret symbol of freedom.

The ring was all Liv had of her mom now. All she had left. She had worn it every day since the hospital. Every day for two years.

But what could she do? What choice did she have? Fighting back tears, she pulled the ring off her finger and thrust it into the waiting bag, abruptly turning away.

Fuck them.

"There's a good girl." Chipmunk smiled matter-of-factly. "Now, off you go into the stall over there and undress. Pass your clothes out under the door."

Too tired to argue, Liv stepped into the stall and slipped out of the hoodie and her by-now filthy shorts and cami-top. She pushed them out and waited, shivering, for her new uniform to be handed over. But nothing happened. She heard a door close. A cold feeling smacked her in the gut.

"All right, Miss Olivia. Step out. We will begin your personal search."

No, no, no. This couldn't be happening. She'd seen stuff like this in the posts about the therapy schools. Strip searches. *Please no.* Liv wrapped her hands around herself defensively. What more did they want from her? She'd been kidnapped and had her possessions confiscated. Now this? The ultimate humiliation.

She didn't speak, already sensing that her words meant nothing here. She was trapped as surely as if she'd been found guilty by a jury and sent to prison. Only she wasn't guilty. She hadn't done anything – at least nothing that deserved this. Had she? Her whole body was rigid, her breath tight in her chest.

"Olivia. You need to step out of the stall, or I will be forced to bring Lomax in to assist. This is standard camp procedure. I'm sure you would rather we conducted the search discreetly and efficiently. It'll be over soon. It's your call."

Just like the doctor. Just like going to the doctor. She said it over and over in her head. But it didn't help. She hated being looked at. She wasn't comfortable in herself. She'd never been comfortable, always preferring oversized jeans and hoodies to hide away in. Just wearing a swimsuit in public was bad enough. But this? How could she do this? How could she step out in front of this awful woman?

But then…what choice did she have?

Swallowing down a wave of nausea, her hands shaking, Liv unlatched the stall door. Taking a deep breath, she stepped out. Her eyes found a particularly ugly strip light on the ceiling, and she locked in on it, blocking out the movements around her.

Her mind dissociated as she was told to turn around, arms out. She kept her eyes up, on the rusty light, a crooked fluorescent tube hanging out of it, loose wires dangling. Chipmunk didn't touch her. Thank God. Liv knew she couldn't have taken that. She wouldn't have – no matter the consequences.

Somehow it was over and Liv was sent back into the stall. She wrapped her arms around herself and backed away from the door, shivering, but not from cold.

A pair of dusty combat boots appeared below the stall door.

Chipmunk was standing outside.

"One last thing, missy," she said. "I know your type. I've been doing this longer than you want to know. I've seen kids like you come and go. You think you know shit. You think you're tough. But you're not. You're just a nobody whose own parents didn't want them around."

Liv backed against the wall, as far as she could get from the low voice. She felt herself shrinking down into the corner of the stall, folding herself around her bare knees as though it might offer some protection from the words coming at her. But it didn't. She still heard them. Every one of them.

"You should know, your folks paid in full, up front, just to bump you to the top of the waitlist. Do you get what that means, missy? Do you understand? Whatever you put those poor folks through, they don't want you no more. Your own family don't want you. You're mine now. The sooner you get that through your head, the better. Toe the line and we'll get along just fine. But cross me and I will ruin you. I will destroy you, inside and out – and I can. You'd better believe it, missy. I can."

There was a rustle, and a pile of new clothes was pushed under the door. A single white envelope was set on top, formally addressed to "Olivia Walker" in her father's handwriting. Footsteps moved away.

Liv wiped at her tears with the back of her hand. Fuck. Fuck. Fuck Chipmunk. Fuck this. She was shaking all over now. She pushed aside the letter and reached for the clothes, gathering them gratefully into her arms. Part of her wanted to stay here, squeezed behind the toilet, curled up tight. She didn't want to move and face anything more. Just hide here and hope the world forgot she existed. There was no good that could come of any of this.

But as the moments ticked away, a bigger part of her fought through the hopelessness, instructing her to get up and get dressed. It had to feel better than this – than the way she felt right now, curled up naked on the floor in a restroom in Utah. It couldn't feel worse. She had to try.

Somehow, she pulled on the grey underwear and sports bra, loose khaki combat trousers and bright yellow T-shirt, finally tucking the letter deep into her back pocket. Somehow, she unlocked the stall door.

When she finally stepped out and caught her reflection in the mirror, a crude smiley face with a tent hat grinned lopsidedly back at her from the oversized T-shirt.

Thankfully, Chipmunk had left now. This was the first time Liv had been alone since arriving at the intake centre. Walking up to the mirror, Liv looked at herself properly. An unfamiliar face stared back – hollowed-out, tight features, pale and drawn with fear buried deep in her eyes.

Part of her wanted to slam something into the mirror, rip the broken light off the ceiling and smack it violently against the sink. Break it – break it all.

But instead, she reached her hand up to her mouth, finally releasing her gritted teeth as she spat out a small silver object. The ring.

Carefully she rinsed it off and slipped it deep into her pocket. If her mom could hide a swallow, then she could too.

Fuck them.

They would not own her – they would never own her.

For the first time all day, she smiled, and her grubby, dirty reflection smiled back.

CHAPTER 6

A large wooden sign marked the entry to Camp Smiling Skies. It was crudely decorated with carved animals: a condor, next to a ringtail, next to a bighorn sheep, next to a terrifyingly oversized squirrel. *WELCOME HOME* was painted underneath in a peeling rainbow of colours.

Welcome home? Great.

Liv sighed and reached up to scrape her hair off her neck and bundle it into a high knot. Dark, wiry strands escaped her efforts, dancing wildly in the breeze.

She was sitting on a bulky backpack in the shade of the sign. Her shoulders burned where the straps had cut into her skin and her legs ached from an hour-long uphill hike. The scrapes she'd picked up at the gas station were stinging from her own sweat. She was not built for this. Her exercise-avoidant lifestyle was catching up with her.

It was mid-afternoon already. The last few hours had been a blur, and Liv's emotions were raw and random. The orientation had wrapped up with a lunch of stale ham and cheese sandwiches, after which Lomax had left on some errand, with the veiled threat that he'd see them "soon enough" at the camp. Then Chipmunk had loaded the three unwilling recruits back into the white van for a two-hour drive to a drop-off in some dusty mountains. That was as far as the road went, so they'd parked the van and been force-marched for an hour to the trailhead, where they were now standing, next to the wooden sign.

Reaching inside the backpack, Liv dug around under all the camping gear for a plastic water bottle. They'd been issued their camp kits back at the intake centre. It was basic stuff: one grey hoodie, a clear plastic rain poncho, one change of underwear (one!), spare socks, a sleeping bag, pillow, towel, toothbrush and a simple mess kit. Liv was pretty sure that none of it was new, apart from maybe the toothbrush. She couldn't bring herself to think about what was missing. Things like soap, deodorant, shampoo and worst of all…tampons. They'd have some here, right? Right?

As she took a long swig of lukewarm water, she looked around.

The entirety of Camp Smiling Skies was nestled in the shadow of a large rock wall. They appeared to have arrived in the middle of the camp, in a large field of scraggly brown grass. There wasn't much to see in the field, just the wooden sign, a fire circle in the centre and a blue tarpaulin off to one side, suspended from two trees at the edge of the woods.

The rest of the camp was divided into two areas on either side of the field, connected by a single white trail. On the left, the ground rose steeply to what looked like an elevated plateau. Here Liv could just make out the tops of a handful of brightly coloured tents. In a clearing nearby were two tent cabins with canvas walls and roofs, built on top of wooden platforms. Clearly this was the sleeping area.

Off to the right of the field, the ground dipped into a shady hollow nestled in trees. She could see a cluster of picnic tables next to a solitary wooden shed. What looked like a crude camp kitchen was set out on a deck in front of the shed. This must be the dining area.

A distant ring of craggy peaks fully encircled the camp, as though they were caught inside a broken bowl. Everything looked desiccated and wild, like it would poke, prick or bite if you went too close.

That was Camp Smiling Skies.

That was it. Everything. For as far as the eye could see.

You might have thought you were alone in the world if it hadn't been for the occasional fly-by of a red helicopter. It had been circling on and off for the whole hike. Chipmunk seemed particularly bothered by it, muttering something that sounded a lot like "I'm going to kill him…" whenever it swooped past.

"Oh my God…you're finally here!" A blond girl had appeared at the top of the field. She bolted in their direction, almost barrelling into them in her excitement. "Welcome to Camp Smiling Skies! I've been waiting for ever for you guys. Seriously! I'm not kidding. *For ever!* It's totally Milo's fault – he told me you'd be here at lunchtime. Not that you should ever trust what Milo tells you. He's like such a doofus." She paused, struggling to catch her breath, looking up at them with enormous brown eyes.

She was cute – very cute. At least, she must have been in her pre-camp days. Expensive-looking platinum highlights had grown out leaving a solid band of dark roots. A sheen of grime covered her light-brown skin, which was liberally dotted with insect bites and scrapes. Underneath, you could still make out her perfect button nose and full lips. Explorer Barbie.

She looked around at them.

"Hi, I'm Ruby Jennifer Clarke. I've been here three months, three weeks and two days and I'm a Condor. I'm from LA – Hollywood really. So yeah, pretty far from here." It all came out with one enthusiastic breath and a perfectly straightened smile. "So, um…like, where are the rest of you?" Ruby looked expectantly at Chipmunk.

"This is all you've got to play with, Miss Ruby," Chipmunk said. "Just three this time around, so make the best of it."

"Just *three*?" The girl appeared to deflate before their eyes. Her disappointment was palpable.

"Don't worry, you'll have your fun with these ones. There are some characters here." Chipmunk shot a dark look in Liv's direction. Liv glared back. Nice to know she'd already made an impression.

"Well, okay," Ruby said, forcing a bright smile. She looked from Lucas to Shasta to Lucas to Liv, and then back to Lucas again. "So, cool. Welcome. Yay."

The low whirring from the helicopter picked up again in the distance, causing Chipmunk to cuss loudly. "Dang that boy!" She turned to Ruby. "When?"

Ruby gulped and shifted nervously. "I'm…I'm not like super sure. Maybe last night? I think Moose might know more—?"

"Oh, he'd better. Where's Moose hiding at?" Chipmunk muttered, glowering at the wooden shed in the hollow. She reached into one of her many utility pockets and pulled out a whistle on a lanyard. Hanging it around her neck, she proceeded to blast it, hard, several times.

Peeeeww-eee. Peeeeeeeeeew-eeeeeeeeeeeeee.

Liv flinched. The piercing sound echoed off the rock wall. A small flock of birds launched into alarmed flight and a cluster of crickets kicked off a loud chorus.

Peeeeww-eee-eeeeeww-eeeeeeee. Peeeeewu-eeeeeeeeeeeeeeeeee

Peeee…

"I'm comin', man. I'm comin'." A man appeared from the direction of the hollow and strolled over, his stained white apron blowing in the wind. As he got close, he wiped his hands on the apron and waved happily at the new arrivals. "Hey, guys. Welcome." He smiled affably, pushing long straggly hair back from his long straggly face with greasy hands. He looked like he was in his late twenties, crinkly and weathered with a prickle of stubble. Clearly the outdoors type. "Hey there, it's cool to meet you guys. I'm Moose, counsellor and camp chef. So, who do we have here?" He grinned warmly at the newcomers.

"Lucas Cole, Shasta Lee and Olivia Walker," Chipmunk said, gesturing in the general direction of the newbies. She glared at him, fingering her whistle passive-aggressively. "Anything to report while I was away, Moose? Hmmm? I noticed search and rescue were out and about."

Moose looked uncomfortable. He swallowed and his oversized Adam's apple glopped up and down.

"Yeah. So...I guess...it's just...Ben went and did another runner." He shuffled on his big feet, awkwardly.

Chipmunk did not seem to be surprised by this news.

"I was away for three days, Moose. *Three.* You couldn't watch him for three short days?" She shook her head and sighed loudly. "Right. Miss Ruby, make yourself useful and escort these trainee rock squirrels to their tents. Let's move it! Need I remind y'all, this is not a vacation. Moose, walk with me," she directed coldly. Moose paled a little but nodded and they walked away, heads down. They were clearly having a disagreement. At least Chipmunk was disagreeing; Moose just followed along, pulling strands of hair nervously.

"So, what's happening over there?" Lucas asked, moving closer to Ruby and nodding in the direction of the counsellors.

"Oh that." Ruby rolled her eyes dramatically. "It's just…Ben. He's like so annoying."

"Who's Ben?"

"Ben Cross. He's the camp troublemaker." Ruby wrapped a strand of hair around her dirty finger and looked coyly up at Lucas. He seemed to have caught her interest more than the others, for obvious reasons. "Ben's one of the charity kids. The WTC has some deal with the State where they have to take on some problem kids for free in exchange for permits. Ben is so bad. He's always running away, and then the Sheriff gets involved, and search and rescue. Then head office gets angry with Chipmunk, and she takes it out on us. It super sucks. Everyone tells Ben to stop. But he won't. He just keeps trying to escape. Though I don't know why – he always ends up back here."

Ben Cross – a not-very-good escape artist. Liv made a mental note to find out more about this camp troublemaker. He could be useful.

"Look, we really should go before Chipmunk gets back," Ruby added, gesturing for the others to follow her. "Ben makes her so angry. She's going to be in a scary mood now and, trust me, you don't want to be around for that. I should find Milo and warn him. Come, come, come…" Ruby about-turned and started up the field, glancing nervously over her shoulder at the counsellors.

The trainee rock squirrels didn't need to be asked twice. *"Chipmunk in a scary mood"* didn't sound fun. They picked up their packs and followed Ruby as she bounded happily up the field and onto the white trail, heading towards the tents. She talked constantly, endlessly, prattling on about any and everything as they walked. Liv was flagging by now, hitting another wall of exhaustion, and dropped back a little to avoid having to even pretend to listen. Only Lucas still had the energy to keep up with the Energizer Bunny, though Liv noticed that his limp was markedly more pronounced after the long hike up from the van.

"Milo, Ben and I are the only campers at the moment," Ruby said to Lucas. She hadn't paused for breath once. "The others just graduated. That's why I'm so happy you guys are here! It's not like super fun with just those two. They're kind of…problematic. But I'm not complaining. Really. It's not so bad. I mean, you get used to it. Well, most of it. I like totally hate the camping part, and the bugs are insane, and bathing once a week at the swim hole is just so, so awful. I can't even. Oh, and Chipmunk is pure evil, I'm not even kidding you. You do not want to get on her bad side. And oh my God, the food is disgusting and for sure you'll get diarrhoea – we all did when we first got here. But, other than that…it's really not so bad."

Well, that was uplifting. Liv rolled her eyes and sighed. A fly was circling her head, intent on getting into her mouth. Damn suicide flies. She'd be happy to assist, she thought, angrily swatting it away.

Shasta had fallen behind, her face red from a combination of overexertion and abject misery. She kept stumbling and tripping over her feet, mumbling to herself. Instinctively Liv dropped back to walk closer to her, ready to catch her if she fell. They didn't speak. Neither of them even tried. There was a mutual understanding that after everything they'd been through, there was really nothing left to say. Nothing good anyway.

"Fuck!" Liv shouted. Something long and dark flew across the path and smacked into Liv's leg, wrapping itself around her ankle. It was heavy and cold.

Shasta screamed.

"*Fuck!*" Liv leaped back, wildly shaking her leg, kicking out so hard she lost her balance and fell back onto the trail. The thing flew up high into the air, coiling as it went, before crashing back down to the ground, right by her face.

A snake. A massive snake.

CHAPTER 7

"Oh my God, oh my God, oh my God—" Shasta shrieked from behind.

Liv reeled backward, rolling away from the snake. Was it following her? Was it moving? She was over a metre clear before she dared to look behind her.

The long green body was flopped loosely in an "S" shape, unmoving – was it in shock? Stunned? Was it dead?

It looked dead. Now Liv could see it clearly, she could make out its flattened head, as though something had crushed it. Had *she* done that? Had she stepped on it?

More importantly – had it bitten her? Quickly she bent forward, examining her legs, her ankles. She didn't see any fang marks, or feel any pain, but she did hear something.

Laughter.

Liv heard *laughter*.

In an instant, she wheeled around. Who was laughing at her? It wasn't Ruby or Lucas. It certainly wasn't Shasta – she had dropped to her knees by the side of the trail and was retching into the dirt.

Then who?

On the far side of the white trail, there was a loud rustle in the bushes, and a boy stood up. He looked East Asian with floppy, black hair falling across his boyishly handsome face.

"Oh my God. That was so funny. You should have seen yourself. I nearly died." He pushed the hair out of his eyes with a dirty, bug-bitten hand and stepped out onto the path, grinning widely. He was very tall and lanky, as though his muscles had sacrificed themselves for those last few centimetres of height. Liv looked up at him, then down at the snake, momentarily confused about what was going on. Her brain was still in fight or flight mode.

"Stop it, Milo. You're such a doofus!" Ruby bounced forward. "Seriously. They just got here. They're not in the mood for one of your pranks. That was so not cool." She turned to face Liv. "Sorry. Milo is so bad sometimes. He gets totally carried away. Just ignore him. Okay?"

It was a *prank?*

"Wait…you did that?" Liv asked the boy, shaking her head as if it would make the pieces fall into place. "You threw a *dead snake* at me?" She said it slowly, her voice tight. She could feel a rising tide of something dangerous inside her, the residual adrenaline from the snake attack was curdling into fury. She knew she should rein it in, but her self-control was at an all-time low, given the kind of day she'd had so far.

"It was a joke already." The boy was still grinning – a smarmy, smug grin. "Besides, I wasn't aiming for you; I was aiming for my camp-wife here." He nodded at Ruby, who scowled back. He held out his hand. "Name's Milo Zhao. Welcome to hell."

No introduction needed. In two short steps Liv walked up to him and shoved him as hard as she could, sending him flying backward into the bush he'd just emerged from.

"What the fuck? Chill!" Milo exclaimed.

"What's your fucking problem?" Liv stood over him, fists clenched at her sides. She was ready to go. Ready to take him down, piece by piece. Enough was enough. She was done. She'd been kidnapped, handcuffed, strip-searched and dragged out here, to the middle of dead-end-fucking-nowhere. No, this boy did not get to throw snakes at her and laugh about it.

"Jesus, what's the big deal? It was a joke! It wasn't like it was gonna bite you or anything. It was dead already." The boy threw his hands up and looked to the others for moral support.

Ruby quickly stepped forward, inserting herself between them.

"He's sorry. Milo is sorry. Tell her, Milo. Please! If Chipmunk hears us fighting…" Ruby looked like she was malfunctioning. Her pouty lips had turned pale, and her fists were gripped into tight little knots. "Please. You know what she'll do. Milo…you know…" She looked at Milo, wide eyed.

Slowly, Milo pulled himself out of the bush and brushed himself off.

"Fine. But I'm only doing this because the wife made me," he grumbled, nodding at Ruby. Turning to Liv, he gave a mock bow. "I'm so totally sorry, newbie. Please, forgive me. Pleeeease…" He didn't look or sound sorry. There was a sparkle of something wicked in his eyes. He grinned.

Liv really, *really* wanted to tell him to shove it someplace dark and lonely. She was already getting the measure of Milo Zhao. She knew his type – the kids who dominated every class in high school. Attention seeking and very, very bored. Everything was a joke to them, because in their own little self-important universe there were no consequences.

But there was something in Ruby's tone that worried Liv. Ruby was genuinely afraid of what Chipmunk would do if she caught them fighting. Maybe Ruby was the sensitive type and overreacting, but Liv just wasn't sure. Today of all days, she didn't want to find out.

"C'mon, guys." It was Lucas. He'd moved forward and was standing next to Liv now. "Nice throw, Milo. Good shove, Liv. I reckon you guys are about even. Hey, Ruby, I'm so down to ditch this backpack. Is the tent far?" He stretched his shoulders out as he said it. As with everything else he did, Lucas made it sound chill, like they were just a regular group of kids on a regular day. Easy.

"Ooh yes, the tents are right around the corner," Ruby said gratefully, smoothing down her blond hair and resuming her position at the head of the pack, clearly relieved that the drama was winding down. Lucas walked over to Shasta and helped her up, hefting her backpack onto his own shoulder. The three of them started up the white trail again, silent this time.

Only Liv held back, pausing to look down at the snake's coiled body, fascination and revulsion mixed in equal parts. Its wide-spaced eyes were blood-red and bulging. Its fangs were smashed at an angle by whatever had crushed its head, protruding from the skin of its jaw. Its patterned skin was scaly, almost beautiful when you looked closely. But she could still feel it folding around her ankle, the cold scales scratching on her skin, the weight of it on her foot. She shivered.

"You know, I did you a favour really." Milo was still grinning. "At least you'll be more careful of snakes now. Rattlers, sidewinders. They're all over this place – scorpions and spiders too. You're in their home now. Better get used to it. This place is a deathtrap."

Liv pointedly turned her back on him and started walking up the white trail after the others. A faint skittering sound could be heard from the bushes ahead. *You're in their home now.*

She willed herself to block out the voice behind her.

"You think I'm joking, but I'm not. People die here. I'm serious. They actually die. You don't believe me? Ask Ben and Moose…or Chipmunk. Ask them about Kevon. Ask them what happened to poor little Kevon Wright…"

Liv kept walking, picking up the pace to get further from him. As she rounded the final corner to the campground, his voice finally tailed off. She stuck her hand deep into her pocket and slipped the ring on her finger, gripping it tightly. But it was already too late. Milo's parting words were fixed in her head on a doom-loop:

"I'm not kidding. This place is dangerous already. Everything's out to get you…you gotta watch your back, girl. Watch your back!"

CHAPTER 8

The bucket.

An orange, plastic, twenty-five-litre bucket – the thing of nightmares.

It was located at the lower end of the field, loosely concealed by the blue tarpaulin hanging from two trees. It was probably intended to be downwind of the campground, but the stench permeated the air everywhere within fifteen metres of it.

So, this was their toilet – the final indignity. Squatting over a bucket. No toilet paper. No way to wash their hands. If the goal of this place was to break them, the bucket alone could do it. But that was the point, wasn't it?

Liv willed herself not to vomit as clouds of flies circled around the bucket's indescribable contents.

It was digging into her worst anxiety. Objectively, she was so scruffy and chaotic, you might not have thought hygiene was important to her. But she was always hyper-conscious of how she smelled: worried about her breath in the morning, worried if her hair wasn't freshly washed, worried if her deodorant was working or not.

Now, here she was, peeing in a bucket, and there was nothing she could do about it.

When she was finally done, she stood up so abruptly that the envelope in her back pocket almost fell into the bucket. She'd totally forgotten about the letter. Seeing her dad's handwriting, she felt a flash of anger and momentarily considered throwing it in the bucket anyway. But she just wasn't quite ready to – not just yet. So, she did the next best thing and wedged it deep in the hollow of a nearby, burned-out tree stump. As far as she was concerned, it could stay there and rot.

Dizzy from trying not to breathe deeply, she hustled away from the stench as fast as she could, wiping her hands over and over on her dirty yellow T-shirt. She was heading for the hollow nestled in the shadow of the rock wall.

It was dinner time at Camp Smiling Skies.

By the time Liv made it to the hollow, the others were already sitting at one of the picnic tables in front of the shed. Apparently, Chipmunk had left on an errand to do with the missing camper – Ben Cross – leaving Moose in charge. He was grilling in the camp kitchen on the wooden deck, happily humming to himself as he cooked.

Shasta was sitting alone on one side of the table, her tears forgotten as the smell of simmering food wafted over them. Lucas was on the other side, wedged between Ruby and Milo, who were hanging off him, talking non-stop, clearly delighted with their shiny new toy. From what Liv could make out of the ongoing conversation, Milo had already ascertained that Lucas was single, bi and emotionally available, and confirmed that he was single, gay and emotionally available. Meanwhile, Ruby had clarified that while Milo called her his "camp-wife", it was just an in-joke and she was actually single, straight and emotionally available. All of which had kicked off a shitstorm of competitive flirting.

Liv slipped unobtrusively onto the bench next to Shasta, keeping as far from Milo as she could. She was exhausted with zero reserves left for small talk and kept her eyes firmly down on the table in front of her.

The surface was crusted with the remnants of several meals, mixed in with dirt and splotches of dried-out bird droppings. It seemed impossible that the last dinner she'd had was at home, sitting at Carianne's immaculate glass dining table. Fried chicken, with mash and a Caesar salad. Her favourite from when she was a kid. *Her favourite.* It hadn't occurred to her before, but her father must have planned, shopped for and cooked her favourite childhood meal on the night he'd arranged for her to be kidnapped. He had actually gone to the food store and picked out the ingredients, all while knowing what was about to happen to her. Then he had sat at that fucking ugly table and pretended to make casual conversation: *How was your day, honey? How was school?* Fuck him.

Something tightened in her chest. Something that made her want to…to what? Curl up on the floor or scream and smash things – she didn't know. Fried chicken and mash. Her comfort food. *How could he?* Pre-fucking-meditated. Every part of it.

For the thousandth time, tears stung the corners of her eyes.

Why didn't he just talk to her and give her a chance to explain why she'd done it? If he'd just sat down with her and tried – no guarantees she would have said anything he wanted to hear. But he'd never even tried.

"Okey dokey, kiddos. Grub's up. Come and get it!" Moose's voice interrupted her thoughts.

She looked up, briefly catching Lucas's eyes. She had no idea how long he'd been watching her. It was uncomfortable. She didn't want to be watched. It made her feel exposed, as though he might have seen a small, secret piece of her. She didn't want anyone to get into her head; it was ugly in there.

Quickly getting to her feet, she turned away, heading over to Moose. Shasta and Lucas soon followed. Milo and Ruby laughed at the newcomers.

"Don't get your hopes up," Milo stage-whispered as they each collected their metal bowls and spoons and headed to the grill. "Moose cooks like a Texan grandpa. Beans, beans and more beans. Keeps us warm in the tent at night, that's for sure."

As if on cue, Moose called out, "Tonight's special is *Beans a la Mode*. A seasonal twist on a fan favourite." Moose was clearly proud of his mush. Using a cup measure, he spooned exactly two dollops into each bowl. When it was Liv's turn, the brown liquid splattered up onto her shirt and face. She roughly wiped it away with her hand. Great, now she smelled like sweat, poop bucket *and* bean juice.

Moose hummed as he scooped the last burned dregs from the bottom of his pan into Shasta's bowl. Liv noticed that Shasta only got one scoop instead of two. Maybe they'd misjudged quantities and run out.

"Um, sorry, but does this have nuts in it?" Shasta studied the mush suspiciously, poking at the burned black crust.

"Nuts? Oh, wait. Yikes. I totally forgot you have a nut allergy, right? Yeah, it was in your file." Moose was suitably sheepish.

"It's like, pretty severe. Um, you know, kind of life-threatening…" Shasta looked even more anxious than usual now.

"Oh wow. Gosh, well I really doubt it has nuts. I mean beans are usually okay, right?" Moose shrugged lamely, as if hoping that would be enough to put the matter to rest. But Shasta just stared at him over the top of her bowl with big eyes. "Okay, you know what, I'll go check the labels. Better safe than sorry, I guess."

Shasta nodded. Duh.

Putting his pan down, Moose sloped over to the shed. Considering that everywhere else in the camp was made of canvas and squashed mosquitos, the shed looked relatively put-together. It had *actual* walls and a real front door. Combined with a steeply pitched roof and the large deck, it had a quaint, cottagecore vibe. Though that impression was quickly dispelled by the words hand-painted in blood-red on the door: *THE SNACK-SHACK – NO ENTRY EVER.* Liv could hear the faint hum of a propane generator coming from behind the building.

Moose pulled a lanyard out of his pocket and fumbled to unlock the large padlock on the door. As he stepped inside, he switched the solitary light on. Liv tried to peek through the door behind him, curious to see what was inside the mysterious Snack-Shack, but all she caught was a glimpse of shelves stacked with cans, before the light flickered out.

"Darn wiring," Moose muttered, followed by some grumbling about a faulty electrical panel and how the WTC never did any repairs. It took him a few minutes to negotiate the dark, and by the time he had made it out, proudly carrying an opened bean can, the others were already seated at the picnic table.

"You're good, Shasta. No nuts," Moose called out, waving the can in the air. Shasta nodded, a look of relief on her face as she picked up her spoon and dug in. "Weird thing though," Moose added. "I was sure I bought cereal bars for dessert. I remember picking them up at the store, but can't seem to find them anywhere…" He scratched at his sunburned nose thoughtfully.

"The food thief strikes again," Milo declared through mouthfuls of mush, clearly delighted with this new turn of events. "One of the great mysteries of Camp Shitting Spies. Someone has been pilfering food from the Snack-Shack. But the only way in is through the locked door and…there's only one key." He nodded at Moose's lanyard.

"Yah, that's right!" Ruby chimed in. "But we all know who's doing it. I mean, it has to be Ben. Obvs. Probably stocking up for his next great escape. It's just no one can figure out how he gets in and out. It's like magic or something."

"Girl, if Ben had magic, I think he'd use it to *actually* escape," Milo added.

"Wait, so Ben never succeeded? He never actually got away?" Liv said it a touch too quickly. She made a mental note to act cooler in future; she didn't want to sound too interested.

"There's like no way out of here." Ruby waved her hand at the craggy mountaintops surrounding them. "You literally can't escape. There are the peaks on one side. You can't climb over them unless you're some freakish free-solo dude or something. Then the other way is worse. The Ochee River runs all the way down the valley. You can't swim across that – you'd drown for sure."

"Just like poor little Kevon Wright!" Milo said gleefully. "He drowned trying to swim across. Ben can tell you about it. He was there—"

"Yah, we're like not even kidding," Ruby added. "There's literally no way out. For sure that's why they built the camp here. We're completely stuck. But, of course, Ben has to keep trying, doesn't he?" Ruby sighed.

"So, er…how many times has he tried to escape?" Liv said, this time sounding much more subtle – at least in her mind. *No way out.* Everyone kept telling her that. But this was actual useful information. This Ben, whoever he was, was testing the limits.

"Since I've been here…maybe three times. But Ben's been at Camp Smiling Skies for nearly a year and apparently he's tried to escape like at least a dozen times…"

Liv dropped out of the conversation mentally after the words "nearly a year". Ben had been here for *nearly a year*? Chipmunk mentioned three months. Three sucky, hellish months. But *nearly a year*?

How was that even possible?

She wasn't the only one thinking it.

"Wait, I thought…I thought that you could leave after three months?" Shasta spoke up, her voice uncharacteristically high-pitched. Liv noticed she had two empty bowls in front of her now. She must have finished off someone else's food, but why would anyone give up their precious ration? Looking around, she noticed that Lucas's bowl was missing.

"Well, you *can* leave after three months," Ruby said. "All the campers I came with graduated a month ago. I just…I guess I did something wrong." For a moment, Ruby looked like a much younger version of herself. She crumpled up her face as she thought about what she was saying. "I mean, I thought I was going to graduate. I was totally looking forward to going home. It's just, somehow…I didn't. I must have messed up."

"Oh my God, wife. Don't start all this again." Milo moved up next to her and slipped an arm around her shoulder.

Ruby pushed him off, muttering something darkly about how

she was not his stupid wife. Milo threw his hands up placatingly.

"Look, Rubes, I told you. You did nothing wrong. You were pitch perfect. It's that bitch-queen mother of yours." Milo turned to the others, a smug smile on his face. "Our Ruby's mom happens to be none other than…*the* Jennifer Clarke."

Lucas's mouth dropped open. Shasta gasped. Liv raised an eyebrow. Jennifer Clarke was the rom-com queen of the nineties. Liv had watched her movie *One Night – Ten Dates*, more times than she cared to admit.

Enjoying their reaction, Milo quickly added, "And get this…her father is Fico Martinez – the movie director. They met on the set of *The Betrayed*. Divorced soon after. But they were together just long enough to make ickle-biddy baby Ruby." He grinned widely, chucking Ruby under the chin like a proud daddy. She smacked his hand away.

So, Ruby had A-list pedigree. Jenn Clarke was a Hollywood movie legend, and Mexican director Martinez was this year's favourite to sweep the Oscars. Now she knew it, Liv could see the family resemblance. Ruby had her mom's petite, girl-next-door charm mixed with her father's brown skin and striking dark eyes. Looks-wise, she really was in a league of her own. So, how on earth had Ruby Jennifer Clarke – ickle-biddy nepo baby – wound up at Camp Smiling Skies with the rest of them?

Milo was still talking to his now fully engaged audience.

"You would never guess it – but turns out everyone's favourite Jenn is the biggest bitch-diva from hell. She's more interested in finding new celebrity husbands than parenting and clearly doesn't want her little Ruby-monster to come home any time soon."

"That's not true!" Ruby exclaimed, her cheeks flushed. She

looked mortified. "Of course she wants me home. I just...I must have forgotten one of the Condor rules or something. It's just... I don't know which one." Ruby's big eyes grew even bigger. She bit her lip.

"Whatever you need to tell yourself, Rubes." Milo held his hands up submissively. "Whatever helps you sleep at night, girl."

"Fuck you, Milo," Ruby snapped. She looked like she was about to cry. "Why do you have to say things like that? Just cos your family are like Silicon Valley tech nerds or whatever, you always think you know everything, but you don't!" She jumped up, flipping him off with her middle finger, tattooed with a small Chinese character. Storming over to the deck, she proceeded to angrily scrape her bowl into a bucket and hand wash it in a tub of water, splashing more water on herself than the bowl.

"Ouch." Milo grimaced, then turned to face the others. "For the record, my parents aren't tech nerds – that's just rude. My mom's in tech, but my dad coaches college basketball. Though they do live in Silicon Valley, I suppose. Look, I'm not being a bitch. I adore Rubes. It's just...the truth hurts."

A cold panic was settling into Liv's chest. This was not good news at all.

"But...but Chipmunk said three months." Even she could hear the pathetic desperation in her voice. But she couldn't stop herself. "She said in three months we could leave if we finished *The Programme*. Right? Isn't that how it works? Our families paid for us to do *The Programme*, so when it's done, we can go home. It's what Chipmunk told us—"

Shaking his head, Milo looked at Liv with something close to pity in his eyes.

"Oh girl, you want to know when you can go home? The truth is, you graduate *The Programme* when your parents want you to come home. So yeah, it could be three months, if you're lucky. But if they have the money and they don't want your ass around, well then buckle up, kiddo – you're here to stay."

Liv felt physically sick.

When your parents want you to come home.

When. She knew what this meant for her. From the minute her father attached himself to Carianne's wagon, Liv had become an unwanted extra; a remnant of the life he had left behind. Money wasn't an issue. They could pay to keep her here until she aged out, if they wanted to.

And they would want to. Liv was under no illusions about that.

The tightness in her chest was expanding; it was getting harder to breathe. She turned her back to the others.

Until she aged out. Until she turned eighteen and became a legal adult. Liv knew what this meant for her.

In the failing light, the crags were dark shadows, their fractured outlines stark against the sky, storm clouds massing heavily over their distant tops. A black cage was forming itself around them. They were trapped in the mouth of a beast, just waiting to be chewed up and swallowed alive.

It was nineteen months until Liv turned eighteen.

Nineteen months.

CHAPTER 9

The campers were sitting around a fire in a loose circle, the firelight flickering across their tired faces.

Liv was struggling to keep her eyes open. Her mind was pushing back on the day's events, shutting it all out and trying to protect its host body. After dinner there had been a blur of chores: dishes, trash disposal and cleaning, followed by a mandatory bucket break. She needed sleep, desperately, but there was one last torture in store for them – a group bonding game to round out their misery and welcome the new recruits to hell.

A ring of half-cut log benches were loosely arranged around the fire pit. Shasta was slumped onto the ground sideways and wasn't even pretending to give a shit any more. Milo was ramping up his attempts to flirt with Lucas, who had assumed a model-like pose next to an old tree stump. Ruby seemed to have reluctantly resigned her stake in the new boy and was sitting next to Milo, picking sadly at a mosquito bite.

Only Liv kept her distance. She was sitting on the end of one of the log benches, facing out towards the dark woods. Night sounds were exaggerated out here, in the vast emptiness. It made her uncomfortable

– it was too connected, too intense; her senses were constantly on edge. This must be what it felt like to be a wild animal, surrounded by potential predators. Always on guard. Always waiting for something with bigger teeth to jump out of the darkness and eat you.

Her thoughts were spiralling. A familiar feeling was settling in her gut. No matter how hard she tried to shake it, it circled back, latching on tightly. It scared her. She had fought so hard against this feeling since her mom's death. But how could she fight it now – here, with no reason to hope, with no control over her movements and actions. Nineteen months. How could she possibly survive?

Moose was walking in slow circles around the fire, attempting for the third time to explain the rules of the game "Werewolf" to the emotionally unavailable newcomers.

"So, two of you are secretly werewolves. One of you is secretly a doctor. The rest of you are villagers. Every round, the werewolves pick someone to kill, and the doctor picks someone to save. But it's all secret, see?" He looked around, scratching at his straggly half-beard. But no one responded. They clearly did not see and were not planning on seeing any time soon.

"Ruby, can you give me a hand here?" Moose looked at her hopefully. "When Chipmunk gets back, she's gonna be fuming if we aren't playing the game. She left super clear instructions."

This got a reaction. Ruby jumped up. Anything to avoid a fuming Chipmunk.

"Okay, listen up. The sooner we get this over with, the sooner we can all go to bed" Ruby said. There was a collective grumbling, but she had their attention. "So, each round of the game has a night and a day. In the night part, the werewolves decide on one villager to kill, and then the doctor secretly chooses one person to save. In the day part, you find out who's been murdered. Unless the werewolves and the doctor happened to pick the same person, in which case no one dies. Then all of us have to vote out someone who we suspect is a werewolf. The game goes on until all the werewolves are voted out, or they outnumber the villagers. Make sense?"

More grumbles. Ruby looked frustrated.

"Oh my God, come on. It's like that reality show my mom did a guest appearance on. You know…a castle, murders…'you have been banished'. Only it's with werewolves…"

A few random nods now. Honestly, Liv wasn't sure she got it. She was struggling to keep up. No matter how hard she tried, her brain kept deprioritizing learning a new game to focus on things she actually cared about, like how to survive at Camp Hell. But she knew she had to try. If she could get to her little tent sooner than later, that was a win.

"Oh great. Here come Regina and The Plastics," Milo said, nodding in the direction of the trailhead.

Three dusty figures appeared out of the dark woods behind the wooden sign, light from their headlamps dancing up and down on the ground as they walked.

The return of Chipmunk. Liv's heart sank just seeing her – the stomping walk, head straight up, defying the world. Her heart sank even lower when she saw who she was with – Lomax. He was dragging someone behind him: a boy, stocky with very short dark hair, his tanned, white skin covered in a thick layer of dirt, bruises and scrapes. Liv didn't need to get any closer to know that this boy was a walking red flag.

"My new friends…meet Ben Cross," Milo muttered, a touch

quieter than before. He seemed a little intimidated by the new arrival.

"Hi, Ben," Ruby said when they arrived at the circle, her voice edged with nerves. "Escape didn't work out for you this time?"

The boy didn't answer. He walked over to the far side of the fire and swung himself down on a log, glowering at the ground in front of him. He hadn't looked once at the new arrivals.

Barely contained anger radiated off Chipmunk as she took up a position in the centre of the circle, squarely in front of Ben. Lomax moved into place behind the boy, and stood, arms folded, looming over him. The firelight caught Lomax's heavy features from below, distorting his face into a sinister grimace. He should have kept his ski mask on, Liv thought. It was less creepy, which wasn't saying much.

"Moose. Status," Chipmunk said. She glared across the fire to where Moose was lurking.

"Um, yeah. For sure." Moose swallowed loudly. "All good here! Super fun dinner. All fed and watered. Just going over the rules of the game, you know... just like you said."

"Okay. Then let's play. Ben and I will join in. Moose, you will be the host. Lomax is going to sit this one out, so he can keep an eye on *things*." She pointedly nodded at the "thing" – Ben – who remained impressively unresponsive. "Let's do this."

Game time.

As directed, they all closed their eyes and Moose tiptoed around the circle, tapping shoulders to assign secret roles. To her relief, Liv wasn't picked as a werewolf or the doctor. Her only goal right now was to be a dead villager, get murdered quickly and doze through the remainder of the game with nothing to do.

Moose was the host and played his role like a nerdy Dungeon

Master, adopting a vaguely British accent. Liv had to hand it to him – he was trying to lighten the mood. It was pointless, but at least he tried.

"'Tis a dark and stormy night in the wee village of…Little Campington." Moose smiled, clearly pleased with his improv. "Rumour has it, werewolves live in the high mountains, and when they get hungry, they stray down to the village to hunt for fresh meat…"

"Fuck's sake. Get on with it," Ben muttered, shifting slightly on the log.

Instantly Lomax slammed his hand down on Ben's shoulder. Ben flinched. Liv flinched too. The memory of those hands dragging her from her bed was still too vivid.

"Sorry, okay. Sorry." Moose swallowed again. He kept looking from Lomax to Chipmunk and back. "So, um, it's night and there are werewolves. All the villagers are tucked up safely in their beds, or so they think! All right, all of you can close your eyes now."

Liv sighed and closed her eyes, wishing to be murdered.

"Good, good," Moose muttered. He was moving around the outside of the circle now, behind their backs. "Now, werewolves only, open your eyes and choose your first victim." Liv caught herself listening with mild interest, but between the loud cricket chorus and sounds of wind in dry tree branches, all subtle sounds were lost.

"Okey dokey," Moose said. "Now, werewolves, close your eyes. Doctor, you can wake up. Choose who you want to save." Another silent pause.

When she was finally allowed to open her eyes, Liv looked around at the ring of faces. No one had moved. They were all silent and watchful, not wanting to give anything away.

"'Tis the morning, and as the villagers awaken, one of their own lies dead in their bed." As Moose said it, a perfectly timed crackle of dry lightning lanced through the distant night sky. Everyone jumped. Somewhere far away, a desert storm was raging.

"For goodness' sake, Moose. Just say it, will you?" Chipmunk snapped. "Who died?"

"Okay. It's…Shasta! Sorry, Shasta, you're dead."

"I'm…dead?" Shasta looked like she might have been asleep with her eyes open. She turned to the circle of faces all staring at her. "So, does that mean I can go to bed now?" she added hopefully.

"No!" Chipmunk said sharply. "We all stay until the end. It's *team-building*. T-E-A-M. There's no 'bed' in 'team'. Are we quite clear?"

Liv bit her lip hard. Someone sighed loudly and Shasta slumped miserably back onto the ground.

"Um, okay…so, back in the village!" Moose said with forced enthusiasm. "As the body is laid peacefully to rest, the townsfolk gather once more. There are murderers among us. Two of you are werewolves. But who? Okey dokey, you now get to vote who you think it might be. If you agree on someone, then they'll be executed and leave the game without revealing if they were actually a werewolf."

Executed? Who picked this game?

There was a painfully long pause, before Ruby spoke up.

"Come on, guys. Let's do this." She sighed, clearly up for the supreme challenge of shepherding them through this as efficiently as possible. "Shasta was voted out. So, who would have a grudge against her? Who would want her dead? I mean she only just got here."

"Maybe someone just wanted to give her a break," Lucas said with a shrug. "No offence, Shasta, but you look exhausted."

Shasta lifted her head, groaned and then dropped it back down again.

"Oh, that actually makes sense. Of course. Well in that case, I think I can guess who at least one of the werewolves is." Ruby turned to face Liv. "I mean, you spent the most time with Shasta, and you seem to have bonded."

Bonded? That was a little strong. They'd been abducted and traumatized in the vicinity of each other. Maybe that qualified as bonding at Camp Smiling Skies.

"Yeah, we're super close," Liv said, with just a hint of sarcasm. She was going for a clean and quick execution here.

"Okay, I vote for Liv," Ruby said.

"Me too," Milo added.

"Yeah, me three. Sorry, Liv." Lucas scratched his nose and leaned back, stretching. His T-shirt rode up, revealing a flash of flat, toned stomach. You couldn't make this stuff happen if you tried. Liv quickly looked away, maybe blushing. Just a little.

Finally, it was down to Chipmunk and Ben.

"Not gonna lie, I'm a little surprised. I hadn't noticed a strong connection between y'all. But to be fair, I've been gone for several hours." Chipmunk was actually playing the game. Ugh. She mooched around a bit, making a big show of her vote before finally agreeing to *execute Olivia*.

"Execute Chipmunk," Ben said instantly when it was his turn, with a short sideways glance at the counsellor.

Lomax moved closer. His free hand smacked down squarely on Ben's other shoulder. Hard. Locked down.

Why did the boy provoke Chipmunk like that? Liv wondered. The vote was over. Liv had already lost. But still he had to go and poke the Chipmunk. Was he stupid? Did he like pain? What was his problem?

Moose stepped back up.

"Okey dokey. So, we are all in agreement. The villagers believe Liv to be a murderous werewolf and she will now be executed."

And just like that, Liv was dead.

Well, that was easy. Gratefully, she pushed herself off the log and lay down on the ground next to Shasta, closing her eyes. God, it felt good.

Round two. Again, everyone had to close their eyes. Again, the werewolves picked their next victim. Again, the doctor saved someone. When they all opened their eyes, Moose announced that this time, Chipmunk had been murdered.

Liv was a little surprised, and maybe a little impressed. Whoever the werewolves were, they weren't afraid to go after Chipmunk. Which made her think that out of the four remaining suspects (Lucas, Milo, Ruby and Ben), the most likely werewolf was probably Ben, with maybe Lucas in second place. She just couldn't see Ruby or Milo daring to murder Chipmunk. They were both too afraid of her.

Chipmunk was clearly annoyed to be knocked out of her own game so early. But what could she do about it? Those were the rules. She made a very immature show about how maturely she was taking the news, before finally, at long last, taking a seat.

Next came the vote to pick which of the four remaining players was most likely a werewolf. It came down to Lucas or Milo. The vote was split, and for this round, no villagers were executed.

With little else to do, Liv spent her time sneaking glances at Ben. His head was firmly down, so she could take her time inspecting him from afar. He was wearing the same T-shirt and combat trousers as the rest of them, but somehow they looked bad-ass on him. The sleeves were ripped off. Two holes had been pierced through the smiley face's eyes, giving it a grim, creepy-clown expression. Definite bad-boy energy.

Round three. Moose and Ruby were the only ones actively participating by now. They were pushing through, trying to get to the end, once and for all. The night murder had a disappointing result when the doctor's vote saved the werewolves' latest victim, effectively cancelling out the murder and forcing yet another round of the game. But at least Milo was voted out and executed.

It was round four with three players left: Lucas, Ben and Ruby.

The final, torturous round of a miserable game. Not to mention the final, torturous end to a miserable day.

Any remaining werewolves selected a victim. Liv forced herself up to sitting, readying herself for the dark trek back to the tents. She was already thinking about her sleeping bag, which was set-out waiting for her. When she was tucked up inside it, zipped into her tent, she would be able to let go. She could stop trying to push through this shitshow. Today was nearly over.

"'Tis the final dawn in Little Campington and all is not well," Moose said with obvious effort, before sighing and dropping the accent. "It's the final round and one of you is dead."

"Just fucking say it already," Ben groaned.

"Please get it over with," Ruby whined.

"Okey dokey. You're dead, Ben," Moose said and flopped down on a log. He'd tried his best.

"Sorry, Ben," Ruby piped up. "Don't blame me though. I didn't kill you. I was just the doctor."

"Whatever." Ben just glared at her darkly. "I don't give a fuck about this stupid game…"

"Aww, what a sore loser," Chipmunk said snidely, still sulking that she wasn't allowed to play her own game. She was on her feet now and moved between Ben and the fire. "Benjamin Cross. Dead. Pity no one's going to miss you. Not a soul alive—"

"*Fuck you!*" Ben leaped to his feet and kicked out hard at a log on the edge of the fire, sending a cloud of sparks spiralling at Chipmunk.

That was all it took. Lomax launched himself forward, clearing the log bench in one leap and barrelling headlong into Ben. They fell dangerously close to the fire, rolling around as they struggled in the embers, thrashing out wildly at each other.

Ruby and Milo scrambled out of the way, falling onto Shasta, who squeaked in surprise.

Liv didn't know what to do. They were almost in the flames. Instinctively, she took a step forward, but felt Lucas's arm blocking her, holding her back. He shook his head. This was not their fight.

There was wild, desperate grunting and panting before Chipmunk stepped in and dragged Ben back by his T-shirt; Liv heard it rip. Lomax leaped up and quickly secured his muscled arm around Ben's neck, pulling tight. He swung the boy hard – too hard – crashing him sideways onto the ground and throwing his immense bulk on top of him.

Ben was pinned down, struggling to breathe.

No one dared to move. Liv could smell burned hair and skin.

It was several moments before Lomax finally edged himself up off the boy. Ben remained on his side, pushed up against a log, coughing.

"Consequences. Let's talk about consequences." Chipmunk's gravelly voice was tight.

Did she ever let things go?

This was the point where she needed to call it. She needed to send them all off to bed. Done. Over. If she wasn't capable of recognizing that, then one of the other counsellors needed to step in. But they weren't going to, were they? Moose was just as scared as the rest of them. As for Lomax, Liv had seen no evidence of a brain. He would do Chipmunk's bidding.

No, if she'd had any doubt before, Liv now knew that this was Chipmunk's domain. Her territory – just like the rattlesnakes, just like the tattooed snake coiled around her arm. They were in her home now, and she knew it.

Chipmunk turned to Ben.

"Dang, I really hate to do this, but you leave me no choice, young man." The firelight flickered; her shadow stretched out behind her, caught in the nearby trees, dancing wildly from side to side as she smiled down at him, and said:

"Moose. Fetch the kit."

CHAPTER 10

The kit? What the fuck was the kit? Liv's mind was jumping ahead. Dark thoughts. Scary, dark thoughts. *What was it?*

All of them sat in absolute silence while Moose ran off to Chipmunk's tent cabin, his head torch flashing from side to side. When he returned, he was holding a metal cookie tin.

Liv glanced at Ben. His hands were resting on the ground. Liv could see them moving, working almost imperceptibly, his calloused fingers scratching in the dirt.

Moose handed the tin to Chipmunk and quickly retreated to the far side of the fire. She popped it open with practised efficiency, pulling out a small white object.

"You know the drill," she said, placing the object on the ground in front of Ben.

Liv was confused. Her tired mind was not up to this. The object looked like a shaver. A battery-operated shaver.

"You do it, or Lomax will assist you." Chipmunk nudged the shaver closer to the boy, with her boot.

It was finally making sense. Was this the "consequence" for bad behaviour – to shave your head? *Seriously?* How was this legal?

It was archaic and humiliating. Liv pictured photos from history books, black-and-white images of prisoners lined up like cattle, shaven heads and uniforms. Was this her life now?

Liv could see the edge of Ben's jaw, the muscles tight, his nails still deep in the dirt.

Say no, Liv willed this strange boy. *Don't do it. Fuck Chipmunk. Just refuse.*

This was abuse. Pure and simple.

"Fuck you," Ben growled, still not looking up. Liv cheered inside.

"Is that your final answer?" Chipmunk picked up the shaver and clicked it on. It buzzed angrily. She handed it to Lomax. He nodded.

No. No fucking way.

"Stop! This is inhumane…and…and probably illegal!" Liv blurted the words out before she could stop herself. "You can't do this. He's not an animal. He has rights!"

For the first time since his arrival, Ben looked up at her, his eyes dark and intense.

Chipmunk wheeled around to face her.

"Well then, are you volunteering to take his place, Miss Olivia Walker?" Chipmunk smiled coldly as she said it.

This was wrong! So wrong. Liv wanted to shout at her – to tell her she couldn't threaten them like this. But her next words died on her lips as she looked at Lomax, the locked-in expression, the buzzing shaver in his hand. Again, Liv felt the chill of fear as her stark reality caught up with her.

She had no power here.

None.

But she couldn't just accept this. She couldn't sit back and do nothing. She couldn't let this evil woman bully them…she wouldn't. It wasn't right.

"Well…?" Chipmunk demanded, eyes narrowed. She seemed to sense the challenge. She seemed to invite it. "What's it to be, Walker? Fancy a new look?"

Liv took a deep breath, steadying herself for what she was about to do. Probably the most stupid thing she'd ever done. But she had no choice. *It just wasn't right.*

Bring it.

She stepped forward…

Suddenly Ben exploded off the ground, snatching the shaver out of Lomax's hands. He turned and without so much as a backward glance, walked off into the dark woods, closely followed by Lomax.

Liv's knees felt shaky. A wave of nausea hit her; she could taste beans again. She felt a hand on her elbow; someone was standing by her side. Lucas.

"It's okay," he whispered.

A faint buzzing sound could be heard from the trees where Ben had disappeared. The crickets jumped into action nearby, loudly joining in the mechanical chorus.

Chipmunk was talking again.

"…stay away…troublemakers like Benjamin Cross…your own healing journey…"

She went on and on, the sound of her voice droning loudly, mixing with the faint buzzing in the woods behind her. But Liv only caught half of her words. She didn't need to hear them to know what she was saying.

Lucas was wrong. It wasn't okay. None of this was okay. She closed her eyes. She couldn't do this. She couldn't be in this fucked-up place.

Not for another day or a week, let alone three months…or longer. She couldn't be here.

Fuck her dad. Fuck him. Fuck Carianne for doing this to her. Fuck.

"…within the rules. It's that dang simple. Y'all do what I say and follow *The Programme*, and we'll all get along just fine." Chipmunk was finally wrapping up her lecture. She nodded in the direction of the buzzing noise, the warning clear.

At long last, and with curt directions to go immediately to bed, Chipmunk turned abruptly and stalked off towards her cabin, an air of victory about her.

With a sad nod of his head, and the weak suggestion that they should all get a good ol' night's sleep, Moose followed.

When they were out of earshot, Liv turned to the others.

"Why do you put up with this?" Anything had to be better than staying here under Chipmunk's sadistic rule.

"What are we supposed to do?" Ruby blurted out, gripping tightly to Milo's hand. "You just got here, Liv. You have no idea what they're capable of. We're completely trapped. If we run, we'll either drown or die…or worse – the Sheriff's deputies will catch us."

"Good!" Liv shook her head, exasperated. "We can tell the Sheriff what's going on here. They'll have to put a stop to all this."

Ruby exchanged a dark look with Milo.

"You just don't get it, Liv. The Sheriff is the worst of them. He knows exactly what's going on. If someone keeps getting in trouble, Chipmunk will send for the Sheriff to come to the camp and help Lomax 're-educate' them."

"*Re-educate?*" Liv swallowed. That did not sound good.

"Military style. It's brutal. They make you do drills until you vomit or pass out. They won't stop until they break you. I'm not even kidding; you do not want to have anything to do with the Sheriff, Liv. Trust me. And you don't want to keep pissing Chipmunk off." There was genuine fear in Ruby's voice. Liv got it. She had enough imagination to know that being "re-educated" by Lomax and this Sheriff person would not be a good thing.

Her nausea was only getting worse. She must have looked like she felt because Milo stepped forward.

"Look, don't worry so much. It's always like this around here. You'll get used to it. Just keep your head down and let Ben take the flack – you'll be fine," Milo said with a forced smile.

"Milo's right," Ruby added. "Ben can take it. Trust me, Liv – he can give as good as he gets. Don't feel sorry for him. He's kinda scary. Rumour has it he killed a kid. That's why he's here."

"Wait, what…?" Liv wasn't expecting that.

Milo cut in, "Apparently, he was in a school fight and lost his temper. He went too far and literally beat a kid to death. It was ruled an accidental death, but he was sent to the WTC right after, probably so he wouldn't kill anyone else. I guess we don't count as anyone important. They don't seem to care about *our* safety."

Shocked, Liv turned to look at the woods. The buzzing had stopped. Ben was out there somewhere, in the darkness.

"That's why we all keep our distance." Milo gave a half-smile. "Listen, it's liveable here. Just do what you're told and don't cross Chipmunk. Okay? And whatever you do, stay well away from Ben." He nodded to the trees. Liv thought she saw a movement, the flash of eyes in the darkness watching them. "Chipmunk was right about one thing when she said he's trouble. *Big* trouble. Our Ben over there…he's a stone-cold killer."

CHAPTER 11

Rare sunlight. Its precious warmth touching a cornflower-blue armchair turned to face a high window with a view across grey rooftops. A soft cough; the rustle of a page turning. Liv knows she's there, hidden behind the high back of the chair, legs curled up underneath her, reading glasses falling low on her nose. Lost in her book, until her tea grows cold.

Liv stands in the doorway and watches silently. If she could just reach out and touch the back of the chair, or step into the warm light. If she could just say something – anything – her mom might look around, might see her. Everything would be okay again. But she can't move – she can't speak. She is trapped in her own body, like so many other nights, so many other dreams. Standing silently by, feeling her mother just out of reach. Always…forever beyond her.

A sound startled Liv awake. The warm, sunny dream slipped away as she opened her eyes to darkness.

It took a moment to get her bearings – the tent, Camp Smiling Skies. It took less than a moment for her heart to drop.

There was the sound again. A small whimper from the sleeping bag stretched out next to her. Shasta was crying.

Liv had no idea what time it was, but there were no signs of daylight yet. It had been a long, messy night, her sleep broken intermittently by strange sounds and dark thoughts. Both she and Shasta seemed to be caught in alternating cycles of misery, taking turns to fitfully awaken.

"Mmmm mmm mmm…"

This time around, Shasta's whimpers were morphing into something bigger. She was losing it.

Reluctantly, Liv poked her head out of the sleeping bag and looked over at her roomie. All she could make out was a dark outline, sitting up now, rocking backward and forward.

"Mmmmm mmmm…"

Fuck. Liv had no idea if Shasta was younger than her, but she looked like she was. She seemed way too gentle for this. Why on earth would her parents send their daughter here, when she was clearly not built for tough love? What had she done to deserve being dragged out of her bed in the middle of the night? Then again, what had any of them done?

Liv ran through her options. She could fetch a counsellor, but that would only make things worse. She could go back inside her bag and try to block her ears. But even as she thought it, she knew she couldn't blank it out. It wasn't just the noise. It was the fact that a metre from her, someone was hurting so badly.

"Hey, Shasta." Liv reached out and gently touched the girl's arm.

"No…no…no." Shasta reacted instantly. "We can't talk. What if Chipmunk hears us…? What if she comes to check on us? I can't…"

"It's okay," Liv spoke quickly and quietly. "If we keep our voices down no one will hear." Liv was projecting all the calmness she could muster. She felt around the edges of her sleep mat for her water bottle and held it out to Shasta – it was all she had to offer, even though the water was lukewarm and tasted of iodine and backwash.

Shasta shook her head – clearly not that desperate – but her rocking slowed slightly.

"So, what brings you to Camp Smiling Skies?" More than anything, Liv wanted to go back to sleep, or at the very least lie in silent misery. But she could tell that talking was helping a little.

"I…" Shasta took a great gulping sob, clearly trying to get her shit together. "I'm fat."

It was so matter of fact that Liv didn't react at first.

"You're…*fat?*" Liv scratched her head. What do you say to that? "What are you talking about?"

"No. I mean, I'm here because my parents think I'm fat." There was not a whisper of insincerity in the way Shasta said it. Liv just stared at her dark outline for a solid moment.

"You mean, your parents sent you here…because of your *weight?*" Okay, maybe her own father wasn't looking quite as bad now. Any way you sliced or diced it, Liv was no angel. But Shasta's parents had thought it was a good idea to incarcerate their sweet girl in what basically amounted to a prison camp…*to lose weight?* "Holy shit. I'm really sorry, Shasta. That's fucked up."

Shasta nodded, her wide-spaced eyes welling up with tears again.

"When we arrived, Chipmunk gave me this." Shasta reached under her pillow and pulled out something. Picking up her head torch, she shone the light on a small white square. Her letter.

Liv's letter, addressed to her in her father's handwriting, was still firmly wedged into a hole in the tree stump next to the poop bucket – unopened.

Carefully, Shasta opened the envelope and handed the letter gingerly to Liv.

It was a quick read:

To our little Shasta Bear,

Please don't be all upset with us. We love you, baby girl. But we just didn't know what else to do. We've tried everything, but nothing has worked! This is the only way. The thing is, you may not understand this now, but one day you will. This world isn't kind to people who don't fit in. Look at you, baby girl. You're still so young with your whole life ahead of you. But your eating disorder is hurting you inside and out, and we can't sit by and watch you throw away your future. We just want the best for you. We know that this time spent in nature will get you moving again. It's a fresh chance to build new, healthier habits. You will feel so much better about yourself when you lose the extra weight. All the boys will like you! We promise. So don't be angry. Next time we see you, we won't even recognize our little Pooh Bear.

Be strong for Mama and Papa. We love you.

Liv snorted loudly.

"Shhh!" Shasta admonished. But then they both broke into giggles. For a solid minute, they couldn't stop themselves, rolling around the tent, tears running down their dirty faces.

"Poor little Shasta Bear…" Liv couldn't help it. Clearly Shasta's folks had the emotional intelligence of kindergarteners. "All the skank boys will like you…" She was laughing so hard, she had to force down the urge to cough.

"And…and the funny thing is," Shasta said, gasping for air. "I don't even like boys! That's how well they know me."

They both fell back, cascading with laughter. It took a solid few minutes and a loud sound from the bushes outside to finally quiet them down.

"Why here?" Liv had to ask. "Aren't there better ways to lose weight than wilderness therapy? Like a gym membership? I mean, isn't this camp for scary problem kids? You know…like me?" She grinned.

"I've been wondering about that," Shasta said thoughtfully. "My parents are really into keeping up appearances, and they'd never live it down if they forcibly sent their daughter to 'fat-camp'."

"And this is better?"

Shasta nodded sadly. "You see, this way, they can blame me. They're probably telling everyone I was depressed – that I *chose* to come here cos I wanted a break or to be in nature or something. But I didn't choose this, Liv. I would never want this. My life is really nice. I have friends and my books, and there's this girl I'm talking to. I wasn't depressed or even unhappy, and I don't want to lose weight. I like myself the way I am. It's just…I guess they don't."

As she lay back down, Liv felt a stab of raw anger. They should kidnap all the messed-up parents who thought it was okay to do this to their kids – the people who depended on them most in the world. Yeah, someone should kidnap *them* and make them shit in a bucket. See how they liked it.

Troubled Teens? How about Fucked-Up Parents?

She rolled over. There was that tight feeling in her gut again. She pushed her fist into her stomach, trying to knead it out. But it didn't help; the feeling was deep inside. The urge to cry was creeping up again. Fuck, this was so hard.

"Liv?" Shasta's voice was so quiet, Liv had to turn to face her to catch the words.

"Yeah."

"I'm not sure. I just. I don't know…I don't think I can do this." Shasta sounded shaky. "I don't think I'll make it…"

Ripples of wind tugged at the fabric roof. A bird caw-cawed loudly nearby, and far away another took up its call. It felt like a warning – a stark reminder that this place wasn't for humans. Enter if you dare. Liv swallowed hard; her fingers reached into her pocket and found her ring. She slipped it on her finger, rubbing her thumb gently over the metal.

What could she say to Shasta? Honestly – what could she say? It'll be okay? It'll only be for three months, as long as you starve yourself enough to impress your stupid parents. Three lean, hungry months for Shasta. But what about *her*? Milo's words were stuck in her head on a doom-loop: "You graduate *The Programme* when your parents want you to come home."

When your parents want you home. When your parents want you…

Liv rolled onto her other side, her back to Shasta, tears falling easily now.

"I know," she finally whispered. "I know. Me too."

CHAPTER 12

It sounded stupid, given everything, but Liv missed her phone so much it actually hurt.

After the chat with Shasta, sleep wasn't happening, and she would have given *anything* to just put on her headphones, her playlist, lie back and escape from here – even just for a moment. Back into her own world, her own life, where there were no Chipmunks or Lomaxes, where she'd never been kidnapped and dragged out here. None of it.

Normal life. It was hard to believe anything would ever be normal now. At some point in her dark musings, it had occurred to her that this was a Friday night – in the real world at least. She didn't know what time it was, but the chances were, she'd be working her closing shift at Woody's Pizzeria right about now.

What would her boss think when she didn't show up for work? Liv was sure her father wouldn't let them know what had happened to her; that would require him admitting what he'd done. She was going to lose her job, wasn't she?

Fuck.

She loved her job; it was a break from school and home life.

She hadn't made many friends in Flagstaff, but work filled that void. Weekend nights were always super busy, but it was a good laugh with her ragtag bunch of coworkers. She didn't want to lose her job. She didn't deserve to. She was a good worker.

This wasn't right.

It wasn't fair.

As if her night wasn't going badly enough, Liv's brain had decided somewhere in the middle of her dark musings that she really, *really* needed a bucket break. She'd tried to ignore it, but her subconscious was locked on one track now, and she knew herself well enough to know it wasn't going to go away.

There was no way she was going to hike down to the bucket-of-despair in the deepest, darkest woods. But she could make a quick stop in a nearby bush. It wasn't like anyone would see her.

Sighing, she pushed herself out of her sleeping bag and, as quietly as she could, unzipped the flap of the tent. The air outside was crisp and cold, but it wasn't as scary as she'd imagined while lying in the dark tent listening to all the night sounds. The moon was out, and a bright, silvery glow touched everything.

Heading to the bushes, she tiptoed past the other tents and was almost at the tree line when she heard it.

"No! Stop!" a low voice shouted.

Liv jumped. *What the fuck?* She looked around at the trees, but nothing emerged.

"No, Dillon…no. Stop. Please, just stop." The words were jumbled, mixed with mumbled sounds and sobs.

The voice was coming from inside the tent she'd just passed. Had she woken someone up? Whose tent was it? Liv looked around, trying to place the tent in her mind. The first tent by the rock wall.

That was Milo. No, wait – Lucas. It was Lucas's tent.

"I'm sorry…God, I'm sorry…" followed by more mumbling. It was incoherent sleep talk. Lucas must be dreaming. "No…no, Dillon…mmmnh."

The name Dillon kept coming up repeatedly. It was clearly Lucas's voice, but he sounded so different from the cool, easy-going surfer-boy from earlier – broken somehow, and clearly lost in a nightmare, locked in his mind.

She understood. Her dream, her mom in the chair, always out of sight, out of reach. The shock of grief hitting her over and over should she manage to fall asleep. Long nights were made for happy people; they served only to torture the sad. An echo chamber for their misery.

"No!" Lucas was sobbing now – great gulping sobs.

It was raw pain – she knew it, she recognized it. She could feel it through the thin fabric wall between them. It resonated in her, and something deep inside reached out to him. Connected with his suffering.

A part of her wanted to climb into the tent and wrap her arms around this sad boy – to hold him until his darkness passed. If she could only give him the one thing she'd needed, so desperately and for so long. The thing she had wished for, night after night after her mother died: that she wouldn't have to be so completely alone.

But it wasn't her place. She couldn't hug some random boy she barely knew. They were strangers in every way that mattered. She was on the outside and he was inside, alone. That was the way it had to be.

She reached out her hand, her fingers softly touching the fabric of the tent between them.

"Mmph…mmm…" Lucas's voice was losing its edge now; he was sobbing softly, the nightmare fading, the sounds muffled into his sleeping bag.

In time he drifted; his breathing slowed to a steady rhythm. There was comfort in the sound. Whatever he was carrying had lifted. His pain floated away on the night air as he fell into the sweet kindness of a dreamless sleep. Doing its work, working its magic. Healing.

Wiping a grubby hand across her face, Liv pushed away tears. Whatever Lucas had been through, whatever this Dillon person had done to him, his pain was still brutally raw. She could see him now; that easy manner was hiding a pit of something dark – maybe something that had brought him to Camp Smiling Skies.

She wasn't the only screw-up here then. She wasn't the only one with a secret. The thought was oddly reassuring. If they'd all been like Shasta – good kids with idiot parents – then she would have been in a league of her own. But no. There was Ben-the-Killer, and now Lucas, hiding secrets behind a perfect smile. Yes, she fitted right in. Camp Smiling Skies collected fuck-ups, and she was one of them.

This was the island of broken toys.

Welcome home, Liv.

Welcome home.

CHAPTER 13

Nothing quite like waking up stiff and sore after a freezing cold night of camping. Character building or torture? There was a fine line.

It took some aggressive whistle blowing on Chipmunk's part to drag everyone out of their tents, but sometime in the grey hour after dawn, they reluctantly emerged – tousled, puffy-eyed and in a collectively foul mood.

At some point in the long sleepless night, the sleeping bag just hadn't cut it, and the cold had seeped into Liv's bones. Even now, after a hot oatmeal-mush breakfast, her hands were stiff, and her nose was running constantly. Not pretty, but she didn't care any more. Between tossing and turning her way through Shasta and Lucas's dark-nights-of-the-soul, Liv had come to a decision.

She was going to get out of here.

Her father had already revealed his hand by having Liv forcibly incarcerated. If Liv knew anything about Carianne, there was no way in hell the unwanted stepdaughter would be allowed home any time soon – if ever.

Nope. If Liv wanted to leave this place before she turned

eighteen, she had to escape. She wasn't sure what she'd do if she got away. Maybe make her way up to Seattle and find Min? If Min's parents weren't able to help her, she could cross the border into Canada. She would figure it out. She just had to find a way out of Camp Smiling Skies first, and to do that…she needed an expert.

She needed to talk to Ben-the-Killer.

So far, all she'd heard were rumours and scare stories about how impossible it was to leave. In all of his failed attempts to escape, Ben must have tested out some of those rumours. If she could just work out where he was going wrong, maybe she could figure out how to do it right.

The morning kicked off with tough drills. They all had to fill their backpacks with logs until they were impossibly heavy – easily half their body weight. Lifting them was challenging enough, but they were forced to swing them up and onto their shoulders, then drop them back on the ground, over and over. Liv was under no illusion about the reason for this exercise. Hiking for miles just wasn't bad enough. Hiking for miles while pointlessly carrying a ridiculously heavy pile of wood was a much better idea. Demoralizing and physically brutal. Perfect.

The thing was – Liv didn't care.

Yesterday, this exercise might have made her want to cry. The futility, the hopelessness of her situation, might have overwhelmed her.

But today? Everything was different.

Her fingers touched the swallow ring in her pocket. She was her mother's daughter, and like a bird she was going to find a way to fly out of this cage. No matter what. She was going to fly free.

The sun was still lurking behind the crags, when the group

finally struggled into their packs one last time, and reluctantly began their first activity of the day – a seven-mile hike with a stop at a swim hole on the Ochee River.

Chipmunk led them. Moose remained at the camp to prep the week's meals, and, to everyone's relief, Lomax had left sometime before dawn to return to town and wasn't expected back for a few days.

This was it – this was Liv's chance to get Ben alone and find out what he knew.

Unfortunately, her escape expert proved to be elusive.

Throughout the hike, Ben lurked off to one side or the other, keeping his distance from the group. He kept his freshly shaven head down, and every time Liv drifted into his vicinity, he drifted in the other direction. He seemed supremely uninterested in the newcomers and hadn't spoken a word since last night. The challenge was going to be getting close enough to even start a conversation, let alone convince him to spill all his escape secrets.

Making things near impossible, Chipmunk was watching Ben at all times. Clearly, she was going to make damn sure he didn't do another runner during the hike.

No – it wasn't going to be easy to pin Ben down. But Liv was committed. No matter how dangerous Ben-the-Killer might be, he had something she needed: information.

It was nearing lunchtime when Ruby abruptly stopped in the middle of the river trail. She uttered a small shriek.

"Oh my God! What is that? That is so disgusting." They were passing through a clearing by the river. Something grey and matted was lying at her feet.

Chipmunk inspected the lump.

"Just the carcass of a baby deer. It must have drowned in the river." She nudged it with the toe of her boot. The sticky mass shifted slightly, its rigid legs sticking straight up in the air. "They do that. Baby animals. Go wading around in the shallows and whoopsie – the current takes 'em."

"It's the curse of the Ochee," Milo said, jumping in on the action, as always. "Rumour has it that there was a village on the banks of the river, just upstream from here. One night, a flash flood swept it away, drowning everyone in their sleep, their bodies carried miles by the floodwaters. Tragic, really. They say, if you come to the river at night, you can see their pale ghost faces, just below the surface, calling you to join them in their watery grave. You might even see little Kevon Wright crying for his mommy…"

Liv caught herself muttering unkind things under her breath, as she glared at the mischievous, irritating boy. Did he ever stop? Was everything a game to him?

"Enough drama from you, Mister Milo. Let's move it along now," Chipmunk barked, reaching threateningly for her whistle.

Grumbling, they kept walking along the trail. Liv glanced reluctantly at the baby deer as she passed it. Something had been snacking on the carcass and large chunks of fur were missing. A fly buzzed lazily out of its open mouth. But despite the decrepit state of it, there was still a childlike innocence to the small body. Its oversized head and scrawny limbs had an aching vulnerability to them. The little glassy eyes stared blankly out at the world. Seeing nothing. Feeling nothing. A life that had barely begun.

It seemed ridiculous to feel sad for a random dead animal, but there was something about the indignity of its untimely death that felt cruel – the futility of trying to protect yourself, when at any moment a powerful current could sweep you away.

Those hollow eyes. Those empty spaces.

Liv kept walking.

It took her a few bends in the trail before she realized that this was the moment she'd been waiting for. Chipmunk was far ahead now, at the front of the line, and seemed to have momentarily forgotten about her nemesis, Ben. The others were following her obediently. Only one person was missing. Ben had dropped behind.

This was it!

Turning, Liv ran back down the trail as fast as she could. She was almost at the clearing, when she stopped. Ben was squatting next to the carcass.

Instinctively, Liv ducked behind a nearby tree. Something told her that whatever he was doing wasn't meant to be witnessed.

Carefully, Liv peeked around the edge of the tree trunk. Her view was limited, partially obscured by ferns, but she could see that Ben was leaning over the deer, doing something with his hands. *What was he doing?* What was Ben-the-Killer doing to the baby deer? Thoughts cascaded into her mind. Bad thoughts. The deer was dead already. Why couldn't he just leave it alone? What was his problem?

She was tempted to intervene. But a small niggling voice in her head kept reminding her that this boy was a known killer. Someone who'd beaten another boy to death with his bare hands. Maybe surprising him in the middle of whatever he was doing wasn't the best idea.

It was several minutes before Ben sat back and wiped his muddy hands on his trousers. For the first time, Liv got a clear look at his face. It had the serious expression of an artist, evaluating their creation – critical and calculating. "Psychopath" popped into Liv's mind before she could stop it. She'd tried not to go there, not to follow those thoughts, but there were too many doubts. *What had he done to the baby deer?*

Abruptly, Ben stood up and brushed the dirt off, turning to go. Liv ducked behind the tree. Her heart was beating hard as she pushed her back up against the trunk, willing herself to melt into the wood, unseen.

There were sounds and rustling noises now. Ben was on the move, coming closer, heading for the trail. Liv strained her ears, tracking every noise, as she waited for him to pass.

Eventually, the sounds tapered off, heading in the direction of the others. Sighing, she leaned back, relieved. Just to be extra safe, she stayed hidden in the ferns for a full minute after he'd gone. Then finally, when she was sure she was in the clear, she stepped out onto the trail.

Fuck.

She wasn't alone.

He'd tricked her.

Ben-the-Killer was standing on the trail, staring right at her.

CHAPTER 14

Liv bit her lip hard and tasted blood.

"Why are you following me?" Ben growled. His voice was low, barely above a whisper. He rippled with physical aggression, his body was taut and tight, fists clenched, poised to dispatch the threat standing in front of him.

Liv glared at him defensively. If she was going to die, she would go fighting, kicking and screaming.

"I need to talk to you." Her voice cracked with nervous energy.

"Why?" His head tipped down, eyes locked on her. It was the first time she'd been this close, and what she saw was far scarier than she could ever have imagined. There was an edge of something in his look – something deeply unnerving lurking behind his dark eyes. Something…unexpected: he had *soft* eyes – warm and brown with long, deer-like lashes.

A killer with kind eyes. Not a good combination.

"Ben…listen," she said, forcing herself to speak calmly. Best to get this over with, one way or another. "I just…I thought you might know how to get out of here. Everyone keeps saying it's impossible to escape, that there's no way out. But I don't believe that. There has to be a way. There has to." There, she'd said it – more like babbled it out. She'd done what she set out to do.

Now he could murder her if he wanted to.

"Why should I tell you anything?" Ben's voice was unchanged – low and dangerous. But his hands released, and he shifted his weight back slightly. Okay, this had to be a good sign.

"You don't have to talk to me. Whatever. It's just…" Liv pulled herself up tall. It was now or never. She needed something from him, and this was her chance. She took a deep breath. "Look, we don't know each other. I get it. But neither of us wants to be here. I can't be here…I have to get out of here. *I have to*." She felt prickles in the back of her eyes. Damn it, she did not want to cry. Not here, in front of this scary boy. "Look, if you tell me what you know, anything, maybe…" Maybe what? She really hadn't thought this through.

In the distance there was a faint *peeeeeeeweeee*. Chipmunk must have noticed that some of her flock had strayed. Ben's eyes flicked up; a guarded, locked-in expression settled on his face.

She was almost out of time. It was now or never.

"Ben…please. I can't stay here. I can't…*I won't*." She sniffed. Stupid Liv. She felt the tears on her cheeks now and firmly told herself to get her shit together. *Stupid*.

Ben hadn't moved. Liv tried and failed to meet his eyes. What was the point? Honestly? What was she expecting from him? She should just go.

"The river." Ben's voice was so low, Liv had to strain to hear the next part. "It's the only way out. Tried the peaks. Nothing but wilderness on the other side. You'd be lucky to survive. Road's too slow, and it dead ends at the drop-off. It's landlocked with no traffic to flag down. It would take a day to hike it back to the main road.

By the time you're down the valley, the Sheriff will be waiting for you. The only way out is the river. On the far side there's an animal track. Runs along the water for a few miles, then heads up over the ridge. Half a day and you'll be in Nevada. Sheriff can't touch you there." He looked at her intently. The softness was gone. "I'm only telling you cos you stood up for me last night, with Chipmunk. Tell anyone else, I'll kill you. This makes us even." He nodded, as if confirming something to himself, and turned to go.

"Wait," Liv blurted out. "The river. The others said it can't be crossed. It's white water. If you swim, you'll drown. Like that boy… Kevon Something?"

Ben flinched. Shit, she'd struck a nerve. Oh God, she forgot. He was with the boy when he drowned. He knew him.

Peeeewww. Peeeeewwwwweeeeeeee. Peeeeeeeewwwwww. The sounds were getting closer.

She looked imploringly at him.

"If the river's the only way out…if it's not swimmable…" *Then there really is no way to escape*, she added in her head.

Ben just shrugged.

"That's your problem, Walker. I never said it would be easy." Was that a smile? A hint of a smile? Liv wasn't sure if she'd imagined it. Before she could ask more questions, Ben turned and walked away up the path. She watched as he went, head down, shoulders up.

Well, that counted as a successful mission. After all, she'd got the information she'd wanted, even if it had just confused her. But now she was more curious than ever to know what Ben – the killer with kind eyes – had done to the poor baby deer.

Quickly, she returned to the clearing, heading over to the riverbank.

At first, she was confused. The carcass was gone. In its place was just a muddy mound of wet earth. Where was it? What had Ben done with it? She stepped closer, for the first time noticing that there were small white wildflowers set out on the top of the muddy mound.

A cross. Ben had made a flower cross.

It was a grave.

Ben had buried the little deer. While the rest of them had simply laughed and moved on, he'd dug a hole and placed the tiny body in it, covering it carefully with mud. The little deer was finally respected; its broken body carefully laid to rest.

For a minute, Liv just stood, staring at the grave, confusion stirring up uncomfortable thoughts. She had come back to find… what? Not this. All her guilty suspicions seemed glaringly shameful now. How could she have imagined such things? She had lurked behind a tree, spying and projecting all her inner darkness, while Ben-the-Killer was picking flowers and gently placing them on the baby deer's grave.

What was wrong with her? What was wrong with her head?

Who was the bad guy here?

CHAPTER 15

The river. It's the only way out.

It was also numbingly cold and muddy with slippery creatures darting about in its murky depths.

The swim hole had turned out to be a pool of river water next to a mudbank, trapped behind a massive fallen redwood tree. The huge tree trunk stuck out several metres into the fast-flowing river, creating a safe backwater, protected from the river's dangerous current.

Concerningly, Ruby and Milo seemed overly excited about this whole swim hole visit and instantly stripped down to their underwear and jumped in. As they explained, this was a once-a-week treat and their only time to bathe and wash their clothes. They were each given a tiny piece of soap and set loose in the muddy water to try and scrub away some of their grime.

Feeling awkward, Liv kept her oversized T-shirt on, only removing her combat trousers and boots. She discreetly slipped her mother's ring on her finger, not wanting to risk it falling out of her pocket. Then she dipped into the icy water, gasping at the cold. It took several minutes to scrub all over with the little piece of soap, and it only took the edge off the ingrained dirt. But that was enough for now. She wasn't overly concerned that it would be a whole week until the next swim because she didn't plan on being around that long.

After the "bath", the campers were fed an underwhelming lunch of stale trail mix and dispersed under strict orders to return in half an hour, when Chipmunk blew her whistle. Milo and Ruby ran off upstream, whispering about some inane thing or other. Ben quietly disappeared downstream, with Chipmunk trailing close behind. Exhausted from the interminably long hike, Shasta lay down under a shady tree, next to Lucas, and fell asleep.

Only Liv had returned to the river. Her fingers were pruned now, her wet T-shirt felt uncomfortably heavy, and her toes were numb. But she didn't mind. She needed this valuable time to plot her escape.

If she strained her eyes and looked at the far bank, she was sure she could make out a small stretch of Ben's animal track: the track that would take her over the crags and into Nevada. It was there. Liv could feel it – this was her way out, with just fifteen…maybe twenty metres of water in the way.

She just had to figure out how to get to it without drowning.

Shifting her attention to the river, Liv half-closed her eyes, studying its flow, trying to assess where the strongest currents might be. The river danced tantalizingly, catching diamonds of sunlight on the surface of the dark, churning water; it looked powerful and dangerous, swollen with rainwater from distant storms.

Admittedly, Liv wasn't the greatest swimmer – but she was good enough. Even if the current was strong, if she took her time, she should be able to make it across, right? How hard could it be to swim fifteen metres?

"Getting ideas?"

Liv jumped, inadvertently splashing a small plume of water into her own face. She spluttered and turned to glare at Lucas.

He was floating behind her, feet up. His blond curls were rat-tailed in the water; his shoulders glistened with ripples of reflected sunlight.

"What do you want?" Liv swallowed. She didn't need the distraction. He was disturbing her plotting time.

"What do I want?" He held his hands up placatingly. "Just swimming. Sorry, Olive Oil – I didn't realize it was *your* river." He said it with a wide, easy smile. He'd been like this all morning: joking around, alternating between cheerful and charming as though he were at a fun summer camp – not incarcerated in an outdoor prison. A perfect boy. Happy Lucas.

Happy Lucas who cried in his sleep.

"Well, swim somewhere else. I was here first." Liv tried to look aloof, but it was hard when your teeth were chattering.

Lucas nodded but didn't move away.

"You do know it's not swimmable." He was still looking at her. Was he reading her mind or something? "It's white water. It looks pretty calm from here, but it'll pull you under before you get halfway. Didn't some boy drown...?"

"Fuck's sake, I know already," Liv snapped. Why did everyone have to keep repeating the same old, same old. A kid drowned, she got it. But maybe this Kevon Wright was a terrible swimmer? Did anyone think about that? As for all the dire warnings – how did anyone actually know the river wasn't swimmable? Clearly, they hadn't tried. If they had, they would either be dead or in Nevada by now. Rumours. It was all just stupid rumours, probably started by

Chipmunk to scare them into staying at the camp. Well, she wasn't buying it. If the river was the only way out, then the river it was.

"Just saying, Olive Oil. If it was me, I wouldn't risk it," Lucas added, drifting onto his back.

Get out of my head, Liv thought angrily.

"Well, you're not me, and my name's not Olive Oil!" It came out stronger than she'd intended. "Stop calling me that. My name's Liv. Liv Walker. Not Olive, or Olivia, or Missy, or…or anything else. Just fucking Liv."

"Sorry, just messing with you." Slowly, he stretched one leg up in the air and massaged it lazily. Liv could see a long, angry scar running along the length of his calf and over the knee. The limp. "You don't like me, do you? What did I do to piss you off, Just-Fucking-Liv?" He was smiling again, a happy twinkle in his eyes. The light caught it and ran with it, his eyes flashing with the colours of the river.

Liv looked at him. Was he *flirting*? No, that wasn't possible. She couldn't remember the last time someone had flirted with her. Not since her Seattle days, at least. Her impressively average looks and unfriendly demeanour were enough to scare off most people.

She turned squarely to face him.

"You're right, I don't like you. You act like this is all a joke – like you're on some stupid vacation or something. We were kidnapped and dragged out here against our will. I don't get how you can just laugh about any of this. What part of this is funny? What part of this is remotely okay?"

"There are worse places," Lucas said with a shrug. But a small shadow crossed his face – just a brief touch of something darker, a crease that was almost instantly gone.

But Liv had caught that little look, and she wouldn't easily forget how he'd sounded last night, in his tent. What worse places? What was Lucas Cole hiding beneath his shiny facade? Who was Dillon?

"Why are you here, Lucas?" She met his open expression head on this time. "Someone sent you here, just like the rest of us losers. Someone paid a lot of money to get you out of their life. So, what was it? What did you do? What's your story?"

Lucas slowly rubbed his leg, his fingers tracing the path of the deep scar.

"You tell me yours – I'll tell you mine." The effortless, sweet, sexy smile was back in place.

"You already know why I'm here. Chipmunk announced it at the intake centre." Liv looked away as she said it. Chipmunk's blunt introduction was still fixed firmly in her head. "I'm here because I'm a low-life, waste-of-space, no-good liar and a thief – *apparently.*"

"Apparently?"

"Yeah. It's only stealing if it's not yours to begin with." An angry fire was starting to simmer inside her.

"What did you take?" Lucas drifted slowly closer, the flow gently nudging them together.

"A painting." She shrugged. "My father gave it to my stupid stepmother for their anniversary. But it was my mom's painting, and it wasn't his to give. So, I took it back, and they weren't happy about it." That was an understatement. They *really* weren't happy about it, and they were even less happy when they found out they wouldn't be getting the expensive painting back. Liv would never forget the horrified expression on their faces as they stood in the backyard by the smouldering grill, watching as the last corner of the canvas crinkled and melted in the fire. It was almost worth getting sent to Camp Smiling Skies, just for that moment. *Almost.*

"Why didn't your mom just ask for her painting back?" Lucas said.

"Kind of hard to ask for things when you're dead." She sniffed and batted at her nose. "It's your turn now." She was done oversharing.

Lucas nodded, but there was something new in his expression. Something uncharacteristically serious.

"I'm sorry, Liv. I lost my mom too. There was an accident when I was little. My family…my mom and dad, my brother—"

"Your *family?*" Liv's face dropped. He'd lost his whole family? What did she have to complain about? "Jesus. Lucas…I—"

Lucas shook his head. "No, don't feel bad for me. It was years ago. Honestly, I don't even remember them. I live with my grandparents, and they're awesome. My life's been good."

Obviously not that good, or he wouldn't be at Camp Smiling Skies now. Liv's mind was throwing up question after question. Was he in the accident? Was that where he injured his leg? What had he done to make his "awesome" grandparents sign him up for wilderness torture?

But before she could ask any of them, Lucas seemed to read her mind yet again.

"It's not my grandparents' fault I'm here. I got in a bit of trouble. I was partying a lot and things got a little wild. They're in their eighties. It was all just too much for them to handle. They were right to send me away – they really didn't have a choice. I get it. It's on me."

He was taking it so reasonably. Full accountability. Very mature and responsible. Liv wrinkled up her nose and looked at him. There he was, all golden and sunshiny, floating in the sparkly water. The picture was perfect. The words were well chosen. But Liv still couldn't forget the voice from the tent – *his* voice. His pain. His grief. This cool, collected boy just wasn't telling her the full story.

So, of course, with her typical lack of social skills, she just had to ask, "Who's Dillon?"

It was as though Liv's words had slapped him – hard. Lucas stood up, water dripping off him, shock imprinted on his handsome features. He glared at her; all warmth now gone.

"How do you know about Dillon?"

"I'm sorry!" she said quickly, though she wasn't quite sure what she was apologizing for. "Lucas, I'm sorry. I just—"

"I asked you – *how do you know about Dillon?*" He was like a different person. Angry. His body language changed; his voice was unrecognizable. Instinctively, Liv backed away.

"Look, I'm sorry, okay? It's just, I heard you last night. You were talking in your sleep and called out 'Dillon', over and over. That's it – that's all."

For a long, awkward moment, Lucas glared at her. His blue eyes looked stark and cold. Empty now. Liv felt herself wilt slightly.

"Lucas…I'm sorry—"

"Fuck you, Liv." Lucas turned his back to her, shoulders taut with anger.

Liv kicked herself. What she'd overheard last night was private. Something painful. It wasn't her place to bring it up. Why couldn't she just act like a normal person and think before she spoke? Maybe if she'd thought about it for half a damn second, she would have realized it wasn't right to mention it. It wasn't kind.

Lucas was already wading towards the shore, head down.

A habitual self-loathing kicked into gear. She knew this feeling well. She was so stupid. Everything always came out wrong. This was why people didn't like her – why they couldn't love her – why her own father didn't want her around. Why couldn't she just mind her own damn business…?

A piercing shriek stopped her cold.

Her thoughts fell away instantly. A shout? A scream?

She looked around. Lucas stopped too. Where had the sound come from?

"*Help!*" The voice was female. There was a loud rustling in the bushes on the bank upstream as a figure broke through the trees. It was Ruby. "Help! Please, someone! *Help!*"

Liv looked at Lucas; he met her eyes.

"What is it? What's happening?" he called out.

"Over there." Ruby waved her arms wildly, pointing to the river upstream. "He fell…he fell in!"

Liv felt a hard rush of fear.

She scanned the tops of the white water upstream, far beyond the fallen tree. The fast-flowing current was pulling something along with it. She could see colour – bright yellow with flashes of something dark, flipping over and submerging.

She didn't need to hear Ruby's next words. She already knew.

"It's Milo… Help him! He fell in…he's drowning! *He's drowning!*"

CHAPTER 16

There was no time to think.

Liv launched herself towards the fallen redwood tree, wading through the water until she was next to its sideways trunk. Digging her fingers into the bark, she pulled herself on top. The trunk was about a metre across and formed a crude bridge stretching far out into the river. She half-ran, as fast as she dared, to the tip of the tree, almost at mid-river.

The yellow mass was heading towards her fast. If she was in the water, she might be able to reach Milo as he was swept past. Lucas clearly had the same thought; he was just behind her.

Voices called out from behind, shouting. Liv ignored them. She had to focus. She was the closest and might be Milo's only hope.

Kneeling down, she carefully lowered herself into the water. The current here was strong and pulled at her, but she wedged her fingers into a hole in the trunk, holding tight.

She looked around for Milo. A flash of yellow appeared briefly – he was close to the edge of the river, just upstream. It could work. If she timed it right, if she leaned out, she could reach him when he was swept past.

This far out, she could feel the immense power of the river. She was in up to her neck now, clinging desperately to the tree trunk, willing her grip to hold.

A hand grabbed her wrist. She looked up. Lucas was lying on top of the trunk with one hand stretched down to her. He nodded. He had her.

The river was churning; the yellow shape ducked in and out of view. Milo was almost there. Liv stretched her arm out, ready – her heart beating wildly. She would only get one chance at this. Milo's life depended on her. She couldn't fuck this up.

The current battered her, but Lucas's grip was strong and reassuring. They could do this, she told herself.

They had to.

It was time. The yellow shape headed straight for her. But just as she was gauging the distance, the current turned, sweeping around the end of the impeding tree, pulling Milo farther out, to mid-stream.

He was too far. She couldn't reach him from here.

Milo was going to drown.

No.

Liv pulled forward, yanking her arm out of Lucas's safe grip. She had to get closer to Milo. She had to. She couldn't let him die.

"Liv, no!" Lucas's voice was almost lost in the roar of the river.

But Liv couldn't stop. She launched herself into a cluster of submerged branches at the crown of the tree, just as yellow flashed up near to her. So close.

Grabbing wildly, she caught a branch with one hand, and reached out with the other, stretching desperately towards Milo.

It worked! She caught the edges of the yellow T-shirt; the fabric snagged on her fingertips. She had him!

She could feel the T-shirt fabric ripping slightly. But it didn't matter. Milo was safe.

Water was pummelling her hard now, pulling her forward. One hand clung to the T-shirt, the other to the branch; she wouldn't let go, but she could feel herself drifting, her legs floating out from under her. Desperately she tried to pull herself back towards the tree, but she just couldn't – the current was too strong.

Lucas was in the water now, still clinging to the trunk with one hand. He reached for her. But it was too little, too late.

Their combined weight was too much for the tree. The branch snapped off in Liv's hand. She felt herself picked up by the powerful current, floating free, as she was dragged out into the river and under.

Her grip on the T-shirt became a desperate grasp. Milo was now her saviour. A float holding her up. She broke the surface, only to be pulled underneath again almost instantly. She was held under, her panicked breath caught. She swallowed water. Choking.

Suddenly she was up again, spluttering for air. Her arms reached desperately for Milo, trying to hold on, but she only felt something hard and rigid.

Under again. Longer this time. She thrashed wildly. She needed air. Kicking out, she couldn't do anything. She swallowed more water. Couldn't breathe.

Then up. A flash of blue sky. Something dark. Yellow. Brief seconds. She gulped for air before going under again. Her arms were weakening. She couldn't hold on to Milo much longer. No air – she couldn't do it. She couldn't do it any more.

Over and over. Up and then under, she saw darkness, her arms were letting go. No strength. Nothing left. No fight. Her fingers slackened, releasing the yellow T-shirt at last. Milo was gone in seconds. It was all for nothing. She was floating away.

She was going to drown. Today. Now.

She was going to die.

CHAPTER 17

Hands. Strong hands.

Liv tried to focus but waves of darkness kept shutting her down. Gasping. Hard to breathe. Too hard.

Words. A voice. Male.

She might have been coughing, spluttering – she had no idea. Her ears were blocked; her eyes weren't working. But somewhere inside, it registered: she was alive.

"Just breathe." Her face was turned; she was on her side. Something was hitting her back, hard. There wasn't enough air. Nothing coming in. Each breath was blocked, obstructed. She couldn't breathe.

More hitting. Something loosened. She gagged.

"That's it."

Vomiting now. She was hacking, coughing up water. Over and over. Retching.

"Okay. It's okay…good." One hand was holding her on her side. One was rubbing her back.

She didn't know how long she lay like that. The dark spots in her vision were clearing. The retching stopped. She felt terrible – weak.

She had nearly died. She knew that much.

It was the closest she had ever come to death. But the full reality hadn't hit her yet. Her mind was blocking everything that wasn't needed in this moment, just to survive.

"Phew," the voice said. "Glad I didn't have to do mouth to mouth on *you*."

It was the first thing that pierced through the fog in her head. Who was insulting her? Now? Liv opened her eyes and looked around. She was lying on what looked like a stack of logs, meticulously tied together – a makeshift raft. Her rescuer was sitting close by, one arm still resting on her back.

Ben-the-Killer.

"Yeah…" She broke into a hacking cough. Her lungs hurt; her chest hurt. She was shaking from a potent mix of icy water and shock. "Me too. If you ever…don't bother…rather die—" More painful spluttering. "How did you…? What happened?"

"I saw you. Heard all the shouting." Ben removed his hand from her back and shuffled awkwardly away from her. For the first time she noticed that he was soaking wet. "Why were you in the river, Walker? Trying to escape?"

"I was trying to rescue Milo!" Liv's tone was indignant, but she didn't care. "He fell in and his T-shirt…his yellow T…" Flashes came to her. The yellow T-shirt, her fingers grabbing it. *Oh God, Milo.* "I had him. I had his shirt, but I couldn't hold on… Is he dead? Is Milo dead?"

"Nope. There was no one else. Just you. Clinging to a log with a T-shirt on it."

"A…a *log*?" What was he talking about? "It was Milo…he was…" What was going on?

There were more voices now, calling her name. The others were on the move, heading downstream, searching for her. Probably expecting to find a dead body washed up along the shore.

What had just happened? Liv forced her brain into gear. Ben said the T-shirt was on a log. She remembered the feeling, her arms clinging to something hard. Wood. So, what did that mean? Where was Milo?

Slowly the pieces were falling together. She'd never actually seen Milo, had she? Just the yellow T-shirt and something dark. But she remembered Ruby shouting for help.

Liv's brain called time. *No thinking, please. Not right now.* She'd nearly died. She would have drowned if it hadn't been for Ben, who seemed to have magicked a raft out of thin air and pulled her out of the river. He'd saved her life.

Wait, she should probably say that one out loud. Without thinking, she reached her hand out and touched it gently to Ben's arm.

"Ben...what you did...you saved my—"

"No. Don't go there. I didn't do it for you, Walker." Ben was looking down at her hand. At first, she thought she must have overstepped, touching him like that. But then she realized he was staring at her ring. She moved her hand away, closing her fist protectively over it.

"So, who'd you do it for then?" Liv wrapped her arms tightly around herself, suddenly aware that she was only wearing a wet T-shirt and underwear. The shivering was getting worse; she actually missed her ugly combat trousers.

"Wasn't personal." Ben stood up abruptly and kicked out at the edge of the raft.

Maybe not to him. Liv sighed. It certainly was to her.

The voices were close now. She should probably call out to the others, but she wasn't sure of her lungs just yet and shouting was a stretch. Plus, what was Chipmunk going to say? This was not going to be pretty. Day two and Liv had almost drowned. Fun stuff. Bet that one wouldn't make the brochure.

Carefully, she sat up. Her throat was burning and her lungs ached. But she was already starting to turn the corner and feel a little more human.

"She's here! Oh my God, she's here!" Ruby appeared through the trees. She looked wildly desperate. Throwing herself forward, she crashed down the riverbank, landing a metre from the raft. "*You're alive!* I can't believe you're alive." Ruby threw herself onto Liv, almost knocking her back down.

One by one, the others appeared, slipping and sliding their way down the muddy riverbank. As soon as she arrived, Chipmunk elbowed Ruby out of the way and grabbed Liv by her shoulders, shaking her hard.

"Holy motherlode of bricks." Chipmunk's face was splotched with dark, angry red patches. "What the heck were you thinking, you stupid, *stupid* girl!"

"I'm sorry." Liv tried to pull back, unsuccessfully. The vice-like grip only tightened.

"If you'd drowned..." she said, adding an aggressive shake to every beat. "If you'd drowned, I would have been up to my dang neck in a whole heap of legal woes. Did you even think about the trouble you'd cause, jumping into the river like that?"

Liv glared at Chipmunk and considered comparing the "heap of legal woes" to being dead. But what was the point?

"I didn't jump in," she mumbled. Why did people keep saying that, like she'd deliberately gone for a nice swim in class-three rapids? "I was trying to save Milo."

A short burst of uncontrollable shivering racked her.

Chipmunk finally released her and stepped back, making large dramatic gestures: hands on waist, hands on knees, hands in hair, as though she was the one who had nearly died.

Shasta quietly slipped onto the raft next to Liv, discreetly slipping her arm around her shoulder and squeezing. The small gesture made Liv feel even more like crying.

Lucas was standing up on the riverbank, arms folded. He hadn't spoken, but his expression was serious and he looked unusually pale. Liv nodded reluctantly at him, avoiding eye contact. It seemed odd, but she was finding the whole "nearly dying" thing mortifyingly embarrassing. There was just too much attention.

Luckily, a movement from behind the trees distracted her and everyone else. A bare-chested and very dry Milo appeared sheepishly from where he'd been lurking behind a bush, just out of sight.

"Not fucking dead then?" Liv said sharply, eyes narrowing. Everyone turned to look at him. He had some serious explaining to do.

Milo tried a half-hearted grin. He walked up and dropped Liv's boots and combat trousers on the raft next to her. A peace offering.

"It was meant to be a joke," he started weakly. "Ruby and I—"

"Oh no, don't you dare. It wasn't my fault," Ruby called out, jumping forward. "It was all Milo's idea. He made me do it."

"Oh my God. What a bitch!" Milo moved up next to her. "You were totally up for it. You said it would be funny."

"I did not. Seriously! Don't even." Ruby held her hand up

definitively. She turned to face Chipmunk. "Milo wanted to prank the newbies. He came up with the whole thing. He put his T-shirt on a log and made me call for help." She looked at Liv, her big eyes growing even bigger. "I didn't think you'd actually believe me and try to *rescue* him. Liv, I'm really sorry…I'm so sorry…" She was tearing up. The potentially tragic consequences of her actions were hitting her.

"Can't anyone take a joke?" Milo was sulking and kicking around at the ground sullenly, his typically effervescent personality on hold.

"You are all in so much trouble," Chipmunk managed between her rounds of self-indulgent posturing. The tattoo snake reared and lunged as she pointed to each of them in turn. "This is getting reported as soon as we get back. I'll make sure all your long-suffering parents hear just exactly what…*the heck is that?*"

The raft. She'd finally noticed it.

With considerable huffing and puffing, she inspected it, flicking at the ties and walking around all sides. It was remarkably well constructed – size-matched branches carefully cut and pruned, tied tightly together with a climbing rope.

When she was finally done, Chipmunk turned to Ben. There was an unnerving look of pleasure on her face.

"Well, well. Benjamin Cross. So, this is what you were up to all those times you ran away. You've been coming here and building this…thing." She laughed sharply and shook her head. Her dyed-black hair floated up in the air.

Ben didn't respond. He was standing at the water's edge, glowering as usual.

With the fog of imminent death still hanging over her, Liv hadn't fully registered what was going on. This was Ben's raft. He must have spent months coming here and working on it. This was his escape plan. His way across the river. His way out.

And he'd given it up to save Liv. That was how he'd managed to rescue her. He'd pulled her out of the water on his precious raft.

Looking at the surly boy, her thoughts reached out to him. She hadn't meant for him to do that; she knew what it meant to escape from this place. Now he'd lost his chance, because of her.

Ben didn't look up. He didn't look at her or Chipmunk. He stood, head down, only a tightness in his posture betraying any emotion.

"Oh, snap. Busted." Milo was back on form in an instant.

"You are a piece of work, Mister Benjamin Cross," Chipmunk said in a low, dangerous voice. "Well, I'm done with playing nice. I'm done. I am so over you, young man. You'll get no food for a week for this stunt. Will you ever learn, Ben?"

Ben just turned his back on her and faced the river, glaring out across the water.

No food for a week? Was that legal – let alone safe? Liv looked around at the others. Ruby was silently watching everything with her big eyes. Lucas looked pensive, standing still, hands in pockets. Milo was clearly relieved to be off the hook and was actually grinning. Only Shasta looked as shocked as Liv, both hands over her open mouth.

"…never learn, do you? You're beyond saving, young man…" Chipmunk was still ranting on, but Liv wasn't listening now. This was ridiculous. Milo had pulled a stunt that had nearly killed her. Ben had rescued her, at great personal risk, but *he* was being punished?

Without noticing it, her shaking had stopped. Anger was overriding the aftershock. This wasn't right. It just wasn't right.

Chipmunk turned to address the others. "All right, cut the ropes and everyone pick up a log from the raft. You'll carry them back to camp to burn on the fire. Throw the rest in the river. You, Ben, will be carrying this." Chipmunk pointed at an impossibly large log that had formed the ridge of the raft.

How was this okay? Liv stood up, wobbling slightly as she got a head rush of dizziness.

"Ben saved my life. You can't blame him for any of this. If anyone should be punished, it should be Milo." Her eyes flicked up. Milo was standing, long arms folded across his chest, sending her a pretty decent death stare. She'd just made a new enemy.

"Really, Miss Walker? You think it's up to you to decide who deserves to be punished, do you?" Chipmunk unfurled. "If I was you, young missy, I'd keep my dang mouth shut. Given all your shenanigans, I would say I've been mighty lenient so far. But I'd be more than happy to reconsider your role in all this."

"My role? What…nearly drowning?" Liv clenched her fists and willed herself to stop. This wasn't the way. Going head-to-head with a megalomaniac like Chipmunk was going to be a losing battle. But at the same time, it was wrong. Just plain wrong.

"Oh, yes. I've been very lenient." Chipmunk narrowed her eyes, focusing their darkness fully on Liv. "For example, Miss Olivia, the rules clearly state the consequences of delinquent behaviour. Now you have deliberately put others in harm's way, aided an escape attempt, and talked back in an aggressive and disrespectful manner to your dedicated counsellor. All of which would earn you a haircut, food rationing and a cooling-off period in isolation. Shall we go there?"

Shall we? Liv felt herself straighten up. She felt her chin lift and her eyes drift upward until they met Chipmunk's eyes directly. Her head was panicking, begging her to back off, but some deeper instinct was driving now.

She smiled and shrugged.

"Whatever, bit—"

"*Are we done here?*" Lucas cut in sharply. He'd moved up next to the now-defunct raft and kicked at it. "Hey, Chippy, can we get our logs and just go?" He had moved into the space between Liv and Chipmunk. With one hand he pushed Liv behind him, out of Chipmunk's line of sight. "I'm so hungry. I'm kind of hoping for beans. Can't beat Moose-beans." He smiled widely, the full Lucas-Cole-charm-offensive fixed firmly on the counsellor.

Chipmunk looked flustered, derailed mid-power-struggle. But the distraction worked.

"Hold your horses, Mister Lucas. You'll get your dang beans." She sighed deeply and turned away from Liv. "Right. Come on, everyone, move! Pick up those logs and follow me. Let's hustle!" She squatted down by the raft and, pulling out her hunting knife, began sawing aggressively at the ropes.

It was over. Liv took a long shaky breath, struggling to centre herself and redirect the furious energy coursing through her. She was kicking herself every which way. In one morning, she had managed to throw herself in a river after a stupid log, nearly drown, mess up Ben's great escape and start a war with the one person who had absolute power over her for as long as she was at Camp Smiling Skies. Not to mention making a new enemy; she winced as Milo deliberately whacked her with his log as he walked past.

One by one they left, following their leader back along the trail, each lugging their piece of the destroyed raft.

Shasta gave her a sad little smile as she walked past.

"Here." It was Lucas. He was propping up a skinny log. "I saved a small one for you."

Liv nodded. "Thanks for changing the subject. I think you saved me several days of hunger. I was just so mad—"

"It doesn't help, you know," Lucas said, hefting his log up onto his shoulder. "There's no point in getting on Chipmunk's wrong side. You've got to pick your battles, Liv. I can see you're not afraid, but if you want to survive you need to be smart too. People like Chipmunk are easy. They can't make it in the real world, so they live in places like this, where they can be a little tin god. Out there, no one respects her. But here, she holds all the power and will use it any chance she gets. You can only survive if you play her game."

"Like you? You're playing *her*, aren't you?" Liv looked him directly in his disconcerting eyes, wondering who else he was playing too.

He met her look squarely, a small smile on his lips. There was a moment – a long moment – when they just stared at each other, before he suddenly laughed outright.

"I do what I have to do to survive, Olive Oil. You might want to try it some time."

And with that, he was gone, walking back up the trail, the slight scent of river-wet clothes floating behind him.

Pausing to pull on her blissfully dry trousers and boots, Liv realized that she wasn't alone.

Ben was standing in the shallows, knee deep in water, still staring at the far banks of the Ochee. There was something about the way he was positioned, weight forward, evenly spread on both feet, hands at his sides – something that made her think of a bird, ready to launch into flight.

"Ben…we should go. Back to the camp, I mean. We should get back…" She tailed off.

He looked at her. She could see he was breathing fast. His thoughts had moved on already and taken him somewhere reckless. His raft was destroyed, but there was still a wild light of hope in his brown eyes. Freedom was so close.

Liv threw her log down. It clattered onto the ground.

"Fuck it. I'm not lugging this back to camp. If Chipmunk wants to make me hike all the way back and get it, fine. It just means more time away from her." Liv wasn't sure what she was saying. Just that she had to say something. She had to connect. She had to bring him back here, to this moment. "This day, right? I nearly died, I mean no biggie, but hey. So…are you coming?" She tried to sound neutral, low-key. But her words weren't having the impact she'd hoped for.

Ben turned away again. The far side of the river was so tantalizingly near.

"Ben," Liv spoke fast, her voice low. "The current's too strong. You won't make it. You won't. Trust me – I just nearly drowned." She could still feel the ice-cold water pulling her under, the unrelenting force, the power turning her over and over like a leaf, a branch. She'd accidentally tested out the river and it wasn't swimmable, no matter how much she wished it was. The others were right. Crossing it would be a death sentence. "Please, Ben. You won't make it. You'll drown – like Kevon."

The name rippled across him. He straightened up instantly, flexing his hands.

The moment was broken. Liv could feel it. She'd got through to him.

Wordlessly and without so much as looking at her, Ben turned and walked away from the river – away from the edge.

When he got to the place where the raft had been, he bent down and easily lifted the huge ridge pole onto his strong shoulder. Then he walked up to Liv and, squatting, he picked up her log as well, balancing it on his other shoulder.

No words, no eye contact, nothing.

With that, he turned his back to her and started walking up the trail, back to Camp Smiling Skies.

CHAPTER 18

Liv had a plan B.

They'd hiked back to camp in silence, giving her plenty of time to think. The fire was set, and Moose had cooked up his latest bean concoction. Over dinner, Liv clumsily fake-dropped her bowl, and quickly ducked under the table, spooning half the beans into an empty can she'd dug out of the kitchen trash bag when no one was looking.

Sticking it under her now-dry yellow T-shirt, she thanked the fashion gods that oversized was in at the camp. The T-shirt was proving to be quite useful for hiding all sorts of things.

After the meal, they were granted a thirty-minute break. Pretending she needed a bucket stop, Liv headed in the direction she'd last seen Ben. Behind the bucket, there was a narrow trail through the trees, around the back of a cluster of large boulders. The scrappy path ended in a clearing with a ledge overlooking the valley.

Two of the largest boulders were propped against each other, forming a small cave opening between them. Nervously, Liv peered into the gloom. She could hear very faint noises from deep inside. Hopefully it was Ben and not a grizzly bear. Stepping cautiously into the cave entrance, she shuffled forward into darkness. Someone had been using the cave for storage. There were random objects propped along the wall: bits of rope, nails, planks of wood, a pile of empty trash bags – implements for escape. This was definitely Ben's lair.

The noises were coming from around the corner. Liv peeked around.

There was just enough light filtering through the crack between the boulders high above to make out Ben, roving around the cave. He had taken his T-shirt off and was squatting down, picking up heavy rocks and carrying them over to a pile on the far side. Working out. Liv smiled. He had made a makeshift gym.

"Hey," Liv said.

Ben jumped, turning sharply to face her. There was always a pent-up energy about him, as though he could snap in a heartbeat. Once again, Liv wondered at the wisdom of meeting Ben-the-Killer alone and out of sight. But she reminded herself that he had leaped into the icy rapids to save her. He wouldn't have done that if he wanted her dead. Would he?

"Peace offering." She lifted the hem of her T-shirt and pulled out the sticky can of beans. It wasn't the most appealing meal in the world, but it had to be better than nothing.

Ben looked at the can suspiciously.

"Why are you giving me that?"

"I figured I owed you…for saving my life." Liv held the can out, feeling like a zookeeper offering a banana to a captive beast. She made a mental note to watch her fingers.

"All right," Ben said. He walked over and reached for the can, his fingers brushing hers, catching on something hard. The ring.

Liv had forgotten to take it off after the river. Ben glanced at it, but then took the can and turned away.

Quickly, Liv stuffed her hand deep in her pocket. Stupid. If Chipmunk had seen the ring, she would have lost it for good. She couldn't bear that. Not ever. She needed to be more careful.

Ben squatted down on a rock and hungrily dug into the can with his fingers, scooping out the beans and licking the juice off.

Okay, this is a good start, Liv thought. The icebreaker was out of the way. She gave him a few minutes to eat in peace before moving on to the real reason she was here.

Fake-casually, she turned to him.

"Hey, so, Ben…"

Ben stopped eating, his fingers frozen in the can. He glared at her suspiciously.

"I've got an offer for you." There was no point in beating around the bush. She could tell he was ready to drop and run at a moment's notice. "I can help you build another raft. If there's two of us, we can build it twice as fast. It won't take long at all."

Ben slowly put the can down and wiped his grubby fingers on his trousers. Something in his movements made Liv even more nervous. Had she made him angry?

"Why would *you* want to help *me*?" he muttered at last.

"Like I said – I owe you." She did owe him – he'd sacrificed his painstakingly constructed raft to save her. But that wasn't why she was here.

"You owe me?" Ben folded his arms and sat back with a knowing expression on his face. "What do you really want, Walker?" Damn him. He'd seen right through her. He probably knew exactly why she was here; he'd probably been expecting her to show up. Maybe, in some weird way, they were more alike than she cared to think.

"All right, look. If I help rebuild the raft, we could…you know, maybe, escape together?"

"No." He stood up, shaking his head. "Not interested. I work alone."

"Yeah, and how's that working out for you?" Liv added snidely. "Just think about it for a minute. You've been here a year, right? And so far you haven't managed to escape one time. Chipmunk has this place on lockdown. But maybe together we can try something new – something she hasn't thought of. It's our best shot. We can do this. I just know it. We can be…partners!"

Partners. It sounded so pathetic she winced.

"*Partners?*" Ben repeated, eyebrows raised. "Seriously?"

Clearly this was a mistake. She hardly knew him, and what little she'd learned about him wasn't good. She would be better off alone. This was another one of her stupid ideas. She should drop it and move on to plan C.

"Whatever. Just forget I said anything." Liv turned to go, her cheeks flushed with irritation. She made it to the mouth of the cave when Ben spoke.

"Your ring. It's a bird, isn't it?"

Liv looked around in surprise.

Ben had stood up. He walked up to her. In the daylight at the cave mouth, she could see marks across his chest and shoulders. Scars, burn marks, all small but noticeable up close. They clearly weren't self-inflicted injuries, and he was rough and scrappy – there was every chance he'd collected them from random fights. But something about them – the number of them, the consistency – told a different story.

She held out her hand. The precious, tiny ring caught the light.

"It was my mom's. She loved swallows – the way they fly free. Mom was an artist – a really amazing one. She always painted a tiny swallow hidden in each of her paintings. It was kind of her secret mark, you know?" A wave of emotion came with those words. Familiar, but oddly raw, even after all this time. Grief was like that. It popped up when it wanted to. Even now after two years.

She closed her fist, gripping the ring tightly, willing herself to put her grief away just as she had done a million times before. Drop it into a box and close the lid.

Ben shifted back slightly, as if aware of her distress, giving her space. Liv could feel him looking at her but didn't turn away. There were those eyes again – pretty eyes, oddly comforting.

"What was your mom like?" Ben asked.

Liv thought for a minute. What was she like? She wasn't perfect, and her mood swings were legendary; Liv and her father had learned to check her expression carefully when they got home, just to see which direction the day was taking. But her highs were so untouchably high, filled with laughter and warmth and so much love. She was everything.

Liv looked at Ben.

"Mom had this blue armchair with white dots on it. She loved that chair so much. She called it her happy place. It's weird…I just keep thinking about that chair; I even dream about it sometimes. Like it's a part of her or something. I know it's stupid. Dreaming about a chair!"

Ben actually laughed. It was the first time Liv had heard his laugh – full, rounded and surprisingly warm. Not like she would have imagined. She smiled and, for a moment, they just stood there.

Outside of the cave, the crickets had started up their evening song again. The sound reflected off the rock walls around them.

"Um…I should go," Liv said, shaking herself out of it. Talking to Ben had cracked the lid open on things that were better kept shut away. Emotions were roiling around inside now, unbidden and unwanted. She knew how this would play out in her head. The darkness had a foothold now; it wouldn't easily be shaken off, especially here, at Camp Smiling Fucking Skies. Best to be alone. She snuck a fleeting glance at Ben's face. He was watching her. She forced a quick smile and turned to go.

"Walker."

Ben turned and pulled up the leg of his trousers. There was a tattoo on his calf. A swallow, intricately detailed, wings raised in a posture of defiance, its distinctive forked tail trailing below.

"A swallow?" She laughed.

"Dunno. Just a bird. I liked the way it looked. It's for my little brother. He's really into birds." As he spoke, a sweetness stole over Ben's hard face, touching his voice. His expression changed and morphed into something uncharacteristically gentle. He clearly adored his brother. "You know, there are a bunch of nests up on the rock wall. On a ledge. Maybe a couple of metres from the top. They've got eggs and all. Reckon they'll be hatching soon enough."

"Really?" Liv smiled. His enthusiasm was touching, if surprising.

"Yeah. If you wanna see them, go up the gully to the top of the rock wall. There's a tree up there. That's the way down to the ledge. If you hold on to the roots, you can climb down like a ladder. My brother would love it up there."

Who was this boy? Not what Liv had expected. Not at all.

"What's your brother's name?" she asked. She liked this version of Ben and wanted to keep him talking.

"Jordan. He's an asshole. Always getting into trouble. Doing stuff he shouldn't. But he's this good kid inside, you know? Kind – like my mom was, I reckon. Not like our dad." A coldness stole into his last words, shutting him down.

"Sorry. Dads suck." Liv wasn't sure why she said it. But she meant it. Her dad sucked.

Ben was watching her again. It was an odd feeling, being in the direct line of fire. His typically avoidant manner usually turned his eyes down or to the side, but now they were fixed on her. Deer-like and watchful. She held his look for as long as she dared before breaking off, blushing slightly.

There was a distant sound of voices. Someone back at the campground was shouting loudly. Break time must be coming to an end. Ben straightened, turning to look into the distance. But he didn't move yet.

"All right." He said it so quietly, Liv almost missed it. "All right, Walker. Let's do this. Partners."

He held out his calloused, dirty hand.

Liv grinned. She couldn't help herself. She grabbed his hand before he could change his mind and shook it firmly, holding on for just a second too long before letting go.

With a short nod, Ben turned away abruptly, heading back up the path towards the camp.

For a moment, Liv stayed in the cave mouth, just listening to his footsteps echoing off the rock walls as he walked away, hearing the others' shouts echoing down the valley. When she'd followed killer Ben out here to his secret lair, the last thing she'd expected to find was a connection.

Grief and love – they could be found in the strangest of places, at the weirdest of times, with the unlikeliest of people. The walking wounded.

Well, she had seen Ben, and he had seen her. And in that moment, she hadn't felt quite so alone.

Partners.

She smiled.

CHAPTER 19

Liv took her sweet time walking back to the camp. She stopped to inspect every scraggly flower and bush along the way, trying to delay her arrival. It would just be more Chipmunk and her threats and lectures. More structured bonding activities. More, more, more. And after they were finally allowed to go to their chilly tents, tomorrow it would be more, more, more of the same.

Until she escaped. With her new partner. Liv grinned.

As she passed the bucket, Liv held her breath. There were still loud voices coming from the dining area. Too loud. What were they all shouting about? The others were standing in a circle at the end of the dining table, where she had left them. Something was lying on the ground in the middle. Chipmunk was kneeling over the dark shape.

Curious, Liv picked up her speed and jogged over, edging into the circle.

Something was very wrong.

Shasta was on the ground, her face red, cheeks flushed and swollen. She was pulling at the neck of her T-shirt, wheezing, gasping for air. Chipmunk was propping her up on her knee.

"Oh God, oh God, oh God…" Ruby kept muttering over and over. She was clinging to Milo's hand. He looked pale and was oddly speechless.

"Jesus. What's going on? Is she okay?" Liv asked, panicked.

"We don't know," Lucas half-whispered, as though being quiet might somehow help. "We were just talking, and suddenly she started coughing and fell over. Like she couldn't breathe or something."

Wheezing and choking, Shasta writhed on the ground. She looked terrible; her lips had a bluish tint.

"Nuts? Did she eat nuts? She's allergic, right?" Liv asked. Her heart was beating hard. This was not good.

Lucas nodded. "Moose says there were no nuts in the food. But this happened right after we ate. Maybe he made a mistake?" Lucas shuffled back on his heels, pushing his hands through his curly hair.

The full implication of this hit Liv. What if Moose had messed up and not checked the labels? He'd seemed pretty confused about the allergy last night. All it took was one mistake. What if Shasta went into full-on anaphylactic shock, up here, in the middle of nowhere? This was bad.

"We need to call someone. We need to get help." Liv looked desperately at Lucas, but he just shook his head.

"We can't. The nearest satellite radio's in the van…" The van that was parked an hour's walk away. *An hour.*

Liv pushed forward, kneeling next to Chipmunk. Ready to do anything she could to help. Words were forming on Shasta's swollen lips, but no sounds came out, just wheezing, gasping breaths. Too short, too tight.

Moose appeared on the other side of Shasta.

"Here. I've got the EpiPen. I've got it." He was holding a yellow-and-white box. Chipmunk took it and ripped it open, pulling out two plastic tubes. It took a painfully long moment for her to decide which was the right one, before finally pulling the lid off. She smoothed out the fabric of the trousers on Shasta's thigh. Then raising the pen high in the air, she swung it down hard, stabbing Shasta's leg.

Liv winced. It looked painful, but Shasta didn't even seem to notice. She was battling something more imperative, struggling to breathe, struggling for her life.

"How long does it take to kick in?" Chipmunk demanded. "*How long, Moose?*" She flung the box at him, focusing on propping Shasta's head and chest up.

"Okay, okay." Moose picked up the box and pulled out the leaflet, but his hands were shaking so hard, he couldn't read it. Liv reached over and took the leaflet from him, quickly scanning the text.

"It starts to work right away, but the full effect takes…er, five to ten minutes. Then it wears off after twenty to thirty minutes." Oh, Jesus. She re-read the leaflet, trying to find something more, something that she'd missed that would make the situation better. But the facts were there. *Jesus.*

Slowly, reluctantly, she looked up at the ring of worried faces. They all knew what that meant. It was an hour's hike down to the road and the van, followed by a couple of hours' drive back to the town with the intake centre. Even if they radioed in from the van and were medevacked off the mountains, it could still be hours before Shasta would get to a hospital, and that was assuming that the small town even had a hospital. If the EpiPen wasn't enough, Shasta was in trouble.

"Okay, everyone take two steps back. Give her some space."

Chipmunk's bossiness was oddly reassuring at a time like this. They all moved back, even Moose, and watched for some kind of reaction or improvement.

It took a few terrifying minutes, but Shasta did seem to ease slightly. Her breathing slowed. She looked around at them for the first time since Liv had arrived, panic and fear clearly marked in her eyes. More than anyone, she must know how bad this was, and just how bad it could get.

Okay. This had to be a good sign, Liv told herself. Any change was good. The epinephrine was doing something. Instinctively she reached forward and took Shasta's limp hand. Her skin was cold. Liv rubbed the hand between her own, willing her strength, her energy to somehow seep across into the girl, to fight against whatever had taken hold.

"Is she going to be okay? Is she okay?" Ruby had taken to repeating everything multiple times, as if that would somehow make more sense. "Is she...?"

"Rubes, for fuck's sake. We don't know, all right," Milo snapped back at her. "Just quit already. It's not helping."

Looking around, Liv noticed Ben out of the corner of her eye. He held back, taking in everything that was happening from near the cook station.

Shasta was murmuring now. She seemed to want to talk, but her voice was weak, faint.

"Need...help..." Her eyes were wild with fear. "Can't...can't... breathe..." She broke into a fit of coughing. Everything sounded too tight, too wheezy.

Fuck. This didn't look good. If the EpiPen was working now, it wasn't doing enough. Not nearly enough. If it was going to start wearing off in twenty minutes, this was not good at all.

Obviously, Liv wasn't the only one who was thinking it. Chipmunk stood up abruptly and turned to Moose.

"She needs to get to hospital, now! We're going to carry her down to the van and start driving for town. Do you understand, Moose? We can radio for emergency help from the van as soon as we get a signal." She was enunciating each word very clearly, making sure Moose understood exactly what was needed from him.

Moose nodded, but he was clearly out of his depth here. Chipmunk was fully in charge.

"We'll carry her between us. You and me. Then you'll drive her to the town. Go and get the van keys." Chipmunk was orderly and controlled. "Go!" she shouted when Moose just stood on the spot, jaw dangling open.

"What can we do?" Liv asked, but Chipmunk just shook her head. What could any of them do? Liv bent down close to Shasta. Her hair was matted with sweat; her face was deathly pale. Her watery eyes found Liv's but there was hardly anything there, they were unfocused and distant. The look of a sick animal, their mind pulling away from their body, trying to cling to life.

Oh Jesus. Was she *dying*?

"Shasta, you're going to be okay," Liv said, her voice shaking. She smoothed the red curls away from the girl's face. "You're going to be okay. I promise. You just have to stay calm and breathe, all right?" How could she promise that? No part of her thought this was going to be okay.

She squeezed Shasta's hand, but Shasta didn't squeeze back. There was no strength left in the girl.

"Oh God, oh God, oh God…" Ruby's backtrack started up again.

Milo wrapped his arms around her, and they buried their heads together. Lucas was kneeling next to Liv now, his hand rested on her back. Ben held out two water bottles he must have retrieved from the kitchen.

Chipmunk nodded and took them, stuffing them firmly into her pockets. She stood up.

"All right, help me!" she demanded. "Lift her." She grabbed Shasta's arm. Liv quickly took the other arm, and with Lucas's help, they pulled her to her feet, propping her upright.

Bending down low, Chipmunk hefted Shasta over her broad shoulders. When she was balanced, she looked around for Moose, who was running from his cabin, arms flailing wildly, the van keys in his hand.

"Let's go!" Chipmunk started towards the trailhead. Kudos, she was super strong. Moose trotted along behind her, trying to support Shasta's head as it flopped up and down on Chipmunk's shoulder.

"You…all…behave…do…you…hear…me?" Chipmunk bellowed back at them, gasping for breath between words. There was a faint murmur of assent, before the three of them disappeared into the woods.

Liv sank to her knees. Fuck. Fuck. Fuck. What had just happened?

For a long time, there was a shocked silence.

"She…she'll be okay…right?" Ruby asked eventually. Her voice sounded small.

"Are you joking?" Milo shot back. "Did you see her? She's a goner. No way she makes it to the van, let alone the hospital."

"Shut up!" Lucas shouted, turning on Milo in an instant. "That's enough. We don't know what's going to happen. All right? None of us knows. So quit talking like that."

Milo sniffed, unhappy at the rebuke. But the point was made. No one knew how this would turn out.

Ruby started sobbing softly. Liv felt like joining her, but pushed it down, turning away from the others to look at the trailhead, where Shasta had disappeared. Her mind replayed the last few minutes, the feeling of Shasta's cold, weak hand, the desperate look in her eyes.

The look.

Liv had seen it before – in her mother's eyes as she lay dying in her hospital bed. There had been a distance there, as though her mom's soul had crept between the living world and the next. A glassy emptiness as her mind and body pulled apart, floating free of each other. Far beyond reach.

She had seen the look then, and she'd seen it now – on Shasta's face.

She recognized it.

It was the look of death.

CHAPTER 20

It would be at least two hours before Chipmunk made the round-trip hike to the road and back. Two hours before they'd get any updates about Shasta.

Liv, Lucas and Ruby were sitting by the unlit fire, the huge logs from the raft propped up in a rudimentary triangle, ready to burn. Ben was lurking next to the wooden sign near the trailhead, away from everyone. Milo had disappeared in the direction of the tent cabins. They were all watching and waiting. No one wanted to light the fire. No one wanted to talk.

There was a cold hollowness in the night air. The possible death of one of their own weighed on them as they each sat with their dark thoughts. No matter how hard she tried, Liv couldn't get Shasta's face out of her mind – the faded look in her eyes. She told herself it was just fear; traumatic memories of her mother's death resurfacing due to the shock. But nothing would shake the feeling that had settled on her.

Shasta could die. Today. She might already be dead. Her life – the really good life that she'd told Liv about – might have been taken from her, here in Camp Smiling Fucking Skies, just because her parents wanted to put her on a *diet*.

It hurt. Liv's head hurt. Her thoughts hurt, physically, as though someone was gutting her from the inside. She just kept thinking of Shasta's words in the tent: *My life is really nice…I like myself the way I am.*

Shasta should never have been here. She didn't deserve any of this. If Liv ever got out of here alive, she would find Shasta's parents and tell them just how evil they were.

"Do you think he's going to run?" Lucas was watching Ben pace backward and forward next to the trailhead. "It's the perfect time. He's got a couple of hours unsupervised. It could give him a solid head start."

Liv shook her head.

"No. He would have gone by now." From what little she knew of Ben, she suspected that this missed opportunity would be killing him. But he'd just lost his raft, and until he came up with a new way to cross the river, there was nowhere to go. A few extra hours wouldn't help.

"I don't want to die here!" Ruby suddenly blurted out. It was the first thing she'd said since Milo left. "People die here. Milo was right. He said it all along. This place is dangerous." She looked around at them, a wild look in her eyes. "I don't want to die here. *I just want to go home.*"

"You and me both," Liv muttered under her breath.

Lucas scooted up next to Ruby and nudged her gently with his shoulder.

"Hey, come on, Ruby. No one is going to die, okay? Chipmunk and Moose are first-aid trained, the van has an emergency radio, and they'll be at the hospital soon enough. Shasta's going to be okay. We all are." His voice was calm and reassuring. There was such an easy confidence to his tone, Liv willed herself to give in to it. If he said it, it would be so. Shasta was fine. Everything was okay. A little faith couldn't hurt, right?

"But what if you're wrong?" Ruby was clearly not up for faith. "You can't just say things like that, Lucas. You don't know what it's like here. You don't know how bad things can get. It's not safe. Accidents happen. People get hurt. *They die!*"

Her expression was lost in the darkness, but her voice carried enough cold fear that Liv shivered. Ruby was a drama queen – that was not in question. But she had also been at this camp for months. What if she wasn't just being dramatic? What if she was being a realist?

Liv's mind started running back over the last several hours, turning over the facts. How had Shasta "accidentally" eaten nuts? She was very careful, and it didn't seem likely that she would just casually eat the wrong thing. Had Moose messed up and added some wild, nutty ingredient to his Beans du Jour? That seemed plausible. But Shasta had checked in with him before dinner again tonight, and he'd said it was all nut-free.

Was it possible there was something more sinister going on here? Someone wouldn't have intentionally given Shasta nuts... would they?

No. It was ridiculous thinking like that. Liv was just tired, and Ruby's scaremongering was making her paranoid. Besides, there was absolutely no reason why anyone would want to hurt Shasta. None at all. At least, none that she could think of.

"Everything's going to be fine, Ruby," Lucas said quietly. "I promise. No one's going to die today." He said it with the same calm assurance as before, only this time the words sounded hollow.

Maybe Ruby was right. How could he really know?

Liv pulled her knees up close, hugging them to her. The darkness had a weight to it tonight. It was oppressive, sinking into her bones, her head, her heart. All these lost thoughts were nothing more than emotions, hardening into little nuggets of fear. She needed to see them for what they were and push them away.

This was not a time for weakness.

"Whaddup, party people!" Milo's voice made them all jump. "Lookee what I found!" He was walking down the field from the direction of the tent cabins. In one hand he had a ukulele, in the other something that looked suspiciously like a large bottle of tequila. "That Moose is a bad boy. Sneaking contraband into camp. Aunty Chipmunk's gonna have to give him a haircut."

He jogged over to the fire circle, clearly delighted with his score.

"Milo, what are you doing?" Ruby sat up. "Seriously, you can't just like go into their cabins and take stuff. We'll get in so much trouble."

"Come on, camp-wife. What can they say? If they accuse us of stealing something, we'll ask them what's missing. Then they'd have to admit they were hiding alcohol. We're clean. They can't touch us." Milo cracked open the tequila and took a long swig. "Besides – considering they might have just killed one of their campers, I would say they've got bigger things to worry about."

"Milo! How can you say that?" Ruby's eyes were round and dewy with tears.

"Girl, that is exactly why we should drink. Look, today has been *dangerous*. We had a near drowning." Milo carefully avoided looking at Liv when he said it. "Then Shasta had her nut accident. Honestly, I think we should drink to surviving this long." He held up the bottle. "To Shasta, our fuzzy little red-haired queen. I may not have known you for long, but I thought you were adorable." He took another long sip.

"Hate to say it, but Milo's right," Lucas added with a sigh. "Fuck this. I'm not going to just sit around expecting the worst. Here, give me that." Lucas got to his feet and walked over to Milo. He reached out and took the bottle, taking a few swigs before holding it out to Ruby.

She managed a stern frown of disapproval, followed immediately by an overacted sigh of resignation.

"Okay, fine. Whatever," she said, snatching the bottle from his hands and glugging it down for a beat too long.

Finally, it was Liv's turn. Ruby held out the bottle.

It felt wrong to sit around drinking tequila while Shasta was in a fight for her life. It felt like they should be doing something more – praying for her, manifesting to the universe, crying…something.

But there was nothing they could do now. Nothing that would help. This was out of their hands.

Maybe Lucas was right after all. They could choose to sit around in misery expecting the worst. Or they could choose to believe in the best outcome – to believe that everything was going to be okay – and drink.

Besides, what was the alternative? Keep feeling the way she was now? No, something had to give.

With a deep sigh and knowing that this was probably a really bad idea, Liv took the bottle. Looking up at the night sky, at the first star rising over the crags, she cast a wish out into the universe.

Starlight, starbright, first star I see tonight.

I wish I may, I wish I might, have the wish I wish tonight.

Let Shasta live. Let Shasta live. Please. Let Shasta live…

CHAPTER 21

Out in the real world, Liv did not like tequila. But at Camp Smiling Skies it wasn't so bad. The warm sensation in her throat was surprisingly pleasant.

The bottle did another round, and then another, and kept going until she lost count. The only one not joining in was Ben. Lucas had offered him a drink, but he hadn't responded, which was hardly unusual. He was still lurking by the wooden sign, his outline barely visible in the dark.

By now Liv could feel the heat spreading throughout her body; her fingers were tingling. The alcohol was shifting something inside her. Now she really thought about it, there was every reason to be optimistic. She was just letting her fears overwhelm her rational mind. Shasta was going to be okay. Of course she was. It was stupid to think otherwise. People had nut reactions all the time. It sucked, for sure, but they didn't die...right?

The group mood was changing along with her – there was a wild edge to everything now, slightly crazy and very stupid. Maybe liquor wasn't the best way to deal, but somehow it was helping, and they all kept drinking as the edges softened. Somewhere along the way, someone had thrown a match on the raft wood and the fire crackled into life. Flames licked and danced before them, the playful light catching on their dirt-streaked faces.

Right now, things just didn't seem quite so hopeless.

Milo picked up the ukulele. He could actually play – not well, but well enough. He broke into a chorus of "Riptide", followed by "I'm Yours", singing along loudly, confidently and a little off-key. It was hard not to smile.

As Ruby's tequila caught up with her, she jumped up and started bouncing around, swaying in time to Milo's latest effort. Lucas joined her, holding her hand and spinning her around, laughing. Crickets provided the percussion, and a few distant birds added their hollow cries as the night finally closed in on them.

"Stick Season". Badly played. Barely recognizable. Lucas jumped up on a log bench. When it got to the chorus, he started singing along, loudly and drunkenly.

"I HATE THIS CAMP, and the reason is IT'S SHIT." Lucas joyfully bellowed out the loosely improvised words at the top of his voice. Somehow, with his big, beautiful smile, he made it seem both embarrassingly stupid and funny at the same time. "I'll drink alcohol till CHIPMUNK's back to fix us... Come on, guys!" He waved them up.

Milo and Ruby joined in, shouting out the nonsensical words loudly.

Call it the alcohol, or maybe the last desperate release of a day that had nearly killed her – whatever – Liv grabbed a nearby stick and started whumping it on the raft wood in time to the music.

"...WE HATE THIS CAMP, AND THE REASON IS IT'S SHIT!" They were all shouting now, laughing. Even Ben wandered closer, hands in pockets. If someone walked into the camp now, they'd think they'd discovered a lost group of feral children. It was stupid, but somehow it felt so good.

Necessary.

The darkness was all around them by the time they finally collapsed, exhausted, on the ground.

Lying on her back, Liv looked up at the sky. The stars were out, brighter and more beautiful than she had ever seen them. It was as though the entire universe was splayed out above her. Strangely though, it wasn't the stars that caught her attention. It was the space in between them. *The big nothing.* Empty and lifeless, as though the light of the world was being sucked in on itself, into the void. It was at once beautiful and terrifying. Up there, "nothing" existed, just as much as "something". It was there. She was looking at it. Yet no one ever noticed emptiness. No one thought about it, or craved it, or bought cute earrings with "nothing" on them. Maybe nothing was the one truly free thing in the world.

And yet, there was value in nothing. It was up there, in the empty spaces, that her mom still existed. Nowhere. But somehow… she was looking at it. It was right there, above her.

Was Shasta up there too now?

Fuck. Liv needed to stop drinking.

The music had finally stopped. Milo was busy escorting a sickly-looking Ruby to the edge of the woods. Too much tequila and dancing – it had to come out one way or another. Ben had wandered off alone somewhere, yet again.

Propping herself up, Liv looked around, her head spinning. Lucas was sitting on a log, elbows resting on his knees, hands clasped together almost as if he was praying. He looked oddly peaceful.

"Can I ask you somethin'?" Liv was slurring; the tequila was doing the talking for her. "Why're you always so fucking nice?"

Lucas laughed out loud and pushed himself forward onto the ground next to her. He lay down on his back, arms folded behind his head, facing the stars. They were so close, Liv could smell him – warm and salty. Like a snack. Like feta sprinkled on fresh, warm bread.

"My mom taught me this trick when I was little." Lucas turned his head to her. She could feel his breath on her cheek. "She said if you think of three things you like about everyone you meet, then you'll never be alone. I reckon she was right. It's like everyone's just trying to do their best with what they've got, you know? We all just want someone to actually *see* us and like us for who we are. You should try it sometime. Just think of three real things you like about someone, and you never know, Liv-Fucking-Walker, you might actually make some friends."

Liv bit her lip. *Three things I like about Lucas Cole.* Now that was easy. In this moment, warmed by the tequila, she could think of a hundred things she liked about Lucas Cole. His eyes, his smile, his laugh…

"Wait…I though' you said you didn't 'member your mom?" Something was ringing bells in Liv's brain, but she wasn't sure what.

There was a pause.

"It's kind of messy, you know? I think I remember stuff, but then I find a photo and realize it was never a memory, just a story my subconscious made up to go with the photo." Lucas looked at her. His eyes caught a shard of cold starlight. "Liv – I might not have been completely honest with you when I told you why I was sent here. Remember the name you heard me saying in my sleep?"

Dillon. Liv nodded, instantly regretting it as her vision took precious seconds to catch up with her.

"Dillon was my best friend, and my first love." Lucas spoke softly. Liv barely caught it, but it was there – a sweetness in his voice, almost lost in the mysterious night sounds all around them. "He died in a car crash, a few years ago, and…I didn't cope well. You know? I was kind of messed up about it. Especially after losing my family. It brought back a lot of memories. I started partying too hard, drinking too much, shit like that. My grandparents didn't know what to do. They made me try therapy and antidepressants and stuff. But it didn't help. I had to go through this thing that was in my head, you know? I had to do it my way." Lucas propped himself up on his elbows, facing her. "I guess I just…went too far. Things got kinda out of control. One night I woke up with two masked kidnappers in my bedroom, and you know the rest."

So, that was why he was calling out Dillon's name. Oh God, poor Lucas. Liv imagined both accidents. First his family, then Dillon, one after the other. So much loss. So much pain. It cut through the drunken fog in her head. She instinctively reached her hand out and touched his arm.

"God, Lucas, 'm so sorry. Losing Dillon…like that…'specially after your family—"

"Shit happens," Lucas said abruptly, shifting away incrementally. Liv's hand dropped to the ground.

She was caught off guard. She pushed herself up to sitting, cursing herself for touching him. God, she hoped he didn't think she was trying anything on. She knew he was well out of her league. There was no way Lucas would be interested in someone like her. She just wasn't pretty enough. She just wasn't *that* girl. It was the way things were – carved in stone on some ancient tablet, now and forevermore. *Know thy place, fool.*

"So, what about you?" Lucas said. He was on his back now, facing up to the sky and the stars. "What was the deal with the painting?"

On a normal day, Liv would have told him it was none of his business. But the tequila played with her tongue and before she could stop herself the words leaked out.

"Was a veeery valuable painting," she said. The world was spinning again. God, she hoped she wouldn't be sick. "Like six-figures valuable, know wha' I mean?"

"Oh!" Lucas nodded. He seemed impressed. "Wow. I can see why they were pissed you took it. It was your mom's, right?"

"My mom painted it. 'Blue Bird'. It was one of her best paintings y'know." Liv could see it in her head, every tiny detail: a soaring image of a swallow, wings starkly outlined against a brilliant sky.

"So, what happened?"

"When they saw what I'd done my dad had me arrested. They were gonna press charges and ev'ything but gave up when they realized they weren't getting the painting back – like *ever*."

"Why not?"

"I burned it."

Lucas laughed outright. "Any particular reason?"

Yes. Every reason in the world. Because every time Liv left the house, she had to look at that painting, at that piece of her mom's soul, her joyful symbol of freedom, incarcerated over the mantelpiece in this other woman's house. How every time she thought of it, she wanted to scream, to grab it and take it far away, to tell them they had no right to look at it. How she had to listen to

Carianne brag to dinner party guests about how valuable it was. How much it was worth. Dollars. Money. Her mom's soul, trapped there, splayed out on the wall to be mocked and devalued every fucking day.

So, Liv had taken it and set it free from the Cariannes and James Walkers of this world, for ever, the only way she knew how.

"'S it matter?" she said, crumpling up her nose in an effort to focus her rambling thoughts. "'m here, aren' I? My own father had to *pay* someone to kidnap me 'n take me here…says it all…right?"

Liv closed her eyes.

Damn that tequila. It had loosened something dangerous inside her. She could feel thoughts that had been bottled up tightly, just tripping over themselves, waiting to spill out. *Pull yourself together.* She didn't want to do this. Not here and not in front of Lucas. She didn't want that. She wiped her nose on her T-shirt, forcing herself to breathe out, slowly. To focus on the big black nothing over her head.

"Liv…"

She shook her head. "'m not good…not good, Lucas. You don' wanna be around someone like me—" *I'm not good?* It wasn't what she was trying to say at all. But she couldn't reach it, she couldn't quite find the words to say what she was really thinking. *I'm not loving? I'm not lovable? I'm not love?*

She closed her eyes, hating herself deeply – intensely. Her drunken thoughts were circling in the air around her, spinning alongside the rest of the world. The closed door to her dad's office. The cold, hard look in his eyes as he stood on his tidy lawn watching while she was dragged away. Discarded. Like the cornflower-blue chair. Her mother's chair, left out on the sidewalk in the heavy Seattle rain, a hand-scrawled *FREE* sign taped to its arm.

Tears were running down her face now. She was a mess, and a lousy drunk. She wiped at her face with her sleeve.

"The thing is, Liv-Fucking-Walker…I do want to be around someone like you." Lucas spoke so softly, she almost missed it. He reached across and gently touched her chin, nudging it towards him until she was looking directly into his eyes. "Someone just like you…"

The alcohol made her do it. It had to be the alcohol.

Before she could stop herself, before she could think, she took his hand, pushing her face into it, holding his fingers against her lips. She could feel his warmth against her skin, taste him. She needed him. She craved him desperately.

Lucas didn't pull away. He didn't resist. He folded himself around her, pulling her into him. His arms held her, his hand was in her hair, their cheeks touched. She breathed him in, deeply, turning her face to him.

Lost in him.

Lost, but just for once – for this one precious moment – not alone.

CHAPTER 22

Ice-cold water hit Liv in the face.

What the…? Liv fell back from Lucas, scrambling to her feet. The shock disorientated her. Water dripped down her neck, down her back.

What just happened?

"That should cool your jets." It was Chipmunk's unwelcome voice. She put down the plastic water container she had just upended over them. "My back barely turned and you all cavorting around here like a pack of disgusting dogs." She spat the words out, hands clenched tightly, indignation pouring off her.

Milo and Ruby were hovering behind her, already in trouble. Ben was lurking in the shadows, glowering at them, his hands deep in his pockets, looking murderous.

Liv blushed. Had her escape partner seen her with Lucas? Had he seen them lying together by the fire? She wasn't sure why that bothered her…but it did.

"*Drinking alcohol?*" Chipmunk spotted the empty tequila bottle. "Y'all are in so much trouble. You have no idea how bad I can make things for you, you screwed-up delinquents." Chipmunk had a particularly nasty air about her – she was dangerous and barely able to control it. Her eyes were red-rimmed and wild.

Oh God. Was Shasta okay?

Lucas said it first. "What happened? Did you make it to the van? Is Shasta all right?" *Is she alive?* The subtext hung in the air. Liv swallowed, terrified of what Chipmunk's next words would be.

But the words didn't come. They weren't needed. Chipmunk just shook her head. Her bravado faltered and she physically slumped. *No.* Shasta was not okay.

"Chipmunk, please. What happened to Shasta?" Lucas asked.

Chipmunk kept shaking her head, over and over. "She wasn't breathing. When we got to the van. I checked and…she wasn't breathing. I tried…I tried, but I couldn't… She wasn't breathing… she was just…gone."

Liv just stood there. At a loss. Instantly sober. She could still see the look in Shasta's eyes, turning in on herself, away from the world. It had been the same look of death two years ago in the hospital. Again now, here on this mountain.

Ruby gave out a keening, wailing sound. It was picked up by some night creature and echoed around the crags. Milo was muttering to himself, pushing his hand over and over through his floppy hair. For the first time, Liv noticed that Ben had moved up and was now standing next to her.

Shasta was dead.

How could this happen?

"Nuts. A *nut allergy.*" Liv was surprised to hear her own voice – her own thoughts spoken out loud. The others turned to look at her, but she was focused on Chipmunk. She should stop now; she knew that much. But that wasn't going to happen. Shasta was *dead.*

Someone had to call it. "You're her fucking camp counsellor. It was in her file that she had a nut allergy – Moose told us. You can't pretend you didn't know. It was your responsibility to keep her safe – your one job. But you just didn't care enough, did you?" Her voice was low and dangerous, her fists clenched at her sides. "That's manslaughter. You know that? Negligence. You shouldn't be in charge of kids. You shouldn't be in charge of anything..."

Her tone snapped Chipmunk out of her stupor.

"*Do not go there,* young miss. Do not speak to me like that." Chipmunk spat out the words. There was cold panic in her voice. She turned on Liv. "Whatever happened here was an accident. *An accident.* Shasta made a mistake and ate the wrong thing. She must have picked some nut off a bush or tree or something and eaten it. This was on her – all on her. *She* messed up. Got that? Anyone of y'all who thinks or says differently – well, I'll make sure you never, ever go home. Do you understand?" Chipmunk was raging, waving her arms around. The snake on her forearm caught the firelight, appearing to rear up, ready to strike, ready to kill to protect its host.

Liv watched with horror, barely able to comprehend what was happening. Shasta was dead, and they were trapped here. They were being threatened. It didn't feel real.

Chipmunk was shouting now. "All of you are going to walk to your tents in silence. Then you're going to go to sleep. I will wake you in the morning, usual time. Moose will be back with the van as soon as he's dealt with things in town. Then we will carry on with our day, just like normal."

Dealt with things in town. Dealt with Shasta's body? A shock of grief hit Liv at the thought. Oh Jesus...

Chipmunk continued her rant, "We will not mention this again. *Ever again.* Do you hear me? *Do you hear me? Now GO!*"

What could they do?

The others turned to go. Milo and Ruby had their arms around each other, clinging tightly as they started back up the path towards the campground. Lucas kicked out angrily at the dirt as he passed Chipmunk. He paused at the edge of the fire and turned to Liv and Ben.

"Come on. Let's just get out of here." He was looking at Liv, but she didn't meet his eyes. Something was shutting down inside her, the way it always did. The way it had to sometimes, just so she could keep putting one foot in front of the other. Keep moving, keep breathing.

Shasta hadn't eaten a *nut* off a random *tree*. It was ridiculous. The girl was quiet, but not stupid, and she was all too aware of her allergy – she had pointedly reminded Moose at each meal. How dare Chipmunk blame her? How dare she? The fucking WTC had a duty of care. They had to keep their campers safe, and they had failed. Chipmunk had failed. She should not get away with it.

"No!" Liv stepped forward. "I will not lie about what happened here. Her death is your fault. She was your responsibility and—"

Two steps and Chipmunk had her by the neck. The snake hand closed in on her windpipe. Liv clawed at it, uselessly. Gasping for air.

"You listen to me, you little bitch. No one will believe a word you say. *No one.* You are dirt – a sixteen-year-old no-good piece of lying shit. One call to your father, and I'll get you sewn up with a diagnosis of being a danger to yourself and others. *Do you hear me?* One word and I'll get you sectioned away in some institution until you rot."

"Hey." It was Lucas's voice. "Hey, come on. It's okay. Everyone's upset. It's late."

There were sparks in the back of Liv's eyes now. She couldn't speak – she could barely breathe. It took all the strength she had to hold the strong fingers back from crushing her neck. Was she going to die too? Like this? One-handedly strangled by Chipmunk?

"Let her go!" It was Ben's voice.

"Come on, Chipmunk." Lucas was close by, his voice calm and controlled. "We're all just freaked out, all right. All just talking shit. We'll go to bed. Right now, okay? We'll go. Just let her go."

"Fucking let her go!" Ben shouted.

The hand suddenly released. Liv dropped to her knees, coughing. The dizziness was back in full force. She felt someone pulling her up, pulling her away. Lucas had her. He steered her around the fire, keeping well clear of Chipmunk.

"Show's over," Chipmunk shouted after them. "That's right, you run off. Go! Get out of here. Get the heck out of here."

"Come on, Liv," Lucas muttered. He kept her moving, kept her upright.

They made it to the trail before something stopped Liv – an instinct. Milo and Ruby were ahead, watching. Lucas was holding her. Something was missing. Someone. Where was Ben? She pulled away from Lucas and turned back.

Ben was still standing by the fire, head down, muscles tensed as he glared at Chipmunk. Chipmunk stared back, the tension between them underscored by a violent, dangerous energy. This was not going to dissipate overnight, if ever. There was blood spilled now. The war had fully begun.

"Ben," Liv called out to him; her voice was weak, her throat hurt. "Ben, come with us." She didn't know why she thought she could make a difference. She was acting on instinct, not thought, her brain still locked into a kind of blank shock.

Ben's eyes flicked up, catching her. She could see the raw anger, the pain and the fear. Somehow, she knew he could see it in her face too. She nodded, willing him to hear her. There had already been too much damage done. Too much loss.

They needed to end this day.

"Ben…*please*," she called to him, desperate to get through. This time she saw it. As she said his name, he softened, just the smallest amount. Just slightly. "Let's get the fuck out of here. Come on, Ben."

"Let's just go," Lucas added. "She's not worth it."

Understatement.

At long last, Ben moved, finally unlocked.

"This is not over," he growled as he passed Chipmunk, edging around the fire and heading for the trail.

"You're dang right it's not over. You hear me? Y'all hear me. This ain't over. Do not mess with me. I will take you down. Each and every one of you freaking delinquents. I will take you down…" Chipmunk was ranting, raging. But she didn't follow them.

Ben passed Liv and Lucas, wordlessly.

Liv's thoughts were all over the place. Shasta. Ben. Chipmunk's threat.

Could Chipmunk do that? Did she have the power to silence them, to get them locked away? What if they all argued against her? Would anyone believe their word against the counsellor's? Even as Liv thought it, she knew.

They were all card-carrying fuck-ups, the unwanted. Sent away to the island of lost toys. No one really cared about them. If they had, they wouldn't have been sent here. They had no power. None. Because no one loved them. Not really. They were an inconvenience.

The cold hard truth was, Chipmunk could do whatever she wanted to them, and there was absolutely nothing they could do about it.

CHAPTER 23

For what felt like hours, Liv lay awake in the dark, listening to the unknowable night sounds just outside her tent. Her thoughts were racing – dark, sticky thoughts that spiralled through her night fears, fuelled by strange noises, tequila and Chipmunk's chilling threats; always circling back around to the fact that *Shasta was dead.*

Liv lay facing away from Shasta's side of the tent. Even with her back turned, she could still feel the empty space next to her; Shasta's belongings, her sleeping bag and pillow set out for someone who would never come.

The letter was lying on her pillow where Shasta had left it that morning. It occurred to Liv that Shasta's parents must know what had happened by now. They must have been informed that their daughter was never coming home again. They'd sent her away, against her will, and now she was dead. Jesus – how could they live with that? How could they ever forgive themselves?

Enough. Liv pushed herself to sitting, wiping at her tear-streaked face. Enough now. She couldn't keep doing this to herself. She couldn't stay here with ghosts.

Clambering out of her sleeping bag, Liv grabbed her flashlight and unzipped the tent flap, stepping out into the cool night air. She was still a little drunk, and wobbled slightly, catching her balance by grabbing on to a tent pole.

It was better outside. Much better than in the tight confines of the tent. She could breathe again.

There was no magical moonlight now, just occasional patches of weak starlight from breaks in a growing wall of dark clouds. Everything was still; no one else was up. It was almost peaceful.

Without a plan, she headed towards the white trail that led through the camp. A distant flash of dry lightning briefly illuminated the sky, starkly outlining the rock wall high above her. The storm was still raging somewhere, moving slowly closer.

The white trail was faintly illuminated by starlight as Liv walked along it, pacing herself. She had no idea what time it was or where she was going, but there was no colour in the sky to give her hope that the day was approaching. Off to her left, she could just make out the faint line where the steep gully zigzagged its way up the face of the rock wall. Maybe she'd climb it to the top and sleep up there, high above Camp Smiling Skies, and Chipmunk. It must feel safer up there, high above—

Crack.

Liv jumped. What was it? The sound was loud and close by.

Crack.

Fuck. Something was out there. Something big. It wasn't her imagination. She was sure of it. Something was moving down the white trail ahead of her.

Crack.

Oh hell no.

Another momentary flash of lightning lit up the scene in front of her – and that was when she saw what was making the noises. It wasn't an animal. It was human. A dark figure. *Someone* was sneaking along the white trail.

Liv held her breath. Who? Why?

Peering carefully through the trees, she watched as the figure approached the top of the field. As they broke out of the trees, she could see that their head was covered. Maybe a hood? Or a hat? They were careful, pausing to look around before moving further along the trail in the direction of the Snack-Shack.

What were they up to?

Her rational brain pushed back. It was probably nothing, probably just one of the others on a bucket break, probably someone else who couldn't sleep. But something about the person's furtive movements was setting off alarm bells; the way they kept looking around, as though they were checking they weren't being followed. Someone was up to something, and they didn't want to be seen.

Liv didn't even consider going back to her tent. Not now. There was no way she could zip herself back into that claustrophobic bubble with Shasta's belongings and try to pretend she hadn't seen this. She wanted to know who was sneaking around in the dark, and why. They hadn't seen her, so if she was quiet she could follow them, keeping in the cover of the dark woods. They'd never even know she was there.

Carefully, she moved down the white trail, tiptoeing along the starlit path in the direction of the mysterious figure.

By the time she'd reached the top of the field, where she'd last seen them, she was out of breath. Pausing, she listened intently. There were no sounds now. She didn't dare use her flashlight to look around. She would be spotted in an instant.

Instead, she just waited.

A cloud passed over the stars, briefly blocking the weak light. Everything fell into darkness. There were flittering sounds on one side, a creaking noise on the other. Eyes – small critter eyes – caught the dim light, blinking out of the woods at her.

Suddenly another bright flash of distant lightning crackled through the sky, lighting up the world around her.

Liv gasped.

The person was still there. They were crouching three metres away, silently watching her. A black outline, barely distinguishable from the trees.

She fell back, too afraid to speak. Something about their posture felt predatory, like an animal paused to pounce.

The figure slowly stood up, raising itself to its full height. Slowly, deliberately, it lifted its arms up, high over its head, hands bent forward like claws.

Then she heard it. They *hissed*. Low and threatening. Feral, like a beast.

The sound was terrifying.

Liv turned and, stumbling in fear, sprinted back along the trail, crashing into boulders, catching on roots. She didn't care. She could feel the unseen eyes following her as she ran.

Her mind was racing. Who was it? *Who the fuck was it?*

By the time she reached the campground, her hands and knees were covered in scrapes and bruises. She only slowed when she was far from the trees, falling on the ground near her tent, her heart still thumping hard in her chest. She had a clear view of the tree line from here. If someone, or something, came after her, she'd see them.

It had to just be one of the others. Maybe she'd surprised them.

For all they knew she might have been a mountain lion, or a bear. That must be it. That was all it was. She'd surprised them and they'd reacted.

But, despite her bravado, something about the way they had lain in wait for her in the dark woods, the way they had stood like that and *hissed* – it felt horribly wrong. They must have seen her – she was out in the open, in the starlight, but still they didn't say anything, just that chilling, animal noise. What they did wasn't normal. It was deliberate and threatening.

It was as though they were trying to scare her off.

Well, they'd succeeded. She was scared and nothing would possess her to go back out there alone. Not tonight. No, she would stay by the tents, close to the others, and she would watch, all night long if she had to.

Just in case whoever was creeping around in the dark decided to come creeping back.

CHAPTER 24

Finally dawn.

After her unsettling encounter, Liv had dragged her sleeping bag out of her tent and sat sentinel through the remainder of the night, watching the tree line for any sign of the mystery night-crawler. A few times, she dozed off. A few times, she thought she heard a sound. Once, she was sure she saw a dark shape lurking at the edge of the campground, but by the time she'd switched her flashlight on and shone it in the general direction, it had disappeared.

But still, she'd made it through another sleepless night at Camp Smiling Skies. Although the tequila and lack of sleep really hadn't done her any favours. By morning, a solid hangover was mangling her sleep-deprived thoughts into a painful, throbbing headache.

Standing up, she threw her sleeping bag on the ground, wobbling a little as a wave of nausea hit her. She couldn't sit there any more. Her thoughts would not allow it. There was nothing good to be found in thinking today. Only grief and fear. She needed to get moving and she needed food.

It was a chilly day. The clouds from last night had formed a dull grey blanket across the sky. Darker clouds were massing at the edges, over the crags. It looked like one of those distant storms was finally rolling in.

No one else seemed to be up yet, so Liv made a quick bucket stop, then wandered along the white trail, grateful for the time alone with her thoughts.

Chipmunk's tent cabin was quiet. The wooden platform and deck had been cleared for the night. The window flaps in the canvas walls were rolled down and tied shut. Only the canvas door was open and loosely flapping around in the breeze. No sign of Chipmunk. Liv was relieved. She was dreading facing her after their run-in last night. Chipmunk's parting words had echoed around and around Liv's night fears: *I'll get you sectioned away in some institution until you rot.*

"Hey." Liv jumped at the sound of Ben's voice, coming from high above her. She looked up, squinting against the sky; her partner was squatting on a boulder overhanging the white trail.

"Hey." Liv looked down. Her eyes couldn't do daylight today. "You okay?"

Ben nodded. "Chipmunk's gone."

Liv's heart gave a short hopeful leap, immediately followed by a burst of anxiety.

"Wait, gone? What do you mean *gone?*"

"Looked everywhere. She's not here. Checked her cabin, just to be sure." Ben nodded towards the tent cabin. "Her bed's made, but no one's home."

"Maybe she hiked down to the van drop-off?" Liv ventured. "Perhaps she was planning to meet Moose there this morning. Or maybe she'd arranged to meet the Sheriff or someone, first thing." A touch of stark reality crept in as Liv thought about it. A camper was dead. There would be questions, the police, an investigation. Maybe someone was on their way to close the camp down, at least temporarily. She felt another small flicker of hope.

Ben just shrugged. "She never said anything last night. Don't think Chipmunk's the type to go walkabout."

He had a point. It didn't seem likely that she would leave without telling them. Especially as she was the only remaining counsellor until Moose returned, and as they all knew too well, she took her responsibilities very seriously.

Liv's hungover brain struggled to process the limited options.

"Ben, I did…I did see something, or someone, last night…" Her voice tailed off. It sounded stupid. Ben must have known how drunk she was. Now if she told him someone had jumped out of a bush and *hissed* at her, he'd think she'd lost it. Unless of course…it had been Ben. Shit, she'd never thought about that. She racked her brain trying to think about the night-growler: their build, if the snarl sounded male or female, were they tall or short? The growl sounded low, possibly male, but it had been too dark to tell much else. "Um, I mean, I thought I might have seen someone sneaking around, but I could have been wrong."

Ben frowned, then shrugged again.

"People get up at night. Could have been anyone," he said. His tone was abrupt. Liv looked at him. Was he angry? No, she must be projecting. He was obviously just tired and sad. Of course he was in a bad mood; how could he not be? Of course it had nothing to do with her.

"Maybe we should wake the others and see if they know anything," she suggested, turning away.

As if on cue, they heard faint voices from the campground.

It sounded like Lucas. Liv could just see the top of his head over the bushes, his blond hair tousled after a restless night's sleep.

It was enough to stir something in her. A flash of memory that had been buried in the drama of last night. The feeling of his hand on her face, their cheeks pressed together. Was it even real? Had she imagined the whole thing? How drunk had she been?

The others were on the move now, talking as they walked down the white trail, heading towards the Snack-Shack.

Liv was feeling fragile, and her hangover was pure evil: her right temple pulsed with pain every time she moved her head, and her eyes kept swimming in and out of focus. She wasn't sure she was ready to face Lucas. Quickly she went around the boulder and scrambled up the back to stand next to Ben. He gave her a short, sidelong look, then turned his back to her, arms folded defensively across his chest.

For some strange reason, Liv felt even worse than before.

She pointedly walked to the furthest edge of the boulder from him and sat down. The view from up here was immense; as though they were trapped inside a snow globe, encircled by the crags and filled with scrubby trees and half-starved critters. Two buzzards circled high above them. It was a place of death – harsh, rangy and cruel. Out here survival was a fight, not an expectation.

Maybe those two buzzards could sense the passing of a life in the dark night and were patiently waiting to claim their prize.

Fuck. Liv shook her head as though it might dislodge those thoughts. It wasn't good to go there. Today she had to keep her head screwed on right. Show no weakness. Not after Chipmunk's threats last night. Today, they were at war.

They could hear the voices again. Lucas was talking, gesturing. Probably trying to lighten the mood.

"You can't trust him," Ben muttered. He still had his back turned to her.

"Trust who?" Liv frowned.

"Lucas." Ben shifted slightly, uncomfortably. "He's not who he says he is."

Liv blushed, feeling mortified. So, Ben had seen them by the fire last night. He'd noticed and his tone reeked of disapproval.

"What is that supposed to mean?" she asked sharply.

"You know."

"No, I don't. Do you want to tell me?" She glared at his back. Whatever happened last night – and she wasn't totally sure she remembered all of it – wasn't Ben's business. "Look, if you have a problem with—"

"I'm not the one with a problem." Ben half-turned, head down. He glowered at her. "*He is*. Lucas Cole. I know his type. You can't believe a word they say. It's bullshit – all of it. I thought you would see that."

"Do you even hear yourself, Ben?" A flood of emotion and anger mixed into the sharp pain in her head. It was enough to try not to sink under the grief of what had happened to Shasta, let alone the fear of what would come next. She didn't need this. "What's your fucking problem? What…are you jealous?" Liv wasn't sure where that had come from and as soon as she said it, she wished she could take it back.

Ben held her eyes – dark and forceful. She held back – angry and confused. Locked in.

Footsteps approached. Voices. The others rounded the corner of the trail below. Liv turned away from Ben, still simmering. Why had she said that? Why hadn't he answered?

"Hey." Lucas waved at them. "Is everyone okay? What's going on?" He was squinting up at them, eyes narrowed.

Liv forced an awkward smile, trying to shake off the conversation.

"Yeah. We're fine. Chipmunk's missing." She scrambled down off the boulder, getting as far away from Ben as she could. Avoiding Lucas's eyes, she gave an update on the absentee counsellor.

The others listened, asking questions and speculating on where Chipmunk had disappeared to. It was late enough that they all agreed something was definitely off. But any relief that their tormentor had gone was tempered by fear that she might be up to something worse. Her threats from last night were still weighing on them. Could she have decided to get ahead of her "nut-accident" story? Maybe she'd intercepted Moose on his return and was on the satellite radio right now, blaming them for Shasta's death. Perhaps she was already trying to get them sectioned and locked away for good. At least if she were here, they would know what she was up to. Right now, she could be out there, anywhere, doing anything – and that was truly terrifying.

But what could they do?

It was out of their hands.

One thing that couldn't wait was food. The hangovers were in full force. Ruby was so pale she looked almost two-dimensional, and Milo didn't seem capable of formulating a full sentence. With Moose away and Chipmunk missing, it was decided that they would have to take breakfast into their own hands and visit the Snack-Shack.

When they got to the deck, everything was where it had been abandoned the night before. Moose must have been mid-clean-up when Shasta fell ill. There were still some dirty pots and pans in a plastic tub with soapy water set out on the table, several drowned bugs floating belly-up in it. Something had been snacking on leftover crumbs of food and there were animal footprints across the deck.

Lucas went straight up to the Snack-Shack door and started inspecting the padlock.

"I'm not sure about this," Ruby said, her pale face lined with worry. "We'll get in so much trouble."

"Girl, we're already in so much trouble." Milo nudged her. "We might as well be in trouble and fed. You heard Chippy last night. Snake-lady is on the warpath. She's probably out there right now, trying to find a nut-tree to back up her alibi."

Ruby sighed. Milo always seemed to get his way with Ruby.

"Okay, but for the record, this was not my idea, and I want no part of it." Ruby raised her hands. "I'm not losing my Condor status for this. I just want to get out of here." She looked like she was about to cry.

"Come here, you sweet thing." Milo put his arms around her. "Once a Condor, always a Condor. Am I right?"

Ruby nodded and forced out a brave little smile.

"You don't need to worry," Lucas said, turning away from the lock. "You won't get in trouble. We'll just say Moose left the Snack-Shack unlocked." He looked at the ground around the deck and picked up a small stick, testing it between his fingers. Bending low over the padlock, he inserted the stick in the lock and wiggled it around. It took a few minutes before they all heard a click. He stood back, smugly holding up the open padlock.

"How did you do that?" Liv blurted out. It was a cool trick, but not something they taught in high school. How many people just happened to know how to pick a lock?

"YouTube," Lucas said, shrugging it off as though it was no big deal. He set the lock down on the wooden stairs.

Ben coughed. Liv shot him a dark look.

"Well, all I can say is…thank you, YouTube!" Milo looked around at the others and did a little theatrical bow. "Ladies, breakfast is served. Let's find out what delicious treats that naughty Moose has been keeping from us. More tequila, anyone?"

A collective groan followed him. Lucas cracked open the heavy wood door and one by one they stepped into darkness.

CHAPTER 25

"Light's not working," Lucas said, flipping the switch by the door. "Maybe the generator's out. Jesus – it smells really funky in here. Anyone else smell that?" He was not joking. As Liv moved forward, the smell got stronger. Meaty and acrid. What kind of food was making that stench? What had Moose been feeding them? The thought made Liv's stomach churn.

"Oh my God," Milo said from the doorway. He seemed reluctant to enter further. "The truth is revealed. Moose has been keeping dead critters in here and feeding us pieces of their carcasses. That would certainly explain his cooking."

"Eww, gross…" Ruby gagged as she stepped inside. "I can't even… we've been eating this? Oh my God, I am actually going to vomit." She turned around and dashed out of there as fast as she could.

"I'll go with her," Milo volunteered, hustling out after her.

It was impossible to see anything in the darkness. The light from the doorway barely penetrated the gloom. Liv's eyes began to adjust a little, but all she could make out were faint rows of shelves.

"This is hopeless. I can't see a thing," Lucas said, bumping awkwardly into a shelf. "I'm going to see if there's a flashlight in the cook station." He followed Milo out.

Ben didn't seem as bothered by the smell as the others. He pulled his T-shirt up to cover his nose and pushed forward, disappearing into the darkness. There was a dull thud, followed by a loud crash and a groan. A couple of loose cans rolled out of the dark.

"You okay?" Liv asked, wincing.

"Fine," Ben grunted, sounding just a little embarrassed. "I tripped. There's something…" He tailed off.

"What? What is it?" Liv asked nervously. Visions of dangling carcasses hanging from hooks, stripped of flesh, popped into her head. What had Moose been doing in here?

"Shit," Ben muttered.

"*What?*" She shuffled forward into the darkness, arms reaching out in front of her, every nerve on edge. "What is it, Ben?" Without any warning, her foot caught on something. She had no chance of catching herself and fell headfirst, crash-landing onto the ground and rolling onto something warm. Squealing, she pushed herself off.

It was Ben.

He was breathing heavily, still lying on the floor where he'd fallen.

"Ben, what the fuck…?" Liv said. The smell was worse here, pungent with a burned edge, like day-old barbecue. Liv gagged, covering her face with her hand, willing herself not to retch. This was quite possibly the worst thing to do with a hangover.

"Liv…" Ben's voice sounded strange. Maybe he'd landed badly or was winded.

"Are you okay?" It was hard to talk without tasting vomit. Liv rolled onto her knees to stand up, but Ben reached out a hand, holding her gently but firmly down.

"There's something here." His voice was barely above a whisper.

There's something here?

"What? What do you mean? What is it?" An animal? A person? Fuck, what was it?

"I don't know…but we're not alone."

"*What the fuck is it?*" Liv squeaked, curling in on herself. She looked around in the impenetrable darkness. Pointless. It was impossible to see anything. She imagined things leaping out of the corners at her. Venomous spiders, rabid mountain lions, creepy fucking clowns.

Lucas's outline appeared in the rectangle of light through the open doorway.

"Here. No flashlight, but I found matches."

"Oh my God! Light the fucking match. Hurry up! There's something in here." *There's something in here.* Without realizing, Liv had grabbed on to Ben's hand. Neither of them dared move.

There was a small, scratchy noise as Lucas scrabbled with the matchbox in the darkness. It took about three strikes before one of the matches caught. He held it up and, for a few seconds, its weak light flickered on the walls before it burned out.

In that one brief flash of light, Liv saw rows of shelves with a selection of tins and boxes, a cabinet…and a dark shape on the floor near the back wall. The thing Ben had tripped over.

The match went out.

Liv and Ben were on their feet in seconds.

"What is that?" Liv knew her voice was shaking but couldn't help it. "*What the fuck is that?*" She pointed down.

"I know," Ben muttered, as they both instinctively sank back, away from the mass.

"Hold on," Lucas said, striking and breaking a match. The next one lit. He held it out, and this time Liv knew exactly where to look.

Lucas dropped the match. Darkness.

No one moved.

"Fuck." Ben was off to one side. He backed further away. *"Did you see it?"*

"Yeah," Liv muttered. She didn't need to say anything else. They'd all seen it. The thing lying on the floor, unmoving. "Lucas, light a match." Her heart was beating wildly as her mind leaped around, trying to make sense of this, sense of the glimmer of something pale she'd seen. The meaty smell. "Lucas…" Her tone was low and urgent. It couldn't be what she was thinking. It couldn't be.

"All right, give me a second," Lucas muttered as he fumbled the matchbox, hands shaking. The box fell, matches scattering across the floor. "Fuck!"

Liv bent down next to him, feeling around on the splintered wood for the box and a match. She finally retrieved them.

"I've got them," she said. Carefully, she struck the match against the box. Once, twice…the third time it took. Leaning forward, she lowered it over the dark mass.

There it was. An outline, soft. Not fur. Clothes. Two large shapes. Feet? Legs, maybe? In the final precious seconds of light, Liv moved the match up, away from the feet.

The match flickered and went out. It had done its job.

Liv fell back. How could this be happening? A body. Pale skin. Hands blackened with dirt, fingers curled. The weak light had caught the edges of a dark snake, crawling up pale flesh, wrapping itself around its unmoving host's arm.

It couldn't be, and yet it was. *It was.*

Chipmunk was dead.

CHAPTER 26

How was this possible?

First Shasta, now Chipmunk.

They were all on the deck outside the Snack-Shack. It had taken seconds for Liv, Ben and Lucas to scramble their way out of the dark storage shed, tripping over themselves and falling onto the deck. It was many more seconds before they were able to speak and tell the others what they had just discovered.

Chipmunk's body.

Oh God. Liv hugged her knees into her chest. She kept seeing the pale arm, flopped out, with the snake's eyes staring up at her. The overpowering, fleshy smell was still in her nose, her hair, all around her. Inescapable. The smell of death.

"*What? How…?*" Ruby and Milo were drilling them with questions, too afraid to peek inside the Snack-Shack for themselves. "How do you know she's dead? Are you sure? Did you check? Did you take her pulse?"

"No, we didn't fucking check," Ben snarled. He looked pale and tense. "She was dead. You could see. You don't believe us, go look. Unless you're too scared."

"I'm definitely too scared…there's no way…I won't go in there." Ruby's words were running together in her panic to get them out. "I've never seen a dead body… Shasta doesn't count…she wasn't actually dead when we saw her…wait, was she?" Her big eyes had taken over her entire face, rounded with fear and shock.

"Ruby, just stop! For the love of God. Stop talking, girl. You're scaring me." Milo put his arm around her and pulled her into a lanky hug. She disappeared into his arms, her head just peeking over the top of his shoulder.

"Look, I know we're all scared." Lucas stepped forward, turning to face them all. It was the first time Liv had seen him genuinely worried. He pushed his curly blond hair back, a serious expression on his face. "I know this is so fucked up. But this is happening. Let's just slow down here and take it one step at a time." He looked at Ruby and Milo. "You asked how we knew she was dead. Well, it was obvious, the way she was lying there…the smell."

"But if you didn't check her pulse…maybe she's unconscious or—" Ruby said hopefully.

"She's fucking dead," Ben cut in sharply. "I saw her face. Her eyes were open, just staring. They were all weird and cloudy. She's dead." Liv couldn't see his expression, but his shoulders were squeezed tight, his hands clenched into fists.

"I just can't believe this…" Ruby looked around desperately. "What do we do? Chipmunk's…she's…her body…oh God. We're trapped here. With her…like that. *What do we do?*" Her voice rose sharply in pitch. Her sweet features were contorted with fear.

"Babe, everything's fine. Come here." Milo reached for her, but she batted him away this time.

"No! It's not fine, Milo! It's not fine at all. They're dead. Don't you get it? We could die. It could be us next…"

"Nothing to be scared about," Ben growled. "Dead can't hurt you. It's the living you got to worry about."

Ruby wailed and slumped forward. Ben wasn't helping.

A shrill, lonely cry pierced the air. Liv glanced skyward. The damn buzzards were circling overhead, closer now. So, they were here for Chipmunk. Liv shivered. Her thoughts were looping like those sick predators above them. Dozens of questions kept going around and around. But she kept coming back to one.

"What do you think killed her?" The wording sounded wrong. *Killed.* Should she have said "how did she die"? It was less accusatory, more open-ended. Liv looked from Lucas to Ben. She was almost afraid to ask what they really thought. The brief flash of light from the match had been enough to show her that Chipmunk was dead. But from what she'd briefly seen of the body, it was intact. No signs of injury or blood. There was just that smell, that foul, burned smell.

Ben shrugged. "I dunno. Didn't see anything."

"Me either," Lucas said. "There wasn't anything obvious. No marks or wounds."

Well, that was something at least. Not a mountain lion attack then. Liv's thoughts went smaller.

"Maybe it was a spider bite? Or scorpion? What about a snake?" she muttered. The image of the snake tattoo on Chipmunk's pale flesh popped into her mind. That would be a twisted way to go, but it had a kind of karmic logic. Out here, everything was out to get you. Milo's words came back to her: *You're in their home now.*

"Makes sense," Lucas said, nodding. "She could easily have put her hand into the wrong hole and been bitten. End of story." The others murmured in agreement, apart from Milo.

He gave a short bark of a laugh.

"You're joking, right?" He looked around from face to face. "Oh my God. You're actually serious. A snake bite? We have two deaths in one night, and you think that it's just some freaky coincidence? How does that make any sense at all? I mean, think about it for half a second."

"Death never makes sense, Milo," Lucas said sharply. He stepped off the deck and started pacing up and down. "Shasta had an allergic reaction. Who knows what Chipmunk got into? Sometimes bad shit happens to people. There's no plan for us. That's just life."

"Look, man. I appreciate you," Milo said. "Seriously, I hear you. But you can't ignore the obvious just because you don't want to know the truth."

"So, what are you talking about here?" Lucas snapped. He was getting progressively more irate. "If the deaths weren't accidents, what were they? *What?* You think one of us *murdered* Shasta and Chipmunk. Is that it? Because if that's what you're implying, then you're an asshole. We're not killers! Look at us."

Liv couldn't help glancing around at the circle of faces. Tight and anxious. Delinquents. Losers, maybe. But killers? No.

"Yeah. You're probably right." Milo stretched his long arms out nonchalantly. "It's probably just me and my stupid imagination, running off again. Obviously, it's ridiculous to think that one of us might be a killer…apart from one small thing."

Everyone was paying attention now. Like it or not, he had them all hooked.

With his flair for the dramatic, Milo walked slowly, intentionally towards the door to the Snack-Shack. He bent down and picked up the padlock from where Lucas had left it on the stairs. He held it out.

"The Snack-Shack was locked when we got here." That was all he said. It was all he needed to say.

Liv stared at the padlock. Her brain had finally caught up with Milo's reasoning. How had she not thought of that before? Chipmunk's body was *inside* the Snack-Shack. Which meant that someone had locked it inside and then lied about it. Why would someone do that, unless…

She looked from face to face. Lucas and Ben. Ruby and Milo. Was it possible? *Did one of them kill Chipmunk?*

Milo was grinning now, clearly savouring the moment.

"Mark my words, kiddos. We all need to watch our backs." He spread his arms wide, turning to be sure he had everyone's full attention. "After all, we've got two dead bodies now, and the only thing we know for sure…is that one of us is hiding a dirty little secret."

CHAPTER 27

All four corners of the deck were now occupied. Wordlessly, they had drifted as far apart as possible. The air between them felt charged and dangerous.

Only Ben had retreated further away and was standing on the grass, still within earshot, but with his back to them, ready to run if needed.

A dirty little secret.

Shit.

This couldn't be happening – and yet, it was. The Snack-Shack had been locked with the body inside. All hope that both deaths were freakish accidents had disappeared. This – whatever it was – was no accident.

"So, what now?" Ruby broke the silence. It was a good question. How do you follow up the revelation that one of you might be a murderer?

There was a long pause. Liv didn't dare to meet the others' eyes. All her worst suspicions were only heightened by the growing awareness that she was a suspect too.

This was crazy. *Insane.* She wasn't a killer, and maybe she was being naïve, but she just couldn't believe that the others were either. It didn't make sense. Even if Chipmunk was hateful and cruel – she didn't deserve to die. And what about Shasta? She'd just arrived at the camp. No one could possibly have had a reason to kill her.

But two people were dead. Fact.

Someone had locked the Snack-Shack. Fact.

They were trapped here alone. Fact.

That was all they really knew – but it was enough.

"*What do we do?*" Ruby repeated, her voice rising. "We can't stay here. Not if one of us is…is a…you know."

"I know this is fucked up," Liv said. "But we shouldn't jump to conclusions. We don't know for sure that anyone's actually a…*you know*." She looked around, keenly aware that overreacting would only make the situation worse. If there was some way to set the tone of this, to avoid everyone launching in on each other – that had to be a good thing.

"I reckon Liv's right," Lucas said, his voice unnervingly calm. "We have no idea what's going on, but we can't do anything. We can't call for help or hike out of here. We can only sit this out. Hopefully Moose will be back before the storm breaks. Then we can get the hell out of here."

"So what?" Milo turned on him. "We just sit tight and hope that whoever's doing this doesn't decide to murder again?"

"We don't know what's happening here!" Liv stepped forward, into the centre of the deck. All eyes were on her now; even Ben turned to watch. "Let's just stick to the facts, okay? We don't want to make things worse than they already are."

Lucas moved next to her.

"Listen, why don't we all just stay together? As long as we keep an eye on each other, we'll be safe, no matter what's going on." He had a point. There was safety in numbers. It would be hard for someone to pick them off if they were in a group. "We can set up in the campground and wait for Moose." Lucas looked around for agreement. Liv and Ruby nodded.

"Sorry, hard pass," Milo said. He pointed at Ben. "Am I the only one who heard Ben threaten Chipmunk last night? I mean, all things being equal, your herd-mentality plan works. But they're not equal. We have a prime suspect. I, for one, am not planning on zipping myself into a tent with someone with a history of homicidal behaviour."

"Fuck you, Milo!" Ben shouted. He was rigid, fists clenched. But he didn't move towards the deck.

"Yeah, well, fuck you too, Ben," Milo retorted. "I'm not staking my life on being polite about this. You are dangerous and if I had my way, we'd lock you in the Snack-Shack with the body until Moose gets back. Safety first."

Oh no. This was exactly what Liv had been hoping to avoid. Everyone had doubts. Everyone was afraid. She could guarantee that they'd all thought about Ben's last words to Chipmunk. If she was honest, she'd circled back to the fact that Ben was the first one up this morning. What if he'd never been to bed? What if he had been up all night…?

"*Just stop it!*" It was Ruby's voice. "Just stop! Milo, you are making everything worse. I can't do this. I won't." She pulled herself up tall, sniffing loudly. "I'm going to the campground, and I'm going to stay there and wait for Moose. If anyone cares to wait with me… well, I will see you there." With that, she stalked off the deck, head held high, heading for the white trail and the campground.

Kudos to Ruby. She'd stopped the negative momentum. Milo looked down sheepishly. Lucas glanced at Liv and gave a little shrug.

"Shall we?"

Liv nodded. It was as good a plan as any.

They started after Ruby, Milo sulkily following behind. Only Ben didn't come with them. It was understandable. Milo's words were tough, but there was truth in them. Ben was the number one suspect. No one was comfortable around him. He was probably better off alone.

When they got to the white trail, Liv paused, letting the others go ahead. She turned to look back at the hollow.

Ben had returned to the deck and was standing by the door to the Snack-Shack, bent low over the lock. She couldn't tell what he was doing – she wasn't sure she wanted to know.

As she watched, he straightened up and stood for a moment, head dropped as though he was listening. Then, with a small sideways flick of the head, he looked directly at her. It was as if he knew she'd be there.

Fuck. Liv tensed up but held her ground. Two people were dead. They were past niceties.

Even over this distance, Liv could feel something charged in the air. She could sense his frustration in the way he stood: fists gripped at his sides and head down. But there was something else too – a connection that had been growing between them over the past two days, with the dead deer, the raft, the swallows. It was all there, in his dark eyes, watching her warily.

Partners, right?

God, she wanted to trust him. But that would be really stupid, possibly even dangerous – the kind of thinking that could get you killed. Right now, with everything that had just happened, she couldn't take the risk.

No. She couldn't let her guard down with anyone, let alone Ben.

As though he'd heard her thoughts, Ben exploded into action. Without a backward glance, he jumped off the deck and ran fast, heading into the woods.

Liv watched until he disappeared among the trees. She almost called out to him. *Almost.* But what was she going to say? Stay? Go? She didn't know.

That was the problem. She just didn't know.

Was he Ben-the-Killer, or the boy with the swallow tattoo? A loving brother or a twisted serial killer? Good or evil? He couldn't be both. It was one or the other.

The real question was…which was it?

CHAPTER 28

The weather had picked up on the general mood, and a light, grey drizzle had settled in over the campsite.

Liv was sitting under the open flap in Ruby's tent, watching the tree line anxiously for signs of Moose's return. Milo and Ruby were tucked up in their sleeping bags behind her, playing Old Maid. It was surprisingly chilly compared to yesterday. The weak rain permeated everything, and a cold wind had picked up by lunchtime. There were ominous rumblings in the darkening sky beyond the crags. The storms were getting closer.

When would Moose get back? She really hoped it would be before the rain really hit. There was every chance the one road up here would become impassable. That might add another day before they were rescued – a thought that sent a shiver of dread through her.

She'd tried to work out how long Moose might be in town, but it was impossible to guess. He was delivering a camper's body; there would be doctors, police, questions. Maybe they'd keep him around to talk to Shasta's parents. Maybe they'd keep him for days. Oh God, maybe they would be stuck here alone with Chipmunk's body until Lomax's scheduled mid-week return. After all, as far as everyone in town knew, they were still safely under the supervision of a living counsellor.

As Liv watched, the bushes at the edge of the campground rustled and shook. A head, then an arm emerged. Lucas. He'd been out in the rain for the best part of the last hour, throwing the frisbee to himself, lost in thought. He seemed to prefer his own company to hanging out in the tent. Only Ben hadn't made an appearance yet; not since she'd seen him by the Snack-Shack.

A distant crack of lightning lit up the tops of the crags. Liv counted, *one-one-thousand, two-one-thousand, three-one-thousand…* A low rumble of thunder rolled across the sky. What was the rule – the storm was a mile away for every second counted? Something like that. She didn't remember. What she did remember was that the last clap of thunder had taken five seconds. The storm was approaching fast.

"Pee time!" Milo wriggled out of his sleeping bag.

"Oh my God, Milo," Ruby said. "You're just saying that because you totally know you're going to lose this round. You're such a cheat." She threw her cards down on the sleeping bag.

"Nature calls," Milo said, grinning. "I need me some one-on-one time with a bucket. If you know what I mean…"

Ugh, gross, Liv thought.

"Ugh. gross," Ruby muttered. "TMI." She rolled over and sighed.

Briefly, Liv considered suggesting that they all go, just to stay together. But if she was honest with herself, she felt safer with Ruby and Lucas in the big open campground, than she would traipsing around the rainy woods with Milo. She barely knew him, and what little she did know wasn't exactly reassuring. There could have been any number of reasons why Milo Zhao was at Camp Smiling Skies. He had zero judgement and even fewer boundaries. If he was somehow involved in Chipmunk's death, then his "one-of-us-has-a-dirty-little-secret" theory was a masterstroke in misdirection.

After a big performance putting on his plastic poncho, Milo finally emerged from the tent. He tossed the frisbee around with Lucas for a few minutes before disappearing in the direction of the bucket.

It was just Liv and Ruby in the tent now. A little awkward. They hadn't spent any time on their own together before now – Ruby was always perma-attached to her camp-husband, Milo.

"So…uh, how are you feeling, you know, about things?" Liv managed to say, throwing out an attempted smile. When Ruby didn't respond, she decided it was probably for the best. But then she heard a snuffling sound. Ruby was crying.

"I…I'm sorry. It's just…so…sad…" She sniffed loudly.

Weird. Ruby had held it together through several rounds of Old Maid, giggling at all Milo's stupid jokes. As soon as he was out of sight, she seemed to fold in on herself. Ruby could flip modes in an instant. She either had some serious mood swings going on or she was faking it – performing for her audience, like her movie-star mother.

"Yeah." Liv nodded. "It *is* sad. Really fucking sad."

For a few minutes they sat silently watching the rain tip-tap on the grey world around them. Lucas had disappeared somewhere. His frisbee lay upside down, discarded, slowly collecting a small pool of rainwater. The birds were oddly silent, probably hunkering down like everything else, sheltering. It was a relief not having to hear their sinister cries.

After a while, Ruby pulled herself to sitting, her big eyes focused on Liv.

"You know, Liv, I wish I was like you. You're so…" Ruby paused. Liv held her breath – her defensive side rose up, ready to shoot down or shut down, as needed. "You're so…strong."

Liv snorted.

"Strong? You think I'm strong?" It was stupid. Ruby didn't know her. This was just their third day together; it wasn't long enough to know someone. Even after everything they'd been through.

"I could never do what you do, Liv. The way you stood up to Chipmunk. The way you just got on with things after you nearly drowned." Ruby shifted forward. Her expression was endearingly earnest. "You're like this kick-ass-boss-bitch and…I think you're kinda cool."

Liv was taken aback. That was not what she was expecting. Somehow it made its way under her shell and felt almost good. She sniffed. Strange emotions were shifting around inside her. Not bad ones. But definitely ones that she wasn't used to. Uncomfortable. Vulnerable. "Well, I, er…think you're cool too," she muttered.

"Really?" Ruby stared at her. "You do?"

Now Liv had to say something. What? What could she say about Ruby? Three things, she told herself. Come on. If Lucas could do it, she could. *Three things I like about Ruby.* How hard could that be? Why was her mind blanking?

"I like your tattoo." She nodded at Ruby's hand. It was weak. Pathetic really. In her panic, Liv had noticed the little Chinese character on Ruby's middle finger. "It's, um…cute."

"Mmm." Ruby looked down at it casually. "Milo always teases me about it. He says it's cultural appropriation, but I think it's super pretty. It means 'heavenly sky'. Milo says they wrote it wrong, and it actually means 'husband'. That's why he calls me his camp-wife – cos I flip him off so much. He's so annoying sometimes." She smiled. Talking about Milo seemed to be helping her mood.

"So, how did you two become friends?" Liv asked, hoping to change the subject.

Ruby shuffled over to the tent door next to Liv, still enshrouded in her orange sleeping bag.

"Oh my God, he pranked me so badly when I first got here. He hid a dead snake in my tent on the first night. I nearly died!"

"You became *friends* after that?" Liv shook her head. That would have been a dealbreaker for her.

"Well, not for a while, of course. But he grows on you, you know? He's like a big puppy sometimes. He just can't stop himself. It's like he has too much energy for the day and if he doesn't get it out in a good way, he gets kinda naughty. He's really close to his mom, but her work's based in China so she's not around much. His dad is like this ex-pro-basketball player and super strict – they clash *a lot*. Milo says he always feels like he's letting him down. I can relate, I mean with my mom, you know?"

Liv nodded. Yeah. She knew a thing or two about being a disappointment. She'd got that one down. She looked out across the rainy field. A small, scraggly bird had emerged from the bushes and was hopping around, scratching frantically in mud puddles, searching for a worm to eat. Survival wasn't pretty.

"Liv, can I ask you something?" Ruby said.

No. Liv would have much preferred listening to the rain in silence, but her politeness-override forced her to say a reluctant, "Sure."

"Do you think you deserve to be here?" Ruby's eyes reflected the rain; the dewy, wet world around them.

Well, that was the million-dollar question, wasn't it? Did she deserve to be kidnapped and incarcerated in a remote wilderness hellhole? She was a fuck-up. Liv knew that. If she was honest with herself, stealing the painting might have been the dealbreaker, but her problems had started long before then, even before her mom died – when she first got sick. That's when things had got confusing; when Liv had started acting out. She didn't know why, or how to stop herself – there were no brakes, no filters.

Yeah, she was definitely a fuck-up. But did she deserve *this*?

"I don't know. Maybe. Probably." What else could she say?

"I'm just asking because, you know, I kinda do deserve to be here." Ruby adeptly shifted the focus onto herself, much to Liv's relief. "I might have done something like *really bad*…with a pair of scissors."

Despite herself, Liv's curiosity kicked in. What really bad thing could you do with *scissors*? Now this was getting interesting.

"The thing is…my family's not really like other people's. You know? It's mostly just me and my half-sister, Jade. Oh, and our Frenchies, Thor and Loki. We're very lucky. Like we have lots of really nice things and all, and so many friends. Especially Jade – she's like super popular." A shadow crossed her face. "But Mom's not there much. You know, she's always going away for shoots or networking. She's amazing; she's like the OG single working mom."

Liv wasn't sure you really counted as a "single working mom" when you were a multi-millionaire movie star with a staff, an entourage and a long string of celebrity ex-husbands. But she didn't say it out loud. Ruby clearly worshipped her mom, right alongside millions of fans worldwide.

"So, what about your dad? Do you see him much?" Liv had to ask, her curiosity getting the better of her. After all, Ruby's dad was on the verge of winning a Best Director Oscar. He was kind of a big deal, back in the real world.

"Nah, we're not close. My parents broke up before I was born. I used to spend summers in Mexico City with his family when I was little, but half the time he wasn't even there – busy on some movie or other. Mom totally hates him. She says he's an arrogant piece of shit. We're not allowed to say his name in the house." She said it casually, as though this was the most natural thing in the world. Maybe wealth and fame didn't guarantee you a happy family, Liv thought. Just enough money to buy yourself a new one.

"Mostly, it's just the three of us: me, Jade and Mom. When we were little, Mom would take us with her when she was filming. It was so much fun. We lived in all these different places for months. We'd have a tutor and hang out on the set. Everyone treated us like royalty – Jenn Clarke's girls. It was so awesome. But after Jade started middle school, Mom stopped taking us, so we would have more stability and all. She would fly back on weekends when she could, but she was pretty busy."

The tough lives of the rich and famous. Liv wondered where Ruby was going with this. Was it a poor little rich girl story? She bit her lip and waited.

"Jade was always fine with everything. She's really popular and looks exactly like Mom – it's freaky. They're so similar. I take after my dad more, I guess. Which is fine, it's just, I'm kinda the odd one out, you know? But Mom always says how proud she is of me. You know? She tells everyone how I'm the easy child. I never cause any problems, unlike Jade. Oh my God, Jade is like always getting into trouble – mostly boy stuff. She's obsessed. But I don't date, and I have like a 4.3 GPA. Mom even decided to take me as her plus-one to the Golden Globes this year. Can you believe it? She's never taken Jade! She usually goes with one of her boyfriends, because it's good for PR and photos and all."

Ruby's face was lit up like Christmas. She was probably picturing the dress she'd worn, the lights and paparazzi, the A-list celebrities smugly flashing their expensive smiles. A perfect daughter, standing on the red carpet, arm in arm with her perfect mother. Desperately wanting to be loved. It all made so much sense now. Ruby Jennifer Clarke – the pleaser.

"So, the night before the ceremony, the house was buzzing. Mom was doing all these treatments. People were coming and going. Even Jade was there, getting into everything. The team from the designer brought Mom's dress for last-minute fittings and touch-ups. They had it set up on a mannequin in her walk-in. I went in and saw it. God, it was so…just perfect. Soft swan grey, hand embroidered with crystals in the bodice, falling like water. It was the most beautiful thing I'd ever seen. I actually cried."

"Wait – I remember your mom's dress! It was super-short with feathered bits, right?" It was all coming back to Liv now. Min was obsessed with celebrity fashion and constantly sent reels of red-carpet highlights to Liv. A few months ago, Jennifer Clarke arrived at the Golden Globes in *that* dress, grey and barely there, crafted by some insanely famous designer. It topped all the best-dressed lists and Min wouldn't stop talking about it (although Liv thought it looked like roadkill). "Wait…was that you on the red carpet? I kind of remember she had her daughter with her…" Liv vaguely recalled a bunch of "mini-me" memes about Jennifer Clarke's daughter – with her blond hair and golden smile. They looked so alike… Oh, fuck. The penny dropped. Yikes. "She didn't end up taking you, did she? She took your sister."

Ruby nodded.

"I found out from our housekeeper. My mom didn't even bother to tell me she'd changed her mind. Apparently, they thought it was good for PR to have Jade on the red carpet. Something about optics and tapping into the mini-me trend." Ruby turned to stare out at the rain, her chin slightly raised. "Mom's always competing with Reese and Gwyneth. I mean, I get it. Jade is perfect for that." She sniffed.

Ordinarily Liv would have found it hard to be particularly sympathetic given the circumstances. Not going to the Golden Globes? It was definitely a first-world problem. But somehow, she understood on another level. The implicit rejection. Liv was very familiar with that.

"I'm sorry, Ruby. That sucks. It must have really hurt."

"Oh, don't feel sorry for me." Ruby shook her head. "I don't deserve sympathy." She pushed herself out of her sleeping bag and crawled through the tent flap, out into the rain. She just stood there for a moment, back to the tent, arms folded across her chest. "You see…I didn't exactly take the news well. It's weird, I don't really remember exactly how it happened. I just remember being so furious with Mom and Jade. I kept thinking about that dress. I couldn't get it out of my head. Like it was taunting me or something." She turned to face Liv; her eyes were perfectly round, imploring. "That's all I remember, until the next morning when they found me in Mom's walk-in closet holding a pair of kitchen scissors…"

Scissors. The dress. Ahhh. Liv tried not to laugh.

"Ruby…"

Ruby just shook her head. "The designer managed to fix it. He turned it into this 'artful feathering'. He even said it ended up better than before! But Mom…oh God, Mom."

Liv could imagine. There wouldn't have been much space for compassion or understanding from a woman who was clearly the centre of her own universe. It all made sense now. Sweet, needy Ruby. The not-so-perfect daughter. A swift departure to a far-distant wilderness therapy camp. No wonder Ruby was out to reclaim her perfect-girl status. No wonder she was desperate to get home to try and fix this. To try and work her way back into her mommy's unavailable affections. No wonder her mom kept kicking back Ruby's release date, rather than bothering to parent her needy daughter. Out of sight, out of mind. Easy.

Liv looked at Ruby. She seemed so lost, Liv wanted to do something for her. But she wasn't sure what or how.

"Well, I think your mom's lucky," she finally managed. "You were too nice. If I'd been there, I would have set fire to that fucking dress and probably taken the house down with it. No fancy designer could have salvaged it. Your mom would have had to collect her stupid award naked."

Ruby stared at her, shocked at first, then a small smile crept across her face. The image of *the* Jennifer Clarke standing on a stage stark naked in front of the entire Hollywood elite was just too good. Ruby broke out with laughter – big, snuffly laughs. Liv couldn't help herself and started laughing too.

That was all so far away from them – another world. Another universe. It was hard to imagine it was still out there somewhere: Jennifer Clarke having brunch with her latest fiancé; Min lying in bed endlessly scrolling on her phone; her dad sitting alone in his home office, doing the thing he liked best – working. All while Liv and Ruby were here in the rain, stuck on the side of a mountain at the end of the world with a dead body locked in a shed. Weird times.

"Thanks, Liv." Ruby sucked up her giggles. "I think I needed to hear that."

Liv wasn't quite sure what "that" was, but it seemed to have done the trick. Ruby was looking like her usual peppy, preppy self.

"Sure." Liv gave her a quick smile, before awkwardly looking around for a way to change the subject. "I wonder where the boys are. I would have thought Milo would be back long ago."

"Oh God, Milo's so hungry he probably passed out in the bucket or something. He doesn't do well without food. I should go look for him."

There was a moment, a quick shy smile, a little nod. Liv nodded back. A connection had been made. Small, but it was definitely there.

As Ruby walked away, heading in the direction of the bucket, Liv watched her go. There was something endearing about the friendship between Ruby and Milo. They were different in so many ways, not to mention annoying. But somehow, they just fit. Maybe their friendship would be the one good thing that would survive Camp Smiling Skies. Maybe.

After a few minutes, the rain started to let up. Restless, Liv picked up the frisbee and, pouring out the rainwater, tossed it up in the air a few times. It must be early afternoon already. Still no sign of Moose, and the storm clouds were massing over the nearest crags now. She had a horrible feeling that Moose wasn't going to make it back in time – that they were in for another night trapped out here, alone in the storm.

Aarghhh. There was a faint cry – in the distance. Maybe the buzzards were finally stirring, sensing the break in the rain. It had been nice not having those creepy harbingers of death constantly circling overhead. She tossed the frisbee up again and caught it lightly.

Aarghhhhhh. Liv dropped the frisbee. This time it was louder. It didn't sound like a bird. Liv looked up at the sky, but the buzzards were nowhere to be seen. Maybe it was some weird-ass mountain critter.

Aarghhhhhh. What was making that noise? The sound was chilling, almost like a low scream. Whatever was making it was clearly in pain, or fear, or both.

Aarghhhhhh…help! Liv gasped. It was one of the others.

This time, she didn't hesitate, sprinting in the direction of the voice, her heart beating hard, adrenaline powering her forward.

They should have stayed together. They should have kept an eye on each other, like they said they would. But they'd stupidly split up, even though one of them might be a killer.

They'd split up and now someone was in trouble.

Again…it was happening again.

CHAPTER 29

Where was the scream coming from?

It was almost impossible to tell. The sounds were coming from all sides now, echoing off the rocks all around. To make matters worse, one of the birds was back in full voice, cawing loudly above.

Aargh… The scream again. It was a male voice.

One of the boys was in trouble – but who was it? Liv thought of Lucas, then Ben. Oh God, who?

There was a crunching sound up ahead. Someone was running fast. It sounded like they were heading straight for the rock wall, towards the gully.

They must know where the sounds were coming from. Liv didn't hesitate, sprinting after them as fast as she could.

The gully was treacherous. A flood of rainwater poured down the narrow crack in the rock, dragging mud and debris with it. Several times, Liv had to duck fully into the icy stream as she struggled to pull herself up, scraping her elbows and knees in her rush to get to the top.

When she finally made it, she scrambled over the rock edge and fell, gasping to catch her breath as she looked around the rocky plateau. It was bigger than she had imagined, and flat like a giant stone tabletop. Lucas and Ruby were on the far side, by the cliff edge. They were hunched over, but she couldn't see what they were doing. Summoning her strength, Liv pushed herself to her feet and ran to them.

"Don't let me go!" It was Milo's voice. But where was he?

Liv slid to the ground next to the others.

"What's going—?" She didn't need to finish her sentence. Lucas's arms were over the edge of the rock, his muscles taut. He looked like he was in pain and was sweating with effort. Ruby was holding him back from the edge, arms around his waist, her full weight on him.

"Help us," Lucas barked.

He was slowly slipping towards the cliff edge.

"I can't hold you, Lucas," Ruby shouted. She didn't stand a chance. Any further forward and Lucas's body weight would be enough to carry both him and Ruby over the edge – over the cliff.

"Fuck," Liv muttered, diving onto her stomach. She army-crawled to the rock edge and peered over. Milo's head was a metre below them, one long arm stretched up, clinging desperately to Lucas's hand, the other clinging to a thin tree root – the only things keeping him from falling ten metres to the rocky ground below.

"Don't let go…don't drop me!" Milo was trying to pull himself up, but he didn't have the strength.

"I…can't…" Lucas said through gritted teeth. He slid several centimetres forward. This was all going in the wrong direction.

"Hey," a voice called out from far below. Ben appeared on the ground under the rock wall, sheltering his eyes from the rain to look up at them. He was pointing at something.

There was no time to worry about him. They were losing this – losing Milo. There would be nothing Ben could do to break his fall, not without getting himself killed. Liv knew she had to do something. She was the only one free to help. But what? She couldn't reach Milo from here. There was nothing on top of the rock wall that she could use to help her. Nothing that she could do…

"Liv!" It was Ben's voice. He kept pointing at something on the cliff, but what?

Suddenly it hit Liv. *The bird ledge.* He was pointing to the ledge. It must be right below where Milo was hanging. You couldn't see it from above; the cliff edge overhung the rock face. But the ledge was there.

That was it. If she could get below Milo, she could pull him onto the ledge. She could do it.

She looked around for a tree – Ben had told her that was the way down to the ledge. But where was it? Where?

"Liv! Help me!" Lucas called out desperately.

"Just…just hold on." She didn't have time to explain now.

Suddenly she saw it, almost lost in the rainy mist. A tiny, scrubby tree growing precariously on the edge of the cliff. Without hesitating, Liv ran to it and, swinging around onto her stomach, she dangled her legs over the edge. Holding on to the tree, she lowered herself, praying this was a good idea. Her feet swung wildly in the air for a second too long as she felt her weight tipping her over. If she'd made a mistake, there was no going back now. There would be two bodies at the foot of the rock wall.

One foot caught on something solid – a tree root. She put her weight on it and eased herself down. Ben was right; the roots formed a rudimentary ladder down to a narrow ledge, no wider than her muddy boot.

Stepping onto the wet strip of rock, Liv breathed in with relief. There was no time to waste. Keeping her eyes on the rock face, she started edging along the ledge as fast as she dared, heading towards Milo.

There was nothing to hold on to, but as long as she moved sideways, keeping her body pressed against the rock wall, she could keep her balance. It took everything she had to focus on her movements and keep her thoughts away from the dizzying fall beneath her. One mistake. That was all it would take. One little slip, or shift, or stumble and she would go over. That easily. She could die.

There were shouts, above and below now. Something was happening. God, she hoped she wasn't too late. What if Milo had fallen, or Lucas had been pulled down with him? Ruby too? What if they were all dead, and she fell and…

She rounded the side of the rock face in a panic. Out of the corner of her eye she could see Milo. Still alive. Still dangling from Lucas's hand, his other hand gripping a small branch growing out of a crack in the rock wall. Thank God, he was okay. She didn't dare turn her head fully to look at him – she had to keep her focus, her balance, one step sideways, followed by another.

Close now.

She stopped by a large root protruding out of the rock. It provided a reassuring handhold. Gripping it tightly, for the first time, she dared to look around. She was barely a metre from Milo now. So close. If she put her hand out, she could almost touch him.

He was hanging directly below the overhanging cliff edge, almost level with her. If he could just reach his feet out, he could touch the ledge. Then she could help pull his weight onto it. This could work.

"Milo, I'm here," she shouted over the noise of the wind and rain beating against the rock face.

"Liv?" Milo sounded shocked.

"There's a ledge. If we can get your feet onto the ledge, you can stand." Looking up, she could just see Lucas's face. He looked exhausted, red with exertion. He didn't have much left in him. They were almost out of time.

Fuck.

Liv shuffled closer to Milo, still clinging tightly to the root as she stretched out one arm, reaching for Milo's swinging legs.

"Milo, *help me!*" she called to him. Her fingers were grasping at air, so close now. But not quite there. She would have to let go of the root to reach him. But the impossibility of it hit her. If she had nothing to hold on to, pulling the weight of Milo onto her would likely propel them both backward off the ledge. Shit. "Milo, you need to swing towards me. I can't reach you."

"I can't. Liv, go back. You'll die." Milo was swinging around precariously.

There was no response to that. Liv wasn't going to stop now.

"*Swing towards me,*" she shouted. Milo swung his legs out and back. She reached for him with everything she had. Her fingertips brushed his trousers. Almost there. "Try again."

"I…can't hold him any more…I can't," Lucas called out. Liv saw him – he was too far forward. Any more and he'd fall. They were out of time.

Gasping with effort, Milo swung his legs out and back. Closer now.

Just close enough.

Liv reached out, grasping desperately onto Milo's trousers. She had him!

In seconds, Milo's hand slid from Lucas's grip, and he dropped. Liv pulled back as hard as she could.

It happened so fast. Milo landed on the ledge. Liv's grip on him released, just as her other hand slipped off the root, flailing wildly behind her as her momentum pushed her backward. She fell back – too far, away from the rock face, the ledge, her arms circling in empty air.

She had nothing. It was over.

She was falling.

CHAPTER 30

"Got you."

It was Ben's voice. His hand gripped her wrist tightly. Liv gasped, pulled up short, still hanging precariously over the edge. He was next to her on the ledge, the other hand holding the tree root. Easily, he pulled her in – pulled her close to him. She caught her balance, her weight safely on the ledge.

She was shaking, pushed up against the wall, Ben's arm around her, holding her. Adrenaline was pulsing through her. This fucking place was going to kill her. Shasta then Chipmunk – she'd be next at the rate she was going.

Ben's face was close to hers, his dark eyes soft with concern.

"Fuck this fucking place. *Fuck it!*" Without even realizing she was doing it, she shifted closer to him, needing something unspoken. Instinctively he seemed to know and pulled her gently into him. She could smell him – dirt and sweat. Earthy and solid. Real. Closing her eyes, she breathed him in deeply as she waited for the pounding in her chest to subside. Even though they were balanced on the edge of a sheer drop, she felt safe here. In this moment, in his arms.

"Maybe don't save Milo next time, okay, Walker?" Ben said.

Liv almost laughed. It was almost funny.

"What's going on?" It was Ruby's voice from above. "Did anyone die?"

"Nope. All alive. Liv nearly killed herself trying to save me," Milo shouted back. "*Again*. Getting to be a habit, Liv."

"Asshole." Liv snapped out of her shaky mood and pulled back quickly from Ben's arms. She was tempted to undo her good work and shove Milo backward off the ledge. But instead, she gritted her teeth and looked at Ben. "Let's get the fuck off this stupid ledge." Ben smiled and shuffled sideways, back the way they'd come.

Liv followed, probably moving faster than was totally safe. But she was over this and needed to get away from here once and for all. Milo trailed behind. For someone who had nearly died – not to mention nearly dragged Liv and Lucas to their deaths with him – he was awfully chatty.

"That was *insane*. I'm not even kidding you. My whole life was like right there, in front of my eyes. Oh my God, just thinking about it gives me chills…"

Liv rolled her eyes and tried to blank him. She would definitely not save him next time.

By the time they'd climbed the root ladder back up to the top of the rock wall, they were all out of breath. Lucas and Ruby were waiting for them anxiously.

"Jesus, are you okay?" Lucas offered Liv a hand, but she didn't take it. She'd had her moment of weakness on the ledge. She was done being pathetic. She was done being a fool. Lucas dropped his hand and stood back, giving her space. "What happened down there? We couldn't see past the overhang."

"We're fine," Liv said shortly. She didn't want to think about it and certainly didn't want to talk about it. She turned to look at Ben, but he'd moved away and was standing near the far edge, watching, arms folded across his chest.

Milo caught the others up on what they'd missed, explaining about the ledge and how he'd nearly fallen, about the rescue. As he described everything in animated detail, Ruby suddenly barrelled into him and wrapped both her arms tightly around his waist.

"Milo, you could have died, you silly beanpole." She seemed genuinely upset – more upset than the beanpole himself.

"Oh, don't be a drama queen." Milo half-turned and hugged her back, kissing her affectionately on the top of her head. "You know I'm only alive because of you. You found me hanging off the edge. If you hadn't come looking for me up here, I would have been a goner for sure."

Ruby looked up at him with big eyes.

"Really?"

"Really. You saved me, Rubes. You actually saved me. You, Ruby Jennifer Clarke, are a hero."

Ruby saved him? Liv rolled her eyes. It was childish. Yes, she could admit that. It wasn't like she'd chosen to risk her life for a pat on the back. But saying that *Ruby* saved him? Now that was just insulting. The last she'd seen of Ruby, she was lying safely across Lucas's legs using herself as a dead weight. Nice job. Very courageous.

"How did you fall?" It was the first thing Ben had said since the rescue. He hadn't moved and was still standing by the far edge, glaring at the rest of them. Liv looked at him – his sleeveless T-shirt had a new rip across the stomach; a flash of tanned skin showed through the hole. Briefly her mind flashed back to the ledge, the feeling of his arms around her, her cheek resting on his chest.

Three things I like about Ben…

Stop. Why was she thinking like that? About Ben? Clearly the near-death experience on top of an empty stomach was making her delusional.

"Well, that's the thing." Milo patted Ruby and straightened up slowly. "I didn't fall."

Instantly, he had everyone's attention.

Milo shrugged. "I was so bored in the tent – no offence, Rubes, but I can only play Old Maid so many times before I'll turn into one. So, after a bucket stop, I thought I might just stretch my legs and look around for any sign of Moose. I came up here and walked over to the edge to get a better view of the road below. But as I was standing there…I heard a noise behind me, a shuffling sound. Before I could turn around, something shoved me hard in the back." He held his two hands out in front of him – palms out.

Ruby gasped. "Wait. You mean something as in a gust-of-wind something? Or a tree branch, right?" she asked hopefully. But her tone was flat. She knew what Milo meant. They all did.

Milo shook his head.

"No, honey. It wasn't the wind. I really wish it was." He turned to look around at the others. "I shouldn't have said that some*thing* pushed me over." He paused for effect here, slowly taking in their faces before at last adding the words none of them wanted to hear. "What I really meant to say was…some*one*."

CHAPTER 31

The afternoon rain had started up again, harder than before. Heavy storm clouds were massing over the crags. Streams of water had sprung up in unexpected places, making their way downhill, through the camp on their way to the raging Ochee. The dusty ground mixed with the rain, creating a red, muddy sludge that clung to everything that came into contact with it.

They were all in Moose's tent cabin, soaked and sodden after their silent scramble down the rock wall. The gully had become a small waterfall. Mud was caked up their legs and arms and spread liberally around the cabin's wooden floor and canvas walls. There was no point in trying to keep things clean. Clean was for regular people on regular days. Not for them – not today.

"So let me get this straight, Milo," Lucas said, his tone laced with frustration. "You have absolutely no idea who pushed you. You didn't see a thing. But you're sure you were pushed."

"Oh my God, Lucas. Yes, yes and yes," Milo retorted sharply. They had been having the same conversation, over and over, since arriving in the cabin.

Milo was bent over a large plastic chest covered in National Park stickers. Moose's stuff. He pulled out random items one by one: a baseball cap with *Jackson Hole* stitched across the front, a photo of a horsey-looking girl in a banana slug T-shirt, a large hunting knife in a worn leather sheath – no food.

No question, their extreme hunger was fuelling their extreme paranoia.

Chipmunk's cabin stood just across the clearing, but no one suggested looking in there for something to eat. Even if it contained a fully stocked mini fridge, they couldn't face rifling through the dead counsellor's things. They would have to be starving to death before they raided it for food, and the Snack-Shack wasn't even mentioned. Not with the body…the smell – not happening.

"Fuck this," Ben said, kicking at a wooden post. Liv understood his frustration. What could they do? They were stuck. There was nothing to eat and nowhere to go, and if Milo was right, then one of them had pushed him off a cliff. But they had absolutely no way of knowing who.

Liv looked at the others. Milo was busy in his exploration of the chest. Lucas was pacing. Ben was standing on the porch steps in the rain, seemingly oblivious to the cold drops of water running down his neck. Ruby was curled up on Moose's bunk with his sleeping bag, pillows and blankets draped over her.

They didn't look murderous. Well, maybe Ben…a little, if she was being honest. She probably didn't look much better – she felt murderous. Liv sighed.

"Okay, let's look at this logically." Lucas stopped walking up and down. "We know someone pushed Milo. But what if it was an accident? Maybe someone was goofing around up there and pushed a little too hard. If that's the case, then just admit it. It's better to come clean now." He looked around at each of them in turn.

There was a long awkward silence. Of course, Liv instantly went into airport-security-panic-mode, blushing a guilty red, but no one seemed to notice.

Unsurprisingly, no one confessed to the attack.

"Could have told you." Milo stopped rifling through the trunk and sat back. "That push was no accident. It was attempted murder."

"Milo, *shut up!*" Ruby shouted from under her pile of blankets.

It was hard to admit, but maybe Milo was right. There was the padlocked Snack-Shack, and now this attack, all on top of Shasta's sudden death. How many people needed to die before they admitted the very real possibility that one of them was behind it all?

There had to be a way to figure this out.

"So, where was everyone?" Liv said. She was sitting in the corner, her back to the cabin wall, just in case. "Where was everyone when Milo was, you know...*pushed*?" The word sounded awkward. But it was an obvious question and needed to be asked.

"I was the first to the top of the rock wall," Ruby said, clearly not realizing that she might be incriminating herself. "I was looking for Milo when I heard him call out. So, I climbed up and he was already hanging off the edge."

"You didn't see anyone else?" Liv asked.

"No. There was no one there when I arrived."

"*No one?*" Liv raised an eyebrow. There was really no good place to hide on the top of the rock wall, and if someone had pushed Milo over and left, wouldn't Ruby have seen them on the way down the gully? "So, it was just you up there, alone?"

"I don't know...maybe? If there was someone else there, I don't know where they went, okay?" Ruby seemed genuine, but then Liv didn't really know her. Maybe she took after her mother and was acting – playing them all. Who knew? "But obvs it wasn't me. Why would I want to hurt Milo? It doesn't make any sense. He's my best friend." She sat back as if that explained everything and she was now officially off the hook for attempted murder. Obvs.

"I am?" Milo cooed.

"Of course you are, silly."

"Aww, honey. Come here." Milo scooted over to the bunk and sat down, swallowing Ruby in his gangly embrace.

So, they had their first suspect. Ruby, by her own admission, was at the scene of the crime with no witnesses.

"I was still in the campground." Liv just put it out there, plain facts. Better to be open and honest about it, rather than look like she was hiding something.

She knew her alibi was going to sound weak – she had no witnesses. Ruby was the only one who could corroborate the fact that she had left Liv at the tent when she'd gone looking for Milo, and even that wasn't rock solid. Theoretically Liv could have sprinted up the gully when no one was looking. She kept her eyes down and hoped she was the only one aware of the fact that she was suspect number two.

"When Ruby left to look for Milo, I stayed by the tent. I was playing frisbee when I heard Milo scream."

"Scream?" Milo said quickly. "I mean, really? More of a manly request for assistance—"

"Milo, it doesn't fucking matter," Liv snapped back. "The point is, we know where you and Ruby were. I was in the campground. What about you guys?" Liv looked at Lucas but avoided Ben's eyes.

Everyone here must be wondering if Ben-the-Killer was living up to his reputation.

"Hiked to the van drop-off." Ben spoke first. No explanation or expansion. He had to know that he was the top suspect. But clearly, he didn't seem to feel the need to explain himself.

He had moved into the doorway, water dripping off him into a large puddle on the floor. Liv had the urge to grab one of the towels hanging on the railing and throw it around his shoulders.

"Okay…any particular reason you voluntarily chose to hike in the rain to the van drop-off?" Lucas was looking more like himself again now. His hair was drying out; little kisses of blond curls were springing up all over.

Ben turned and glared at him.

"Why do you think?"

"Guilty conscience?" Lucas glared back.

"Fuck you, Cole," Ben snapped. "I was looking for Moose. Wanted to see if he was back."

"And? I'm guessing you didn't find him?"

"Road's flooded. Nothing can get through. Not until the rain breaks. Moose ain't coming. Not any time soon."

Moose ain't coming.

Fuck. Liv closed her eyes.

It wasn't unexpected news, given the weather. It must have occurred to each of them that the storm would delay any chance of rescue. But hearing it said out loud like that shut down any lingering hope – like another nail was being driven into the lid of their coffin.

The end date for this hell-on-earth had just been extended indefinitely.

"Well, that's convenient," Lucas said. "And let me guess, there were no witnesses who saw you on your 'hike'. It's just your word that you went there at all." He wasn't asking. *Suspect three.*

Ben narrowed his eyes, his fists tightened. "What about you then, Cole? You want to point fingers? Where the fuck were you?"

"I was on a bucket break."

Ben coughed, loudly. "Right…a bucket break." He glared at Lucas, who just shrugged.

"Wait, Milo – you went to the bucket. Did you see Lucas when you were there?" Liv asked. She hadn't meant it to sound accusatory. It was a logical question – they should have crossed paths. But Lucas shot her a wounded look.

"You don't believe me?" *Suspect four.*

"No! I—" Liv stopped herself. She didn't have to justify her question. They were just trying to gather facts.

"What about you? You say you were by the tent, but did anyone see you? Any witnesses?" Lucas fixed his clear eyes on her with an unnerving intensity.

Liv's anger flashed. "Why are you changing the subject?" Her eyes narrowed. He wanted to go there? She'd go there.

"How exactly is this helping?" Ruby's voice sounded muffled. She still hadn't emerged from her blanket nest. "All this proves is that any one of us could have attacked Milo."

"Apart from me!" Milo grinned, lying back on the bunk. He stretched out and sighed.

Though she hated to admit it, Liv knew that Ruby was right. No one had a solid alibi. Any one of them could have found a way to sneak up on Milo, push him over and then hide. All this arguing wasn't helping the situation at all.

There had to be another way to look at this.

"What about motive?" She hadn't meant to say it out loud. The others turned to look at her. "I just meant, if we're saying someone killed Shasta and Chipmunk, and tried to kill Milo…why? Who would want them dead?"

"We all had a motive for getting rid of Chipmunk," Lucas said with a shrug. "Just think about the last thing she said to us. She threatened to institutionalize us permanently. I reckon she could have too."

Liv nodded. There was no question in her mind: Chipmunk had the power and would have happily abused it. They were all at risk from her angry threats, and they all knew it.

"But what about Shasta? Who would want to hurt Shasta?" Liv couldn't imagine that anyone would actively set out to harm the sweet girl. She was just so nice.

"Again – as one of the victims, I think I can excuse myself from this conversation," Milo said with a smug smile. Liv had to resist the urge to throw something at him.

"Nobody gets excused," Lucas said sharply. "You want a motive? You and Ruby do all these stupid, dangerous pranks. You nearly killed Liv at the river. What if a prank went too far? You could have put nuts in Shasta's food as a joke."

"Is that the best you can come up with? A prank gone wrong?" Milo laughed, a short bark of a laugh. Ruby made an angry snuffling noise from under the blankets. "Okay, fine. Let's go on with this line of fiction. So, Ruby and I accidentally poison Shasta. How does that explain Chipmunk? Please don't say it was another prank."

"She was locked in the Snack-Shack. Maybe you locked her in there overnight, thinking it would be funny. She'd have a rough night, and in the morning, you'd deny everything."

"And what…she just died?" Milo said.

"Maybe she got stung by a scorpion or a black widow crawling around in the dark. We never examined the body…maybe we should?"

"Oh Jesus…" Liv muttered. This conversation was going from bad to worse. There was no way in hell she was ever going near that body again. Absolutely no way. The police could examine it when they arrived.

"Oh my God, do you even hear yourself right now? This is ridiculous." Milo threw his hands up dramatically. He looked at Ruby for moral support. She had partially emerged from her cocoon and was sitting up with an angry frown on her face.

"Look, I don't think Lucas is saying that you and Ruby are guilty," Liv said placatingly. "Just that it's possible. We have to consider everything right now."

"Well, what about you and Lucas then?" Ruby shouted from the bunk. "All of this started when you and Lucas arrived. We were all fine. Then you both show up and people start dying like…rabbits! Why would that be, huh? Explain that!"

She had a point. A good point. Liv avoided Lucas's eyes.

"Okay, fine. Yes. This started after we arrived. I'm not denying it. Which means, we're all fucking suspects." Lucas dropped his hands to his hips and started pacing again. "Is anyone going to bring up the elephant in the room, or do I have to do it?"

Ben. The elephant.

It didn't need to be said. Everyone knew that Ben was the most likely suspect. After all, according to Milo and Ruby, he'd killed before, beating a kid to death in a school fight. He was one of the "problem kids" sent to the WTC as part of the State deal. He hated

Chipmunk and had threatened her the night before she died, and he would seemingly do anything to escape – maybe even poison an unsuspecting girl to create a distraction so he could run again?

Liv couldn't look at her partner. The thoughts were there in her head. If she looked at him, he'd see them in her eyes. She didn't want him to see them.

"*Fuck all of you!*" Ben suddenly yelled, storming back out of the doorway. He kicked at a bucket, sending it flying off the porch.

Liv dropped her head into her hands, regretting that she'd started this conversation. It was pointless. So far, they'd succeeded in pointing fingers at each other but hadn't got any closer to the truth. They were all suspects, they all had motives and opportunity. Back to square one.

Milo was the first to speak.

"Of course, there is one thing we do know…"

Liv glanced up at him. His smug smile was back, fixed on his smug face.

He looked around, making sure he had everyone's full attention before continuing. "We have two bodies, right? First Shasta – victim number one. Then Chipmunk – victim number two. Shasta – one. Chipmunk – two. Get it?" He held his fingers up, one and two, in a gesture that seemed to imply that he was making an important point, rather than stating the obvious.

Liv had no idea where he was going with this, and from the looks of it, she wasn't the only one. She sighed and sank lower on the floor, wishing that she was anywhere else.

"Anyone…?" Milo frowned with the pained expression of a high school teacher. "Okay. Let's try it this way. Who remembers the game of Werewolf?"

"We all do," Lucas said shortly. "What's your point, Milo?"

"Think about it. Round one, Shasta is killed by a werewolf. Round two, Chipmunk is killed. Shasta *one*. Chipmunk *two*." His fingers went up again.

Liv snorted. She had finally caught up with his thinking. He must be joking. If not, the guy was firing on half his cylinders.

"Oh, come on." She looked at Milo, shaking her head. "You're not actually trying to say that you think this has something to do with the game, just because it happened in the same order? Milo, you've lost it. I swear, you should just go back to your tent and sleep it off."

"Liv's right. That's ridiculous," Lucas said, walking over to the door flap and looking out across the crags. "I can't believe we're even having this conversation." Behind him, through the doorway, Liv could see the mid-afternoon sky, heavy with darkening storm clouds.

Milo stood up and walked into the middle of the tent. "Not gonna lie, I thought it was just a coincidence at first too. But then…I was attacked." He held out his hands one more time. "Think about it. Shasta dies in round one; Chipmunk dies in round two. What happened in round three? Anyone? Help me out here…"

"Someone was attacked and saved," Lucas said, frowning.

"Yes! Do you get it? There was a failed attack…*three*." The dots connected.

The third round of the game. Someone was attacked by the werewolf but saved by the doctor. Milo was attacked on the rock wall and then saved after Ruby found him hanging off the cliff.

Shit.

Liv dropped her head into her hands.

She felt sick.

They all fell silent, the immensity of Milo's words hanging in the air. The rain was beating hard now; a gust of wind threw a torrent of water against the side of the tent.

"It's got to be a coincidence," Liv muttered. "I mean it has to be, right? If it was the game…if someone was…" She couldn't finish. She couldn't say the words out loud. If it was deliberate, and someone was playing the game for real, killing them off one by one…

She looked around.

They were all there – the five of them. Lucas, standing in the doorway, leaning back against the post, hands in pockets. Milo in the middle of the tent, long arms folded across his chest. Ruby's head poking up from the top of the sleeping bag. And Ben – who had moved out to the edge of the porch as far from the others as possible, head down and fists clenched tightly.

Five of them. Problematic. Delinquent. Rejects. But were they bad enough to kill?

Was it possible?

Was there a werewolf among them?

CHAPTER 32

The mood in Moose's cabin declined quickly. Everyone was on their feet, standing in different corners, tense.

In the middle of the floor, names were scrawled on the rough wood boards in chalk. Shasta was crossed out.

MILO ~~SHASTA~~ RUBY CHIPMUNK

LUCAS LIV BEN

"This is so stupid." It was Lucas's voice, raised to be heard over the heavy rain drumming on the canvas roof. "We're seriously going to go with this game theory, rather than look at the actual facts?"

"Respectfully, Lucas – get over yourself," Milo said, holding the chalk in his hand. He pointedly turned to the others. "We never found out who the werewolves were, thanks to Ben picking a fight with Chipmunk. No one has confessed, so now we'll have to work out who they were by a process of elimination. That should give us our prime suspects."

"Jesus, this is ridiculous," Lucas said. He was pacing, head down, with barely concealed frustration.

Lucas was right; it was a pretty far-fetched theory that the killer was playing out the game. But still, the deaths, the attack…if there was even a small chance that Milo was right, shouldn't they consider it? Their lives were on the line.

"So, let's start with the doctor," Milo said, ignoring Lucas. "Anyone?"

"Yah, that was me, remember?" Ruby piped up, raising her hand. "I was the doctor. Which was kinda fun, cos I got to save people. Plus, it proves I'm not a werewolf."

"Unless you're lying about it," Ben muttered under his breath.

"Oh my God, I literally told you it was me, right after the game. Remember?"

"I remember," Milo confirmed. "It's true. She admitted as much at the end of the game. Okay, so we know that Ruby was the doctor." Milo looked around.

Liv vaguely recalled something about that, and no one else said anything.

So, Milo squatted down and drew a line through Ruby's name.

MILO ~~SHASTA~~ ~~RUBY~~ CHIPMUNK
LUCAS LIV BEN

"Just think for a minute. *Why* would someone do this?" Lucas said. "Assuming that your stupid game theory is right, if a werewolf was the actual killer, then why would they follow the game? They'd be giving themselves away. It doesn't make sense. It's just not logical."

"We're talking about a *serial killer* here," Milo said. "They *kill* people for fun. It's all a game to them. There is nothing logical about murder."

Ruby nodded vigorously, but Lucas just shook his head in exasperation.

"Then why wouldn't they just kill random people? Or maybe they're—"

"Have you got something to confess?" Milo smiled coyly. "Because it sounds like you're trying really freaking hard to convince us of something here. Who were you in the game, again?"

"Fuck you, Milo. Who were you?" Lucas shoved a nearby wastepaper basket hard. It rolled, its contents spilling out across the floor.

"Temper." Milo laughed and knelt down by the names again. "Shall we continue? So, Shasta dies, and Liv is voted out of the game by the villagers. Of course, that doesn't mean she wasn't a werewolf, so we don't cross her name out."

This was basically a witch-hunt, with Milo leading the charge. Out the werewolves – then what? Pitchforks at dawn? Burning at the stake?

Thank God she wasn't a werewolf, Liv thought nervously. She was pretty confident Lucas was one, though. He'd lasted to the end of the game and was arguing against Milo's theory way too hard.

"In round two, Chipmunk dies, and no one is voted out. So, Chipmunk is, by default, innocent." Milo scratched a line through Chipmunk's name.

MILO ~~SHASTA~~ ~~RUBY~~ ~~CHIPMUNK~~

LUCAS LIV BEN

"Round three, there's the failed werewolf attack that was countered by a Dr Ruby save. Then I was eliminated." He bent down and struck out his own name.

<del>MILO</del>   <del>SHASTA</del>   <del>RUBY</del>   <del>CHIPMUNK</del>

LUCAS   LIV   BEN

"Wait! What are you doing?" Lucas took two steps forward and snatched the chalk from Milo's hand. "You were eliminated. That doesn't mean you're not a werewolf—"

"Ah yes, but I was also the person that Dr Ruby saved. Which, of course, makes me a villager." Milo took the chalk back, grinning widely.

"You are so full of shit, Milo." Lucas shook his head. "How do we even know you were the person Ruby saved? You could be lying about that."

"Am I, though?" Milo turned to Ruby. "Doctor, please reveal who you saved in round three of the game."

"Seriously? Do I have to?" Ruby rolled her eyes and sighed, a deep, end-of-the-world sigh. "Whatever. I saved you, Milo. There, can you leave me alone now?" She dived back under her pillow pile.

"Ha!" Milo crowed, getting right into Lucas's face. Any possibility of future flirtations between them officially died on the spot.

"You could both be lying," Lucas said.

"Only we're not." Milo shrugged. "And the way I see it, the only one who can say different would have to be a werewolf. Got something you want to admit to us, Lucas?"

"This is all bullshit," Lucas muttered, but turned away.

There was a bitter taste in Liv's mouth. She forced herself to look at the remaining chalk names: Liv, Lucas and Ben. Two werewolves. Liv knew she wasn't one of them. Which meant…

Her eyes drifted up.

Lucas and Ben. It had to be them. *It had to.* She'd already guessed Lucas. But Ben? What if Milo's theory was right? That would mean one of them was a killer. She looked at Ben, who was standing with his back against the doorframe. Oh God…it made sense. It really made sense.

"Which brings us to…" Milo looked directly at Lucas this time.

Lucas glared at him but didn't speak. He must have realized it was useless. He laced his fingers behind his head, pacing again, pent-up energy pouring off him.

"Round four." Milo smiled.

Before he could say more, Ben suddenly pushed past Lucas and snatched the chalk from Milo's hand. He stood looking down at the words on the floor for a moment, before kneeling and striking out his own name:

~~MILO~~ ~~SHASTA~~ ~~RUBY~~ ~~CHIPMUNK~~
LUCAS LIV ~~BEN~~

Wait. That couldn't be right. But it was. Liv hadn't thought ahead. Ben was the victim in the fourth round. That's what started the fight between him and Lomax. But then that meant…

Liv shook her head. No.

There were two names left. Two suspects. Two werewolves.

But Liv wasn't a werewolf, and she wasn't the killer. Something was wrong. Someone was lying. She swallowed loudly. She could feel the others looking at her.

"No…this is all wrong," she said, trying to meet their eyes. "I don't know how. It's wrong. I'm not—"

"Looks like we have our suspects," Milo said with a small flourish. "Lucas and Liv. Makes perfect sense. Everything was just fine at Camp Smiling Skies until you two arrived."

No, no, no, no, no. This couldn't be happening.

"This isn't right. I'm not a werewolf," Liv said, her cheeks burning. "I was a villager. I was! I'm not lying." They didn't believe her. She could see it. Her denial was just making things look worse.

"This is bullshit," Lucas shouted suddenly. His frustration had boiled over into rage. "You think I don't know what you're doing?" Milo retreated with a small yelp, backing towards the bed. Lucas kept moving towards him, fists tightly clenched. "Milo's lying. He's making all this up."

"Milo's lying?" Ben moved forward with surprising speed. He stepped between Lucas and Milo. "You want us to think Milo's lying, when all along it was you. You and Liv. Lying about being werewolves. *You're the fucking liars!*"

Lucas faltered.

Wait, this was madness. Why were they all buying into this?

"Just stop!" Liv stepped forward. She had to make them understand. "It's all wrong. I'm not a werewolf, and this whole thing – it's not a fucking game. I mean, it could be a game…but it doesn't have to be. Don't you get it? *It doesn't have to be!* Any one of us could be the killer." She was messing this up. She knew it. She could hear herself.

"Says the *werewolf*." Ruby half-emerged from her cocoon. Her voice was uncharacteristically hard; lucky there were no scissors nearby. "It was you all along, Liv? Oh my God, I hung out with you alone in the tent. I trusted you. How could you?"

"Wait, no—" Liv looked around desperately. Her eyes caught Ben's. His expression was wary. He didn't believe her either. How was this happening? How had she suddenly become a murder suspect? "Guys, come on. I'm not a werewolf...or a fucking murderer!" It was pointless. Liv knew it the moment she said it. The more she tried to deny things, the worse it looked for her. They were all following Milo's logic.

"Ruby." Lucas moved forward but was instantly blocked by Ben and Milo. He backed off, hands held out placatingly. "Okay, okay. Everything's fine. I just want to ask Ruby one question. Just tell us, who did you really save in round three?" He pointed a finger at Milo, his movements careful and slow. "Was it Milo? Are you sure you saved Milo? Because if you're lying..."

Ruby glared at him from behind Milo's back.

"Yes, it was Milo," she squeaked.

"Come on. Just tell the fucking truth. *Who did you really save?*"

Ruby stared at him. Her eyes growing bigger.

"You can't bully her into lying for you." Milo ducked down to one side and started digging in Moose's plastic chest.

"Fuck's sake, Ruby!" Lucas shouted, pointing to the names on the floor. "Why are you lying?" Lucas's voice was desperate. He edged forward. Ruby gave a small shriek and grabbed Ben's arm. Ben stepped in front of her, squaring up. Ready for battle.

"It was Milo. I saved Milo in round three," Ruby shouted. "Now just leave me alone!"

"They're both lying. Can't you see?" Lucas addressed Ben now. He was scrabbling. It wasn't working. He sounded desperate, trying to deflect the blame any way he could.

Liv had never been surer – Lucas was a werewolf.

"You and Liv need to leave," Ben said, shuffling close to Lucas, chin up, fists clenched.

"Wait, Ben…" Liv wasn't sure why she said it. What she thought she could do.

It was hopeless. He wouldn't even meet her eyes; he wouldn't look at her. This was bad. It was dangerous. It was wrong. They'd got it all wrong. How could they be so stupid? There might be a real murderer here, and it could be any one of them.

Lucas was thinking along the same lines.

"You think Liv and I are behind this? Whatever. You've signed your own death certificates. Because if you're wrong – and you are – then you're ignoring the fact that one of you is the murderer." Lucas moved towards Ben – a step too far.

Ben was on him in an instant, sending him reeling with a violent shove. Lucas found his feet and turned back, throwing himself towards Ben with a roar.

Ruby dived for the bunk. Liv jumped forward, trying to stop Lucas, but was pulled off her feet by his momentum. She stumbled, struggling to get her balance. When she looked up, everyone had stopped, frozen in action.

Milo was standing between them, holding a knife at Lucas's throat.

"*Back the fuck off!*" he shouted. He cradled the large knife in his long fingers. A leather sheath was lying on the floor by Moose's crate. It was Moose's hunting knife.

Lucas held up one hand. With the other, he held Liv back, pushing her behind him.

Ben and Ruby didn't move.

"Back off and fuck off. Get the fuck out of here," Milo shouted, shaking the knife in the air in front of him. "I will fucking use this if I have to. Do you hear me?"

Lucas didn't move.

Liv's eyes were on the blade – its vicious, serrated edge caught the light. Made for gutting wild animals. She felt sick.

"Listen to me." Ben's voice was low and dangerous. He inched forward, coming closer to Milo – closer to the knife. "You two need to go. Now. Go and stay away. Do you understand?"

Liv was frozen to the spot. All she could think of was that knife, pressed against Lucas's neck.

"Liv?" Ben said sharply. "Do you understand? Get him out of here." He nodded towards Lucas. Liv pulled herself up, fixing her eyes on Ben. There he was – his deer eyes staring at her intently. "Go now. Stay away. Don't come back until Moose gets here." He slightly nodded his head.

Okay. She nodded back. She could move again, think again. Unlocked.

"Yeah. Got it. We're not wanted here. We're leaving, okay? You won. All of you. You can put that fucking knife away already."

She grabbed Lucas's arm and pulled him back. Together, they backed away through the canvas door, not daring to turn their backs on the knife. Not even for a second. It was only when they reached the bottom of the porch stairs that they looked away.

The rain was pelting them heavily. The light was failing, and they could barely see the others inside the dark cabin.

"Fuck them. Come on, Liv," Lucas muttered, pulling on her arm. But she shook him off and turned back to the cabin.

"For what it's worth, I'm not a werewolf and I'm not the *fucking killer*," she shouted at the dark doorway. "Which means that one of you is, and one of you is lying." Ben appeared out of the darkness, head down. He stood impassively, watching her. Liv's next words were directed at him. "Good luck sleeping tonight with that knife between you. Better watch your back – *partner* – cos there's a werewolf among you."

With that, she turned and started running as fast as her legs would carry her, away from the cabins, away from the others and far away from *that knife*.

CHAPTER 33

It must have been early evening, but it felt like night.

The storm's darkness had fully enveloped the camp. A rainy mist swallowed the crags and mountains in a grey shroud. Even the roaring sounds of the Ochee were lost as gusts of wind battered the shrubby trees and bushes around them. No wildlife, no birds; they were all hunkering down, surviving.

Liv and Lucas were sheltering at opposite ends of Ben's cave. It was too cold to sit out in the rain, and the only alternatives were Chipmunk's tent cabin, the flooded tents or the Snack-Shack with Chipmunk's body. The tent cabin was too close to the others for comfort, and the other two options did not appeal. So, Liv had led Lucas along the cliff trail to the cave, keeping a guarded distance between them. Now they were both shivering inside, trying to avoid looking at each other as intermittent drops of slimy cave water fell on them from above.

Ben's stash had moved since the last time Liv was here. She had been hoping to make a rain jacket out of the pile of trash bags, but they were missing, along with the rope and most of the cans of beans. Luckily, a solitary can had rolled to the back of the cave and been left behind. With a nail and a stone, they'd managed to knock enough holes in the lid to prise most of the beans out, sharing them preciously between them, bean by bean.

It was hard to tell if it was from the cold or the shock, but Liv was shaking from head to toe. It felt pathetic, but there wasn't much she could do to stop it, and it was possibly keeping her just the tiniest bit warm. So, she just sat, arms tucked inside her oversized T-shirt, and focused on keeping her teeth from chattering out loud.

Her mind was jumping wildly from thought to thought. She was shunned, cut off from the safety of the tent cabin, in a remote cave with the only known werewolf and top murder suspect. Maybe coming here was a really bad idea. Maybe she would be safer hiding out somewhere alone. But at the same time, the idea of spending the upcoming night completely isolated felt even more risky. If she separated herself out, she would be an easy target to pick off – whoever the killer was.

No, there were no good choices here. But with three possible suspects outside the cave, versus one inside, the odds supported staying – for now. She would just have to make sure she kept a close eye on Lucas at all times. Just in case.

She snuck a sideways glance at Lucas's profile.

Was it possible that Lucas Cole was a killer? If you thought about it, the only thing she really knew about him was what he'd told her, and he could be lying. What if his charm and apparent good nature were a cover for his true agenda? After all, they had only just arrived when the killings started, and she knew she wasn't the one doing it.

It was just…he didn't *seem* like a cold-blooded murderer. He was kind and funny, and so warm. Of course, that didn't mean much, did it? It wasn't your looks and manner that made you capable of killing another human being – it came from a dark spot on your soul, a crack hidden inside. Being beautiful and charismatic just meant that you'd get your own Netflix documentary if you ever got caught.

"Liv?"

She jumped. Lucas had turned to face her. His clear eyes were almost translucent in the dim light – could they be hiding murderous secrets?

"Listen, I know this is messed up," he said, shifting awkwardly. "You have no reason to trust me. I mean, we've only known each other a few days, right?"

Liv narrowed her eyes and didn't answer. Whatever he had to say, he should just say it.

"The thing is…I'm not the killer. Honestly. You don't have to believe me. But I swear on…*Dillon*, it's the truth."

Words. Just words. Liv sighed, a long world-weary sigh, and turned back to watch the rain, keeping Lucas safely in her peripheral vision, just in case. A huge, ferocious crack of lightning lit up the sky, followed several seconds later by a thunderous roll. The universe was getting in on this game, playing along for fun.

"Look, we need to stick together if we're going to get through this. One of the others is likely a killer, and we both have targets on our back now. I know we'll be okay if we work together. Just tell me what I can do to prove myself to you – to show that you can trust me. Anything. I'll do it."

"Fine. You can start by telling me who the other werewolf was." Liv gave him a sidelong look, watching his reaction closely. "You know it wasn't me. So, who was it?"

Lucas nodded.

"Okay, I'll tell you everything I know." He shifted closer, rubbing his knee. The cold seemed to be bothering his old leg injury. "Milo is the other werewolf. He wasn't attacked in the game. He's lying about it. In round three, Milo and I picked Ruby as the victim, but, as it turned out, she was the doctor and had been saving herself all along. I don't know why she lied and said it was Milo. Maybe she's confused, or scared…or maybe Milo threatened her? I don't know – but I do know that she's lying. They're both lying."

Or Lucas was lying.

Liv had no idea whether to believe him or not. Milo was the one who'd been attacked on the cliff, and he'd led the werewolf hunt. There was no reason to suspect that he was secretly a werewolf. But there was one thing Liv did know for a fact: someone else *had* set her up to look like a werewolf. Someone else was lying. At least Lucas's half-assed explanation covered the bases. If he was telling the truth, it would explain why she was now sitting in this freezing-cold, miserable cave.

But was that enough to trust him? Then again, did she have a choice?

Lucas was still talking. "Listen, I know you have no reason to believe me. But we'll get through this night, I promise. You and I, okay? Tomorrow, Moose will be back, and this will all be over. If we can just stick together – we've got this."

Liv turned back to look out at the tree line. In a few hours, the last of the dim, grey light would be gone from the sky, and it would be night. Pitch-black night. She shivered.

There were no right answers here. There was no way to prove or disprove what Lucas was telling her. All it really came down to, in this moment, was choosing what would help her survive the night. No question, she was safer in the cave than out in the storm alone, and safer allied with someone else who could help watch her back. Maybe that was all she had to go on.

For now.

"Okay." She nodded. "I'll work with you. But that doesn't mean I trust you. That's the best you're going to get. So, just stay back, and keep to yourself. All right?"

"I'll take it." Lucas smiled, moving back slightly. It was progress.

Gusts of wind were picking up outside now, whistling into the cave entrance. Liv ducked her head inside her T-shirt, arms wrapped tightly around herself. It was going to be a hellishly long night.

Her mind was probing. Four suspects left. Lovely Lucas, Ben-the-Killer, Milo-the-Prankster and Dr Ruby. Four possible killers. Could she eliminate anyone?

Every instinct told her good-girl Ruby couldn't be a killer – her whole life revolved around trying to please people. But that wasn't fact-based evidence. Best not to count anyone out just because of an instinct, especially someone whose mom was an award-winning actor. What if Ruby was putting on the performance of a lifetime? Or maybe she simply didn't remember what she'd done? After all, she'd admitted to blanking out during her scissor attack on her mom's dress. What did that say about her mental state?

What about Milo? He just seemed like an annoying prankster. Was he really capable of pulling off two murders and then faking an attack on himself? If Lucas was to be believed, Milo was the second werewolf. In which case he was a cold and calculating liar who had manipulated everyone into thinking that he was innocent and Liv was guilty. All of which would put him right at the top of the suspect list.

Of course – there was Ben, her "partner". Just thinking about him made something seize up inside her. His hands – his strong fighter's hands. Were they a killer's hands? He had shown how easily he could lose his temper and snap and, according to Milo and Ruby, he had a history of homicidal behaviour. Plus, wasn't he with Kevon Wright when he drowned? Was it possible that Kevon's death wasn't an accident?

And yet… She touched her swallow ring. Something didn't feel right. There was another side to Ben…a gentle side that loved his little brother and put flowers on a baby deer's grave. A killer? She just wasn't sure.

But once again, she knew it wasn't safe to rely on her instincts. Not with this much at stake. She needed to stick to the facts, which moved Ben back to the top of the suspect list.

The storm was getting stronger, and the wind was shifting. What little shelter they'd had before was not cutting it any more. Rain was everywhere now – driving in through the cave mouth, pouring down the rock walls, dripping on them from above, below, sideways.

Without saying a word, they'd both retreated to the back of the cave, and were now huddling together in the one remaining dry corner between two large boulders, side by side. They were close enough that Liv could feel the heat radiating off Lucas's arms.

Her shivering had become uncontrollable by now. She had given up trying to stop her teeth chattering. Whatever part of her still distrusted Lucas was weakening in the bitter night. More than anything, she wanted to lean into him, to curl up against him. She craved that shared body heat, that connection, that touch.

Maybe Lucas was feeling it too.

"Not gonna lie, this wasn't what I was expecting camp life to be like." Lucas shook his head.

Despite herself, Liv smiled. "Maybe our folks paid the WTC for the premium camp service. Bonus upgrade: your kid might die and never come home."

Lucas laughed. His sweet laugh. The air felt a touch warmer.

He looked sideways at her, and just for a moment her shivering stopped.

"So, what do you think, Olive Oil? If we'd met in the real world, like at a coffee shop or something, would we have liked each other?" Lucas smiled. Liv could just make out his dimples in the weak light.

It was off the wall. The thought of standing in some bougie cafe, deciding what iced coffee to order, with Lucas in line ahead of her, was delicious. Liv smiled, warmed by the thought.

"No way. We have like *nothing* in common. You wouldn't have even talked to someone like me…and you know it." She hadn't meant it to sound rude, but it was an honest assessment. Lucas would have arrived in a coffee-scented cloud of admiring glances. Liv would have been hoping that the too-cool barista noticed her existence long enough to take her order.

"You're wrong, you know." Lucas was still looking at her. "I would have noticed you."

Liv snorted. "Maybe if I spilled coffee on you." This was killing her. But at the same time, it felt so good to be thinking about something else, somewhere else, so far from Camp Smiling Skies.

Lucas laughed.

"You don't think much of yourself, do you?"

"Fuck off, Lucas." Liv rolled her eyes. This was not the time for therapy. "I don't think much of you either."

"Fair enough. I mean you made that obvious. You pretty much

accused me of being a killer." Lucas's voice dropped as he said it. He held her eyes. Open and clear.

Well, what could she say to that?

"Did it ever occur to you that *I* could be the killer?" she asked, narrowing her eyes.

"Come on…" Lucas gave a short half-laugh.

"You never once asked, did you?" A small voice in the back of Liv's head told her to shut up.

"Yeah, but…you wouldn't hurt anyone," Lucas said, with a small, irritatingly know-it-all smile. Liv felt a flare of indignation.

"Yeah? What if you're wrong?" Oddly, the banter was making her feel better. Her heavy mood from minutes before was lifting at the edges. "Maybe I'm the killer. Maybe I have a rock behind my back right now, ready to smack you over the head if you keep annoying me." *Stop*, said the little voice in her head. *Stop – do not speak any more.*

"Well, do you?" Lucas turned and faced her straight on now. He was studying her expression, watching her closely, the small, irritating smile still playing on his lips. "Okay, show me what's in your hand, Olive Oil."

Smug bastard. If she could have felt around and grabbed a rock, she would have. Just to prove him wrong.

"Don't tempt me."

Lucas moved forward, so close now. He reached a hand around her back.

"So…are you going to show me your murder weapon…or not?" Those angel eyes, staring into hers. That small, irritating, beautiful, perfect smile.

Three hundred things I like about Lucas Cole…

"Why don't you come and get it," she half-whispered. The voice in her head officially quit. She was out of control. Someone get that girl a square meal and a good night's sleep.

Lucas laughed outright. He paused, a quizzical look on his face. "Wait…was that an invitation?"

It was. She hated herself for it, but it was.

Two deadbeat murder suspects in a bitterly cold cave. A raging storm, with nowhere to run and nowhere to hide. It was definitely an invitation.

This was insane. He could be a murderer. He might have killed two people already and tried to murder a third. For all she knew, she was victim number four, and the flirting was just his way of playing with his food before eating it. *She knew all this.* So, why was she flirting back? What was wrong with her?

But even as she thought it, Liv knew – she was past caring. It was all too much. Too scary and sad and cold and depressing and miserable and everything bad in this shitty world. Something else was taking over, a wild impetuous need. She wanted to be held. To feel safe. She wanted warm arms wrapped around her. To forget Shasta and Chipmunk, to forget Camp Smiling Skies and the cave and everything, just for now. Right here, in this chaotic moment, in this miserable damp cave – she wanted Lucas Cole.

Slowly, she raised her eyebrows, just enough. The message was clear: *Well? What's it to be? Ball is in your court.* She held her breath.

The sky lit up with a crack of lightning. The cave walls rumbled with thunder.

Lucas kissed her.

CHAPTER 34

Too cold. Way too cold. Unbearable. The storm had temporarily released its chokehold, and an all-encompassing gloom had taken over the sky. It was almost dark already.

Liv was sloshing through ankle-deep mud on her way back from the campground. Lucas was walking just ahead of her. They had raided the water-soaked tents, looking for supplies so they would survive the upcoming night. So far, they had collected two damp sleeping bags, four pillows, three flashlights, a selection of random socks and as many water bottles as they could carry between them. Sadly, there was no food in the tents. This was bear country and everything edible was safely stowed away in the Snack-Shack at all times. But at least they'd had their lonely can of cave beans. It was looking more and more likely that that was going to be their last meal at Camp Smiling Skies.

Lucas was walking a couple of metres in front of Liv, his arms filled with his stash bundled neatly in a rain poncho. Watching his back, the way his rain-soaked T-shirt clung to his broad shoulders – Liv couldn't help it – a small corner of joy was holding its own in her heart.

Despite everything, a perfect moment had snuck through the

cracks of this evil place. The impossible had happened. *Lucas Cole had kissed her*. They'd kissed.

Oh, she knew it didn't mean anything. She wasn't stupid. Desperate times made desperate people do desperate things.

But honestly, did it matter why he'd kissed her? Did it matter that out in the real world, he wouldn't have looked twice at her? Or that he might be a serial killer, and that there was a solid chance she wouldn't survive the night? Okay…yeah. But maybe this one time, she'd enjoy the win, however short-lasting. Real or not.

They were near the bucket. Liv could still smell it despite all the rain. Looking around she saw the orange container, upended by the storm. Its foul contents had flooded and spread around the entire area, sinking into the ground. Nice.

As she passed by the blackened tree stump where she'd hidden her father's letter, she paused. She'd almost certainly be leaving Camp Smiling Skies as soon as they were rescued and the deaths were reported. If any small part of her wanted to retrieve the letter, then this might well be her last chance. *If*. Walking over, she peeked into the hole in the trunk, half hoping that the letter would be gone – turned into squirrel bedding somewhere. But it was still there, surprisingly intact and relatively dry. Liv could see her dad's handwriting on the front.

Did she even want it? It had to be filled with a load of excuses justifying what he'd done (*we didn't want to… it was for your own good…*). She knew that. There was no way it was going to be more than that – maybe an apology, or even an explanation (*Carianne made me do it… I never wanted this…*). Of course, no part of her imagined for even a second it might say something sappy (*I love you, I miss you, I'm sorry…*). Of course not. She fully knew that. One hundred per cent.

Still, she yanked the envelope out of the hole and, folding it tightly, she tucked it in one of the retrieved socks and shoved it deep into her back pocket. No need to overthink it. She could always throw it away later. It didn't mean anything.

The only bright light in the camp was radiating from Moose's cabin, its glow flickering merrily through the trees. It looked deliciously cosy and dry. The others must be so snug in there. If they weren't busy trying to murder each other, then they were probably bundled in blankets, drinking tequila, while the undesirables were forced to scavenge in the cold, just to stop themselves from freezing to death.

She looked down. Her clothes were clinging to her – soaked through. The sleeping bag she was holding smelled damp and mouldy. This night was only going to get colder, darker and scarier. What she wouldn't give to be in there right now, tucked up in an actual bed.

Not fair. Not okay.

A figure briefly appeared in the doorway. Ben. He stood for a moment, hands in pockets, seemingly looking out at the darkening world outside. Liv wondered redundantly if he could somehow sense he was being watched, sense her presence. It almost felt as though he was staring right at her in the dim light. She stared back, across the rainy void between them, defiantly willing him to see her standing there, soaked to the bone and shivering, carrying a pile of miserable wet supplies. She wanted him to think about her. She wanted him to wonder if she was okay. She wanted him to care.

A bird cawed and he turned away, walking back through the open doorway and disappearing inside the warm cabin.

Of course he didn't care. What was she thinking? He was just killing time.

"Hey." Lucas had stopped walking and was waiting for her. He was shivering too now. "Sucks, doesn't it?" He nodded at the cabin. Clearly, he'd been thinking along the same lines. "Maybe we should go full-werewolf and throw them out. Make them stay in the cave. See how much they like it." He grinned at the thought; his teeth were chattering.

"Yeah, if it wasn't for the knife, I reckon we could take them on," Liv said.

She didn't really. Milo and Ruby would be no problem, but she suspected Ben could snap them both in half and eat them for breakfast. Raw.

There was a short burst of laughter from the cabin. It sounded like Milo. What did he have to be happy about? Two people were dead. He was playing house with two possible killers. Unless he was the killer, playing house with two possible victims. Either way, there was nothing funny about it.

Her curiosity was stirring. What was going on in there? What were they talking about? They must be suspicious of each other. Even though they'd banished Liv and Lucas, they had to be wondering if they'd made the right call. Would they dare to try and sleep, or turn their backs on each other? Who had the knife?

Of course, if they could get closer, they could listen in. Maybe they'd get some of the answers to all those questions.

"Lucas, do you think...?" Liv nodded at the cabin.

"You want to spy on them?" Lucas looked at her; he must have been thinking the same thing.

"It's almost dark. If we're really careful, we could probably sneak up on them without being seen."

"Great idea." Lucas nodded, no hesitation. "I'm in."

"Yeah?"

"Hell yeah." He smiled. Liv grinned.

It definitely wasn't a great idea. There was a solid risk of getting caught, just on the off chance that they might hear something incriminating. But if someone in the cabin was the killer, then who knew what might happen tonight. This way, Liv and Lucas could keep an eye on things and stay one step ahead of their enemy. It was a risk worth taking.

Liv smiled. She could feel the first warmth of the night, a small fire of excitement growing inside. It felt good; it felt like they were finally taking control.

Decision made, they stashed most of their supplies under a bush and headed to the rock wall so they could approach the cabin from behind, just in case someone looked out of the open front door. When they got close, they both instinctively paused. The cabin's warm glow shimmered through the falling rain. They could hear talking, voices raised. Through the cracks in the canvas walls, they could see shadows moving about.

Liv paused; a moment of indecision hit her. Was this crazy? Were they taking an unnecessary risk? Milo had held a knife at Lucas's throat the last time they were here. What would happen if they were caught sneaking around the cabin in the dark?

But she pushed those doubts away. They would be careful. They wouldn't get caught, and if she could just find out what they were thinking…

Lucas nudged her and nodded. She nodded back.

Whether it was wise or not, they were decided. They were doing this – together, both irresistibly drawn to the light, just like moths to an open flame.

CHAPTER 35

It was amazing what desperation could do to you.

This was a new low. Possibly worse than the bucket.

Liv and Lucas were under the cabin, hiding out with all the spiders and scorpions and who knew what else (*please not snakes…*). The thought of what was lurking in the darkness made Liv's skin crawl. Even the miserable cave was starting to look a lot more appealing right now. But she just had to suck it up – after all, it had been her great idea to come here.

There was about a metre-high crawl space between the ground and the underside of the wooden platform that the cabin was built on. Creepy things kept catching on them every time they moved, so they'd settled in a corner close to the cabin door. Liv had brought one of the sodden sleeping bags with them and they had it wrapped over their shoulders as they sat silently hunched over, listening.

Loud footfalls shook the floorboards above them. Cracks of faint golden light from the cabin's lanterns illuminated the dusty air in strips. A few larger holes in the wood made perfect spy holes if they needed a better view. It was uncomfortable and filthy, but dry, and they could hear every word from over their heads. Good enough for now.

"Well, this is fun." Milo's voice was unmistakable. "Crazy thought here, but maybe if you stopped pacing up and down like a manic tiger, we might actually be able to chill a bit. It's going to be a long night as it is."

"No. I need to keep a lookout." Ben's voice came from directly over their heads; he must be pacing in front of the doorway – guarding it. Every step he took launched another small cloud of dust. Liv pulled her T-shirt over her mouth to avoid coughing.

"You seriously think Lucas and Liv are going to sneak up and try to murder us? We're three against two – though to be fair, Rubes should only count for a half." There was a faint rumble of distant grumblings as Ruby protested this weakly.

Liv grinned under her shirt, glancing at Lucas and rolling her eyes. He shot a quick smile back.

"I'm not gonna underestimate them." Ben's pacing sped up as he talked. "Two people are dead. You nearly died. I was killed in round four of the game. If you're right about all this, then the killer's coming for me next. So don't tell me what to do."

"Whatever," Milo said. There was a long pause and some shuffling noises. It sounded like Milo was on his feet and moving around now too. "So, who is it? Who do you think is the killer? Lucas, or Liv? My money's on Liv. That girl has a darkness about her. She has a way of looking at you like she wants you dead…"

Unbeknownst to him, Liv shot him the darkest, most murderous look she could muster through the floorboards. What an asshole! She heard a noise from Lucas. He had his hand over his mouth and was trying to stifle a laugh. Great. So fucking funny. Liv kicked him as hard as she dared.

Milo wasn't done yet. "Or maybe Lovely Lucas is a serial killer who came to camp to pick off unsuspecting victims in the night. He charms us all into trusting him and then murders us one by one, in our sleeping bags. I mean, if you think about it, wilderness therapy camps are the perfect place to get away with murder. They're unsupervised, unsafe and inescapable."

"Milo, stop stirring." It was Ruby's voice, calling out faintly from somewhere inside the cabin. Probably tucked back up inside her enviably cosy nest of blankets.

"I don't know. Don't care either," Ben growled. "But it's gotta be one of them. They lied right to our faces. They were the werewolves all along. Working together and all. I don't trust either of them. So, they'd both better stay the fuck away from me."

A shot of something went through Liv. After everything – the conversations about her mom, his brother, the moment on the ledge. After all that, her partner still thought she might be a *murderer*? It had all felt so real – to her at least. As though they had connected just that little bit below the surface. Yet he thought she was capable of poisoning Shasta, killing Chipmunk, and pushing Milo off a cliff – capable of coming after him now.

Fuck him. Liv pulled herself up. It didn't matter what Ben thought about her. As far as she was concerned, he was the top of her suspect list too. It didn't matter what they'd shared, he was the obvious choice. Messed up, angry and dangerous.

"Whatever, just trying to make conversation." It sounded like Milo had moved over to Moose's bunk, near to Ruby. He sounded bored. Milo had an amazing capacity to not be bothered by life-threatening situations. Even after his near-death experience on the cliff, he'd managed to make it all seem like a fun adventure. It could have been called admirable, but Liv wouldn't go so far as to say brave. Did it take courage to do something dangerous if you lacked the imagination to be afraid of it in the first place?

"I totally wish we'd played a different game," Ruby said. "I mean if we'd played the Balloon Game or something, maybe no one would have died."

"Not sure that's the best choice," Milo muttered.

"You know what I mean, Milo." Ruby sounded frustrated. "Just something without a werewolf. If there was no werewolf, then we wouldn't be in this situation. Right?"

"Optimistic at best, girl. But I dig your enthusiasm."

"Well, at least I'm safe." Ruby sighed loudly enough to be heard from under the floorboards. "I think being the doctor was the best role for sure. That way I could make sure I'd survive each round. Which totally wasn't a big deal when it was just a game. But now…"

Ben's footsteps stopped.

Liv frowned.

Had Ruby meant to say that? Out loud?

"Girl, give it a break," Milo said, with what sounded like a yawn but could have been an exasperated sigh. "Do we have to talk about the game all night long?"

"Just saying. If I hadn't saved myself, I would be totally freaking out right now. Sorry, Ben – no offence."

Liv closed her eyes and focused on listening. Had she heard that right? If it was true, it changed everything. Clearly the implications weren't lost on Ben either.

"You saved *yourself*?" It was Ben's voice, low and menacing. Something in his tone set alarm bells ringing in Liv's head. He was primed and dangerous.

She felt a knot in her gut. Ruby needed to stop talking. Milo needed to stop her.

"Yah. Of course I saved myself! I mean, who wouldn't, right?" Ruby carried on, oblivious.

"You saved yourself in *each* round?" Ben was clearly focused on this, and Liv knew why. This was not good. Not good at all.

"Duh – yes. Why do you keep asking?"

"Oh my God, can we move on already?" Milo cut in, a little too abruptly, his voice edged with tension. He must have finally caught on to what was happening here. "Rubes, for goodness' sake, girl, let's talk about something else. Why don't you tell us some gossip about your diva, bitch-queen mom?"

Liv opened her eyes and looked at Lucas. This was what she'd needed to hear; Lucas had told her the truth. Ruby had saved herself in each round. She hadn't saved Milo in the third round of the game. Just herself. They'd both lied about it. But why?

There was a low thud, and the floorboards directly over Liv's head creaked.

Quickly Liv moved up to one of the knots in the wood. The hole was big enough for a clear view; Ben was kneeling above her, staring at something on the floor. For a moment she thought he was looking through the hole – that he'd seen her. She froze, panicking. What would he do to her if he caught her spying?

But before she could go there, Ben turned his head slightly. He wasn't looking at her. He was looking at something else. The names. The chalk names.

Liv thought back. She could picture it. She knew what Ben was thinking.

~~MILO~~ ~~SHASTA~~ ~~RUBY~~ ~~CHIPMUNK~~
LUCAS LIV ~~BEN~~

If Ruby saved herself, then Milo was never the victim. If Milo wasn't a victim, he could have been the second werewolf. Lucas was telling the truth. Milo had lied. Ruby too.

Which meant Ben was locked in the cabin with two liars, a possible werewolf and a knife – and he was next in line to die.

"It's not what you're thinking, Ben." It was Milo's voice. He moved forward into Liv's limited line of sight. He must have realized Ruby's mistake.

The floorboards creaked as Ben stood up, slowly.

"Are you a werewolf?" His voice was almost a growl.

"You just need to let me explain, okay?"

From where she was sitting, Liv couldn't see Ben's face any more. She needed to see his face, to gauge where his head was at. Carefully, she crawled over to another knot, trying not to make any noise. Lucas was still listening intently.

As she peered through the new hole, Liv caught the edge of Ben's profile. His head was down but his eyes were turned up, watching Milo talk. His jaw was tight.

"Look, Ben, I know what you're thinking, but I wasn't lying. I mean, not really. I was just messing around. Everyone was so serious about the deaths, I figured I'd lighten the mood with the whole 'there's a serial killer playing werewolf' thing. Honestly, I never thought anyone would be stupid enough to actually believe me."

"What are you talking about?" Ben said coldly.

"I mean it was a *prank*! Just a prank. I thought it would be funny if I tricked you all into thinking it was the game. After Shasta and then Chipmunk died, it was the perfect set-up! Round one and then round two. All I had to do was fake round three and you'd all be shitting bricks."

Liv didn't have a clear view of Milo's face, but she could feel the insouciance radiating off him. He was proud of himself. *Proud.*

"It was super easy to set up a fake attack and be saved by Dr Ruby." Milo kept on going, just digging his own grave deeper and deeper. "I knew about the ledge on the rock wall. I'm tall enough to stand on it and reach the cliff edge. So, I prearranged to meet Rubes up there, then I climbed onto the ledge and started screaming for help. Easy! Honestly, I never thought anyone would actually believe it. I mean, come on. *Werewolf?*" Milo laughed – too loudly.

Liv's mind was racing. She pictured the ledge, Milo's legs dangling, swinging wildly in the air. Was it true? If he'd stretched out, could he have reached the ledge and just…stood up?

Jesus. She felt like the wind had been smacked out of her. *Jesus.* She'd nearly died trying to save the fucker's life. *Twice.* All for shits and giggles. Milo had better be glad she wasn't in the cabin right now. She was ready to get her hands around his scrawny neck and teach him how it feels to have someone mess with your life.

"*Are you a werewolf?*" Ben was not letting it go.

"Don't you see? It doesn't matter, Ben!" Milo's pitch was rising. "What are you not getting here? It doesn't matter if I'm a werewolf. It was just a joke. I pranked you all into thinking it was the game. After the others died, I thought it would be funny. I didn't think for a second anyone would actually believe me. I mean, come on—"

"You held a *knife* to Lucas's throat—"

"I was scared. He was threatening me!"

Creaking. Milo was backing away.

From what she could see, Ben had hardly moved, but there was still a predatory tension in his posture, in the way he was standing, head down. Milo should be afraid. He really should.

"Listen, Ruby knows everything! She pretended to find me hanging off the cliff and agreed to lie and say she'd rescued me in the game. Ask Ruby. Ask her! She was in on all of it."

"Oh my God, do not go there, Milo!" Ruby's voice came from near the door. She must have moved from her bunk and was clearly heading for the exit…just in case. "It was all your stupid idea. Just like the river prank. I should never listen to you. Ever!"

"I'm going to ask you one more time." Ben was on the move. He spoke slowly, his tone low and dangerous. "*Are you a fucking werewolf?*"

Oh God.

This was not going to end well. She was with Ben on this – heart and soul. No question, Milo deserved what he had coming. But two people had died already. The madness had to stop.

Liv looked at Lucas and pointed up. Should they go in there? Lucas shook his head, holding out his hand. He mouthed the word: *Wait.*

Liv understood. If they scrambled out from under the cabin, miraculously appearing out of nowhere, the others might think it was a surprise attack. It could make things much, much worse.

Ben had moved out of her limited range of view. She shifted over to another knot, then another, desperately trying to see what was going on.

Milo was still talking, his usual cockiness wilting under pressure.

"You need to listen to me, Ben. You're not getting it. It doesn't matter if I'm a werewolf or not. Don't you understand? It doesn't matter! I've no idea how the others died. None. But it wasn't the game. That was just a stupid joke. A joke!"

They were near Moose's trunk now. Liv crawled closer. One of the floorboards was split, and through the crack she could see movement – feet and legs. Milo was by the trunk. Ben was facing him, approaching slowly. Liv heard footsteps outside on the deck. Ruby had run outside. Smart girl.

"I'll take that as a yes," Ben said quietly. Too quietly.

A thrill of icy fear went through Liv. Desperately, she moved around from crack to crack, trying to get a clear view.

A pause. No movement. No words.

At last Liv found a spot. A small hole. She put her eye up to it. She could see behind Milo's back, his arms and hands, playing with something. Something hidden. Something shiny.

Moose's hunting knife.

Milo was holding the knife.

Liv gasped.

There was a shuffle, a creak. Ben stepped forward.

"Stay back," Milo shouted. "Stay the fuck away from me!" His grip on the knife tightened.

Another creak.

"No!" The word escaped Liv. She banged on the floor, hard. "No – stop! *Stop!*"

There was a crash; the floor shook. Clouds of dust flew into the air. Liv dropped down, dirt in her eyes, coughing. Frantically, she rubbed her eyes, scratching at them. What was happening? What was going on? She had to see.

The noises were terrifying. Grunts, thuds, a scream.

It ended too soon. In seconds. Silence.

Liv's eyes were streaming. Blurry images were coming through now. Strips of light. A dark shadow blocking them, outlining a shape above. She blinked, trying to focus.

Someone was lying on the floor directly above her.

Who? *Who was it?*

Something dropped onto her arm. Then again. Something wet.

Liv held her arm up, shaking, confused. She moved it into a strip of light. Dark red liquid was dripping onto her. Dripping through the cracks in the floor. Blood.

Some instinct pushed her; she rolled onto her knees, looking for Lucas. His face was lit up by a spot of light from above. Pale and shocked. She nodded to him. They needed to move now.

In a blur of panic, Liv scrambled out from under the cabin, followed by Lucas. She could feel the blood rolling down her arm.

Whose blood? Whose?

Please not Ben. The thought was in her head. Over and over. She couldn't shake it. *Please not Ben…not Ben…not Ben.*

CHAPTER 36

It took precious moments to pull themselves out from under the deck. Liv half-fell onto the cabin stairs, scrambling forward, only stopping when she reached the canvas doorway. Lantern light cast eerie shadows over the scene before her.

She staggered slightly, reaching for the door post.

It was Milo.

He was on the floor, leg bent at an angle, hands clutching his stomach. Blood was seeping through his yellow T-shirt. He was cradled in Ruby's lap – alive, but deathly pale, pain wrought onto his face.

Ruby was silent, mouth open, shock frozen on her lips.

Ben was gone.

Relief smacked her hard. Guilty, shameful relief. Ben was gone, which meant he was alive – at least for now.

Lucas pushed past her. He slid to the ground at Milo's side, instantly in action. Doing what he needed to do.

Ruby was talking fast, her voice high. Lucas was asking Milo questions, but there was no response. Liv just stood there, suddenly aware of herself. Aware of what was going on around her. Milo was alive. Ben was gone.

"What can I do?" She forced herself forward and knelt beside Milo. "Ruby...what do you need?"

"I...I don't know." Ruby was out of her depth. "Um...I don't know."

Lucas looked at Liv.

"Help me get him onto the bed," he said. Liv nodded. She took Milo's feet, gripping his ankles tightly, while Lucas lifted him under the arms. On three, they hefted him onto Moose's bed. Despite his height, he was surprisingly light.

Lucas took a deep breath. "Okay. We need water, towels, clean sheets. Anything you can get your hands on." He bent down and placed his hands on Milo's stomach. The long, serrated knife lay on the floor at their feet, tipped with red.

Liv looked away.

This was a time for action. Not thinking.

A camping first-aid kit was hanging on a hook by the door. Liv pulled it down and unzipped it, setting it on the floor next to Lucas. A laundry basket by the bunk was full of clean linen, so Liv grabbed what she could: a pillowcase, a T-shirt and two towels. She tossed them to Lucas and ran to a large water container propped on a wooden crate. It was too heavy to drag alone.

"Ruby, come here. Help me move this," she called out. But Ruby was still on the floor, staring transfixed at her blood-covered hands. Shock. "Ruby! Snap out of it!" Liv abandoned the water container and walked over to Ruby. Kneeling down, she took her by the shoulders. "Ruby, look at me. Milo's okay. He's going to be okay. You need to come and help."

Ruby shook her head. "I saw it all. Milo...he tried to... he swung the knife at Ben. He didn't mean to. I know he didn't mean to. But Ben…he grabbed the knife and…and they fell. Oh God. Oh God!"

Without thinking, Liv threw her arms around Ruby. The shorter girl folded, collapsing against her, sobbing now.

"It's okay, Ruby." Liv stroked her hair gently. "It's okay." It wasn't and might never be again. But what else could she say? "Milo's alive. Let's get him some water and help with whatever he needs. Okay? Let's help Milo. Let's get him better."

Her words were helping. Ruby took a few last gulping sobs before pulling herself up to her feet. She nodded shakily.

"Okay…sorry. What do you need? Just tell me what to do."

It didn't take long for the two of them to drag the water container next to Lucas. Then Liv piled up some more towels and sheets ready to go, while Ruby was set to tearing pillowcases into usable strips of bandages.

At last, Liv sank onto her knees next to Lucas. Milo was breathing hard, eyes closed. His skin was tinged with grey. Lucas had a towel pushed hard against the wound, already soaked through with fresh blood. It didn't look good.

"Can I get anything else?" she asked.

"No. I don't think there's much more we can do," Lucas said.

"What are you thinking?"

"I don't know." Lucas looked at her. His eyes were clear and focused. He was pale but functioning better than anyone could expect, given the circumstances. "I guess we just try to stop the bleeding and hope for the best."

Liv nodded. She wasn't sure how to say the next part.

"Lucas…I think—"

"You're going after Ben." Lucas said it flatly.

Surprised, Liv looked directly at him. He met her eyes – no emotion.

"It's fine. Go," he said.

"Are you going to be okay?" Liv wasn't sure why she said it. Of course he wasn't. None of them were. Least of all Milo.

"Just go," Lucas said, more firmly this time. "There's nothing you can do here. You go and find Ben. He needs help and might listen to you."

For some strange reason, Liv felt like crying. She nodded.

"Thanks." She wasn't sure what else to say. It felt like she was deserting them. But there was nothing to do here. Lucas had said it himself.

Ben was out there somewhere, in the rain, thinking that he'd killed a boy. If she could get to him. If she could talk to him…

She stood up and gently touched Lucas's shoulder, pausing, feeling the warmth of his skin, the strength in him. He was okay, she told herself. They were good here. Safe. Milo was going to be fine. They had this.

Before she could change her mind, she turned and ran out into the rain. She knew where she was going, where she would find Ben. There was no doubt in her mind.

There was just enough dull light to make out the path ahead as she ran, as fast as she could, towards the river trail.

She was heading for the Ochee.

CHAPTER 37

The river was swollen with storm run-off. The path that they'd hiked along just yesterday was knee-deep under water, the current now torrential. Liv had to scramble through bushes, clinging to trees to prevent herself from being swept away as she made her way to the swim hole.

Occasional crashes of lightning pierced the air, lighting up the world for precious seconds. Each time she looked ahead, desperately searching for any sign of Ben, praying that she wasn't too late. But she saw no one. Just the trees swaying wildly in the wind.

Her thoughts were fleeting, terrifying. Images hitting her over and over. Milo gripping his stomach. The knife – its serrated edge glistening red. The growing pool of blood on the wooden floor.

How had it come to this?

"Ben!" she shouted, uselessly, her voice lost in the storm. "*Ben! Where are you?*" She had to find him. She knew where he was going because she knew what he was going to do. She had to stop him. There was no other way. She had to.

A core of fear powered her forward, slipping and sliding as she went. Please let her get to him before he did something stupid.

If she could just talk to him – tell him that Milo was alive, at least for now. If she could let him know that he wasn't alone.

At last, she broke out of the trees and into a familiar clearing. This was it – the beach. She stumbled down the riverbank, plunging into the icy water.

Everything was different now. The sand was gone, washed away by the floodwaters. The river was dark and churning with silt and debris from upriver. It was nothing like the swim hole from yesterday. This was a place to fear.

"Ben!" she called out. Her voice was taken instantly by the powerful roar of the river. "Ben, it's me." It was pointless. He wouldn't hear her. She wouldn't hear if he answered. The roar was terrifying, all-encompassing.

She looked around but couldn't see far in the failing light. She pushed the rain out of her eyes. Where was he? He had to be here. She had to be right. This was where he would come, she was sure of it. But where was he?

Wading forward, arms out, she headed in the direction of the fallen tree. She could feel the river water lapping at her ankles, then her knees, pulling at her trousers. It was breathtakingly cold, but she couldn't go back. Not now.

Another bolt of lightning lit up the sky.

That was when she saw him. Waist deep. He was near the end of the tree, at the edge of the fast river current. There was still time.

"Ben, stop!" She pushed herself towards him, wildly splashing through the freezing water. "Ben, please don't. It was an accident. A mistake. Don't go. Please…"

He didn't turn; he didn't look around.

The roar was louder now, the river was pulling hard, violently.

The floodwater was incessant, dangerous, powerful. She was scared. She didn't want to move into the current. She didn't want to get taken again, pulled under again. But she had to stop Ben.

"*Ben!*" she shouted loudly but the river stole her words.

Another step, and she fell, knocked over by a large branch. She went under, the current taking her as she struggled against it. Panic hit. Her clothes were weighing her down and she was disorientated, flailing. But then something caught her arm and in moments she had righted herself, her feet finding the riverbed.

She surfaced, coughing.

Ben had her arm. He was holding her up.

"Ben…" she gasped, trying to catch her breath. "Ben…please. You won't make it across. Please don't do this."

His head was down, bent low over her, sheltering her. Rain ran down his face, off his chin.

"You shouldn't have come," he said. "You shouldn't be here."

"I was there, under the deck. I heard everything. I heard Milo taunting you. You were scared. He had a knife. You did what you had to do."

Her words were pouring out now. Desperately. If only she could get through to him. He couldn't go; he couldn't try to swim the river. He didn't stand a chance. Not with the raging floodwaters, the ferocious current pulling at them. He wouldn't survive.

"Ben, we can go back and wait for Moose. It'll be okay. I'll tell everyone it was an accident—"

"No one will believe you." Ben shook his head. "People only think what they want to think. I'm a killer…remember?"

"I don't care what people think!" Liv grabbed on to his arms. "And I don't care what you did before. I know you, Ben. *I know you.*

You saved my life – twice! *You're good.* I know it. You're good inside." She was babbling desperately, half her words lost in the roar of water.

"But you don't know me, Liv. Not really. I didn't kill anyone, but I did put a boy in hospital. He hurt my brother, and I swear, I could have killed him. It's in me – I felt it. I could have done it. I wanted to do it…and now this…Milo…" Ben shook her hands off and took a few steps back towards the current. "I'm my father's son. I'm not good. You don't know me, Liv. You don't want to know me. Just go back to the others. Go back to Lucas."

"Please…Ben, please." She was crying but the rain was hiding her tears. He didn't respond. Head still down, he took another few steps back. The water was up to his chest now.

She couldn't lose him too. Not after everything, after everyone. Ben was good – she knew it in her heart. Beneath the fear and pain and anger. He was good. She could see it in his eyes. His brown eyes, filled with warmth as he talked about his little brother.

What was his name? What?

"Jordan!" She had it. "Ben, think of Jordan, the…the *asshole*. Jordan – he needs you, Ben. He needs his big brother. I know he is thinking of you. He's waiting for you to come home."

"If I stay here, I won't be going home. Not now. Not after what I did to Milo." Ben shook his head. His face was wrought with grief. "Liv…I'm finished. Don't you see? They're gonna lock me up for this. This is my last chance. If I can escape from this fucked-up place – if I can make it home before they catch me – I can get Jordan away from that house, away from our bastard father. I can protect him and make sure no one ever hurts him again. I'm all Jordan has. I have to try."

"No! You won't make it. Jordan will have no one. You can't help him if you're dead." Liv reached for Ben. But the current was too strong and he was too deep. She tried to move forward, but she could feel the water pulling at her, trying to steal her feet out from under her.

"I can make it. I can get to the other side. I know I can."

"Ben, *please*. Don't go, please. You'll drown, just like Kevon Wright." She was sobbing now.

"Kevon made it."

"What...?"

"He made it, Liv. He swam to the other side, and he found the animal track. Kevon escaped – he was free. But then he came back. He tried to swim across again...and this time he couldn't... Liv – Kevon came back...for me."

Ben faced her. She could see him – his eyes filled with grief. He shook his head.

"The thing is – it wasn't for nothing. I know that now. He showed me the way out. He swam the Ochee, one time. That's all it takes. One time. It can be done. He did it, and now it's my turn. I can do this."

He stepped back; the water was up to his neck. So close, he just had to turn, to swim, and the current would take him.

"Ben..." Liv plunged forward, reaching desperately for him. "The river's flooding; you won't make it. Just wait. Think about this. Please, don't go. *Please. For me...*"

But he just shook his head. He was crying.

"I'm sorry, Liv...for everything. Be careful, okay? It wasn't me. I'm not the killer. Look after yourself. Please. Look after yourself—"

"*No!*"

He stepped back, slipping soundlessly into the powerful current.

Liv watched, helplessly. She saw him – flashes of his head pushing forward, his strong arms striking through the water. She watched as he was pulled under – once, twice, then again, this time longer. He was fighting to stay afloat, to swim, but he just couldn't. *He wasn't going to make it.* He went down. This time seconds went by. She thought she saw him, just a flash before black licks of water pulled at him, ghost hands dragging him deeper, stealing him away with a ferocious roar.

Swallowing him under.

Until finally, he was gone.

Gone.

"*No!*" Liv cried, her voice taken from her. "No… Ben!"

What was the point? The purpose? The reason? Ben was good. He loved his brother. He didn't deserve this. *He didn't deserve to die.*

Grief tore at her. Liv stood, pulled forward, the icy water swaying her, taunting her to take another step. To follow Ben.

She closed her eyes. She could hear the voices in the water now. Calling her. Summoning her to them. Maybe she would go with Ben, with the voices. Just let go. It would be so easy. She could just let them take her away…

"*Liv!*"

The sound of her name called her back. What was she doing? She recoiled, stumbling away from the fast-flowing current.

A hand grabbed her arm.

"Liv, here, hold me. I've got you." It was Lucas. His hands reached around her waist, dragging her away from the edge, from the voices, from Ben. "Liv—"

Somehow, he pulled her back. Somehow, she was on the

riverbank. Back in the mud, and the rain – the bitter cold rain. Lucas was holding her.

"Oh Jesus. Liv. Oh Jesus." Lucas kissed the top of her head, rocking her backward and forward. "Oh Jesus."

She realized she was crying. Great, messy, gulping sobs.

Ben was gone. Everyone was gone now. Lost.

She leaned into Lucas. The rest of the world was cold and dead. But as they lay there, she felt the warmth of life in his arms, wrapped up in each other. Lost in their shared grief, in the moment, in the pain.

Lost.

CHAPTER 38

The hike back to Moose's cabin was a blur of muddied confusion. Stunted by shock, Liv was barely functioning. Her feet were moving, but they felt disconnected from the rest of her. If it hadn't been for Lucas – his gentle arms guiding her, pulling her forward – she would have curled up on the banks of the river and never left.

When they both finally stumbled up the stairs onto the cabin porch, they fell to the floor, too exhausted to move.

Liv closed her eyes, her breath fast, her heart pounding. Her head was still at the river – with Ben. She could still see him, standing before her, facing out towards the river and his final escape.

It was over. He was gone. Dead. Taken by that cruel, black water. Hadn't it had enough victims over the years? Was it still taking its dues, sucking the life out of anyone who came within its reach? Everything about this felt wrong. How could Ben be dead? He was just here. Strong and capable. Young. None of it mattered in the end. Her mother had withered before her, stumbling blindly into death. But this was different. Shocking. Raw. Impossible.

He didn't deserve to die. The boy who loved his brother, who climbed along a narrow rock ledge to watch birds nesting.

The deer-like eyes that could soften in a breath. Maybe the others were right about him. Maybe he was bad – he'd stabbed Milo and was in Camp Smiling Skies for attacking another kid. But that wasn't the whole story. Not for her. Not from everything she knew about him, and not from the way he made her feel.

Liv closed her eyes and scratched her nails into the splintered wood floorboards, trying to pull herself back from the edge.

This night wasn't over yet. Milo was badly hurt, and they were stranded. She still had a job to do. It wasn't the time for grief. She needed to get herself up off the floor, go inside the cabin and do whatever she could to help Milo get through this horrific night.

Liv forced herself up to sitting, brushing away her tears. She took a long shaky breath.

"Wait, Liv." Lucas said it quietly, but there was something about his tone that set alarm bells ringing in her mind. "I followed you down to the river, because there's something… I need to tell you something…before you go inside." He nodded to the door. The angles on his face caught the light from the cabin; he looked almost hollow.

Something flipped inside her. She didn't want him to say any more. She didn't want to hear what was coming.

"After you left…" Lucas wasn't meeting her eyes. He seemed to be struggling to find the words he needed. "After you—"

Fuck, was he crying?

"No, Lucas." Liv held up her hand. He needed to stop. As long as he didn't say it, it wasn't real. She didn't want to know. She didn't want to hear the words. Enough. There had been enough death.

"Milo was bleeding. There was so much blood…I couldn't… We couldn't do anything. He just…he just stopped—" Lucas dropped his head into his hands.

No. No. No. Please God, no.

This couldn't be happening. Shasta. Chipmunk. Ben. Oh God. No more. *No more.*

Liv pushed herself to her feet, wobbling slightly as she turned to face the canvas doorway to the cabin. The golden light, once so enticing, now cast a sickly glow over everything. Long shadows stretched out across the deck.

Through the half-open flap, Liv could see Ruby's feet, her knees curled up. She was sitting on the ground at the foot of Moose's bunk. Bloodied towels and sheets were strewn across the floor next to her. So much blood. Too much blood.

Liv hardly felt herself step forward. Her movements were on autopilot. She reached up to push the loosely hanging canvas door to one side.

And there he was.

Milo was lying on Moose's bunk, where she'd last seen him. His long limbs were stretched out from top to bottom of the frame, like a cold statue resting on a tomb.

Someone had covered him with a bloodstained sheet that didn't reach past his ankles. His dirty, socked feet stuck out the bottom, almost like an afterthought. One hand had fallen off the mattress and was dangling limply over the side, long fingers stretched out towards the floor.

Unmoving. Unseeing.

Milo Zhao was dead.

CHAPTER 39

Time was moving differently now. Chunks of it were lost as memories merged into the present. Laughter silenced. Brown eyes closed for ever.

Liv sat on the floor next to the doorway, arms wrapped tightly around her knees. She might have been there for minutes or hours, she couldn't tell any more.

What she did recognize was this feeling – disjointed, dissociated.

She'd felt it in the hospital when her mom died, and in the weeks after. She'd felt it at her mom's funeral, when she'd had the irresistible urge to giggle. Again, at the wake, which she'd spent on the roof smoking weed. There was a disconnect between what everyone expected from her and what she was feeling. She didn't want to cry. She didn't want to scream at the universe. She felt guilt and shame. What was wrong with her? She couldn't even grieve the way she was supposed to.

It was only much later, when she looked back, that she understood that she had shut down. Her mind was defending itself from an attack too big and too painful to survive head on. In time, the tears and the grief would come; when they did, they were relentless, beating her at the very core of her soul. In some sad, strange way, they'd never left.

Here she was again. Shut down. When she thought of Ben, her mind went blank, she couldn't see him, as though someone had blurred his face. It was the same with Milo. Even though his body was lying right in front of her, she couldn't remember how he had ended up here, the fight, the blood. The idea of it was there, in her head, but the details were fuzzy, and the emotions felt empty.

But she'd been here before, and this time around she knew that the numb feeling was a respite. No need to rush through it – the pain would come, and she'd better be ready when it did.

Lucas was sitting on the floor next to Ruby.

"Can I get you some water? You should drink something." He spoke in a muted whisper, as though he didn't want to wake Milo from a long nap.

"I'm not thirsty." Ruby shook her head. It was the first thing she'd said since Liv had arrived back from the river. There was a set, hard tone in her voice. "So, is he dead?"

It took a moment for Liv to realize she was talking about Ben.

"Yeah. He went into the river," Lucas said quietly. "He tried to swim across. I saw him get pulled under."

"Ding dong, the wicked witch is dead," Ruby said coldly.

"Jesus." Liv felt like she'd been slapped. The callous statement ripped through her. She jumped to her feet and walked to the door, staring out at the empty night, willing it to take some of this breathless pain away.

She could taste blood in her mouth from where she'd bitten her tongue, forcing herself not to retaliate. Ruby was in shock. They all were. This wasn't the time to pick fights. It wouldn't help. Not now.

Not with Milo's body lying right there in front of them.

"What? Do you expect me to feel sad that Ben's dead?" Ruby said flatly. "I'm not sad, Liv. I'm happy. Ben murdered Milo. He deserved everything he got. *He deserved to die.*" Ruby shouted this last part; something seemed to have cracked open inside her.

"Milo started it. He had the knife and went for Ben. Ben was defending himself." Liv turned on Ruby, unable to hold her words in any more. The anger was back. This time it wouldn't settle.

"*Defending himself?* Oh my God. You have got to be kidding me." Ruby was on her feet now, her face red. "Ben was a psychopath! Why won't you just face it? He killed Shasta and Chipmunk. He killed Milo. He beat some kid to death before he was even sent here. He probably murdered Kevon Wright too – and those are just the ones we know about! How can you stand there and—"

"*He just died!*" Liv's anger and grief were boiling over. "Ben just died! I just…I watched him… We don't know if he killed Shasta and Chipmunk. Kevon Wright drowned trying to rescue Ben. You have no idea what you're talking about." Hot tears now. Fuck.

"I have no idea? *What the fuck is wrong with you?*" Ruby was shrieking, out of control now. There she was – the girl with the scissors. "You weren't here when he stabbed Milo to death in front of me. I saw everything. He murdered Milo. He murdered my best friend, and I will tell everyone what kind of monster he was. I will tell everyone—"

"*That's not true!* Milo had the knife. Milo started the fi—"

"Aarrgghh!" Ruby screamed it. "Aarrgghhh. Aarrgghhhhhh!" Over and over. At the top of her lungs, wildly, out of control. "*Aarrgghhh!*" She smacked her head with her hands, hard.

"Ruby, calm down!" Lucas was next to her in an instant. He had her hands, holding her tight. "It's okay. You're okay. Just breathe. Okay. You have to breathe."

A wave of bitter emotion gripped Liv. She needed to move – to get out of here. She was only making things worse. She wiped a hand roughly over her face and stepped out of the open doorway.

"Liv—" Lucas said.

"No," she told him. "I'm okay. Just…just take care of Ruby. She needs you."

She almost tripped down the porch stairs in the darkness. Her thoughts were reeling.

How could Ruby say those things? Was that it? The legacy of everything that had happened here, the blame for each death would all be put onto Ben's shoulders whether he was guilty or not.

Ben the Killer.

She thought of Jordan. The little boy who was about to be told that his beloved big brother was never coming home. That he was dead. That he deserved to die because he was a murderer. It wasn't right. Ben loved his brother more than anything in the world. He loved him and was thinking about him, right up to the end. Jordan needed to know that. No matter what else he was told about his brother, he needed to know that.

She ran, distracted. She was outside Chipmunk's cabin. Her earlier squeamishness about going inside was long gone. Everything was different now.

Walking up the steps, she went in, fumbling in the darkness. It took minutes to feel her way to a lantern propped on a low shelf; her cold fingers struggled to switch it on.

Finally, welcome light flooded the room. She looked around, only half taking in what she was seeing. The cabin was well stocked and decorated like a college room with sarongs hanging from the walls and cushions stacked on the bunk. Chipmunk's belongings were messily spread across the floor, her clothes spilling out of a large basket in the corner. Camo Crocs, an American flag towel, her worn toothbrush. Objects with no owner now. All junk.

Exhaustion was catching up with Liv. She felt wobbly. But it was okay. Maybe she didn't have to be strong any more.

Walking over to Chipmunk's bunk, she kicked her boots off and slumped down onto the mattress. With great effort, she pulled herself into the sleeping bag, dragging it up and over her head. The lining smelled faintly of sweat, but Liv didn't care. She curled up into a tight ball, gripping the neck of the bag closed over her, sealing herself into the warm darkness.

Then she cried. Sobbing as memories washed over her. Thoughts and images. Grief. Sadness. There was no hope, no wishing death away, no second chances. Death was the end. The finish line. The one thing in this life that you could rely on.

Over and over, she pictured Milo's fingers hanging limply, the bloodied sheet that didn't quite stretch to his ankles, his mocking laugh now silenced for ever.

Over and over, she replayed that final moment at the river. Ben standing in the water, rain running down his face. His eyes. The desperate hope.

Over and over, she heard Ben's voice, his words, the last thing he said to her. The last thing he would ever say:

Be careful, okay? It wasn't me. I'm not the killer. Look after yourself. Please. Look after yourself.

CHAPTER 40

Liv sat bolt upright, clutching at her throat, gasping for air.

It took moments for her to realize where she was, the stifling air in the sleeping bag heavy around her. Pulling it off her head, she looked around. She had no idea how long she had slept for. The lantern was still on, casting long shadows on the tent walls around her. Through the cracks at the edge of the door flap, she could see darkness. It was still night. Still Camp Smiling Skies. Great.

Her skin felt clammy and sweaty from the sleeping bag. Throwing it off, she stood up, for the first time aware that her clothes were still damp from the river. She looked longingly at the pile of clothes in the basket. Would it be so bad? Chipmunk didn't need them now. And it wouldn't be as if she was wearing them for fun. It was survival.

Besides, she would rather be rifling through a dead person's personal belongings, than sitting in Moose's cabin, trying not to look at Milo's body, while listening to Ruby's relief that Ben was dead.

No, this was just fine. She could worry about the ethics of it later. Right now, she had her eye on a cosy pair of grey sweats, sitting on top of the pile of clothes.

It didn't take long to change into the sweats and an oversized hoodie, tucking her damp letter into the back pocket so she wouldn't forget it. The clothes were basic and only semi-clean, but damn… they felt so good. Liv had taken her sweet time picking out the thickest pair of woolly hiking socks, pulling them gratefully onto her aching feet. She slipped her boots on over them.

Next, she headed to a propped-up plastic water tub with a spout. There was a tin cup by the bed. Liv took it, filled it and drank, one cup after another. She hadn't realized how thirsty she was. She couldn't remember the last time she'd eaten or drunk anything.

When she was finally done, she turned to look around. The little cabin was surprisingly cluttered. Besides the bed, there was a makeshift desk and canvas clothes closet, even a bedside table and a stack of plastic drawers. Every surface was filled, with random objects spilling from all the drawers and cabinets. Messy, hoarder's things.

This wasn't camping. There was nothing utilitarian about it. Liv couldn't help feeling that she was looking at all of Chipmunk's worldly goods. There clearly wasn't a parent's attic somewhere, filled with boxes of her belongings, lovingly waiting for her to come home. No. This was it. This was all she had. Dragged up a mountain to the middle of nowhere. Home.

There was something deeply sad and lonely about it. Chipmunk's bluster rang hollowly as she looked around – all her proud stories of survival from a tough upbringing. This was a damaged person, hiding away from the real world, in a small corner where she could control her tiny little domain. This wasn't living. It was barely surviving.

The lantern flickered and dimmed a little. Liv wasn't sure how long she'd left it on for, but clearly the batteries were running low. She didn't want darkness. Tonight, she needed light.

Chipmunk probably had a stash of batteries somewhere in here. But it was hard to know where she would keep them in all this chaos. Liv looked around.

The drawers were the most obvious place to start.

She opened the top one. It was filled with random bits and pieces. A bandanna, rope, rolls of tape, Swiss Army knife, boxes of tissues and scented toilet paper for those special moments. No batteries, but Liv took the knife, slipping it into her pocket – better safe than sorry.

The middle drawer had books and notebooks. A well-thumbed copy of *A Game of Thrones* had the corners turned up on the bottom of several pages. Liv flicked through it and saw passages underlined, all Sansa Stark. Clearly Chipmunk's favourite.

The bottom drawer was hard to open. It was heavy and filled with stacks of files. Liv almost shut it again but then stopped when she caught sight of her own name scrawled at the top of a manila folder. *OLIVIA WALKER.*

Curiosity getting the best of her, she pulled out her file. It was thick. Mostly stacks of legal contracts guaranteeing that the Wilderness Therapy Camp would not be liable in the event of accidental death. The WTC had better have a good lawyer. Someone was going to be poring over those clauses soon enough.

At the bottom of each page was a space for digital initials. *JW.* James Walker. Her father had ploughed through all of these documents and clicked his initials on every page, indemnifying random strangers from responsibility should his daughter die in their care. These weren't Carianne's initials. They were her father's.

As Liv scanned page after page, anger coursed through her. Her father's notes on her mental problems, her behavioural deviance, listed by a man who had barely taken the time to know her, who had barely looked her in the eyes over the last two years. Suddenly the expert. There was nowhere for her father to hide here, in all these papers, no excuses. He knew exactly what he was doing. Everything was in there. He had sat in his office and read this, then gone downstairs and asked her how her day had been, knowing exactly what he was about to do to her.

He was a fucking liar.

Liv threw the file across the room in disgust. She didn't want to cry. The bitterness had pushed out any possible tears. This was a betrayal. This weak and needy, selfish pig of a man was not her father. She would hold on to that. Maybe her mother's death had made him lose his mind. Maybe he had cracked and let the wolves inside. It didn't matter. Either way, her real dad was gone. Dead, like her mom.

Fuck.

For a moment, Liv just sat on the floor, hugging her arms to herself, breathing fast. Her body felt electric, as though the thoughts had somehow charged her with their toxic energy. Name that emotion. That's what her therapist would tell her now. But was there a name for this? There was anger and sadness in equal parts. A feeling of raging power while her heart was ripping in two deep, deep inside.

Without noticing it, she gripped the swallow ring tightly, turning it around with her thumb. Fuck him. Her mom would always be with her. Maybe her old dad too – an amiable, warm presence in the background. No one could take those memories from her. Not even this *JW* – this new middle-aged man squeezed into skinny jeans and lathered in hair-growth serum, styled by his gold-digging trophy wife. Weak, foolish, selfish. No. She would keep the memories of the man he used to be. A better man.

Those memories were hers. He didn't own them.

And he didn't own her. Fuck him.

The universe agreed. A rare break in the clouds flooded the world with moonlight. Through the tent flap, Liv saw trees, the distant crags, all cast in silver. Long shadows stretched across the floor as the light tipped into the cabin. The files were lit up, the names stood out. They were all there: *SHASTA LEE, LUCAS ROBERT COLE, RUBY JENNIFER CLARKE, MILO ZHAO*. Many more. Other names. Previous campers. Prior delinquents.

BENJAMIN CROSS.

Liv stared at the name. She could feel tears prickling behind her eyes.

Taking a deep breath, she reached for the file. Flicking through the first few pages, she found a photo. Liv pulled it out and held it up in the moonlight. It was a photo of two boys. A young-looking Ben was standing holding the hand of a mini-me little boy. Ben looked different in regular clothes with long, floppy hair. Undeniably cute, but there was still that raw, dangerous look about him. He would have been the cause of many bad-boy crushes at high school.

The smaller boy – Jordan, she guessed – was the image of his older brother; tough and cute but with one major difference – he was smiling. There was something about the way they stood together that caught at Liv. The bond between them was so clear. Jordan looked happy under the protective wing of his adoring older brother. It must have hurt so badly to be separated. It had broken Ben.

Ben.

It was getting hard to breathe. Liv's chest was tight. Without thinking, she folded the photo in half and slipped it into her back pocket. She didn't want to look at it any more, but she wasn't ready to let it go.

She threw the file back on the floor and sat, just for a minute, trying to calm herself. Her thoughts kept looping back to the river. To the last time she'd seen Ben. The look on his face – desperate and sad. So sad.

Everything was messy and confusing right now. Emotions were hitting her from all directions. But there was one thing Liv knew was real. Ben – his death, her grief; none of that was going away any time soon. A part of him would be with her for ever now. Somehow, she was going to have to learn to live with that, and to live with the pain.

But not yet.

It would have to wait until she was safe. Until Moose returned and she got the hell out of Camp Smiling Fucking Skies once and for all. Then she would let herself go there. Only then.

Forcing herself back into the present moment, she looked around. Her eyes fell on the remaining folders. One file stood out. It was much thicker than all the others. *LUCAS ROBERT COLE.*

Surprised, Liv thumbed through the pages. Mostly dry paperwork, parental contracts. But what was different was how many sets there were. Three at least. All the same documents but repeated over and over. Liv looked at the initials. All the same initials, but the dates changed between sets: one signed a month ago, one six months ago and another six months before that. Confused, Liv pulled apart the sets. The contracts were all with the same organization, WTC, but the camps were different: Camp Smiling Skies, Camp Happy Vistas, Camp Hopeful Trails.

This didn't make any sense. Lucas had never mentioned being at other camps before. Liv's mind quickly ran through past conversations. Was she missing something? Was it possible that it just hadn't come up? That maybe he didn't want to make a point of it, maybe he was ashamed?

But any way she looked at it, even if he hadn't outright lied, he hadn't been truthful by omission.

It was such a big thing; she couldn't just brush it off. Liv thought back to the van on that first awful night. Lucas in his grey hoodie. At the intake centre. He'd been so chill about it all. She'd put it down to his easy nature. But now she could see why. This wasn't new to him. This was his third camp. He hadn't been kidnapped in the middle of the night. He was just relocating.

Liv dropped the file on the floor and squatted down next to it, a cold feeling in her gut. She picked up the Camp Happy Vistas file and flicked through the first pages. There was a photo pasted on a form titled *Background*. It had a group posed together. Lucas, maybe a few years younger, standing next to a smiling middle-aged woman and two pretty girls, one older looking, one younger. All blond and tanned, all with distinctive clear blue eyes. They looked so alike, there was no question that they were related to Lucas. They looked happy, and affectionate, their arms around each other in a natural, easy way. Sisters? No, that wasn't right. They must be an aunt and cousins or something. His parents and brother had died years before this photo was taken.

But the attached form listed their names. *Mother: Lindy Cole. Siblings: Maya and Cara Cole.* No father listed. No brother.

Something was really off. Lucas had lied. He'd told Liv that his family died. He'd made it seem like he had gone off the rails when his boyfriend tragically died in a car accident. That he had been sent to camp by loving grandparents who wanted to help him recover from his grief. He seemed happy and well-adjusted and easy-going. A kid who had no business being at a camp for losers. Someone who would return home and thrive.

But none of that was true – was it?

A creak behind her made her jump. She looked around quickly, the weak light from the lantern disappearing uselessly into the dark air. The porch was empty – it must be just the wooden frame creaking. The door flap caught a gust of wind and flapped loosely.

Liv turned back to the pages on the floor. She picked up Camp Hopeful Trails. From the dates, this must have been Lucas's first camp. Again, she went straight to the front sheets, flicking through the filled-out forms, the pages of writing with the camper's history and medical records. An extra sheet was stapled to the back of this set. It looked like an official document, a report of some sort.

As she read it, Liv gasped. She slumped back. This couldn't be real. How could it? *How could it?*

There was another faint sound behind her, from the doorway. This time she was sure – she was not alone.

"Liv?"

She jumped to her feet, the report still in her hand, and turned to face the door.

Lucas was standing in the opening, flashlight in his hand. He looked at her, standing in a pile of folders, papers strewn across the ground. Her hands were shaking badly, the report crumpled in her fist.

"You okay? I'm sorry, I know you wanted space. But I just wanted to make sure you're all right." He stepped into the cabin but didn't move out of the doorway.

She forced herself to nod.

"Fine…I'm fine." Her voice was shaky. She hoped it wasn't giving her away. "You should go now. See Ruby. I'm good here. Alone. Please."

There was no way he wasn't suspicious. No way at all. She was the world's worst actor.

Lucas frowned. He looked around, his eyes lingering on the files at her feet. She could almost hear his thoughts ticking over, figuring out what was really going on.

"Liv…has something happened?" His eyes flicked up; their icy blue caught the lantern-light.

"You lied…" Liv blurted out. Maybe stupid. But she couldn't hold it back. Who the fuck was he? *Who was Lucas Cole?*

Instantly, Lucas's expression changed. His smile dropped; his head dropped. His eyes dropped, down to her hand – to the single sheet grasped tightly. A dark look settled on his even features. He didn't speak. He just stood there, watching her.

"It was you, wasn't it?" Liv shook her head, trying to clear her thoughts. This was pure danger. Ben's words were playing out in her head, over and over. *Be careful. It wasn't me. I'm not the killer.* "It was you all along… I know everything. I know all your lies. Your family didn't die in an accident. Did they?" She was shouting now. "They are alive and well. They put you here, and in all those other camps. They don't want you because you are fucked up and dangerous. You're a pathological liar and…and…" She couldn't say it.

Still, Lucas hadn't moved. The beam from his flashlight lit his features from below. He looked dangerous, scary.

She couldn't say the words, instead thrusting out her hand, holding out the sheet of paper. He didn't take it from her. He knew what it was. He knew the truth. He'd known it all along. And now she knew it too.

"You…you killed Dillon."

CHAPTER 41

"Who the fuck are you?" Liv shouted. Her shakiness was morphing into rage. "Who even are you, Lucas? Huh?" She held out the sheet of paper – the police report. "You lied to me about everything. When you were fifteen you went to prison for a year – to juvie, for killing Dillon, your own boyfriend. Then when you got out, you were bounced between institutions and therapy camps until you wound up here. You are a criminal and a murderer. Not to mention a fucking lying bastard."

Lucas didn't react. He just stood there impassively, watching her. No smiles now.

Gusts of wind rattled the flimsy tent walls. The canvas door was flapping wildly behind Lucas. But he didn't flinch.

Fuck. She was in trouble. She was standing in a cabin, in the middle of nowhere, with a convicted killer and pathological liar. Instinctively she slipped her hand into her pocket, feeling for the Swiss Army knife. Her thumb pushed against it, ready to go, just in case.

It was so obvious. It has been there all along. All the pointers. The murders started when he arrived. He was the werewolf, and a liar. But she hadn't seen it because…because she didn't want to. Because it was Lucas. Charming, sweet, funny Lucas.

Lucas who was standing before her now. Not charming, sweet or funny. Not any more.

"*Who are you?*" she asked again.

"I told you." Lucas's voice was low. It was hard to hear over the rattling walls. "At the river, I told you that you didn't know me. That you didn't see who I really was. You saw what you wanted to see. Just like everyone else."

As he was talking, Liv's animal brain was working overtime, assessing the ways to escape. Lucas was blocking the door flap. But the nice thing about canvas walls was that you could make a new door. The canvas was thick and would be hard to rip, even if she could get her knife open in time to try and cut through it. The eyelets in the canvas were lashed firmly to the cabin frame with thick rope. But the lower corners were loose. The last few holes had been left open and there was just enough room for someone small to crawl through – she hoped. It looked about her size anyway… Besides, what other choice did she have?

She took a small step back. Keep him talking. Keep him distracted.

"This isn't on us, Lucas. You're a liar and a killer…"

This time Lucas stepped forward. "It's not what you think, Liv. Let's just take a minute. Sit. I can explain…" The wind flipped the door flap up. Liv looked through longingly at the darkness behind him, escape – just out of reach.

"Don't! You don't need to explain anything to me," she said. "I know enough."

"What do you think you know, Liv?" Lucas's tone was measured.

He was looking at her cautiously. Watching her.

"I know you were a werewolf, and that you picked off your victims, one by one. Starting with Shasta." *Shasta*. Liv's mind was working hard, filling in the blanks. She pictured Shasta and Lucas, sitting at the picnic table that first night. They hadn't talked much. But there was something between them – when Lucas shared his food with Shasta. How kind it had seemed at the time, sharing his undersized portion with her, cheering her up. Now, seen in a new light… Liv gasped. "It was you! You put nuts in your own bowl, didn't you? Then you shared it with Shasta, just like on the first night. Of course, she would have eaten it and not suspected anything. Oh my God. That was it. That was how you did it – how you killed her."

Lucas just laughed and shook his head, but there was darkness in his eyes.

"Come on, Liv. That's all just bullshit. I know you don't really believe that. You're tired, your mind's playing tricks on you—"

"*Don't fucking gaslight me,*" Liv snapped. Fuck him and his schmoozing, fake-easy, lying ways. "I'm done being manipulated by you." She edged back, just a step, towards the hole in the corner. Hopefully he wouldn't notice and would think she was being reactive. The closer she got before she went for it, the better her chances would be.

"Okay, fine." Lucas held his hands up. "If you think you have this all figured out, then tell me. What happened next? How did I do it? How did I kill Chipmunk?"

Liv's face creased in a frown. There was no way she could know that. They had never found out the cause of death. Just that there was a lack of blood or obvious injury, the stench of barbecue and the body with its glassy eyes and dirt-covered hands, the tattooed snake staring up at them. That was all they knew – that and the fact that when they'd arrived at the Snack-Shack, they'd found it locked from the outside.

Correction – Lucas had found it locked. *Lucas.*

Why had she missed this before? It was so obvious now.

"You know how to pick locks. Which means you could have got in and out of the Snack-Shack any time you wanted." She shook her head incredulously. He'd been one step ahead of them at every turn. "You could have killed Chipmunk and then locked her body *inside* the Snack-Shack. Of course, I was so stupid. I should have seen it all along."

The cabin rattled, down to the floorboards. The gusts of wind were whipping around now.

"Wow. Honestly, I'm impressed by myself. I'm clearly not just your average, everyday serial killer. I'm smart too. You're really giving me credit here, aren't you?" Lucas had dropped his hands into his pockets. What did he have hidden in there? Her thoughts flashed to Moose's knife – the long, serrated blade.

Please, not the knife. She squeezed her hand tightly around the little Swiss Army knife as she carefully backed away – to the corner, to the small open flap, to escape. If she could just string Lucas along a little longer, this could work. She might make it.

She looked around desperately; her mind was blanking, reaching. The file was on the floor, pages scattered around. The photo.

"What about Maya and Cara?" That got a reaction. At the mention of their names, Lucas straightened. His eyes flashed icy silver in the flashlight beam, eyes that had seemed so clear they couldn't hold secrets or lies. Now cold and empty. "Your sisters are really pretty. They look just like you." Liv nodded towards the photo on the ground.

Lucas looked down, frowning, momentarily confused. He spotted the photo, his attention briefly engaged.

This was her chance. Before Lucas could react, Liv spun across to the farthest corner of the tent, diving for the small hole. Her guess was right and she fitted perfectly, squeezing through and tumbling headfirst onto the muddy, wet ground. She was out.

She started towards Moose's cabin. But then skidded to a stop. If she ran in there to warn Ruby, they would both be trapped in the cabin. They would have to stay and fight, and like it or not, even the two of them against Lucas were not great odds.

No, the best bet would be to lure Lucas away from Ruby. She didn't know the truth about him, so he had no reason to hurt her. Liv was the only one who knew his secret. He would have to come after her.

Turning to look at Chipmunk's cabin, moonlight lit up the view. Lucas was standing in the doorway. He saw her too. He started running for her.

Shit, she had to get out of here. Now.

Without thinking, she turned and ran in the only direction she could think of. The only possible way out of this hellish nightmare. She ran towards the wooden sign and the trailhead, heading for the road.

CHAPTER 42

Stumbling, falling and crashing forward, Liv ran along the trail that led to the road.

She had lost all sense of time. It was endless. Terrifying. She had fallen so many times, she was bruised and scraped from head to toe. At one point she smacked her jaw so hard on a tree root, she felt a hard edge of tooth where she must have chipped it.

Thank goodness Lucas had a bad leg. She looked behind several times but only caught glimpses of him through the trees. He seemed to be having as much trouble as she was and wasn't gaining on her. Not yet.

As she ran, short bursts of panic cut through the fear.

How could this be happening?

Who was Lucas? A psychopath? Just moving from camp to camp killing off random kids for kicks? Perhaps he'd developed a taste for murder after killing Dillon. Perhaps there was a whole string of "accidental" deaths following him around wherever he went. Perhaps he'd always managed to charm his way out of it. After all, he'd almost got away with these murders. They had looked like accidents at first. But now Ben would be blamed, and no one would ever know what really happened. Unless she stopped him.

Liv pictured him sitting at the picnic table, in the cave, by the swim hole, endlessly smiling, his charm dripping off him. Lying over and over to her face. Jesus, how fucking stupid was she to fall for it? He was always too shiny and perfect. Fake. But she'd let him get under her skin. She'd trusted him.

The kiss. That should have been enough to tell her he was a liar. She knew that boys like him didn't waste time on girls like her. Not without an ulterior motive. *She knew it.* But she had let herself hold on to that feeling; that small, stupid, pathetic hope. He must have known she could be manipulated. All that time, she thought she was projecting her strength and pride, but he had seen right through her and smelled her weakness and vulnerability. He knew a loser when he saw one.

Fuck. She lost her footing on a wet, slippery rock. This time she couldn't break her fall and tumbled headfirst, rolling over and over, down the trail, crashing hard onto a large boulder. She lay there, winded. Her head was spinning, confused; darkness clawed at her vision. There was a loud ringing in her ears. Was she okay? There was pain. A lot.

She tried to lift an arm, but her limbs weren't obeying her. Nothing was working. Jesus, her head hurt, and she could taste something strange in her mouth. Salty, metallic. There was blood. But where? How?

Through the confusion, she sensed something more. Danger. Shadows. The sound of something crashing forward. Lucas was catching up.

But there was nothing she could do.

Move, she told herself. *Move. You're going to die here. You need to move, Liv.* With difficulty, she lifted her head. Lancing pain went through her temple and down her neck and she gasped. Her vision was blurry, even in the dark. But she could still make out the shadowy outline running towards her. Lucas was close now. She needed to do something.

Sensation was returning. She felt in her pocket for the Swiss Army knife. But it was gone, probably lost when she fell. Her hands reached around her for anything she could use as a weapon, but all she came up with was mud and twigs. She couldn't fight him off.

Lucas was almost upon her. She tried to recoil, to curl up into a ball and protect herself, unable to do anything to stop him.

But just at the last second, he turned to the side, running on.

The path turned. Liv hadn't seen it in the fall. She had landed in the bushes to one side. He hadn't seen her in the darkness.

She fell back, relief surging through her.

Just breathe. Breathe. Calm down. She had some time now. It could be minutes before he realized she wasn't ahead of him any more. Time to pull herself together.

Her vision was working now and she could move – slowly, at least. The searing throb in her head was lifting, but a new pain in her left arm was kicking in. By the time she had made it to sitting, she was pretty convinced her wrist was broken. Any movement sent a vicious pain up her arm and into her shoulder. She didn't dare feel around it to work out what was going on. Instead, with a gasp, she pulled her hand close to her and cradled it with her other arm like a makeshift sling. The less movement the better. She could figure out the damage later – if she survived.

There was blood on her face from her head injury. Using her shoulder, she rubbed some of the blood away, pushing it out of her eyes until she could see well enough to get moving.

For better or for worse, she had a plan. She would follow the trail, watching out for signs of Lucas as she went, and try to make it to the road. It couldn't be that much further along now. There she could find a safe place to hide near the van drop-off and wait it out until morning. Until Moose's return.

Hopefully Lucas would run on, thinking she had started down the road. It could work. Either way, in the state she was in after her fall, she didn't have a lot of options. Hiding out seemed like the best way.

The hike down to the road was a blur. She wasn't running now she wasn't being chased, but her shifting vision and the blistering pain in her arm made it equally challenging, and she kept falling painfully, stumbling around like she was drunk or high.

The clouds were patchy overhead, and welcome bursts of moonlight broke out intermittently, giving her the chance to stop and look around, checking for signs of Lucas. But she didn't see or hear him. He must have run on, chasing shadows.

Maybe the knock to her head was messing with her, but she kept imagining people in the darkness: her mom. Ben, Shasta, Milo. Just brief impressions of them, standing by, silently watching her. Dead, but not scary – not ghosts or memories exactly. Just a calm sense of their presence and the weird sensation that she wasn't alone. She did wonder, more than once, if she might be dead too. Maybe her body was lying in the bushes where she'd fallen and her soul was wandering free, unaware that she had died. Perhaps the spirits were here to guide her to the next world. God, she really hoped it was the head injury messing with her.

The last part of the hike was lost in a mess of confused thoughts. Disorientation was back and settling in like a heavy fog in her head.

It took everything she had just to force herself to move forward one step at a time, clinging to her arm and trying to stay upright. Trying to keep going.

By the time she saw the damp grey of the road through the trees, she was about ready to give up. But somehow, knowing she was here, at the drop-off, gave her hope. The same place where she had arrived just three days ago.

As she broke out of the trees and stepped onto the road, she dropped to her knees. She could have kissed the ground. The cracked, asphalt road was physical proof that she was still walking the earth. There was hope. The spirits would have to wait – for now, at least.

Her whole body was shaking. The pain from her arm had radiated and seemed to take over her, inside out. But she didn't care any more. For the first time, there was a faint light in the distant sky. A kiss of dawn on the eastern clouds. It felt like an omen. A good omen. She had come this far and almost made it to the new day – almost survived the night.

Almost.

She'd jumped ahead of herself.

There was something else out there; she could make out the faint outline on the far side of the road. His blond hair caught the edges of the light.

Lucas had stopped running. He'd figured out that she was no longer ahead of him and had waited for her. He must have known she would head here, to the end of the road, hoping for rescue.

Well, now he had her.

CHAPTER 43

"Stay away from me," Liv shouted, pointlessly. He'd chased her all the way down here for a reason. She knew he was the killer. He needed to add her to his list of victims before she could tell anyone else.

Lucas started walking towards her.

"No! Stay the fuck away from me!" She scrambled to her feet, wobbling, her head spinning as she backed away from him, heading down the road. If she was going to run, she was not running back towards the camp. She was heading out of this hellhole in the direction of town. She would rather die here, like roadkill, than in Camp Hell.

"Liv, you're not thinking straight." Lucas was holding his hands up, placatingly, his face open. She knew that look: winsome, engaging. *Manipulative.* Playing with his kill. "You're hurt. There's blood on your head. Let me help."

"You killed Dillon." Liv said it straight up. There was no way in hell she was falling for more of his smooth talk. Never again.

"I…yes."

"You told me he died in a car crash." Liv kept moving, facing him, backing along the road.

"He did. I just didn't tell you all of it."

"Yeah, you left out the part about going to prison for killing him!"

"It's…complicated." Lucas was keeping pace with her, moving step by step as she backed towards the bend in the road.

"*Complicated?* You killed your boyfriend. You lied about who you are – about everything. You murdered Shasta and Chipmunk. Milo and Ben are dead because of you. Just stay back. Stay the fuck away from me." Liv backed further away. Her head was throbbing; her vision was still unfocused. She might have been slurring. She didn't know how much longer she could hold out.

"Fine. We can wait here for Moose. You can tell him everything you found out about me. Okay? Just…let's sit. For a minute." Lucas moved forward, hand out, too close.

"No!" Liv backed up, almost tripping. "Stay back!"

"For fuck's sake, Liv." Lucas kept coming towards her. He kept coming.

There was nothing for it. Liv turned and ran, down the road, heading for the bend. He could catch her, even with his bad leg. She was stumbling and dizzy, but this was her last shot. Her only chance. She had to try.

Her feet almost tripped over themselves as she ran with everything she had in her. She could hear his footsteps close – too close. He was catching up; he was right behind her.

"Liv!"

There were lights.

His fingers caught at her sleeve.

Lights, a rumbling sound.

She turned the corner, spinning out straight into the middle of the road – straight into the path of an oncoming van. Brakes screeched. Dirt skidded in the air. A scream.

She froze, locked in the headlights. There was nothing she could do, no way to avoid it. She was going to get hit. The spirits *were* waiting for her. They knew.

She was going to die.

She closed her eyes.

CHAPTER 44

Silence. Darkness and silence.

No great white light, or some shimmering afterlife. Just an average, dull, early-dawn kind of silence.

Still alive then.

Liv opened her eyes. She was lying on the road. Lucas was lying half on top of her, his arm around her. He had dived in front of the van, pulling her out of the way seconds before the van hit.

The two of them lay, together, not moving – both breathing heavily. It had been so close. Too close.

Lucas, the killer who had chased her down the entire trail, had just risked his life saving hers. This was…confusing.

She lifted her head slightly and looked at him. He was on his side, his face close to hers. He met her eyes. His clear blue eyes. Looking right at her.

"Hey." He smiled. *Smiled.*

Confusing.

Slowly, Liv sat up, wincing as she moved her arm. God, it hurt. Everything hurt. The dramatic dive hadn't helped.

There was the sound of a door slamming. The van. She'd almost forgotten.

"Jeez, you guys okay there?" Moose's voice was the best thing she'd heard in days. Liv looked around, blinking in the bright headlights. The van had stopped in the middle of the road at an angle, tyre burn marks trailing behind it. "Man, I totally thought I was gonna hit you both. What the heck, man?"

Liv couldn't help it. She laughed – and maybe cried a little at the same time.

Lucas grinned.

"That's funny, is it? Wait, did I do that?" Moose pointed to Liv's forehead. She knew she must look like a wreck. Moose was staring at her like she was roadkill. She shook her head, causing a brutal pain to shoot through her temple.

"Nah, Liv did that one to herself. Running away from the scary werewolf." Lucas sat up next to her. The deadly killer. He brushed some gravel off his trousers and smiled at her. His hands and forearms were scraped raw from the dive – the dive to save her from being run down. All right, what was going on? It couldn't all be confusion from the head injury.

"Phew. Well, that's good then. I mean not good. But…you know." Moose grinned sheepishly.

"It's so fucking amazing to see you, Moose!" Liv looked up at him. "You have no idea."

"Yeah, I'm guessing…" Moose scratched his man bun. "Sounds like there's a lot to catch me up on. Like why you were running down the middle of the road at dawn. Where's Chipmunk? I bet she's pissed as all hell at you two."

Oh God. Liv hadn't thought this far ahead. The idea of rescue was the furthest her fantasies had got. What now? They had to explain three more deaths. How was this going to sound out in the real world? Fuck.

She didn't have to worry about it for long.

There was a scraping noise behind him as the van's side door slid open. Liv glanced at Lucas, then stared at the doorway, even more confused now. Who was with Moose? She'd just assumed he was alone. Oh God, please not Lomax, coming back to check up on them. When he found out about Chipmunk…

There was a brief pause, the sound of a seatbelt unclipping, and then one long leg emerged, followed by another. A girl slid out of the van and stood, innocently, on the road.

She gave a small wave and smiled shyly, pushing her curly red hair back off her face.

"Hey, Liv. Hey, Lucas. How's it going?" said Shasta.

CHAPTER 45

They were all sitting in the parked van.

Oddly, they'd taken up the same positions they'd been in three days ago, on that fateful drive through the night.

Lucas was behind the driver's seat. Moose was in Chipmunk's seat. Shasta was behind him, and Liv was near the back, a large Band-Aid on her forehead, her wrist bundled in a spare shirt. Moose had radioed into town, and help was on the way.

The van was warm and cosy, the windows misted with condensation from their wet clothes. Liv and Lucas were hungrily sharing a box of cheesy crackers that had been left in the glove compartment. This was the closest they had been to civilization in days. It would have felt good, apart from the obvious. The lurking truth of what had come before. Of those they had lost.

They were taking turns to catch each other up on the last few days. Shasta had gone first and was unusually chatty, bubbling over with words, with Moose interjecting an occasional "so true... totally". She'd had quite an adventure, and Liv and Lucas were content to listen, waiting as long as possible before they would have to break the news of what had happened while she was away – of the deaths. After all, Shasta's adventure had a happy ending.

She'd started feeling better on the van ride down the mountain. She could breathe consistently and wasn't getting any worse. At that point, she said that she wasn't worried any more. She'd had worse anaphylaxis before, so she knew she'd be okay. At the hospital they had pumped her full of epinephrine and put her in a bed with an oxygen mask and an IV for overnight observation. The next day, when the storm rolled in, they'd let her stay an extra night until the roads were safe to travel. She'd been treated like a princess and spoiled by all the sympathetic hospital staff as she lay in bed, watching TV and fielding anxious phone calls from her parents, who immediately pulled her out of the WTC programme and started the long drive up to Utah to pick her up.

Pre-dawn this morning, Moose and Shasta reluctantly headed back up the road to Camp Smiling Skies to collect Shasta's few belongings and say her goodbyes, before her parents arrived to take her home.

"I still can't believe you're okay," Liv said when the story ended. "The way you looked…the expression in your eyes when you left camp. I was sure you were half dead already."

"Right, and Chipmunk told us you'd stopped breathing when you got to the van," Lucas added. "We all thought you'd died."

Shasta blushed a little, glancing up to check in with Moose. He gave her a reassuring smile.

"If I tell you something, will you promise not to tell Chipmunk?" Shasta looked at them with her wide-spaced eyes. Liv glanced at Lucas – that was a promise they could guarantee to keep. They both nodded.

Shasta continued, "So, it's just possible…I might have…faked the whole nut thing."

"Wait…what?" Liv looked at her, then at Moose, who clearly already knew what Shasta was about to confess.

"I was just so unhappy. I knew I couldn't bear to stay at the camp another night. So, I decided to fake an accidental nut poisoning to escape. I knew that my parents would never make me stay in a place that wasn't nut-safe. They're way too controlling. This was a guaranteed way to get home. I've been micro-dosing as part of my nut allergy treatment plan, so I knew exactly how much to take and what it would do to me physically. I took enough to look really bad and then acted up the rest. It was easy. I was hospitalized for anaphylaxis when I was nine, so I knew exactly how to make it look real. At the van, I held my breath when Chipmunk was checking me, just to be really convincing. Maybe I pushed it too far, if she thinks I'm dead? I'm really sorry; I honestly never meant to scare anyone. I just really needed to go home, you know?"

Liv shook her head. It was brilliant and surprising at the same time. Shasta really was a dark horse. She had seemed so quiet, while secretly hatching a masterplan to escape, achieving what Ben and the others had been unable to do.

"So, you knew?" Liv looked at Moose.

"Shasta told me at the hospital." Moose shrugged. "I thought like, cool. Whatever. Seemed like a good plan to me."

"We made a deal," Shasta added. "I would say I'd been hungry and secretly ate one of the cereal bars, not realizing it had nuts. That way, no one could blame Moose or sue the camp. In exchange, he agreed to keep my secret."

Wow. Liv laughed. The whole thing had played out perfectly. Almost perfectly.

Because Shasta's escape had just been the beginning. It had set off a whole chain of events that hadn't been as innocent. A chain that had led to all the suspicion and fear and death. How many times had they argued over who had killed Shasta? Looking around at each other with fear and distrust. Who was the killer? They were all suspects. All potential murderers, and yet there had never actually been a victim.

Liv looked out through the misted glass. The dawn was clear and fresh, the world washed clean in the rain. Raindrops on the window captured tiny upside-down images of the world around them. Miniature universes. But this was the one she was stuck in. The reality where Ben had swum off into the Ochee, accused of Shasta's and Chipmunk's murders, of stabbing Milo. The reality where she had believed that Lucas had murdered several people, including the girl sitting contentedly in the seat across from him.

"So, what about you guys?" Moose asked. "Did we miss anything?"

CHAPTER 46

Lucas had done most of the talking. It sounded odd hearing a play-by-play of the events of the last few days. Shasta cried most of the way through. Moose looked ill. When they explained how Chipmunk's body was found in the locked Snack-Shack, Moose shook his head.

"Chippy would go there a lot at night," he said. "She'd get hungry and go sneak some food when she thought everyone was asleep. I used to hear her, but I never told her I knew it was her."

"Chipmunk was the food thief?" Liv asked, shocked. She remembered the dark figure she'd followed that second night at camp. How they'd hissed at her from the top of a boulder. Of course, it was Chipmunk, the snake lady, interrupted on her way to sneak a midnight snack. She must have seen Liv following her and tried to scare her away. "Why didn't she just take what she wanted? She was in charge; she didn't need to steal food."

"She was a real stickler for the rules, you know?" Moose scratched at his man bun. "She wouldn't let anyone else break them, so she couldn't exactly go around breaking them herself. She thought I didn't know that she was the one stealing food. I pretended I thought it was one of the kids. But I started keeping the key on me at all times. Cos, she could eat. I mean, one time she ate through the entire week's breakfast rations, and we had to get by on a daily handful of dried granola till the next food run." Moose pulled out the key. "I was worried cos I forgot to leave the key at the camp, with all the drama with Shasta here. But then I remembered how Chippy had a secret way in, through the crawl space at the back. She had no idea I knew about it, but I reckoned in a pinch she could get food out while I was gone."

"So that was why the Snack-Shack was locked on the outside," Lucas said. He shot a quick look at Liv. She blushed, remembering how she had accused him of killing Chipmunk and locking her body inside. Some of the other things she'd said to him came rushing back. Oh God. Not good. She had been so sure he was the killer. She was going to have some serious apologizing to do.

"Did you find out what happened...how she died?" Moose asked, looking pale.

Lucas shook his head. "There were no obvious injuries. At least, we couldn't see anything. But it was dark in the Snack-Shack and, to be honest, none of us were up for looking too closely. Ben said her eyes were open and cloudy. Other than that, nothing. But it smelled really bad. Like cooked meat or something. We wondered what you'd been feeding us..."

"Cooked meat?" Moose looked thoughtful. "You said it was dark in there. What happened to the lights?"

"Not working. The electricity went out that night and hasn't worked since."

"Oh...oh no." Moose went even paler. Clearly something had occurred to him. "Where was the body? Near the back wall, by the electrical panel?"

"Yes! How did you know...?" Liv said it, but before she even finished her question, her brain had caught up. Under the electrical panel. *The faulty electrical panel.*

"It should have been fixed. It was on our request list. But it just...it never got done."

The smell of burned flesh; the blackened fingers that she'd thought had been dirty. Had Chipmunk touched the wiring? Had she accidentally electrocuted herself, crawling around in the darkness? As she thought it, Liv could almost smell the burned fleshy smell: repulsive, nauseating. "I just...I—"

Liv pulled open the sliding door and jumped out of the parked van.

She ran to the side of the road, falling on her knees. Doubling over, she vomited. Again and again.

It was hitting her, hard. Shasta's death was faked. Chipmunk's death was a stupid accident. Milo's death was the result of his own sick prank, trying to trick them into thinking they were playing the Werewolf game. None of it was real. *None of it.*

Apart from Ben. Ben's death was real. It was real.

Oh God.

There wasn't much food in her stomach, but she couldn't stop retching.

There was no murderer. No plot to kill them off. No game.

The way they had looked at each other – convinced that they might be capable of murder. The way they had so easily believed that they were among killers – evil, vicious killers.

Just a sick kid, a tragic accident, and the fact that they thought they were bad. Bad enough to kill.

Liv pushed herself to her feet, holding her injured arm tight against her.

Slowly, she walked away from the van, down the road. The crags looked sharper, clear in the dawn light. Everything was harsh, washed clean, like the world was in focus for the first time. This place was hard, cruel and deadly. This place was not for them, and they needed to get out of here. All of them. Once and for all. They needed to leave.

A sound stopped her. A sound she'd never wanted to hear again. A sinister cawing. The buzzards were back, circling around again, further down the valley. Back on the hunt for the dead. Back for more.

Who was it this time?

Milo? Ben?

Was it Ben? Had his body washed up on the banks of the Ochee somewhere, waiting to be picked apart by those fucking evil birds? No one had believed in him. No one had truly seen him. God knows, he probably didn't believe in himself. He was bad, written off, discarded. Even she had let him down. Her heart had told her the truth. He was good. He was good all along. He just wanted to get home and protect his brother. She should have trusted her heart and fought for him, stood with him. But she hadn't. And now she never could.

Liv bent forward. She was sobbing. Grief, guilt and pain. She knew the names for these emotions.

No one believed in any of them. That's why they were here. Whatever had brought them here, whatever messed up or screwed up mistakes they'd made, they had been judged and sentenced. You are bad. You are unlovable. You are hopeless.

She saw her father, standing on the lawn, turning away from her. *Past saving. Out of control.* She saw Carianne, waving goodbye, protecting Mattie in her arms from the evil girl. *Unwanted. A troublemaker.* She saw herself in the mirror of the intake building. *Ugly. Undesirable. Unlovable.*

She stood on the road, curled over on herself, her body racked with tears.

They were bad. The world believed it. The world had told them that, over and over. And that message had got inside each and every one of them – into their heads and their hearts – until they saw themselves the same way.

They had let it in, and it had destroyed them.

I'm bad. I'm bad. I'm bad.

CHAPTER 47

Eyes closed, Liv breathed in the reassuringly antiseptic smell of the hospital room. Clean and sterile. No dirt, mud or bean juice. Not here.

She was wearing a blue gown; the clothes she had borrowed from Chipmunk's cabin had probably gone into some hospital furnace. Best place for them. She could lie here all day and happily listen to the buzzing and beeping noises of a regular every-day in the hospital ward. A rumbling low voice, a laugh, the sound of little footsteps running fast down the hallway.

Now *this* was heaven, and she hadn't had to die to get here.

She smiled and stretched out her feet to the furthest corners of the bed, wiggling her toes with pleasure. At least wilderness therapy had taught her to appreciate the little things in life.

Liv's wrist was fractured in two places and was propped next to her in a comfortable splint. Honestly, if she didn't move, she couldn't feel it. The nurse had given her enough pain medication to knock out a horse, and she was feeling exceedingly chill. The doctors had been more concerned with her head injury. Apparently, she was showing signs of confusion and slurring (how wssh sheee t' know?), so there was a likelihood of a few days of observation in the hospital.

She wasn't complaining. This place was perfect. And the longer she stayed, the longer she could avoid thinking about the future and whatever would be next for her.

A bang made her open her eyes. The door had opened, and Lucas was standing in the doorway.

Too lazy to sit up, Liv coolly pushed a button and let the bed slowly lift her. She was getting far too attached to this shiny, clean hospital bed.

"Okay if I come in?" Lucas asked, a little awkwardly. Liv nodded a little awkwardly, wincing at the sharp pain in her head.

This was the first time they'd seen each other since their return to town. A group of police and paramedics had hiked up to the camp with Moose to rescue Ruby and collect the bodies. Thankfully, Liv, Lucas and Shasta hadn't gone back with them. They had been taken to town in separate ambulances and checked into the hospital.

Lucas walked over in that quiet, careful way people have around sick people. He gently propped himself on the edge of her bed. He looked completely different. All polished and new. His dirty blond hair was dirty no more, and his face was scrubbed clean. Both forearms were wrapped in bandages, wrist to elbow, where he'd scraped them on the road. Only his bright eyes looked the same. Always the same.

He looked really good.

"How are you?" he asked.

"Fine. You?" It was polite and formal. Especially after everything they'd been through together. But it had occurred to Liv, somewhere in the juggle of her brain injury, that she had accused him of being a murderer, before he'd had the chance to explain, and had nearly got them both killed trying to run away from him. So, yeah – a little awkward.

"Good." Lucas smiled. A different smile today. Not showy – more vulnerable. He looked down at her wrist, her pink fingers poking out from the end of the cast. His hand was close to hers. Her fingers twitched as though trying to escape and reach him. "I just got done with the police. They talk to you yet?" he asked.

Liv nodded, then regretted it. Her vision couldn't keep up with the movement.

"They tried. I think they're going to come back tomorrow. Apparently, I wasn't making a lot of sense." She gestured to the bandage on her head.

"Does it hurt?" He looked genuinely concerned.

"Not as much as my ego. Listen, Lucas…" God this was uncomfortable. How do you apologize for accusing someone of being a serial killer? "I'm just…I'm so sorry… Those things I said… about you—" Fuck, this was hard.

Lucas just shook his head and laughed.

"Don't worry about it. It wasn't personal. That place just really did a number on us." He looked sideways at her. "You know, back in the cave, when you said you might be the killer and were hiding a rock behind your back…honestly, I was a little worried."

Oh God. Liv would have buried her head in her hands with embarrassment, if it hadn't hurt so much to move. Lucas just smiled at her.

"Liv, can I tell you something?"

She nodded (ouch) and pushed her favourite bed button, raising herself a tiny bit more, so she was almost sitting upright.

"I wanted to tell you…about Dillon. If you promise not to run away this time." Lucas kept his eyes down, focused on the space between their fingertips. Liv blushed a little and made a mental note to be a better listener in future. "Dillon was my first boyfriend. He was the coolest and the funniest guy. We were best friends and then it became something more. I just…I loved him so much. But I was kinda wild back then. I had, like no boundaries and just got into whatever shit was going on."

Lucas stood up and walked over to the window. Bright stripes of sunlight cut through the hospital blinds, outlining him softly. He ran his hand through his curls, pausing to find his next words.

"One night, we'd been at a party and were both drinking and stuff. Dillon was a junior and already had his driver's licence. But he got so toasted, he couldn't even walk straight. I was fifteen and didn't even have my permit, but I was so fucking stupid, I said I'd drive us both home. We were laughing about it. We thought it was funny, you know?"

He kept stopping, struggling to find the words he needed, his expression pained and unfocused – lost in the past. Liv wished she was closer. She wanted to reach out and touch him; to let him know she was listening. But she could only watch silently. She knew what was coming, but this was his story to tell. Hers to hold.

"The thing is…I don't really have to say it, right? I was goofing around, drunk. Showing off and speeding and doing fucked-up, stupid stuff. We crashed – badly. *I* crashed. I don't remember much about how it happened – only after." Lucas took a long shaky breath. "I…I was upside down…the seatbelt was caught…I could smell gas. I couldn't see Dillon. Not at first. I managed to…crawl out. My leg was fucked. I couldn't walk. I was calling Dillon…but there was nothing."

Liv looked away. His pain was so clear, in his bearing, in his tensed arms, his clenched hands. She could feel it, and she didn't want to. She had the sense that he wasn't in the room any more; his head was somewhere else, a dark terrifying place. The place he had gone to in his dream that night in the tent.

"When I finally…found him, he'd fallen out of the car. Halfway. He was…his head was…I…I tried, but he was already gone. I could see it. *I could see—*"

It took a while before he continued.

"I was arrested and charged with vehicular manslaughter. I deserved it. It was a first offence and all, and as we were both being stupid and drunk, I only got sentenced to a year in juvenile detention. My family and lawyers all said it could have been a lot worse. Only it couldn't. Not really. Because the worst had already happened.

"When I was in juvie, I was in a really bad place. I was spiralling about Dillon, and about what I'd done. It was…tough, but that was okay. I deserved it. The kids were all fuck-ups, and I was just one of them. I've been in therapy camps since then. Every six months there's a new one. Sometimes I just start fresh and become someone different. I can be whoever I want to be. This guy? This 'Lucas Cole' is a good guy. I have a whole backstory for him. An orphan who partied too much to cope with his grief, loving grandparents who raised him. This Lucas – the one you know – isn't real, Liv. He never was. He's fiction – good, kind and dependable, he'd never hurt anybody. I can see why you like him. This Lucas – *your* Lucas…his hands are clean. He never got into that car two years ago and murdered his best friend…"

Lucas broke off, his voice cracked with grief.

Fuck it. Liv pushed herself up out of her lovely bed and carefully lowered her feet to the floor, her head only spinning a little. She walked up to him and reached out her one good arm, to gently touch him on his back.

At the feel of her fingers, Lucas turned and pulled her to him. He dropped his head onto her shoulder, burying himself in her. She held him close. Two broken toys. Their incompleteness fitted together, their jagged edges slotting into the empty spaces in between them.

The feeling from the trail was back. The feeling that she was not alone, that the spirits had returned. She could sense them in the hospital room's sterile air. Her mom, Milo and Ben. Ben was there. Ben was always there now. Not in the way he should have been. Not in the room with her, alive and real, his warmth and strength in equal measure. But somehow, he was there.

Liv could feel tears on her face – gentle, soft tears.

They stayed like that for a long time. Life went on in the corridor outside – high-speed, high-stakes hospital hustle. Noises and voices. Someone else's drama. But neither of them moved, until the sunlight through the blinds shifted, falling over the white bed sheets in golden strips, as time moved them gently on.

Slowly, Liv's dizziness was creeping back. Too much vertical time was not working well for her. Reluctantly, she pulled back from Lucas. Reluctantly, he nodded and let her go.

"So, look…I should probably get going. Moose will be picking me up any time now—"

"Wait, you're leaving already?" A short burst of panic hit Liv. It was too soon. She wasn't ready. The campers had been notified that they would be returning home, but she hadn't thought about what that would actually mean.

Lucas just nodded, avoiding her eyes. "There's a programme in

Colorado that can take me on short notice. More of a residential treatment facility, but hey, I'm good with having flush toilets for a while. Moose is driving me to the airport." He raised his eyebrows and shrugged. "I wonder who I'll be this time around? Maybe I'll be you. Tough, snarky with the biggest fucking heart." He turned to go.

"Fuck you, Lucas." Sad. Liv felt sad, confused and pissed off. Was this it? Was this how it ended for her and Lucas? Back to their little lives. So long and thanks for the memories. The thought of him climbing into a van and driving off into the sunset, starting over with a fresh group of fuck-ups – *it hurt*. How could he put everything that had just happened behind him – just add it to his pile of unresolved trauma? Would he forget about her and move on to the next loser?

She didn't want that. She wasn't ready for that. Not yet.

When he reached the doorway, Lucas paused.

"Liv, I just…I wish, more than anything, that we had *really* met. You and me. The real Lucas. I wish I'd been braver. I wish I'd given us a chance." His eyes were focused on her. There was something there. Love maybe? She didn't know. But she felt it. The full force of his feelings. "I guess it's too late now."

The dizziness in Liv's head was mixed with a heady sensation.

"Lucas, I…" What? What did she want to say? It had all been an act, right? He had a point. She'd never met the real Lucas Cole, until now, if this was really him. She didn't know who he was. But they had been through so much together. Life and death stuff. She had seen him react, unplanned, to everything that was thrown at them. Was it possible his mask was fixed on so tightly that in all that they'd been through, she hadn't sensed his real character? How could she know?

Her words were stuck somewhere inside. She wasn't sure what

to say or how to say it. She just looked at him. This boy. The boy she'd kissed. A stranger and yet not.

Lucas nodded. He seemed to have taken something from her silence. He smiled, a small, tight smile.

Reaching into his pocket, he pulled out a yellowed, creased pile of envelopes. She recognized the letters he'd been given on their first day. Her letter was in a Ziploc bag with her swallow ring and other personal belongings, in a locker at the far end of the bed.

He tossed them lightly into a trash can next to the door.

Then without turning back to look at her, he muttered, "Goodbye, Liv Walker."

And with that, he was gone.

CHAPTER 48

Boys.

Were they worth the drama? Probably not.

Liv walked over to the trash can and pulled out the pile of letters. If Lucas hadn't wanted her to read them, he shouldn't have left them behind. It was hardly an invasion of privacy. It was more of an invitation.

She perched on the end of the bed and took the top letter off the pile. It was dated from a few months ago.

Hi love,

We got your message that you want to stay at camp. Lucas, can I come and talk to you about this? It has been such a long time since I've seen you, and a year since your release. Your sisters and I really miss you and wish you would come home. Maya graduates from high school soon and will be heading off to college. I know how sad she'll be if she doesn't get to see you before then. Cara has been learning to bake, and our freezer is full of all the cookies she's saving for you. At least call us. Please, love. We need to talk.

We all love you so much,

Mom xxxx

The next letter was dated a few weeks later.

Lucas,

I'm so sorry. That call was so upsetting for all of us. Please forgive me if I made things worse. We love you. We are not "better off without you". How could you ever think that? You've always been so hard on yourself. What happened was a terrible mistake. I'm begging you to forgive yourself and move on with your life. It's what Dillon would have wanted. He loved you and would hate to see you torture yourself like this. You are a wonderful, loving, kind boy and your home is with us. Please come home, Lucas. Please. We all love you so much and miss you desperately.

Love always,

Mom xxxx

The final letter must have been written just before they started at camp.

Hi love,

The WTC reached out. At your request, they have found a new placement for you in Utah at Camp Smiling Skies. It sounds nice. If this is what you really want, I will of course sign the paperwork and pay for it. You've made it clear that you feel this is the right thing for you, and I will respect that. More than anything, I just want you to be happy, and if this is what you think is best, I will support you.

Please just know, when you are ready to come home, I will be here for you. Always.

I love you,

Mom xxxx

Liv sat back, tears in her eyes. It couldn't have been more different from Shasta's pathetic letter, with her parents justifying their misguided choice to incarcerate their sweet daughter. This one was all heart. She could feel both the love and pain in every stroke of his mom's pen.

Even if he couldn't forgive himself, Lucas had a home. He had a place in the world. He was wanted.

Her eyes fell on the locker. What would her letter say? Would her father ask for forgiveness and tell her she was loved? Would he beg her to come home? When the WTC had called to inform her parents of the tragic events at Camp Smiling Skies, her father had elected not to make the drive up to Utah, claiming that it would be best to give her space to recover, and that he'd just get in the way. Of course, he'd "generously" offered to pay for whatever she needed, for as long as she wanted, just so he wouldn't look like a bad father. To be fair, he had called once, but Liv hadn't picked up. What could she say? Really?

But this was different. The letters lying open on her bed told a different story. Lucas *was* loved. He *was* wanted. He had a chance for something that was worth fighting for, whether he felt he deserved it or not. He couldn't throw it away. He just couldn't.

Liv got to her feet, checking in with her head. Not too bad. Not too wobbly. Lucas had a few minutes' head start, but she could still catch him if she went now. She could stop him – or at least try to.

It was a little mortifying, running down a hospital corridor barefoot, wearing a hospital gown with her arm in a sling and a bandage on her forehead. She half expected a security guard to catch her and send her back to bed. But fortunately, the hospital was a busy place with zero interest in anyone capable of walking.

No one paid her any attention, and she made it to the stairwell in record time.

At the ground floor, she banged through the lobby exit doors and stepped out into the parking lot, blinking as her eyes adjusted to the light. It was obscenely bright and sunny – not a great thing for a concussion. The sunlight felt like needles poking into her retina.

There was no sign of Lucas. She sheltered her eyes as best she could and looked around, but he wasn't there. The dizziness was getting worse. If she stayed like this, she'd either pass out or vomit, and that would attract the kind of attention she really didn't want.

There was a smokers' bench nearby with one shifty-looking orderly sucking hard on a vape pen. Liv headed over, trying to walk in a straight line, and sank onto the other end of the bench, disappointment coursing through her.

Maybe she had been overly optimistic. Lucas must be on his way to the airport by now. Even if she'd caught up with him, he probably didn't want to hear what she had to say.

Jesus. Stupid Lucas. Stupid idiot. He was choosing to be institutionalized because he felt too shitty about himself to go home. He didn't believe in himself. Well, that just made no sense.

Sitting back against the wall, she closed her eyes and felt the hot sun on her face. She could feel Lucas's letters, tucked safely inside her sling.

This was all so wrong. All of it.

Belief. It came down to that, didn't it? All of this? *Belief.*

It was more than a word. It had incredible power. They had been sent away from their homes, their lives, and told they were no good. But the part that hurt the worst, was that somehow that belief had sunk into them. It had got inside, through their skin, past their defences, their defiance, the walls they'd carefully built around their hearts. It was in their core. Each of them. Ben, Lucas, Shasta, Ruby and Milo.

But where did this end? How?

Liv knew the answer.

It was the easiest thing in the world, and yet the hardest.

They had to believe in themselves. Each of them. Including her. Somehow, she needed to find a way to look at herself in the mirror and say, *I fucked up, but I'm trying*. Somehow that had to be enough to get on with the rest of her life. She had to choose to believe in herself. As perfectly imperfect as she was. She had to believe that she was enough, that she was doing her best, that she was all right. She had to because nobody else was going to do it for her.

"Hey, Liv! S'up." A voice snapped her out of her thoughts.

She turned around and saw the white van. It pulled up alongside her, the front window rolled down. Moose was in the driver's seat.

"You're up! Feeling better already?" Moose was clean shaven, wearing a flannel shirt, his long hair loose on his shoulders. He looked a lot better than the last time she'd seen him. Then again, he had been escorting a team of paramedics up a trail to retrieve the dead body of his colleague. Probably not his best day.

"Yeah, I'm good," she mumbled, scanning the van for Lucas, but it was empty. "How about you?"

"Oh, you know. Doing my thing. Moving along." He smiled. He was trying his best to be cheerful, but Liv couldn't forget the devastated look on his face when they'd told him Chipmunk was dead. Whether he'd liked her or not, he'd lived with her for the best part of a year. "Super pumped to see you up and about! Heard Ruby's doing okay too."

"Yeah." Liv nodded. She'd been getting regular updates on Ruby from her nurse; she was still in the hospital. Apparently, when the emergency services found her in the cabin with Milo's body, she'd been hysterical and needed to be sedated for twenty-four hours before she was coherent enough to speak.

"Moose, have you seen Lucas?"

"Nope. He's not down yet. I'm supposed to take him and drop him at the airport. He's transferring to another programme. He's still inside if you want to catch him. If he's not with you, then he's probably saying goodbye to Ruby."

Of course. Lucas would want to see Ruby, for sure. After everything, he'd want to know she was going to be okay.

"So, er…how are things going with you? Did you talk to the police?" Part of Liv didn't want to ask. It had been easier just focusing on her own recovery than thinking about the giant shitstorm that had been kicked off by the events at Camp Smiling Skies. That would come later.

"Sure did. They had a whole bunch of questions. Told me I gotta stick around for a while, just in case they need to talk to me again, or something. Though, as all the really bad stuff happened while I was in town with Shasta, they're pretty chill about things. I reckon I'll be good to go in a month or so. Just glad to see you looking all perky." He smiled – a sweet, genuine smile.

"Thanks, Moose." Liv knew she had questions for him – things that had swum in and out of her confused brain while lying in the hospital bed. There were far too many to cover now. But one question had stood out above all the others; something she needed to understand.

"Moose…why did you stay at Camp Smiling Skies? It was just so awful. Chipmunk was…" Liv tailed off. No point trash-talking the dead. "I mean, we couldn't leave, we were stuck there. But you could have left any time. Why didn't you just quit?"

A shadow caught Moose's long face. He scratched at his chin uncomfortably.

"Aw, Liv. Not gonna lie, I thought on it. I really did. Pretty much every day. The WTC sure wasn't what I signed up for. I wanted to be a park ranger and teach kids about the beauty of nature, y'know? But I didn't get an internship so I thought maybe I could do some good here. But turns out the WTC sure weren't in the business of teaching kiddos.

"You should've seen Ben and Kevon the day they arrived. They were wild and bursting with hellfire – you would've liked them. Not bad kids; just scrappy and hurting – kinda like you." He smiled at her, sadly. Liv blushed. "But Chippy made it her mission to break those two boys from day one. Now this isn't me making excuses but – full candour – I was outta my league. I tried standing up to Chippy but never got far. This don't add up to much, but I had my resignation letter all tucked up in my pocket and good to go…the day Kevon died." His face seemed to age as he spoke. Weathered lines grew deeper. His deep tan greyed at the edges.

He continued, "You see, after that day…I couldn't go. I couldn't leave Ben alone with Chippy. She was dang scary and outta control. Kevon's accident just made her ten times worse. There sure wasn't much I could do, but I promised myself I'd stay until the day Ben finally made it outta there. I promised." He swallowed; his Adam's apple ducked up and down. "I'm guessin' in some way…that's what I did."

Liv looked away; it was easier than looking at Moose. People were getting on with their days, bustling in and out of the hospital entrance. A siren piped up as an ambulance pulled away. A hospital security guard stood in front of the doors, arms folded, glaring in their direction. Clearly, they were infringing on some rule or other.

So, Moose had stayed for Ben. It made sense somehow. He had recognized his own limitations – his total inability to control the situation and handle Chipmunk – but at least he'd felt a duty of care for the kids in his charge. He'd tried to help, the only way he was really able to. He'd stayed.

"So, what's next?" Liv asked, pushing out a smile. "Where are you going after all this is over?"

"Me? Aww yeah. I'm thinking about taking my Astrovan up to Alaska. Always wanted to see polar bears." The hospital security guard was heading in their direction now, waving Moose along with an irate frown. "Well, reckon I'd better go find me a legit parking spot. Don't wanna cause any trouble." Moose waved affably in the direction of the officer. "Sorry, sir! I'm movin' along here. Hey, Liv, if you see Lucas, can you tell him to hustle already? We're gonna miss his flight if we don't leave soon."

Liv smiled sadly. "Sure – and good luck in Alaska. Look after yourself, Moose."

"It's Clay by the way. My real name's Clay, like the mud. Reckon it's time to retire 'Moose' for good."

A thought occurred to Liv.

"What was Chipmunk's real name?" It felt fitting to know the name of the dead woman.

Moose just shrugged. "Strange thing is…I never knew it. She never told me. As far as she was concerned, it was Chipmunk all the way. So long, Liv. Take care of yourself, all righty, and don't forget to stay in touch." With that, Moose put the van in gear and pulled away.

CHAPTER 49

Ruby's hospital room was at the furthest end of the corridor from Liv's.

For the last few days, Liv had come up with a string of excuses to avoid making the trek down the corridor to visit Ruby. Clearly Ruby hadn't been inclined to visit Liv either. After all, the last time they'd seen each other, back in Moose's cabin, things hadn't ended well.

But the need to talk to Lucas had overruled Liv's reluctance and now she found herself lingering outside Ruby's door. If Lucas was inside, then this might be her last chance to see him.

Taking a deep breath, Liv opened the door. Ruby was sitting up in bed, wide awake and talking animatedly on what looked like a brand-new cellphone. She was fully made-up, wearing a preppy, pink pyjama set, comfortably propped up on several pillows. Gift bags, cards and flowers littered every surface around her.

Lucas wasn't there.

Relieved, Liv turned to go, but it was too late. Ruby had seen her and held up a finger, gesturing that she should wait.

Caught.

"Okay…yah…yah…oh my God, yah." Ruby was grinning widely at the phone screen.

It was the first time Liv had seen Ruby out of camp-mode, and it was hard not to stare. She was glowing as though she'd just got back from a relaxing Caribbean vacation. All the mosquito bites and bruises had artfully disappeared under a skilled layer of concealer, and her immaculate hair was silky-smooth and two shades lighter without the layers of dirt. Even her manner was different, now she was back in her natural element – confident, bubbly. There was no sign of the highly strung Condor that Liv had come to know and tolerate. No sign of the grief-stricken girl who had just lost her best friend.

"'Kay. Bye, Mom. Love you. Love you. Yah. Byeee." Ruby's fingers made a quick, practised flick through several phone screens before she finally set her phone down on the bed sheets. Her smile rigidly fixed itself in place as she turned to Liv.

"Hey," she said brightly. Too brightly.

"Hey," Liv answered. Long pause. God, this was awkward. Complicated.

"So, like how are you?" Ruby nodded at Liv's sling. "I heard you like broke your arm or something?"

"I'm fine." Liv shrugged. "Thanks. You?" As far as she knew, Ruby hadn't been physically injured but had been kept in hospital for shock and dehydration. That made sense, given that the last time she'd seen her, Ruby was screaming at the top of her lungs, over and over, while standing next to Milo's body. Shock would do it.

"Oh, I'm like totally fine. Just waiting here for Mom to come and pick me up. She's flying in on her private jet. That was her on the phone. She's like so worried about me." Ruby's face lit up manically as she talked. "She's been on the phone like twenty-four-seven, making sure I've got everything I need. It's like so sweet of her."

Liv was confused. Was Ruby high? Had the hospital pumped her full of opioids or something? She seemed to be in a great mood, given everything they'd just been through. Then again, maybe this was her happy ending? The traumatic events had finally made *The Jennifer Clarke* sit up and pay attention to her needy second daughter.

But at what price? Where was the damage hiding?

"Hey, so I'm just looking for Lucas," Liv said, feeling the need to get out of there. "Was he here? I wanted to catch him before he heads out."

"Yah, he's picking up an iced vanilla latte from the cafeteria for me. You can stay and wait for him, if you like?" Ruby had picked her phone back up and was scrolling as she talked.

"Oh. Um. Okay." Liv nodded, moving closer to the door.

For the first time, Liv noticed the TV was on in the background. Some local news channel was playing; an overly made-up newscaster was standing in front of the entrance to a familiar grey building, under a sign with the word *INTAKE*. A large, recognizable man was standing guard in the doorway, arms folded tightly across his broad chest. So, Lomax was still working for the WTC. Liv glared at the screen. The volume was turned down too low to hear what the newscaster was saying, but the closed captions were trying to keep up along the bottom of the screen.

AS YET NO COMMENT FROM THE WILDERNESS THERAPY CAMP CORPORATION

CAMP HAS BEEN SHUT DOWN

INDEFINITELY PENDING FULL INVESTIGATION

No shit, Liv thought darkly. Camp Smiling Skies should be shut down – permanently, pending nothing. The whole therapy camp set-up was abusive. Incarcerating kids against their will? In what universe was that ever okay? Kids had died there; that had to be enough to get some press attention on what was happening in these camps. That had to be enough to get them closed down once and for all. Didn't it?

The news had moved on and was now showing footage of a river; flood damage and washed-up debris were strewn across the banks. Liv felt something tightening in her chest.

SEARCHING THE OCHEE RIVER FOR THE BODY OF MISSING CAMPER SEVENTEEN-YEAR-OLD BENJAMIN CROSS
LAST SEEN ON THE NIGHT OF THE STORM

Fuck. Liv wasn't ready for this. She wasn't ready to think about this. She tried to look away from the screen, but her eyes kept dragging her back to it.

DIVE TEAM CONDUCTING A SEARCH AND RECOVERY OPERATION ALONG LOWER RIVER, CONFIDENT THEY WILL LOCATE THE BODY IN THE NEXT FEW DAYS

Okay, she told herself. This wasn't news. It didn't change anything. Not yet.

She knew that the search had been delayed by another storm that had rolled in. She knew that today was the day they were going out to look for him.

But as long as they hadn't found his body, she could still picture him out there, standing in the river – the way he had looked at her that one last time. Alive.

Fuck. Liv wiped at her eyes with her good hand.

"Liv—?"

The sound of Ruby's voice pulled Liv's attention away from the TV. She had no idea how long Ruby had been watching her.

"Um…yeah," Liv muttered, embarrassed. "What?"

"Do you remember…back in the cabin…what I said…that Ben deserved to die…that I was happy?" Ruby's red eyes were betraying her. "You know I really didn't mean it. It was just…Milo…"

And there she finally was. Ruby Jennifer Clarke – Condor. Her facade crumbling just a little, just at the edges. Her eyes widened, tears trying to force their way through her impenetrable wall of make-up. Her mouth fell open silently, lips trembling.

It was. Just Milo. Just Ben.

Liv got it.

Without overthinking, Liv walked up to the bed and put her good arm around Ruby. She could feel the girl fold into her, tucking her head into Liv's shoulder, the way she used to with Milo. They stayed like that for a while as the faint sounds of the TV played out over their heads, strangers dissecting what had happened to them, piece by piece.

Liv didn't speak. Were there words for this? For this feeling? Everything was just so messed up and confusing. Sadness and grief were mixed with disbelief and guilt, maybe a little shame and a kicker of bitter anger. There was nothing worth saying today. Nothing good, at least.

Eventually the bed sheets buzzed as Ruby's phone went off.

Wordlessly, they both pulled back. Ruby quickly picked up her phone, checking the screen.

"It's Mom. She wants to FaceTime in a minute." She reached for a tissue to tidy her make-up. "Oh my God, I must look so bad." Out came a make-up bag and mirror, Q-tips and a full armoury of weapons in sweet-smelling tubes.

Liv walked to the door. She would wait outside for Lucas.

But there was just one last thing. A stupid small thing that had been stuck in Liv's head.

"Ruby, can I ask you something?"

Ruby nodded, without turning away from her mirror.

"Why was Milo at Camp Smiling Skies?" Liv wasn't sure why it was so important to know – it just was.

"Milo?" Ruby shook her head, dabbing efficiently at the make-up under her eyes. "I mean, it was stupid. He didn't like to talk about it. I think he was embarrassed."

"What was it?" Drugs? Stealing? Running away? What had Milo done that was so bad he'd paid for it with his life?

"He got dropped from the basketball team."

Liv blinked.

"*The basketball team?*"

"Yah, he said that was like the last straw with his dad. He was always messing up and getting into trouble. He kept being late and missing games, so the coaches cut him mid-season. His dad was so angry. He thought Milo wasn't trying and figured he needed some discipline. So, he sent him to Camp Smiling Skies." Ruby paused. Liv could see that her mirror had dropped a touch. "It's just, Milo once told me that he only messed around because he couldn't do stuff right, no matter how hard he tried. He always screwed up and forgot things. He just couldn't focus for like two minutes. He said he'd rather they thought he was lazy than stupid because if he was lazy, he could change. But if he was stupid, he'd be a disappointment to them for life."

A disappointment for life. Now in death.

Jesus. Poor Milo.

Liv's breathing felt shallow, the way it did when she thought too much these days. Almost as though a deep breath would be too painful to bear and might crack her open deep inside. She just nodded.

A loud celestial chime filled the air. Instantly, Ruby turned away from Liv and grabbed her phone, holding it out just long enough for Liv to see a brief flash of the queen herself on the screen.

"Hey, Mom. Yah…yah…yah. Wait, seriously? For real? Dad said that? The Oscars? No way! Oh my God…what am I going to wear?"

Liv smiled and watched for a second longer. Maybe Ruby would paint her face and hide in her mom's entourage, or on her dad's red carpet, all glammed up and gorgeous to the eyes of the world. But scratch the surface – even one time – and the darkness might leak out. The damage was all there, and it wasn't going to go away just because Ruby wanted it to. Like it or not.

Turning, Liv stepped out into the busy corridor and pulled the door shut behind her. With everything left in her heart, she wished Ruby all the best, wherever life, money and private jets would take her.

This was goodbye. They wouldn't stay in touch.

CHAPTER 50

It was several minutes before Lucas finally appeared down the busy corridor. He was carrying an enormous iced coffee.

He stopped when he saw Liv, sitting on an orange plastic chair, just outside Ruby's door.

"Oh…hey." His cheeks flushed slightly.

"Lucas, can I talk to you for a moment?"

He nodded, then, indicating the coffee, he tapped on Ruby's door and took it in to her. Through the open doorway, Liv could still hear Ruby talking happily on the phone with her mom.

When he came back out, Lucas sat down one seat away from her.

She pulled the letters out of her sling. "I read these. Sorry." Liv set the letters down between them. "You know what I'm going to say?" she asked.

"That I should talk to my mom. That I should go home." Lucas turned to her. "I've heard it all before, Liv. Counsellors, therapists. Even Chipmunk said it. But it's just not going to happen. I can't go home. Not now, not ever. They're happy. My mom and my sisters have got this perfect little life, you know. Small house, crazy dog and so much fucking love. I don't fit there any more. I'm toxic, you know? There's just so much…darkness inside. I'm not the son or the brother that they remember. Not any more. They're better off without me. I'll only bring them down."

Liv could see the pain in his face. The way he talked about his family, his lost life pre-accident – it was the way she remembered her life in Seattle. Maybe it was an idealized version. For sure it was. But they were both grieving the loss of something irretrievable. The day her mom died, Liv's childhood ended. The day Lucas crashed a car and killed Dillon, his childhood ended.

But the difference was, Lucas's family wanted him back. It wouldn't be the same. Not ever. The past was gone. But it could be something new, if Lucas let it. He *had* to let it. If you were lucky enough to have a family who actually cared about you, you didn't throw that away, no matter how fucking hard things might be. You didn't give up on your family, the way her father had given up on her. You just didn't. What else was there?

Lucas stood up.

"Thanks, Liv. It means a lot that you tried. But there's nothing you can say to change my mind. I love my family too much and I will never hurt them. I won't go back. Ever."

He turned to go.

No. Liv stood up and took a deep breath. Lucas still had a chance here and she wasn't going to stand by and let him throw it all away. *One life. Live it.*

"Three things." Liv said it quietly, but Lucas heard her over the shuffle of people walking past. He paused, and turned to look at her, a slight frown on his face. Liv continued, "Three things I like about the *real* Lucas Cole."

"Okay." He gave a half-smile. "Are we really doing this? Here?"

"Number one." Liv looked at him directly. No shying away now. "When Shasta was sad and homesick that first night, you gave her your own food, even though there wasn't enough to go around and we were all starving." No reaction. He was watching her, guard still up.

"Number two. After I accused you of being a serial killer, you threw yourself in front of the van to save my life, even though we could have both been killed." Lucas hadn't moved. Was she getting through to him? She couldn't tell.

One last shot.

"Number three. On that first, freezing cold, fucked-up night in the van, when I didn't know what to do and I felt like my whole life had ended…you gave me your hoodie."

A reaction. Lucas hadn't expected that. Something softened a little in his eyes. He blinked a few times. They both remembered.

"You weren't acting then. That was all you. The real Lucas Cole. No matter how fucked up you think you are, your heart is good." There was no point in tiptoeing around any more. "You need to go home. Go home and do the work. Use that loving heart of yours to make your family's life better. Be there for them. Love them. Support them. It won't be easy, I know. Life isn't easy. We've both learned that the hard way. But you can't keep running away. It's time to go home, Lucas. Your family needs you."

Lucas was crying now, tears running down his face. A few curious passers-by slowed down to look at them, sympathy on their faces – they looked too young to be in a place like this. A place of endings.

Neither of them spoke. There was nothing more to say.

Reaching down, Lucas picked up his letters, then with a short nod, he turned to go. No words.

Liv watched his back as he walked down the long corridor, head hung. Would he go home? She really hoped so. But while she'd done what she could, she also knew that you couldn't fix someone else. At the end of the day, you could only fix yourself.

She sank down into the creaky plastic chair and reached back into her sling. There was something else she had carefully stashed in there along with the letters.

For the first time since leaving camp, she unfolded Ben's photo. There he was. Ben – half smiling, his brown eyes crinkled with warmth, his fighter's hand gently holding his brother's little one. Not a killer. A brother. Someone who had been dealt a shitty hand in life and left to fall under the weight of it. No help. No love. No second chances.

Liv stared at the photo. At the boy. The pain was starting up inside. Grief was back, like an old engine warming itself up. It was time to let it in. It was time to be brave.

Any way she looked at it, she was one of the lucky ones. She had escaped the camp of broken toys. Life had given her the second chance that Ben never got. She owed it to him to take it.

Her life was hers now.

There was no way to run from it.

It was time to go home.

CHAPTER 51

The perfectly coiffed lawn was unchanged. Ostentatiously green and overwatered in the desert heat, complementing the columned facade of the accompanying McMansion.

No one was waiting for Liv when she stepped out of the Uber. Unsurprisingly. It had been less than a week since her "family" had waved her off in the back of the white van, hoping to get her out of their lives for several months at least. Now, awkwardly, she was back, and she was pissed.

Liv had no luggage, just a bag from the hospital gift shop containing a bottle of water, her phone and two envelopes. She was wearing used clothes donated by the hospital: baggy jeans and an oversized pink hoodie that read *I hiked Zion National Park* in big letters on the front. Her arm was in a sling, and there was a small line of tape on her forehead, covering a row of stitches. But she didn't care what she looked like. She didn't care who saw her, or what anyone thought of her. Fuck them all.

Taking a deep breath, she walked up to the door and rang the bell.

Footsteps. Muttered voices. They were gathering on the other side of the door, preparing themselves to face her. What would it be? They really only had a couple of choices. They could play innocent: *Camp? What camp?* Or maybe: *Oh honey, we were only doing what we thought was best for you...* Or they could dig in: *Any more of your shenanigans, young lady, you'll be right back on the next white van.*

Honestly, it didn't matter either way. They could say what they liked. Liv was calm. She'd taken her time getting to this moment. She was ready and almost excited that she was finally here. Bring it.

The door swung open and there they were.

Her father and her gold-digging step-witch. No smiles. They both had locked-in, defiant looks on their tense faces. Clearly, they'd told themselves and the world what they needed to, in order to justify sending her away, digging themselves into their little trenches. No surprises there.

"Dad. Carianne." Liv nodded, keeping her tone neutral, giving little away. She didn't have to make any of this easy on them.

"Liv," Carianne said coldly. "Why don't you come inside? Your father just made dinner." She glanced furtively at the neighbouring houses, clearly worried about appearances. The neighbours must have seen Liv being escorted away. They would have nodded and ahhed sympathetically along to Carianne's stories about her out-of-control and dangerous stepdaughter. A stepdaughter who was now back, like an escaped prisoner, standing in their precious cul-de-sac. Just a little awkward.

"Actually," Liv said, shaking her head. "I'm good right here. There's something I want to say to you." She directed it at her father.

Wow. The fear in his eyes was hilarious. He was actually scared of her. Honestly, it was pathetic. Laughable. So far, he hadn't dared to say a word. He just stood, slightly tucked behind Carianne, arms folded defensively over his golf shirt. Coward.

"We'll talk inside," Carianne said sharply, stepping aside and indicating the way with a short nod of her head.

Liv snorted and wondered what part of Carianne's little brain thought that she had any authority left over her. Respect was a two-way street.

"No, thanks." Liv focused on her father. What she had to say was for him alone. "I wanted to give you this."

Reaching into her gift bag, she pulled out one of the two envelopes. It was muddy and water-stained from its time stashed deep in her pocket, what seemed like a lifetime ago. She pointedly held it out to her dad. Carianne looked like she wanted to snatch it away but seemed to reluctantly understand that this might just be overstepping. She glared at the letter, then at Liv.

But Liv didn't care. At this point, Carianne was irrelevant to her, a footnote in her life.

Slowly, James Walker unfolded his arms and reached out to take the unopened letter.

"I didn't read it," Liv said, facing him directly – the man who had once been her dad. "Whatever it says, whatever you've written in there, that's for you. Not me."

"Now, Liv…" His voice was small. Had he always been this pathetic? "Now, Liv, you need to understand. This has all been very hard on us. We did what we had to do. We didn't want to, but—"

We. Liv held up her hand to stop him, shaking her head. *Who even was he?* Who was this nondescript, balding man? He barely resembled the dad she used to know. He had sunken into domestic servitude, gratefully and comfortably. This was his happy place now.

"Do you remember Mom's chair? The blue armchair?" It wasn't what she'd planned to say.

James Walker's face shifted; his eyes narrowed the smallest amount, confused. He hadn't expected her to say that, and it took moments for him to recalibrate.

"Of course…yes. Your mother's chair. I remember it. Why are you bringing up the chair?"

"Do you remember how she used to call it her happy place? Most days, when I got home from school, she would be sitting there, curled up with her latest book, drinking tea. She was always smiling in that chair." Liv paused. She wasn't sure she wanted to ask the next question, but she'd started now. Might as well finish. "Do you remember *us*? Do you ever think about how good we were? How much we loved each other? We were a *family*." She searched his face, but his defences were unflinching. He knew he was vulnerable and under attack, and he simply wasn't strong enough to go there.

"Now, don't be silly, digging up old things like this. It doesn't help to remember, Liv. You need to move on with your life."

But Liv did remember. She remembered the house in Seattle. A home filled with sunshine and squabbles and giggles. It was real and it could have lasted a lifetime, longer even. It could have been passed on through generations, the memories and joy. *The love.* But as it turned out, it had died with her mother. Too soon.

"When Mom died, I felt like you died too. You just…gave up on me. You latched on to the first money-grubbing woman who came your way and forgot I even existed."

"Liv, don't talk to your father—" Carianne cut in.

"*My* father. Stay out of this, Carianne," Liv warned her. Her voice was low and even, but there was no mistaking the raw strength there. She was not going to be messed with or bossed around. Not any more. Any residual parental authority had long since dried up. They were equals now. They all knew it. The power had shifted.

Carianne stepped back slightly, hands on hips, chin raised defensively. But she didn't speak.

Liv turned back to her father.

"Since Mom died, you have barely spoken to me. You dragged me out here and let your new wife treat me like dirt. I was grieving and heartbroken, but instead of loving me, like a father should love his own daughter, you just moved on. Yes, I acted out, I was so fucking unhappy. But I'm not bad, or delinquent or broken. I just needed my dad. But he never showed up."

"Now, Liv. You're being very unreasonable."

She wasn't getting through to him. She knew this might happen. He was so far gone, so locked down, that he just couldn't hear her. But it was okay. It was okay because she didn't need him to love her any more. She didn't need *him* any more.

She shook her head.

"No. It's my turn now. You made your choices. Now, I've made mine." She pulled out the second letter. It was clearly addressed to James T. Walker & Carianne B. Walker, with a Seattle return address of Wei Legal Associates, Inc.

Carianne snatched it from her hand. She ripped it open, scanned it, then held it out to her husband, one eyebrow raised archly. He took it and ponderously read through the first few lines. It was enough to get the gist of it.

Neither of them said anything.

Min's parents had been more than happy to help her when she'd called from the hospital. After she'd told them everything – about the kidnapping and the camp, about the deaths, it had taken them less than twenty-four hours to file a legal motion for emancipation. No judge in the land would question the filing when they heard what had happened to her at camp. She was sixteen years old, and she was divorcing her loser family. She didn't need them any more. She was better off alone.

Liv had played out this moment so many times in her head. The letter. What she would say. What her father would say. But honestly, there was nothing there. No reaction. No emotion. Nothing.

Nothing.

And there it was. Everything she'd needed to know.

A wave of exhaustion hit her. She was at the finish line now. Something that had started in the hospital on the day her mother died was finally coming to a close. She took a deep breath.

"Let's just call this what it is, all right? I just came to pick up my things, and then I'll be out of your hair," Liv said.

Carianne had taken back the letter. Liv had no doubt that when she wrapped her head around it, she would be delighted. She would see it as a victory, finally getting rid of her unwanted spare child. Just as long as she could keep it quiet. A legal emancipation wasn't a good look, but if this was all kept discreet, it would be just fine.

As for her father? *Her father.* Liv knew exactly what he would do the minute she walked out of the door and out of their lives. He would retreat to his office and switch on his computer. Any confusion or messy feelings would simply be put away, in favour of work. Just like the day her mom died. He would shut Liv and her mom up together in a tight little box in his tight little heart, while he worked and cooked dinner and drove Mattie to her ballet lessons. The saddest part? He would be just fine.

This was over.

Almost imperceptibly, Carianne moved to one side, clearing the doorway for her.

Liv nodded and walked inside, up the stairs and into her bedroom for the last time. Barely aware of what she was doing, she grabbed a bag and threw handfuls of clothes into it. That's all she wanted. Clothes were expensive and she was going to be supporting herself now. Everything else could go to charity as far as she was concerned. The only thing that mattered to her had been left in Seattle. Left in the rain on the sidewalk with a *FREE* sign stuck on it.

It took less than five minutes to pack up her life here.

As she walked out of her room, she saw a little face peeking at her around the corner of her door. Mattie.

She smiled.

"Come here, pumpkin." She held her good arm out wide, and Mattie burst through the door, tumbling into her embrace.

"Liv…I missed you. Where was you?" Mattie looked up at her sister, her big, beautiful eyes round with happiness.

"I missed you too." Liv stroked her downy-soft red hair. "I love you very much, okay? I have to go away now, but I want you to know, if you ever want me, come and find me. I will always be your big sister. *Always.* And I will always love you. Okay?"

"'Kay." Mattie nodded. Confused. She wouldn't remember this conversation. She probably wouldn't remember who Liv was – and if one day she asked who the dark-haired girl was in some old family photos, the answer wouldn't be kind. But maybe, sometime in the future, when little Mattie was Liv's age and Carianne was sucked into the maelstrom of a midlife crisis, maybe Mattie would need to get away too. Maybe she'd need help, and if she did – Liv would be there.

Liv kissed her on the top of her head, breathing in her sweet baby-shampoo scent for the last time. Then she stood up tall and walked down the stairs, past her ex-parents and out of that tacky, loveless McMansion for the last time.

The Uber was waiting as she'd asked it to. She climbed in, and without a backward glance, they pulled away.

EPILOGUE
SIX MONTHS LATER

The car's engine spluttered to a dead stop just as Liv pulled into the driveway.

It was a nineties Jeep Cherokee that was running on fumes. Half the time it randomly wouldn't start, and the roof leaked rainwater onto the backseat. But Liv didn't mind; she loved her car, and she needed it to get between her two jobs and community college in the Seattle traffic.

For a while, Liv just sat in the driveway, hands on the steering wheel, listening to the pattering of heavy rain on the car's roof. She was exhausted and smelled of grease and sweat. Her closing shift at the pizzeria had dragged on and it was nearly three a.m. already. Classes started in a few hours, so it was going to be another day fuelled by caffeine and willpower.

Through the rain-streaked front windscreen, she could see her little guest house tucked into the backyard behind the Wei family home. Min's light was still on upstairs in the big house – she never slept! Liv smiled, and briefly considered messaging her to see which crush she was "talking" to now, but when she pulled out her phone, she saw all her missed notifications:

Tofurkey? Was that even a thing? Liv grinned. Honestly, they could give her a peanut butter and jelly sandwich, and she would be just fine. She loved Lucas's family. They had taken her under their wing in a way that she couldn't put into words, endlessly grateful that she'd convinced Lucas to finally go home.

Lucas. Liv smiled.

Slowly, gathering up her things, she took a deep breath before making the cold, wet dash to the front porch. The mailbox was full, so she grabbed the contents and quickly unlocked the door and stepped inside. Switching on the light, she looked around, the way she did every time she came home, breathing it in. *Home.* Her home.

It was perfection – a tiny little studio with a kitchenette tucked in one corner opposite her IKEA sofa bed. On the far side there was a bookshelf she'd crudely constructed from planks of wood, next to a ratty-looking blue armchair dotted with tiny crescent moons that she'd found at a yard sale.

This was Liv's favourite place on earth. It wasn't chic or fancy, and nothing matched, but it was hers. The Weis wouldn't even let her pay rent. They said she'd been through enough, and when she graduated, they could talk again.

Throwing her bags on the floor, Liv hurriedly flipped through the mail. It was all junk addressed to previous renters. Nothing else.

There was the usual flash of disappointment. What was she expecting? Someday she would have to get her head around the fact that there might never be more, and that was okay. She already had what she needed.

Dropping the junk mail in the wastebasket, Liv glanced over to a small shelf by the door, where a postcard was carefully propped up.

She didn't need to read it – there was nothing to read. The card was blank on the back, with just her address handprinted in blocky writing. On the front there was a photo – a picturesque cathedral looming over a crowded sunny plaza, with the word *Valladolid* printed underneath in bright pink letters. The photo was generic and unremarkable, apart from one small detail. At the top of a tree, in the top right-hand corner, were two tiny birds, hand drawn.

Reaching up, Liv softly touched the card, the way she did every night, reassuring herself that it actually existed, that it wasn't just in her imagination. She paused, resting her fingertips on the corner of the image, over the scrappy little birds.

No – she had exactly what she needed right here. The postcard was more than she could ever have hoped for. It was real – and it was enough. It had to be. For now, at least.

Liv nodded to herself and smiled.

Kicking off her trainers, she walked over to the kitchen and switched on the kettle. While the water was boiling, she threw on her pyjamas and washed her face, before finally carrying a cup of night-time tea over to the old armchair and flopping down into the deep cushions. She curled her tired feet up under her, holding the steaming hot cup carefully in both hands, and sighed deeply.

This felt so fucking good. So right. The broken toys were fixing themselves, piece by piece. Patching their little lives together. It wasn't easy – it certainly wasn't perfect. But it was a start, and that was enough.

Blowing on her tea, she finally let her eyes settle on the solitary painting hanging on the wall next to the armchair.

It was a large painting in a cheap-looking wooden frame. The bottom left corner was missing where she'd cut it off with a pair of kitchen scissors – a small but necessary sacrifice – and there were vertical lines across the surface from a few weeks rolled up in a garbage bag in the hot Arizona sun. But the brilliant colours and images still lit up her heart, melting into each other. The dark outline of a blue bird flew high against a vibrant sky, wings reaching out as if they could touch the face of the sun. Its forked tail trailed behind as it soared endlessly upward.

Liv could feel it; she could catch onto that tail and let it take her with it, higher and higher – up into that wide-open sky. Where she could fly. Where she could breathe.

Where she could be free.

She took a sip of her tea and smiled.

"Goodnight, Mom," she whispered.

ACKNOWLEDGEMENTS

Writing this book got me through a rough patch in my life. For a while it felt like everything was upside down, and writing was a safe retreat from the world. Liv became my proxy, and her on-page adventures helped me find the words I needed to hear. To me (and Liv), this is a story about broken toys learning to believe again – with maybe a murder or two thrown in, just for kicks. I will always have a soft spot for this story, and I hope you enjoy it too!

Thank you to my brilliant editors: Becky Walker, who started this journey, and Amelia Mehra who picked it up and ran with it all the way across the finish line. Your talent and passion made this book fly higher than I could ever have imagined. I am so grateful to get to work with you both. Also, thank you to Sarah Stewart, Debbie Sims, Jenny Bish, Kath Millichope, Kat Cassidy, Jessica Feichtlbauer, Hannah Reardon Steward, Fritha Lindqvist and the incredible team at Usborne who brought this book into existence with all the care in the world.

As always, none of this would exist without my agent, Ludo Cinelli. You are my champion in the mysterious world of publishing, and your passion and commitment are second to none. Also, thanks to the talented team at Eve White Literary Agency – Eve, Steven and Emmanuel.

A huge thank you to Annie Berger, Gabbi Calabrese and the brilliant team at Sourcebooks for bringing this book to the US, aptly titled *The Betrayed*.

Of course, none of this would be possible without all the incredible booksellers, librarians, influencers, bloggers and readers out there. Without you, writers would be nothing more than annoying daydreamers and our books would just sit on shelves looking pretty. You bring the words and the characters to life – thank you!

To Mum, Dad, Susie, Bob, Paul and all the rest of my incredible family, all over the world: for the longest time, I assumed that a close, loving, endlessly supportive family was typical. Well, I've finally learned that it's not, and I won the lottery with you. If I don't say it enough…*I love you guys x.*

To my friends: how did I get so lucky to have you in my life? Your love, humour and support make anything possible and it's a privilege to walk alongside you. Thank you!

And to my three favourite humans in the whole wide world: Nat, Jack and Gemma. It is the best thing in my life to exist in your orbit. I am in awe of each of you, for different reasons, and will happily spend the rest of my days sitting on the sidelines in the sunshine, watching your very great adventures.

Lastly, to all the broken toys out there – you're not alone. When the time is right, you will start putting those pieces back together again, one by one. It might take a while, but you will fix yourself – you will. Just, hang in there and *believe*. It gets so much better.

 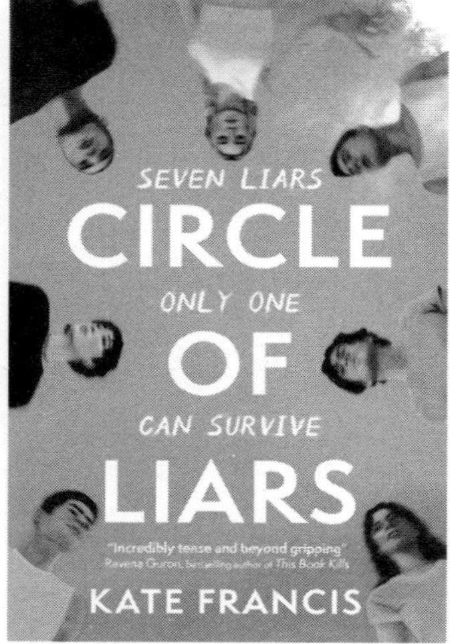

KATE FRANCIS is an English-American writer and architect. She graduated from Edinburgh University and the Bartlett School of Architecture, and worked as an architect for several top design firms in London. Her debut YA thriller, *Circle of Liars*, was published internationally and translated into multiple languages. She now lives in California with her three kids. When she's not building something, she enjoys kayaking, walking the dog, and crafting interesting ways to kill off fictional teenagers.